THE STONE PICKER

CHRIS LEANDRO

ISBN: 978-1-4834-4891-6 (sc)
ISBN: 978-1-4834-4890-9 (e)

Lulu Publishing Services rev. date: 4/15/2016

For Amanda, Mika, Louis, and Luna

PROLOGUE

He had been missing for five days and no one gave much hope for his survival. The unfortunate fool had accepted to go on an unauthorised archaeological reconnaissance, out in the wilds of a war-torn Maghreb — and disappeared.

He should never have come up here. The captain said that this would be the solution to all their problems but he was beginning to feel that his life had not been all that bad lately. He had his salary and had saved up a fair whack to take home when this tour was finally over. The heat was intolerable out here, especially on the south side of the Mountains. At least in Algiers he could always have a cold beer. He wasn't able to move about the city as he wished, no one could, thousands had been killed, some said hundreds of thousands. Only a week ago a bomb had killed two more of their Arab soldiers in the city and injured several civilians. But out here they would have to be really unlucky to get into any trouble. That did not stop him from worrying, even though the war was all but over and De Gaulle had said that they would soon be going home. He couldn't wait; he was desperate for green fields, beef and fresh milk.

Ever since they had left the jeep he'd had the worrying feeling that someone was following them. He carried his service revolver on his hip and its weight reassured him. It wasn't far now, he could see the cliff above him. But they still had a way to go, they needed to get there soon if they were to get back to the vehicle before nightfall.

He was the second son of one of the many small dairy farmers in the Périgord of southwest France. His parents were simple, hard-working folk. No one could have hoped for better parents, but the little farm could support no more than one family. They had pigs and poultry, eggs of course and milk from the cow, cages of rabbits and plenty of pigeons, even a small vineyard. They could always feed themselves but it was clear that the three youngest boys would have to look for a living elsewhere if they ever wanted to raise families of their own.

When the call-up papers came through for Serge, the eldest brother, their parents had been dismayed. Serge had become indispensable to the farm and the harvest was about to begin. Serge had been disappointed. He had fallen heavily for Emily, the baker's pretty young daughter and he had no desire to waste the next two years away in the army. Apart from the hair, the older boys looked alike, though there were nearly two years between them. They were both big lads but Serge had always been the bright one and it was he who had the idea. His mother laughed at first then worried when she heard what they had decided. But his father had agreed. They were going to swap identities, he was to take the train to Limoges with his brother's papers and join up! He would become Serge, Serge who always came first, whose handed-down clothes he had always had to wear. It was a dream come true.

The military service was a blessing in disguise. It got him out of the farm for the first time, and when he knew he was being posted to North Africa he had visions of seeking his fortune in unknown exotic latitudes. But it turned out to be mostly drilling in the barracks parade ground under a merciless sun, and interminable nights on guard duty. That and having to put up with the bloody Arabs, always gawping at his red hair marking him out as a Martian or something worse. He had caught them making crude gestures behind his back.

He had been doing some driving for the captain lately and they had become almost friendly. The captain wasn't as stuck up as most of the other officers and had asked about his family back home and his hopes and fears. They had joked together and got quite chummy, and then he had asked Serge if he wanted to get involved in something a little more lucrative and far more exciting than guard duty.

The sweat had soaked through his shirt and shorts by the time they reached the opening. At least the captain had been right about the location. He had followed the dry riverbed until the military jeep was struggling so much he was afraid it was going to get bogged in the sand or to blow a gasket. He wasn't especially mechanically minded, that was one of his brother's skills. But then he was always good at everything, the clever one; he himself hadn't been good at much at school except sports. He liked it when things were uncomplicated. As it was, they would never be able to turn round, they would have to back out.

Struggling up the dusty hillside he heard stones shifting somewhere below him, probably disturbed by their passage. Looking up there was a bit of scrub clinging to the rocks, but hardly any other vegetation: it was really desolate out there. A big bird of some sort, a vulture no doubt, sailed out above them, wheeling. Serge shivered despite the heat.

As soon as he ducked into the cave the temperature dropped dramatically. He took out his water bottle and drank deeply, then handed it to Jacques. Just a quick look was all they came for. Bright spots swam before his eyes in the darkness and he felt disorientated. Jacques wiped the neck of the canteen on his shirt tail fastidiously before drinking. He belched loudly in the echoing space.

"So this is what we came here for — it looks empty." He sounded disappointed. Jacques was an annoying little bugger, short for a soldier but with a high opinion of himself.

He couldn't gauge the size of the cavity they had entered, but knew it was large with a high ceiling. Fumbling around for the big torch, he found it in the side pocket of Jacques' backpack, not that Jacques had bothered looking himself. When he managed to get the thing to work, the weak beam hardly broached the darkness. But his eyes were becoming accustomed to the dim light penetrating from outside. The captain had told him that there were supposed to be some kind of ruins up there but he had not expected anything like this. The red sandstone of the cave wall appeared to have been carved into a kind of pillared temple, with an ornate doorway worked into the back wall.

On either side of the opening on high red sandstone plinths stood two large pale statues of half-naked women, their hips draped in thin skirts hanging down to their bare feet. They were wonderfully proportioned, their arms were outstretched in welcome or perhaps entreaty, their proud, sad-looking, pretty young faces streaked with black tears. They were almost identical, too, the same woman each in a slightly different pose. The one on the left was missing a hand, broken off at the wrist.

He heard the liquid sound of stones trickling down outside and said to Jacques:

"Okay we've seen, come on, let's get back."

"No, wait!" Jacques cried out, his eyes bright in the darkness, "Let's take a look inside." He was getting fed up to the back teeth with Jacques, who seemed to get more arrogant by the minute. He claimed that though his father was French his mother was Swiss, her family was in banking or something, and he was only here for the experience, then he would be going back to join the family business. Devil-may-care Jacques had been getting on his nerves.

"You must be joking, we aren't equipped for potholing."

"Just a look, come on, bring the torch." Jacques made off across the smooth stone floor to the shallow stair that climbed up six or seven steps to a dark doorway. Serge followed reluctantly. Close up, the statues were smaller than he had at first thought, about life-size, beautifully made. He was drawn to them, he wanted to touch, to run his hands over those proud breasts, encircle their slim waists and lay his head on a cool, hard stomach. They climbed the steps together and he went over to the figure on his left and ran his fingers over the stone. To his surprise it was smoother than he expected, not granular like the stone of the temple and far paler than the elaborately carved doorway.

"What the hell is this place?" he whispered, beginning to feel intimidated by the silence.

"Captain said Roman ruins, except they don't look too ruined, do they? Just old and dusty and, slightly damaged, a bit of cleaning and a few repairs and they'd be good as new"

Jacques approached the doorway, he could see that the wood had rotted, leaving only a few splintered scraps clinging to the rusty bands of the ancient hinges to bar the entry.

"Maybe the ruins are inside, Serge, take a look at what's left of these doors." Serge was on his knees scrabbling around in the dust by the steps.

"What you doing Serge? Come over here with the torch and let's take a look inside."

"Just a look was what he said! It's getting late, we're going back." He got to his feet and made his way back to the entrance. Jacques grumbled about the wasted opportunity, but followed all the same, not caring to be left alone in that eerie place.

"Let's come back tomorrow then, Sergio, now we know where it is; we'd need to set off earlier though if they'll let us."

Then he noticed that Serge was carrying something out of the cave and wanted to see. Serge held up his prize: outside in the sunlight the stone was a bloodless ghostly white, it was the weeping woman's hand, broken off at the wrist but otherwise intact and, held open, it seemed to be imploring.

"It was in the dust at her feet," said Serge, taking the backpack off his shoulder and tucking his souvenir away. He didn't feel comfortable until they were back in the jeep and heading for home. He had felt observed on the exposed hillside and times were still dangerous.

The captain had been guarded but he was obviously overjoyed with Sergio's find, and said it looked like it had come from a Roman marble or perhaps an even earlier culture. He wanted to organise an expedition to explore the temple.

But they were at war, still struggling to defend France's economic interests in Algeria and it was all going rather badly, so their trip would have to wait. Perhaps they could go together to visit when he had a bit of leave — but it was splendid news. Serge had never asked how the captain had found out about the site. But not far from there they had driven past the extensive remains of an ancient ruined town sprawling down the scrubby red hillside and the captain had always been interested in old stuff.

They had been told to keep their mouths shut about the temple but one thing was sure: if they intended to take out anything large like the statues, they would need more help. Not all the Arabs were fighting against the French: many worked with them and the barracks were full of Arab soldiers. But Serge guessed the captain would not want any of them knowing that he was planning to somehow spirit away part of their national heritage. When he asked about the moral aspect of the venture, the captain had said that the museums of the world were full of treasures plundered from those unable to recognise, appreciate or protect them.

"We will only be liberating some otherwise unknown antiquities in the same way Napoleon did when he took his army into Egypt. What's good enough for Napoleon's good enough for me."

The captain had that reassuring air of calm confidence that put him at ease. Not that he really cared. He couldn't even see why they were out here: the French had been trying to civilise and educate this hopelessly lazy race for four or five generations to little avail. They didn't deserve to keep the weeping women, who anyway were probably weeping because they were being kept against their will.

It was several weeks before they managed to organise a trip back up into the mountains. The captain had brought ropes, lamps, and a pick and a shovel which Serge suspected he would be carrying up there and of course wielding. But he had also brought a picnic and wine and a little camera; he had not been able to send any photos back home since he had been there and hoped to persuade the captain to take some shots of him, perhaps picnicking at the mouth of the cave. They would look good; and it would put his mother's mind at rest to see him relaxing in the shade beside the remains of a good meal. It was early morning when they set out and the sun still lacked the fierce intensity that made any kind of movement a torment later in the day.

Before they even got close Serge could see that something had been going on in the dry river bed that took them to the foot of the escarpment leading up to the cave. He pointed out the tyre tracks and how some of the bigger boulders had been moved out of the way to allow a larger vehicle through. The captain was agitated when they finally stopped and climbed down from the jeep, and told Serge to bring only a canteen of water and a torch. They could see the cavity up above and to the right of them. The captain went scrambling up ahead, making short work of the climb. Serge came behind, noticing how the ground had been levelled here and there, holes filled and rocks pushed aside. There were footprints everywhere, mostly smooth-soled, probably sandals, but there were boots among them too.

He hadn't known what they expected to find as they had not entered the space behind the broken doors the first time. So he couldn't guess what the people who had got here before them had come for. As his eyes became used to the light he let out a low groan.

"What, what can you see?" the captain turned towards him, his face twisted with anxiety and frustration.

"The women, the statues have gone."

That was when things became confusing. There was a small rock-fall at the mouth of the cave. When he went to see, there were two traditionally-dressed Kabyl tribesmen, heads wrapped in cloth turbans, standing outside with a couple of heavy old wartime

Lee-Enfields levelled at them. The captain pulled back into the shadows and brought out his revolver, but Serge was not quick enough. The men ran up and jabbed their guns into his ribs. He raised his arms and they relieved him of his weapon and gestured him outside, still keeping their eyes on the deep shadows that hid his companion.

He knew that the captain would not be far behind, he saw no other Arabs and shouted out to him that there were only the two. But the captain never came to his rescue. Serge was forced to climb up behind the cave until they came to a narrow winding track where a small boy was waiting with three sway-backed, moth-eaten donkeys. When he saw the child his hopes rose a little: no one would kill a man in front of a child, would they? But one of the tribesmen chopped him hard in the kidneys with the butt of his rifle and he fell gasping to his knees. The child screwed up his face and Serge thought he was going to cry, but instead the kid spat in his face. He looked around desperately for any sign of the captain. But before he had time to see if he was coming one of the men grabbed his arms and the other wrapped his head in a stinking old hessian sack.

P en awoke as he often did these days, alert, listening to the sounds of the house, the tiny creaks, and the regular ticking of the heating overlaid by Sophie's soft snoring. It was still dark. They had always slept naked and Pen resisted the temptation to turn into the warmth of her familiar body for a few more minutes. Through a gap in the curtains he could see that the day would have trouble breaking. He was aware of the odd drip of rain falling from the tiled roof into the zinc guttering outside the bedroom window. It had rained in the night, but had it rained enough?

Peeling back his side of the bedclothes quietly he rose and dressed in the light from the landing, pulling on the clothes that lay rumpled over the chair where he had chucked them the night before. Sophie's lay neatly folded next to them like a reproach; he touched the soft material lightly then stole down the stairs to the back door. A slow excitement was building in his gut. It was not yet light enough to see properly but it felt like there had been a good downpour. Somewhere a jay gave a dry rasp which started off an argument with its neighbours and there was a brief squabble in the wet branches of the oaks surrounding the garden.

There was no time for breakfast. Pen rooted around in the larder and found half a packet of biscuits. Those and a banana from the fruit bowl would have to do. He checked his pockets for change, tobacco, his lighter. Then, grabbing a green plastic raincoat and his rubber boots, he was out the door. He felt guilty taking the little Peugeot, leaving the girls the truck for the school run. But the truck was too conspicuous and prone to getting bogged down once it went off-road — he had found that out too many times, to his annoyance. He was resourceful as one had to be, living the kind of isolated life they did, and had always managed to get the vehicle out of trouble, but sometimes it had cost him the morning and what it might have brought him.

The old Peugeot was ideal. A small powerful car, an inconspicuous dark green, it could be parked anywhere without attracting attention. Day was finally attempting to assert itself, and a narrow band of pewter light clearly outlined the wooded slopes to the east around the property as Pen pulled out of their muddy track.

He could see now the standing puddles of rainwater gleaming promisingly in his headlights as he hit the poorly maintained tarmac and shifted up into third gear. He knew exactly where he wanted to go, but was undecided as to which route to take. He was beginning to have a good feeling about today.

As he accelerated out into the dawn he was visited by thoughts of his mother. She had become a ghost, slowly wasting away in that terrible home back in Suffolk. Guilt took a small bite out of him, almost ruining his mood until he shrugged it off.

When he looked back on that day, as he frequently would, he could see that it was the starting point. That was to become one of the last carefree days he could remember; his brief unease when setting out that morning had been like an unheeded warning that augured disaster. If the yet fairly innocent Pen Williamson had had the slightest inkling of the events that were about to unfold around him like the slow beating wings of his troubled pubescent dreams, he would have appreciated those last quiet moments for the haven they were. Afterwards he was forced to wonder, had he known where events would lead them, would he have acted any differently? Passion is a strange master, not easily denied. Pen would have liked to think that, given the same choices today, he would have done the right thing. But he couldn't be sure.

It was late autumn, and across the south of France it had been a hot season that year. The Indian summer was making up for an atrociously wet and miserable July and August. The leaves had turned suddenly, giving a wonderfully festive feel to the end of the year. It had been dry since the harvest, and the stubble had stood in the fields for weeks on end. But lately there had been a flurry of activity as the farmers had ripped over it in preparation for ploughing. They needed rain to soften the soil for that to be possible. Pen had watched patiently, secretly happy that the ploughing had been held up, giving him time to get on with his new job. The rain had eventually come, but by then most of the farmers were occupied with other work.

By mid-October he was beginning to wonder if the bulk of the ploughing might end up getting done in the spring. The traditional farming methods were slowly being abandoned as ever-bigger machinery came onto the market. It was becoming common for the time honoured methods of removing stubble, weeds and even old pasture before ploughing, to be replaced by chemical defoliants like Roundup, or Agent Orange as they called it in the Vietnam war. He shook his head at the thought. To what avaricious lengths would those powerful multinationals not go to get the salt of the earth to poison their own land? It was exasperating.

He swerved and stamped hard on the brakes, swearing creatively as the small fallow-deer leapt out from the woodland and disappeared into the trees on the other side.

"This road gives about as much traction as a greased eel's arse!" Last year, when Pen had hit a deer, his insurance just didn't want to know. It hadn't been the first time he had turned up at Rémy's door with a carcass to butcher in the boot of his car, but the repairs to the Peugeot had to come out of his own ragged pockets.

He slowed down, realising that in his haste he had become distracted. He remembered one recent afternoon driving to pick Alice up from school behind a heavy beat-up Massy-Ferguson tractor equipped with a mud-caked five-blade plough and thinking, "They've started..."

That was two weeks ago. Since then Pen had been out most days checking on which fields had been worked. This entailed an enormous amount of driving. The Périgord is huge, with long valleys that divide the countryside into a series of ridges. Most of it is wooded, so that even with the pair of binoculars he kept in the car he often had to get up close to a field to see what state it was in. Still, he did not begrudge the driving — there was always something new to discover.

He had come to France for the first time in the late 1980s, on an impulse. He badly needed a break after the drawn-out, painful ending of his first real relationship. So he took his worn-out little English Morris Mini-Traveller down to Bordeaux. The old city could not be called pretty, but it had a stocky elegance and the wide boulevards one associates with France, it had a comfortable feel to it. He loved the shady, paved squares with their central fountains and the heavily populated terraces in front of the cafés and bars surrounding them. Many of the tall, well-made limestone buildings were strung out along the west bank of the wide muddy Garonne. Pen knew that the city and the region of Aquitaine had belonged to the English crown until the middle of the fifteenth century. To him Bordeaux had an exotic feel, just what he needed: France seemed to exude history. In the Musée d'Aquitaine he was drawn to the prehistory wing, the carved bone and the engravings of naked goddesses on stone plaques fired his imagination. He had read so much about the amazing find, by three school kids in the 1940s, of the prehistoric painted-cave site at Lascaux in the Périgord that he had decided to drive down there and see for himself.

Arriving in late July to the sound of crickets and cicadas, Pen had fallen instantly in love with the place. He felt at home in its tightly folded, bleached-out landscape, so often clad in deeply shadowed woodland. There were unspoiled medieval hamlets tucked into most of its valleys and plenty of fairy-tale chateaux. He took immediately to the gentle pace, where everything seemed to be set to a soothing, unhurried rhythm. It reminded him of his childhood in the garden with Guinevere, his mother, he ended up staying. To his chagrin Lascaux had long since been closed to the general public. However it was just one inaccessible jewel in the barely credible trove of treasures that the Périgord would reveal to him over the years.

He needed to get up onto the plateau to the east of the small village of St Léon. His first destination was a long narrow strip of land that was sown with maize most years. But last year he had been surprised to find that it had been made over to wheat, a mixed blessing.

As he came up over the crest of the hill he spied the bootlace of the Vézère river glinting in the middle distance, sluggish as molten lead as it snaked down through a wide plain of tidy freshly-worked farmland. Tall Lombardy poplars lined the river's banks and separated some of the fields, dark shadows glowing a dirty yellow in the early light. Turning into a well-maintained lane he could see the grey-slated spires and rooftops of the château looking like the folded plates of some slumbering dragon behind the trees. Smoke plumed up beyond it as a hearth fire somewhere got going.

Pen pulled in to a lay-by he knew well and killed the lights. The rain had turned it into a shallow puddle of muddy ruts, but he knew it would be hard enough under the surface for the Peugeot.

Since arriving in the area, he had spent the years scraping a living as an artist, trying his hand at everything from sculpture, ceramics and print-making to drawing up building plans. When times were hard he had had to fall back on agricultural work at the neighbouring farms, helping out with the tobacco and strawberry harvests. He had even gathered walnuts for a season but had found it back-breaking; the ground was far too low down for his gangly frame. No wonder so many of the old French farmers' wives were bent permanently double, their spines ruined by years of stooping. The local people had been wonderfully welcoming and generously rewarded his work with friendship and good food. Those mid-day meals were always long, copious and festive.

Rémy Saliner had become a dependable friend over the years. He was patient with Pen's stumbling French and had turned out to be intelligent, informative and well-versed in local history. Even from the beginning, sweating under the weight of bales of dark pungent tobacco in the dusty, sun-drenched fields loading the trailers destined for the drying sheds, they had chattered away endlessly.

Sign-language came naturally to Rémy, as with most French people. Tie their hands behind their backs and you're essentially gagging them — Pen often thought — so communication was mostly sign-language. Pen's open good nature and willingness to work endeared him to these people who showed their gratitude with ridiculous ten-course lunchtime meals, well irrigated with rather poor local wine. Rémy refused to drink water — he said he found it too bland. By two o'clock they were back in the fields reeling from the effects of the food and wine and a liberal dash of *eau de vie* in their coffee. The pay was pathetic, but it was better than nothing and Rémy was an invaluable source of intelligence.

It was that first day, when he had turned up at the imposing but unlovely modern farmhouse, that Pen was to be smitten by the virus that was to afflict him for the years to follow. He was apprehensive when he heard the sudden cacophony of hunting dogs as he knocked on the scraped and peeling front door.

Rémy had torn the door open wide as he hurled an incongruous falsetto voice over his shoulder at the dogs. Then turning his attention to Pen, he had said:

"Oui?"

"Er," replied Pen, in English, "I'm looking for work."

Rémy raised his almost transparent eyebrows. The man that stood before Pen looked about his own age, thirtyish, tall and thin, half a head taller than him with a whip-like toughness that must have come from his outdoor life. The knuckles of a large brown hand stood out like knots of wood where they rested on the doorjamb. The untidy fair hair had been bleached blond from hours of work in the sun and his soft grey eyes seemed full of humour.

Pen was ushered into the hall, the dogs leaping up to greet him with their unbearable dog smell and their sharp scraping claws.

"Ulysses! Attila!" screamed Rémy, and the dogs scampered through an open doorway and settled under the kitchen table. Pen could see an old couple who he guessed were Rémy's parents sitting there shelling beans into a saucepan.

His eyes were drawn to the plain glass-panelled display case that took up half the hallway. It was well made in blond oak, placed there to be seen by visitors. It was packed full of prehistoric flint implements. The prominent display spoke eloquently of a collector's pride.

"Wow, did you find these?" Pen mimed, unable back then to find the words in French.

"No, no," gestured Rémy. Bit by bit, Pen worked out that it was Rémy's father who found the flints when he was out working the land, where they grew like mushrooms.

Pen slipped from his car taking care not to slam the door. The château stood on a promontory dominating the valley below. Over the years he had discovered that this was exactly the kind of site our distant ancestors had chosen to occupy. He now knew that a large part of France had been inhabited by successive hominid species more or less constantly for close on a million years. It was staggering. What was more astonishing was that those long vanished people had left behind thousands upon thousands of their stone tools. When you knew how to look for them, they could be easily found, as they patently had been by Rémy's old dad.

The long field behind the château had been ploughed two weeks ago, Pen had searched it in vain for flakes of flint, But the earth was too dry, and needed a good soaking to wash them clean. Last night's rain should have done the trick. The nice thing about a ploughed field was that you need not worry about damaging someone's work, and just concentrate on the flint hunting. If the farmer spotted you, he wouldn't get in a twist because you were walking on his seedlings, and until recently would merely consider you a little eccentric for wasting your time in what for most people was a pointless pursuit. The downside was that a ploughed field is one of the most difficult terrains to walk over. It was not for nothing Pen reflected, that the battleground of Agincourt, like many other medieval battlegrounds, was purported to have been ploughed up by the defenders before combat. For all the good it did them on that occasion.

As he stepped out into the field, a familiar calm came over him and his mind slowed its headlong monologue, his thoughts draining away, he was at one with the present. These moments seemed the only time these days that he found the profound peace he had known as a young hopeful artist working away for hours on a canvas oblivious of time, free of need. He stood for a moment while he rolled a cigarette and surveyed the results of the rain.

The field rose up the hillside from the lane, but it had a few dips and a prominent high spot quite close to where he was standing. Many were the fields that Pen had walked from bottom to top, finding nothing of interest apart from one small spot where he realised that there must have been a settlement, however brief. That little rise in front of him was one such place. He set out with exquisite anticipation. This narrow field had brought him many of his most interesting finds.

The stones scattered everywhere must have been deposited when the land had been either seabed or perhaps an antediluvian coastline.

They were mostly rolled pebbles in smooth yellow ochre and jasper reds that contrasted with the fine sandy soil. In some areas like the one he was looking at, the underlying limestone had been brought up by the plough in small flat slabs. The flakes of flint, of which Pen could see there were many, were bluish or shiny grey in the early light.

He picked up everything, scrutinising every small flake for signs of workmanship. This was time-consuming but Pen had a soft spot for a well-made little scraper or borer.

Often those were the only things he took home with him after a long morning's hunting — but not today. When the moment came he showed no reaction, other than to stop his slow advance over the long abandoned campsite. His eyes were sliding over and over the exposed edge of what he knew to be a buried hand-axe. He had learned to savour these all too rare moments.

The sinuous edge that presented itself to him was distinctive in that it was a warm caramel colour, unlike the local flint which was black when freshly broken but weathered to all shades of blue-grey or white depending on many criteria which he had learned to read. He knew that this toffee-coloured flint was common the other side of the river at La Chapelle towards the medieval city of Sarlat where Sophie had her handicrafts stall. It had been carried a long way to get here. He bent down to pull it from the ground it had lain in for perhaps a hundred thousand years. Instinctively he held his breath. This looked like it could be a good piece — but was it going to be intact?

Too many of the larger, most impressive of the prized hand-axes he had found were inevitably damaged by the passage of heavy farm machinery. The machines that had brought them to light invariably destroyed them. The longer they lay uncollected after being dislodged by the plough, the more chance they had of being damaged by the successive passages of the tractor in the course of farming the land. Pen had long despised superstition but believed in luck: his motto was 'Seek and ye shall find'. The luck came in two parts: first, did the object happen to be just where you were looking? and, most important, would it be intact?

His hope was that this piece had lain undisturbed until two weeks ago when the land was worked, the plough having perhaps being set a little deeper than usual, flipping it up as the soil was turned. It came free with no resistance. It looked good. Wiping off both faces with the heel of his right hand, he scrutinised it with an expert eye.

"You little beauty!"

Pen had been right to savour the moment. The French called these tools '*biface*'. This one was magnificent. Without washing it he could not be quite sure, but he thought it was undamaged. Taking a slow drag on his cigarette, he gazed thoughtfully at the museum piece that had just come into his hands. He resisted the urge to go back to his car to rinse the mud off in the puddle, and slipped it into an empty coat pocket.

He had to finish this field quickly and get to the next before one of the other flint hunters beat him to it. There weren't many of them, but most were at least as badly afflicted as him, and he could count on coming across the footprints of someone who had already picked over a spot before the day was done.

He stiffened as he heard the sound of a motor turning into the lane. When he had started collecting he had visited most of the farmers to ask permission to wander across their fields. One or two had refused, on the grounds that they collected themselves, which he thought fair enough. There had been no reply when he had rung at the wrought-iron gates of the château. He had asked a farmer whom he had spotted working the land one day. But the man did not live on the property and said that Pen would have to ask the owner, who lived in Paris. He had never got around to it. He hated confrontations with irate owners and now considered ducking down out of sight. The vehicle slowed and pulled into the lay-by behind Pen's car.

"Shit," breathed Pen. Discarding his smoked roll-up he turned to see what sort of a nuisance this might be. It had already broken his concentration and was destroying his peace, but he could easily be bawled at and thrown off this rich site for ever.

Some of the tension went out of his shoulders as he spotted a curly mop of light brown hair coming up the bank from the lane. With a hop in his stride, his old mate Noël strolled up towards him.

"God, you're out early," said Noël, trying to hide his disappointment: "Find anything yet?"

"No, I just got here myself," Pen lied easily.

"Had any breakfast?"

"No. You?"

"I've got some grub in the car. Let's have a bite while we talk."

Pen was hungry, he didn't argue. Besides, he had his most determined competitor with him now so no longer had to worry where else he might be hunting.

Noël was a small man, his finely boned face had a handsome, lived-in look, and his intelligent blue eyes didn't miss much.

"It's just there, the site. Where you were standing," he gestured, finger outstretched like a cocked gun.

"I didn't know you'd found this field," said Pen.

"Last spring just after the sowing, I found that small grey triangular biface right where you were standing, you know the one."

"Yeah, I know it," Pen grunted back "I've found a few here myself. I've never spotted any footprints though so I thought I was alone. I see I'll have to get up even earlier now to get here before you."

"Nah, don't worry," said Noël "There are other fish to fry."

"Not many," said Pen, "the sites are getting emptier every year and the farmers have stopped clearing woodland, so there won't be any more to look forward to."

They shared their food by the cars. Noël was well prepared with a fresh baguette, cheese, apples, orange juice and a bar of chocolate. Pen was happy to eat. Sharing his meagre fare with his friend he decided to relent and slipped the new find from his pocket.

"*Putain!*" groaned Noël in grudging awe. "What a beauty." Pen bent down and rinsed off the flint in the puddle to reveal a symmetrical, almond-shaped hand-axe larger than his own hand, its surface finely flaked all over with what he had come to recognise as the soft-hammer technique. The flint was a dull orange in the increasing morning light; but as he turned it over they both saw that it was a pale cream on the other face.

"Double patina," murmured Noël reverentially. "That's one hell of a piece, man. Can I come over to your place later to have a proper look at her?"

"Yeah, come and eat with us," Pen offered as they both took out their tobacco.

"Where are you off to now?"

"Fanlac," said Noël climbing into his old Peugeot estate.

"I'll bring a bottle of *rouge*. Good hunting."

"Same to you, mate." Replied Pen. With that the big car swung out into the lane, turned slowly and then accelerated away.

Pen went eagerly back to his field-walking, but his mind had unconsciously taken him back fourteen years to when Sophie was still living with Noël. If he had got to know them better as a couple, Pen was sure that he would never have taken advantage of that moment of weakness when their relationship was tottering on the edge.

He had been pretty broke, as usual, but had had an idea for a sculpture and was hoping to find a model who was prepared to work for a pittance. He pinned up an ad in the local bar without much hope, but you never knew. Sophie and Noël had moved to the Dordogne to escape a cloying past as well, but he did not get to hear about that until a good while later. When Sophie heard that an English artist was prepared to pay for someone to sit around in his studio all day, she came to visit. It was early summer, Pen remembered that evening. He had just finished smoking a little joint when a woman's voice called through the open barn door:

"*Bonjour.*"

Pen was not expecting anyone to drop by and was chilling out after spending a frustrating day trying to work out an idea in three dimensions.

"Hey, smells good in there," she called.

"Oops," thought Pen. "Er, hi."

"Hi, *Monsieur.*"

"I'm not *Monsieur*, I'm Pen," he said.

"*Bonjour, Monsieur* Pen," she said. "I heard that you were looking for a model." Pen was stunned for a moment. The evening sun backlit this strange woman, her light hair glowed, a golden nimbus hung around her head, and he was having trouble making her out.

"I'm Sophie," she said. "It smells good in your home."

"Hum?" fumbled Pen, stepping around his workbench and moving towards her across the concrete floor.

"Is there any left?"

"Any what?"

"Your grass."

"Er, no, I finished it,"

"Shame," said Sophie with a sad smile. "I came looking for work."

Pen had trouble believing his eyes. She looked not much over twenty, with an athletic figure. There was a neglected sophistication about her. Had she deliberately dressed unflatteringly for this unusual job interview? It took little intuition to see that even a potato sack would look good on her sleek frame. She had a distinctive face too, once it came into focus, high cheekbones and a straight nose with nostrils that curled up to each side giving her a feline look. Her narrow lips were pulled into a serious little smile. Though she wore no makeup that he could discern, it still looked as if those dark questioning eyes had been lined with kohl.

"Come on in," said Pen, trying to cover his self-consciousness. "Have you ever done any modelling?"

"Not at all," replied Sophie.

"Hum, do you mind if I ask how old you are, Sophie?"

"No, I don't mind."

"Well, how old are you?"

"I'm twenty-six," she said, giving him a coy grin. "You need someone?"

"Yes, I've been asking around, but I didn't expect it to be this easy. Do you know what I need you to do?"

"I suppose I just have to sit around all day with no clothes on."

"Yes, something like that."

"Something like, or that?"

"No, no, look," said Pen, leading her over to the desk where several large drawings lay scattered amongst the mess of crayons, teacups and objects that Pen brought back from his regular walks in the countryside.

"They're lovely," said Sophie, "but a bit sombre, no?"

The drawings in red and black depicted the same woman lying in different contorted poses with a look of desolation — or was it boredom — on her face, when it was visible through her tangled hair. Pen had thought that his period of convalescence was well over. The separation with his ex had been a bit like surviving a motorway pile-up, involving people you never expected to hurt, and leaving a dreadful crop of lasting scars.

Looking at his work through Sophie's lovely eyes, he realised that he had yet to move on from those dark musings.

"These are old drawings. Besides, if you don't mind, I would like to start with some photographs."

"Oh, photographs! Why not?"

"Would you mind if I photographed you?"

"Not really, no. I suppose not. Look, there's your joint in the ashtray. It's not really finished. May I light it?"

Pen was taken by this friendly young woman, with whom it looked like he would be working, and said,

"No, it's finished. But you can roll one if you want." He fished under the desk and brought out a shopping bag half full of pungent weed. Sophie's face lit up as she took the bag, plunged her hand into the dried flowers and brought a fistful up to her nose.

"Oh, it looks good. But you didn't dry it properly. It smells a bit like fresh hay."

"What?" said Pen, surprised at her assumption that he had dried the plants and therefore grown them.

"We grow our own too, but there is never much left by the summer. Would you sell me some?"

"Shit," thought Pen "this girl might be trouble."

"I don't sell grass," he said "it just grows in the garden."

"How many plants did you grow?"

"I had three but two were males, so I pulled them up."

"And you got all this?"

"There is more," said Pen, "but I don't keep it here."

"More?"

"Where I grew them, the last owner used to keep chickens. The soil was so rich the plant just went crazy!"

Pen had scraped and saved and begged and borrowed all he could, and had managed to buy the old tobacco-drying shed the year before. In those bygone years the building and planning regulations were supple enough to allow him to camp there for a few years and renovate it. The broken-down wire chicken-run had turned out to be an amazing garden once he had got it cleared. He was in the process of converting the space inside the wooden building into a studio with living space at the back, but it was slow going, mainly because he never had two coins to rub together.

Sophie was saying something, but he had missed it.

"Sorry?" he said.

"I would be happy to work for your grass," said Sophie. "It's better than money for me."

That evening, before Noël turned up, Pen arranged his day's findings all freshly scrubbed on the kitchen table. Sophie was clattering around between the sink and the stove with a large ladle in her hand, a cast-iron pot was steaming away on the wood-fired range. It was already dark and the lights had been left on in the studio. They heard the big doors sliding back as Noël let himself in. There was a rap at the door between the two adjoining rooms, and without waiting for a response Noël pushed it open. His arms were full and Pen relieved him of a bottle so that he could brace himself to lever off his still muddy boots. Tucked under his left arm was a small crate.

There were warm smiles and kisses all around.

"Smells good," remarked Noël: "Roast veg! Parsnips, or squash?"

Sophie smiled at him.

"You'll have to wait and see."

"What will you have to drink, Noël?" said Pen. "Gin-and-tonic, wine?"

"Yes, I think we need to celebrate this," said Noël, leaning across the table even before putting down his box and picking up the morning's prize.

"Sumptuous."

Pen had scrutinised the piece many times already. It was without doubt the most beautiful biface he had ever found. He had even put it back down on the ground once to re-live the moment he had first seen it. He could discern no damage at all. Apart from the patina, it was as it had been the day it was made, which was unusual. Its edge bore none of the distinctive steps that re-sharpening produced. It looked as if it had never been used all.

"So flat, no cortex, made on a large flake of Bergerac flint, not from La Chapelle," proclaimed Noël knowledgeably, "sexy as hell."

"You guys are sick," observed Sophie "I'm going to have a drink. I've been cooking all evening. Come on."

By the time they had settled down and started in on their gin, Alice had come downstairs. She was supposedly doing her homework.

"You can turn that stupid computer off now." Sophie said, "We're going to eat." Alice seemed not to hear and went and sat on Noël's lap.

"Did you find anything, Noël?" she asked.

"I don't really know, sweetie. I don't think there's anything left. Your papa has found it all. There's always stuff like that." He waved dismissively at the few grey flakes on the table. "But there was something unusual today." He took a long pull at his gin and then started unpacking his box.

On the top was an old sock. They both used these to protect pieces of any worth. It had an egg-sized lump in it down in the toe. He put his hand in and pulled out a piece of lettuce-green stone and handed it to Pen.

"My god, it's a piece of jade!"

"A piece of a polished jade axe I think," said Noël sadly. "If only she was whole. Look, she's flat on this side and then curved." He drew the nodule in the air with precise hand gestures.

"Where did you find it? We don't get much Neo in this part of the Dordogne, and I've never seen anything of this quality here."

Noël hesitated. They had always been fiercely competitive with their collecting. Pen wondered if that had something to do with their relationships to Sophie, an unspoken rivalry. They rarely asked precise provenances and almost never offered up the sites of their most-prized finds unless the other already knew of them. Then Noël's eyes sought out Pen's and he smiled, crinkling up the crows-feet around them.

"After I left you I went to Fanlac, but some irate peasant saw me in the field and started shouting from his car."

"Crazy buggers! Probably don't collect anything but parking tickets themselves."

"Or stags' heads," said Noël.

"They've become so jealous. They reckon we're getting rich from the sweat of their brows."

"But they just grind everything to gravel with their massive machinery! They never get down off their air-conditioned tractors to pick them up." Pen looked pained.

"No, and it's getting worse."

"Anyway, I couldn't stay there so I went back to St Léon, but by lunch-time I only had this."

Noël was unpacking his little box of findings. Three scrapers, two points, the nicer one broken, a large side scraper and two good nuclei which were the waste-products from making the points. But these larger pieces were also damaged. The best find came out last, a good-sized biface with a narrow blade and thick ergonomic base. It was milk-white on the face that had been exposed to the air for untold millennia, but a dark grey with faint red veining on the side that had lain in contact with the heavy clay soil: thus sheltered from the atmosphere, it had been effectively protected from ageing.

Pen groaned as he picked it up. The point had been freshly snapped off. He could discern the darker, near-black of the original flint in the break. Noël looked disgusted.

"Looks like it came up just now, like yours, but it wasn't so lucky."

"Yes, but it's much older. Looks Acheulean. Mine's Mousterian, it's much more symmetric."

"Neanderthal stuff, that is what nearly all of this is," said Noël, gesturing once more at the table.

"So who made this?" said Pen, looking down at the well-made Acheulean blade in his hand. "Erectus, Heidelbergensis?"

"It's hard to say, but it's old, two hundred thousand years at least, maybe lots more." Noël's eyes sparkled in the light of the candle burning amongst their clutter on the table. Pen reached out and picked a thumb-sized flat flake from the table. The end had been worked into a perfect curve.

"And this is us, Cro-Magnon."

"Homo sapiens?" said Noël.

"They are all Homo sapiens, we are Sapiens sapiens."

"God, why did they make the taxonomy so complicated?"

Alice yawned loudly. Sophie picked the big pot off the gas-ring with a pair of oven cloths.

"They will make a good table-mat for the soup I think."

"All right," said Pen, "we get the message."

After dinner, still around the table, they were enjoying the end of the wine when Noël got to his stockinged feet.

"Hey, Noël, man, let me get you a pair of slippers."

"Not to worry," Noël replied, beginning to gather the dishes.

"Noël, leave that, Pen will do it. You can roll a joint."

"Okay, but we need the space," said Noël.

"Oh, you two!"

The piece of jade glowed quietly between them on the table, its surface slightly cloudy in the diffused light. "This has been broken for a long time, it even looks rolled."

"Yes," agreed Noël, "I found it by the river."

Pen looked incredulous. They rarely hunted down on the plain as the sites were usually buried too deep for the plough to reach them. On the high land, by contrast, the earth was constantly eroded away and the sites were often only centimetres beneath the surface.

When the time was right, as it was now, they were always to be found roaming the elevated sites that they had spent years exploring on those hills.

"Where exactly, Noël?"

"I came back. I took the bottom road below the château where we met this morning. I guessed that if they lived up there they would have to come down to the river for water. I didn't find anything, of course, but I went right down to the river. I found this embedded in the bank, the water is high since the rains, it had been washed out. I thought it was a piece of pottery at first."

They both knew that European jade is extremely rare. The main deposits are now known to have been in the southeast-facing Italian Alps in the Piedmont. Jade was highly prized during Neolithic times for its seductive beauty. It was used to make ceremonial axes and jewellery, and the deposits were thought to have eventually been worked out completely. The evidence that they existed was only discovered in the late twentieth century. Before that, Pen had read, it was believed that the ancient jade in Europe must have been imported from Burma or China. He had also read that in the late nineteenth century a prominent German archaeologist had offered a respectable sum of money to anyone able to bring him a single chunk of native European jade in the hope of proving this theory wrong and finding the source. The prize was apparently never claimed.

Like most self-respecting flint collectors, both Pen and Noël dreamed of owning a Neolithic polished jade axe. Pen scanned the press hoping to hear of one of them coming up for auction just to see one change hands. Many had been found, of widely varying qualities, mostly dug out of burial mounds. But most of those were now in museums. Pen had seen his first one in the British Museum, a long triangular axe, beautifully symmetric in a smooth deep green jadeite, and so thin. It had a sharp pointed butt and a wide, perfectly curved blade.

That axe had been found in Kent, but is believed to have been already old when it came over from France. It had perhaps spent time in Brittany, where so many jadeite axes have been found. It seemed a fragile object to have survived intact, changing hands, being treasured for generations. The jade must originally have come from the Alps, like the piece he was now turning thoughtfully over in his fingers.

"Listen," said Pen, holding the stone up to the light. "This must have come from a burial mound. "We need to find out where it was."

"Well, perhaps you could start with the washing-up, my little Pen."

Sophie had hit the nail on the head. Where the hell were they to start looking on the vast cultivated flood-plain of the Vézère Valley for a six-thousand-year-old burial mound?

"I'll dry," was all Noël contributed.

Alice had retreated back upstairs. There was no school tomorrow and she was shouting down for a story. Sophie came to the rescue with an old story tape that Pen had salvaged from another life, along with his old tape player. He was hoping to cultivate a little love for English literature in his daughter. Noël went upstairs to say goodnight.

"What's this?" he asked when the dramatic music came on.

"The Hobbit," said Alice, eyes wide. "Have you heard it? It's in English."

"Ah Tolkien, it's my favourite, my little elf." He grinned at her conspiratorially. "This story is full of little people like you."

"Maman says it's too violent for me, it gives me the willies," she said, giggling with anticipation, "but I need to see how it ends."

"Mm, she's right little one, she wants to protect you. But life is full of strangeness. It's easy to lose what you love the most."

"Like Gollum did? I don't like Gollum."

"Perhaps... perhaps a little." He bent over her and kissed her lightly on her hair, turning softly out of the room as the story captured her attention.

Noël's mood had changed; he looked more serious and was lost in thought. He was quietly starting to pack his stones away when Pen came downstairs from saying his own goodnights. He pretended not to notice the transformation.

"We need to take a look, Noël. What are you doing tomorrow?"

"Tomorrow I sleep! It has been there for six thousand years, it'll wait another day or two."

3

Sophie had seemed preoccupied and grumpy after Noël left. She had gone to bed leaving Pen to clear up and fill the wood burner. She had been a long-suffering victim of premenstrual tension and he had always known when the storm was due. But he refrained from saying anything these days as she tended to fly into a temper at his implication that she should be able to recognise the signs and control her moods. He just called her Grumpy-Bum. But he knew her period had just finished.

Now he lay on his back next to her, looking up into the dark. He had been thinking back to a conversation with Rémy's father after he had decided to begin collecting. The older man had found his flints in the course of his work, Pen had asked him if he could give some idea of the best places to look. Claude was so unlike his son in appearance, short and stocky, a broad smile showing silver teeth often spreading his ruddy cheeks. Only his probing eyes were like Rémy's, their heavy lids hiding an unexpected intelligence.

"Well," he began, his thick accent making it even more difficult for Pen to follow him, "they are easier to find when there are no other stones in the field to hide amongst." That particular condition had turned out to be one of the most infrequent that Pen had encountered in the thin soil of the hilltops. Down in the valleys the deep rich farmland was often pretty stone free, but then there weren't many flints either, most of those rolled by repeated seasonal flooding of the rivers and effectively ruined. He soon worked out that valleys were not good places for field walking.

It had been difficult at first for him to pick up enough prehistory to make sense of his finds. The subject was full of new terms, and although Rémy's dad had found plenty of artefacts he seemed to know next to nothing about them. He realised that his smattering of geology was insufficient, there was going to be a lot to learn. Visiting museums had helped, but it was slow going.

He got his head down and begun to read about the new subject, discovering that all those valleys had been cut by massive rivers in spate, many of them dwarfing any that still existed now. The water had been locked up for millennia in the immense ice-sheets that covered most of northern Europe, and sea-levels were sometimes more than a hundred metres lower than today

In a series of alternating warmer periods the melt-waters created rivers of such ferocity they cut deep wide channels down through the limestone bedrock in order to reach the sea.

In his mind's eye Pen saw boulders crashing down the swirling torrents while unfamiliar mega- fauna roamed the higher plateaux in wandering herds. The landscape of the region had been sculpted by these waters. The dramatic limestone cliffs that lined the narrow fertile plains were the results of more than two million years of glaciation. Pen knew that the ice-age was not over: we were just enjoying one of those warmer periods, and the ice was due back.

Sophie snuggled tantalisingly into Pen and began to snore softly. She often snored these days, especially when she had been drinking. Behind the tang of gin Pen wistfully inhaled the fresh scent of her. He let a hand slip over one of her grumpy buttocks. He was as horny as hell with the grass they had been smoking, but she often rejected his advances these days, with greater or lesser grace. He considered the alternative, and then forced himself to visualise the site where Noël had found the jade.

The château occupied a cliff-top overlooking the river. The land below had been shaped into two distinct terraces. He knew how it would be. Regular flooding had either scoured away or deposited thick layers of silt over most of the prehistoric sites in the bottom part of the valley. The higher terrace was more promising because it may have been inhabited since the river had ceased to wash over it. But the part that interested Pen was boggy. There was some sort of a spring there, and the land had been planted with poplars. That left a narrow band up above the track that wound down from the château at the foot of the cliff, but they should be looking for a mound or a dolmen.

Hopefully the relatively recent age of the Neolithic culture that had left that fragment of jade might mean that something could still be left of a monumental structure, if such a thing had been built down there.

Up early next morning, the smell of toast filling their luminous kitchen, Pen ate breakfast with Alice. She was a joy in the mornings, chatty and eager to get to school. Pen couldn't understand where that had come from. He had sort of liked school at one time, but not for long, and Sophie was not a morning person at all. It was comforting that their cheerful little daughter had not inherited all of their failings.

"Come on Papa, aren't you going to pour my juice?" said Alice, the anticipation showing on her face.

"Don't you want to try Aly? I'm sure you'll be fine."

"It's your thing Papa, come on, do it."

He had noticed the curious phenomenon years ago, and at first always tested it, but he had grown so used to it that he now took it for granted. He realised that when he had a bottle, jug, teapot or anything else with some liquid in it — not full, of course, that would be ridiculous or magic — if he up-ended it, emptying it completely into the recipient he wanted to fill, he could always count on filling it without overflowing or spilling any, often to within a whisper of the top. It was not an earth-moving experience, not something that had ever impressed anyone he told about it. Even Noël was unimpressed, and he had shown him dozens of times. Only Alice seemed to get as much pleasure from it as he did and it had become one of those quirky things that defined him. But despite his pragmatic nature he had stupidly become superstitious about it, fearing that one day some juice or milk would be left in the cardboard container or wine in the bottle or worse, spill from the glass spreading over the marble worktop, and his luck would change. Of late the fear had made him careful, checking what was in the bottle before daring to pour, or just pouring a half a glass. It made him feel foolish but he couldn't help himself.

It was a bit chilly as they left the house. Alice was eager to be off. He reminded himself that he had to cut some wood from the stack out the back. He did not mind the regular chore now that they were heating most evenings, but his chainsaw needed sharpening, which made the whole operation far more tedious.

The old car sprang to life reassuringly. He saw that he would have to stop in the village for fuel — he certainly did a lot of kilometres these days. Pen gave Alice a kiss at the school gate and felt a little tug at his heart-strings as she instantly took up with a girl in the playground and they skipped off chatting gaily. He and Sophie would probably be out of her thoughts all day. It felt strange, the way she was gaining a little more independence each day.

Without any conscious decision to do so, Pen found that he had taken the long way home to check out a couple of fields. He didn't have the time, but the virus wouldn't be denied.

Driving back from his unproductive foraging he passed not far from Rémy's place and decided to drop in. As he pulled into the muddy yard the dogs set up their infernal racket. He could tolerate Rémy's dogs now as they had got to know him, and had never been trained to attack humans. As soon as he climbed out of his car he heard Rémy screaming at the top of his voice at them to calm down. Then he appeared from between two barns with a gun in his hand. Rémy was a woodsman and a hunter, and they often served venison and wild boar at his table. But Pen had never seen a gun like that one around here. Rémy waved greetings when he saw Pen and gave a toothy smile, stretching out a big hand as he approached. Pen put up both of his own hands in mock fear.

"Shit, Rémy, what the hell's that?"

"Oh this, strictly speaking it's an unauthorised weapon."

"I'm not surprised. What are you doing with it?" It was a vicious-looking rifle with a well-polished wooden stock hanging in his loose grip, the oversized mat black barrel pointed at the ground. As he lifted it for Pen to see, he detached the intimidating cylinder with a twist of his hand.

"A silencer." Pen whistled with admiration.

"Yes, I've been shooting pigeons off the barn roof for my mum and this old .22 makes such a racket. I get one, and the others all fly off. I found it on the internet, works a treat." Pen had a bit of a fascination with weapons himself and they shared an interest in well-made knives and edged tools, which ran over into the flint collections.

Pen's parents had been absorbed by the Arthurian legends and had named him Arthur Pendragon Williamson, Pen for short. His early life haunted him increasingly. He had spent much of his childhood in a make-believe world charging off on quests in an assortment of glittering tin foil and cardboard armour and generally trying to be chivalrous. His parents peopled those years like half-remembered ghosts playing the parts of heroes and villains and princesses in distress. Since then he always had a sword or two around the place. Rémy had been impressed on his first visit to his home by the interesting assortment of blades Pen had built up over the years.

Apart from a couple of regimental swords and a bayonet bought from the flea markets there was a late Samurai katana, a sublime piece of metal-work called a kriss from Indonesia, and a brutal looking Ghurkha kukri which he had slung by his bed in its distinctive scabbard. Most precious of all, though, was a wicked-looking straight blade from Sumatra, supposedly forged from a meteorite centuries ago; the metal had something viscous about it, like oil on water. It was sheer magic. These last three had been presents from his friend Martyn, back from various extended trips abroad. He knew Pen's exotic tastes and had been rewarded with unstinting quantities of choice Dordogne bud and board, a buffer between ancient Asian romance and hard European reality.

Rémy had been brought up with guns. He loved them, and had a big gun-case on the wall in his kitchen. Among the strangely domestic-seeming double-barrelled shotguns were a couple of large game rifles kept lovingly well-oiled, and even a spare cattle prod in black leather, like something out of S&M Monthly. These particular weapons had proved so persuasive that a more powerful version was being issued to the French police now. The difference between Pen's collection and Rémy's was that Pen didn't use his to kill anything. Killing and butchery were a part of rural France that Pen hadn't come to grips with. Here was a new example of the clandestine side of country living. In the Dordogne he knew that plenty of farmers ran their cars on the cheaper red diesel only officially used for heating and tractors. He had been introduced to poaching, illicit distilling, truffle filching, and now the use of unauthorised weaponry. He could see why silencers were illegal even though, as Rémy had pointed out, they had some justifiable uses. His bit of dope-growing seemed tame stuff in comparison, but Pen didn't doubt that it would be considered a more serious offence by the rural gendarmerie if he were ever caught with his little drying-room full at harvest-time.

"Where are the pigeons then?" asked Pen.

"I hung them in the barn; they need to hang for a few days before they can be eaten."

"You're joking — they'll rot."

Rémy seemed surprised that Pen didn't know of this obviously commonplace practice.

"It's not a joke, Pen. If it isn't a bit rotten it's too tough and doesn't taste as good."

"Ugh!" said Pen grimacing, "remember not to invite me round when your mum serves them up!"

They got to talking about flints, and Pen asked him about the farmers who worked around St Léon. Rémy knew everyone and seemed to think that he would be safe enough hunting around the château, as long as he stayed out of the grounds. They would be unlikely to throw Pen out of the fields, but just to be sure he should go either early in the morning or between midday and two o'clock when any self-respecting Frenchman is having lunch.

Pen left Rémy promising he would drop back soon for a little apéritif, though he knew that "little apéritif" was a euphemism for a hefty piss-up. He was working for a new wealthy client, and needed to get on. There was something Pen felt he hadn't worked out yet about the guy, but he paid well and for Pen money was always tight. He had cursed his creative talents more times than he could count. Though he had never questioned his choice until he had to try and make a living out of it.

At art school he'd had few friends; he liked people, but just never went out of his way to meet them. Until they got to know him better though, those who liked him in return found his enthusiasm for the slightest insect or fallen leaf a little exasperating. He felt they wondered if he was a little simple — or perhaps he'd got god? He knew nobody else who found anything extraordinary in being alive. But when he suggested that we are the consciousness of the universe, they looked around to check that his nurse was within easy call.

Naively, he had thought to make his life an artwork by collecting and displaying, everything that he had in some way or another consumed in the living of it.

That first year had ended in disaster when he exhibited the work in a large classroom cleared for the purpose. He had collected all the items he had used, owned or possessed that year; from his bike and his few sticks of furniture, pots and crocks to a heap of food wrappers and used toilet-roll tubes. There were the books he had consulted, pencil-stubs, filled notebooks, shoes and socks, mostly clean, his best jeans and winter sweaters. There was all the music he had listened to, bus and cinema and even a couple of ice skating-rink tickets, stuck onto coloured sheets of cardboard, jostling for place amongst his drawings on the walls. He had thrown almost nothing away from that first year, and it was all packed into that darkened room lit with precise little spotlights. Empty tin-cans had been washed out and displayed together. Many of his objects were mounted on pedestals, giving them a pop-art feel, or hung with reverence; and on the door was a hand-printed sign announcing 'Pen Williamson, The Dappled Grove'.

His tutors thought he was taking the piss. His reaction to their rejection was to close in on himself, which made things worse because he refused to defend his concept. Pen would have walked out then if it hadn't been for one professor of sculpture, a discreet but intimidating, bearded fellow with whom Pen hadn't dared exchange two words all year. He seemed to find the whole thing hilarious as soon as he laid eyes on it, and genuinely found the idea ingenious.

Despite growing up alone and many years of terrible insecurity, it had taken this event to shake his native optimism. He had observed with incomprehension the current trend for pessimism and for the first time conceded that there might be grounds for a certain circumspection regarding this complacent post-war era. From that point on he spent a lot of time in the sculpture studio, though now he wondered if it was time well spent. "I could have been an engineer," he moaned out loud, "or an osteopath".

The wealthy client was a retired Belgian businessman with the unlikely name of Renault. He had been brought to Pen's workshop by Vincent, one of Pen's better-off flinting colleagues. He never knew how far he could trust Vincent, whose practiced charm always seemed condescending.

Vincent had a collection that had left Pen speechless the first time he had seen it. He no longer went stone-picking, if he ever had, but he was skilled at finding old collections. Being a local lad he knew everyone. He had gone to school in the village, as Alice did now, and was known as a passionate flint freak even as a child. That was years before Pen turned up.

Vincent had never told him, but it was common knowledge so Rémy let him in on it, that he would buy up farmers' cumbersome piles of old stones.

"Sort of do them a favour; find the stones a safe home while turning them into a modest sum of hard cash, something anybody could understand."

During the sixties and seventies, the farmers were stripping the densely wooded hillsides to grow strawberries or tobacco on the virgin woodland soil, or just to create pasture and more arable land. The flints that were turned up, sometimes in large numbers, were considered a legitimate crop, though even then they knew it would have to be a clandestine one. There were laws about archaeological finds — but what could the authorities do? The whole of the Dordogne was one big archaeological site. Private collections existed, usually owned by people of means, sometimes even government officials. They would claim that the collections were old, made before the restrictive laws came out in the forties. Vincent had been involved in the trade that had supplied them. He once boasted that if he assembled all the best flints he had owned, they would cover his living-room floor ankle-deep. *Biface,* meaning worked on both faces, were the most sought-after and held a unique fascination for collectors: they possessed a faceted, jewel-like completeness; a well-made one had a smooth, elemental simplicity. Pen had heard that those who were foolish enough to begin collecting often develop a craving and he was now in a position to confirm it. One could never acquire that final perfect piece that would round off the collection. They were all different, many were beautiful, and there were always more. Vincent had had the pick of the countryside for many years.

Unexpectedly for a foreigner, Pen turned out to have a sound instinct for a likely site, and a good eye. He worked for himself and so could usually be free to go out when the conditions were right. Even though he had turned up at the end of the bonanza, he had built up a respectable collection over the last few years and in the small world of flint enthusiasts word had got around. People often visited him at his workshop.

He called his studio the workshop for two reasons: because *un studio* also means a small flat in French, and because many of his friends worked in the building business and had workshops. His arty-farty status seemed a bit pretentious to some and, if truth be known, to him too. He rarely got the kind of work that merited it and his own stuff had not taken off. He was considered eccentric. People saw him wandering the fields alone, head down. Even if there were still a few stones left to find, was it worth traipsing through the mud all day long to find them? A disgruntled farmer once said to him, "You stone-pickers are like snails, you only come out when it rains." Pen had laughed, but the farmer wasn't joking. And of course everyone knew Pen did not have a proper job, which didn't help his image.

The day he met Maurice Renault, Pen had been mulling over ideas for an ancient Greek-style mural, a commission for a restaurant. He was about to roll a joint for inspiration when Vincent had turned up. In the fine weather the big doors were usually wide open and people could be seen approaching, if Pen lifted his head to look. But he was engrossed with the purple bud in his fingers, bopping his head to Miles on the big sound system, when he noticed a change in the light.

Vincent stepped in through the doors followed by a tall, distinguished-looking slightly older man. It was a warm day. Pen remembered being in t-shirt and jeans. But Renault, whom Vincent introduced, was in a jacket and well-pressed slacks. Tall and balding, with an eroded widow's-peak exposing a broad forehead, he looked over the lenses of his glasses with a shrewd gaze.

Pen zapped the volume of the music with the handset and drew a sheet of paper with practised ease over his makings.

"Call me Maurice," said Renault, holding out a substantial hand. Pen expected it to be firm, but the handshake was limp and a little damp.

For a second Vincent looked unsure how to continue, but Pen welcomed the interruption and smiled encouragingly.

"You look like you've got stones on your mind, Vincent."

"Yes, I was wondering if you had time to show some of your stuff to Maurice." Pen looked into the expectant face of his visitor and saw passion written all over it. It was always gratifying to show his collection to a new enthusiast.

"You flatter me Vincent, but what I have is nothing next to your hoard."

"Perhaps, said Vincent evidently agreeing, "but you should not be so modest. You've found some remarkable stuff. Besides, between the three of us, it is Monsieur Renault here who has the most impressive collection."

"Ah, you collect, Maurice, then I should make a condition: I'll show you mine if you show me yours." Renault gave a self-deprecatory little smile and frowned slightly. "I am not here often, but of course, you must come to the house with Vincent."

Pen led them through a door at the back of his work space into a small room lit by a couple of neons. There was no window and the walls were lined with narrow shelves. On the floor under the shelves were piles of dusty orange boxes and other containers brimming with Pen's lesser finds. Renault exhaled audibly:

"Yes, this is good."

Pen was proud of his flints. They represented thousands of hours of field-walking but also an ability to put himself into the mind of his prehistoric ancestors. Most of this stuff was Neanderthal; the oldest were pre-Neanderthal, and some went back five hundred thousand years.

Renault was turning one of Pen's most treasured bifaces over in his hands.

"This is magnificent, Pen. Would you be prepared to sell it to me?"

"Sorry?" said Pen, feeling foolish. People often asked him to sell pieces and he always refused, but had given dozens of the lesser ones away. Renault was supposed to have a fabulous collection of his own which meant that he must have it bad. Anyway that biface was special.

"I am trying to gather all the local material that I can to create a comprehensive collection. I will give you a good price for all your stuff."

"You're kidding me!"

Renault looked deadly serious. "How much do you reckon your stuff is worth?"

"I have no idea. Anyway, I couldn't sell it."

But Renault had squatted down and was going through the boxes. He held a small shoe-box in his hand with a blue fox printed on the lid. A few years ago it had held a pair of Alice's first proper little shoes; now it was so full of packets of arrow heads that the lid would not stay in place. Pen had found a few of those delicately-made points, but others he had picked up all over the place. Some of them came from the Davies Street antiquities market in London. He relieved Renault of the box.

"I can't sell these either"

"How much will you sell?"

Pen was always short of funds, but had resisted selling because people always wanted the best pieces.

"I like my collection, Maurice. I am not flush, as you can see. What I really need is work."

"Ah, Vincent told me that you are an artist. Well, when you come to the house you must tell me what you can do for my place, or perhaps the garden. You can make me a proposition. Now, my boy," Renault smiled expectantly: "What about it?"

"I shall have to think about it. But one thing is for sure: the stuff on the shelves is not for sale."

Vincent had been examining a large lustrous biface, his back to them, seeming to take no interest in the exchange. He looked put out when he turned around. Why? Because Pen had always refused to sell to him, or because Renault had appealed to Pen's vanity in offering him the kind of proposition he was always hoping for? Vincent's face was usually easy to read, but this time Pen couldn't tell what was on his mind. He guessed he didn't know that Renault was going to make him an offer, or that if he did, Pen would refuse him outright. Renault, it seemed, had a very persuasive manner.

Pen was glad they had not arrived after he had smoked that spliff. He would either have felt insulted and thrown them out, or more likely seen a quick way out of his troubles and accepted Renault's offer. He had a momentary image in his mind of a black-and-white photo from a Pink Floyd album he had once owned of a glamorous naked woman sitting with her legs tucked up to one side. In her hand she held a small bird while two more poked their heads out of her pubic hair. A bird in the hand...

They went through the motions of looking through a few more things, but it seemed clear that Renault, having made his play, had his mind elsewhere. Vincent looked a little embarrassed.

"We'll let you get back to work, Pen. Give me a call tonight and we will organise a visit to Maurice's house."

After they left, Pen couldn't get his head around Bacchus and Aphrodite any more.

Sophie was visiting her sister Denise, who suffered from bouts of more or less debilitating depression. Perhaps, now that the days had started drawing in, she was over-sensitive to the seasonal lack of light. Denise was a lovely girl, but could not seem to pull herself out of a series of crises that Sophie found wearing. She was surviving for the most part on tranks, booze and Sophie's sympathy. Sophie had an excuse to cut her visit short today because she would be picking up Alice from school, but she always came back drained — Pen thought it a good moment to visit Noël and find out what he made of this new turn of events. But first he would finish rolling his spliff. He felt he needed it.

That had been almost two years ago. Renault had turned out to be true to his word and offered Pen far more than he thought possible for his orange boxes. He even bought all the dross, stuff that Pen brought back from the fields that never made it into his little museum but piled up in drifts around the place. There was enough for Pen to change his truck and put long overdue solar panels on the workshop roof. More important though, Renault had given him work.

What Renault called his house was not far short of a château. Built out of pale dressed limestone, it had two large neo-classical wings. The central part had three storeys, and the high façades had a score of huge regularly-spaced shuttered windows. There was a warren of cellars and several decent dressed-stone outbuildings, some with arched open bays supported by stone pillars. There was an orchard, but very little farmland, Renault not caring to burden himself with the personnel necessary to tend it. At the bottom of the once ordered garden the wide river flowed sedately by.

One wet Sunday afternoon Vincent finally took him there. When he saw the place as they turned out of the woods, sitting at the end of a long rutted drive, Pen's first thought was that this would be a really cool place to put some of his work. It had just the right sort of run-down opulence. Close up, the place showed a few signs of neglect. The grass was over long and full of weeds, the shrubs in the forecourt were overgrown, and the maroon paint on the shutters was peeling, allowing the grey undercoat to show through.

Since that first visit, Pen had always had some project on the go for Monsieur Renault. Right now he was doing some ceramics for an abstract mosaic in one of the wide hallways. Renault took no nonsense. He liked contemporary stuff but it had to be the result of good craftsmanship. He allowed Pen free reign to develop his ideas but rejected them when they did not appeal to him. He liked big, imposing things.

On his most ambitious project, Pen had been able to employ one of his oldest mates, Alec, an energetic, easy-going English metal-worker who had lived there for years. Like Alice, his children were born there. Pen loved the whole family though he was a little intimidated by them — they were so intense. They always had a dozen things on the go and seemed to juggle them effortlessly. He wondered where they found the time. But then, he supposed, they didn't waste it wandering the muddy fields as he did. Among other things, his wife Catherine did fireworks during the summer season and it was said that she had a mysterious 'way' with burns. People would sometimes turn up at their house with ailments which she would somehow alleviate. Pen wondered if, a couple of centuries ago, those skills, her unruly shock of auburn hair, and Alec's elemental prowess and no less striking appearance, wouldn't have got them burned at the stake as witches.

He and Alec were to build an extensive feature for Renault's garden. Pen had been paid for his ideas and the time he spent, but it was Alec who did most of the work; so he got most of the money and Pen was happy to share his good fortune.

It was Alec who had convinced him to invest in an Internet site to publicise his artwork. Medea, a friend of one of Alec's daughters, put the site together for him. She was good at it, but there was a catch: he had to go to her little flat in town every time he wanted to change the slightest thing. They had spent hours together cramped in front of one of her little screens breathing each other's air, until he realised that she preferred his company to the assignment, so he tended to leave it showing his older work. She was pretty enough though she dyed her hair black-and-white, but Pen was still very much in love with Sophie. The site had been fun to do but had never really brought in any clients. He used it more as a gallery to show his stuff to people who had already got to know him, and had sent the link around to show off his work. It was about as far as Pen cared to go with the slightly daunting technology that was outstripping everything else.

Alec was full of energy, enthusiasm and good ideas, which he applied unstintingly to Pen's project. The work they collaborated on was a succession of monolithic rough plasma-cut iron arches. The elongated curved openings lined up with the summer solstice sunrise. At the western end of this alley, he had created a wide, low iron ring of plates marking the hours with an imposing iron needle at its centre. The needle would be lit for a brief moment as the sun hit it at the appointed hour, lining up with the arches, casting a long narrow shadow with a bright penumbra around it reaching right down to the house. The curves were to allow for the spin of the Earth, so as to keep the sun in line as it rose from the horizon. He called it 'Iron Henge'. Alec, who was used to grafting for a living, scratched his head and called it money for old rope.

It had been more than a year since Pen had worked out the alignment. They had not been able to get it finished for the last solstice so he was still waiting to see the result of his work. Given the stakes Pen felt his apprehension was normal. For the rest of the year the structure remained a dramatic piece of art, awaiting its solar rendez-vous.

Renault had gone along with the idea of a huge sundial from the start, and was often present during the positioning of the thick iron sections. Pen had done a bit of bronze casting at art school and had experimented with acids and other chemicals to give his efforts a rich surface patina. He had thought of trying the technique on the sections of ironwork to accelerate the rusting process but decided against it — the acids were dangerous. Once he had taken a lungful of the fumes and had nearly choked his guts up, his throat was raw for several days. After that he always wore a mask. In time the iron would turn a deep rust-red in the damp air coming up from the river, to resemble the wonderful texture of some of the work of the Spaniard Eduardo Chillida, whom Pen admired.

For the 'erections', as Maurice Renault was fond of referring to the operation of installing the work, he had his man Serge, or Sergio as he called him, bring up the big John Deere tractor with the forks on the front to lift them into place. Serge made it very clear that he did not like Pen. He obviously felt was he was exploiting Renault's good nature and ripping off his boss. He was somewhat younger than Renault, though of the same generation. But he was evidently more vigorous and still looked tough and wiry. He glowered at Pen sullenly from behind an unkempt greying beard that was still mostly dark red. Pen didn't give a toss: maybe it was just Sergio's manner, maybe he was paid to be suspicious. Pen hoped that the metal would take on a similar colour to his hair. Rufus, he thought. Suddenly he felt he was doing what he had always wanted. He even felt grateful enough to give in to Maurice's nagging and let him have two nice flints.

To get to St Léon, Pen would have to take the truck. He could park up at the top and walk down to the valley on the small animal tracks that wound down through the scrubby trees. There would be a bit of scrambling to get to the bottom, but that was par for the course. No pain no gain. Clambering over a last tumble of rocks to the valley floor he felt his mind slide into flint mode. All his anxieties were sent to a place where he could look at them from a safe distance while he inhabited what he felt was his real self. He found himself in the mind of that curious little boy who was still there inside him after all these years. He occasionally asked what he thought he was up to, indulging his whims making art, treasure-hunting, and still smoking dope at his age. But he had a theory that maturity was only a myth created by older people to keep the young in their place. Surely everyone lived with their past lives packed away inside them like Russian dolls. Those lives weren't just sloughed off like reptiles' skins, but might rise to the surface to open and spill out their forgotten contents at unexpected moments, showing that time was not linear at all. It only required the right conditions; even a cabinet minister or a five-star general could find himself back in the wondering mind of a small child. Fat chance of that, thought Pen.

Most men seemed desperate to shrug off the cloying remnants of childhood, and most women had it dragged screaming and kicking out of them in a swath of gore with their first child.

"Come down to earth, man!" Maybe that was why Pen was the way he was, to help keep the balance.

The foot of the cliff was a tangle of shrubs and small trees competing for light in the deep shade. Over the millennia when this wide space was filled with water, the cliffs had soaked it up. Each winter, freezing had caused the porous stone to fracture and flake away, mining into the walls and creating vast overhangs. Some of the resulting rock shelters had been inhabited in prehistoric times. Others had collapsed under their own weight and lay jumbled and strewn down the slope to the flat land below. It was going to make it difficult to recognise a Neolithic monument.

The poplars growing in wide rows between Pen and the river gave off a pungent, metallic smell. Poplars always smelt strongly, but the rotting leaves that had been shed a few weeks earlier intensified the effect. In the spring these trees would be filled with the buzzing of hundreds of bees collecting the resin from the sticky buds to make their propolis. Right now, the trees might be sitting on an important Neolithic funeral mound.

"Shit!" He swore pensively.

Shading his eyes with his hand from the bright afternoon sun, he looked up into a deep clear sky sliced through by a couple of vapour trails. He closed his eyes for a moment, luxuriating in the warmth of the sun on his face. In the past the trees would not have been here and the south facing cliff face would have caught the light for most of the day. Beyond the poplars the land had been ploughed right down to the river. It did not take Pen long to come across Noel's footprints from the day before. He went to the water and found them again at the river bank. It must have been here that he had made his find.

Pen turned and looked back at the high cliff. The château squatted forebodingly up there, dominating the whole valley. In medieval times the river would have been a main thoroughfare; the château could have controlled the trade and been impregnable up there.

Pen knew from experience that vantage points like these had been inhabited more or less continuously from the distant past. The terrain around châteaux like this one would be rich in all sorts of archaeological relics, most now obliterated by the constant re-building and reworking of the land. Pen had found his best biface up there — perhaps there was a Neolithic settlement under the walls of the present edifice. If so it would be lost for good. He scanned the riverbank for another piece of the jade axe without much hope, then headed back to the cliff.

"How the hell are discoveries made?" he wondered. The cliff was now two or three hundred metres from the water. Time and the elements had been eroding stuff down from the top to pile up as sandy ramparts at the base. Anything there would be buried beyond recovery. Wandering back towards it Pen scanned for anything that looked as if it could have got there through human intervention.

The earth at the foot of the cliff had been disturbed recently in a few places, like foxes had been digging. Passing around a great block which looked as if it had come crashing down from above, Pen noticed one place which had been particularly disturbed. He climbed up to take a closer look.

Foxes or something had definitely been there. The fine sand resulting from the eroding of the rock face had been freshly dug into. Pen could see two holes close together which he thought might be entrances to a den. In front of them was a large mound of sand spreading down the slope. Coming closer to the holes, Pen could smell a distinctive acrid odour — faint, but he knew it was fox. Studying the entrance hunting for their paw-prints in the stony sand, he guessed it was deserted. It looked as though there had in fact been no activity here for a while. Pen froze, suddenly unable to believe his eyes: the sand in front of him was strewn with small bluish flakes of knapped flint. He bent forward and picked up a few. The more he looked the more he saw. They were mostly waste flakes but they were definitely man-made. They had the distinctive bulb of percussion just under the striking platform, as he remembered from Kenneth P.Oakley's little book on flint implements, the first book Pen had read on the subject. The clear, explicit descriptions had opened it all up for him. It was not easy at first to tell stones broken fortuitously by natural agencies from those struck by man; but once you got it, it became easy enough.

Pen picked up all the flakes he could see — several tools, scrapers and burins. Cro-Magnon then, they had been made on rectangular blades. The flints were finer than any he had found in the fields, sharp and undamaged. Then he noticed something else. There were fragments of bone there too. There were more fragments of bone than flint, perhaps the remains of the foxes' dinners? Pen picked up a piece of bone that looked like a piece of a rib from an animal too big for a fox to bring down. Fully four centimetres wide by perhaps fifteen long, it sparkled with mica from the encrusted sand. He gave it a wipe with the ball of his thumb and turned it over, and his heart nearly missed a beat.

As excited as at any time in his flinting career, he set off with the encrusted bone held out before him to where the spring bubbled out among the poplars. It was sunny and Pen had not thought to bring his wellingtons, not intending to go field-walking. He went in over the tops of his hiking boots and felt the cold water soak down through his socks from the top. Oblivious, he took one more step, then crouched and slowly immersed the little piece of bone in the clear water. He rinsed the sand away gently then dried the fragment on the end of his t-shirt. Standing up, Pen backed out of the water; he wanted this moment to last for ever.

In his mind's eye he had modelled the first Paleolithic peoples of Europe on the natives of North America. They would have been noble hunter gatherers, living in a mobile society, lacking modern technology for sure, but in no other way inferior to modern man:

Chris Leandro

they were the culmination of seven million years of evolution. Their tools were so sophisticated that without a long apprenticeship they were impossible to reproduce. The tradition that had given birth to that technology had been unbroken for nearly two million years. They had become such skilful artists that when the techniques they had learned in that golden age were eventually lost, it would take almost thirteen thousand years before they would be rediscovered briefly in ancient Greece, then at least another thousand years later in renaissance Italy. When Picasso visited Lascaux he was reported to have said in awe, "We have invented nothing."

In his hand, Pen held an exquisitely executed engraving of a young fawn suckling its mother. He walked up the bank. At the top he bent down to unlace his boots he took them off, and draped his wet socks over a warm boulder to dry. Sitting down in the sun with his back to the great block, he gazed tenderly at the marvel that years of dogged passion and providence had brought him. He took out his tobacco and sat there until he felt the temperature drop as the sun started to slip behind the trees. He knew then what he was prepared to do; but he wanted to share the fun and he knew with whom he wanted to share it.

5

The good weather seemed to be having an agreeable effect on everyone. Sophie was in fine form when Pen got home. The darkening kitchen smelt of thyme: she had harvested a whole pile of it and was separating bunches out onto a drying frame spread with a white sheet. It was early, but Pen turned on some lights. She glanced at him, one cheek fetchingly smeared with a grubby thumbprint. Pen felt a stirring deep down inside

"Pen, you'll have to make some room upstairs," she said, "the grass must be dry now, don't you think?"

In the roof space over part of the workshop they had made a little drying-room. They had access to it through a small, simply-disguised door behind the hangings on their bedroom wall. Since Alice had come along they had to be more careful. Things had to be hidden away from prying eyes and nosy noses.

"Okay, *chérie*," he replied with a smile, moving up behind her and putting his arms around her to cup her breasts.

"What are you after?" she murmured, straightening and leaning back into him.

Mmm, thought Pen, my news can wait a bit, I suppose.

"Pen, I have something to tell you."

"Before or after we make passionate love?"

Their relationship had been a hard one from the beginning, and Pen wondered how they had survived. It was either all bliss or absolute hell. There seemed no in-between, Since Alice the periods of hard-won peace seemed to last longer, but Sophie had a long memory and nothing went unpardoned. Sometimes Pen wondered if it was not cultural. Many French people didn't follow English humour. He was always being taken too seriously — an ironic quip could be read as an insult, or hyperbole as ignorance; he could never work it out. He often found them too literal, tending to over-intellectualise everything. He had heard it said that the French had replaced humour with philosophy, and sometimes he could almost believe it. Off-hand remarks could take ages of subsequent explaining — of course he hadn't meant any offence for god's sake, it could be tiring! To cap it all he had noticed that many French seemed loath, or be unable, to poke fun at themselves.

At almost forty Sophie was still stunning. She had rejected glamour, but now that age was catching up with her she was becoming a bit vain.

"Pen darling, do you think I am putting on weight?" she had called out to him from the bathroom as they were preparing to go out.

"It's all that chocolate," he had replied, and she had gone cold.

Sophie's weight fluctuated by a couple of kilos. Pen actually preferred her slightly heavier, it filled out her curves. Unaware of the gravity of his thoughtless remark, he said,

"But I love you fat, baby." His sweet smile had not saved him from an evening of reproachful sulking. Little things like that could spark off long periods of cool distance between them. These days, he often felt that she was bored with their relationship. Or perhaps it was just a gender thing; males and females were not intended to understand each other, remaining always complementary, somehow destined never to meet. But something told him that this time he must have got it right.

Sophie exhaled deeply, letting her body sag against him, the softness inside her loose clothing delighting him.

"Do you think we have become a habit to each other, Pen?"

"Yes, a very good one."

"Oh, I don't mean that. Listen to me, Pen. I have to tell you something."

"Can't it wait?"

"No, I'm sorry, Pen, but I have to tell you." Pen could feel the moment slipping away.

"I had a long affair with Noël after you and I got together."

Pen looked at her, stunned.

"We stopped when I got pregnant."

"So how do you know who the father is?" Pen was suddenly wondering if his own sense of humour wasn't deficient.

"Look at her Pen, isn't it obvious?"

"Oh shit."

"Pen, we were careful."

"Shit!"

Pen dropped his arms to his sides. Sophie turned and looked at him.

"He was so sad when we split up; he said he was addicted to me. We had been together since I was sixteen."

"Why are you telling me, now?"

"I'm not sure, Pen. Not to hurt you. I can't keep the secret any more and Noël is still in love with me."

"He said so."

"No, but I know."

"So?"

"So nothing. Alice is staying over at Denise's tonight. Will you come to bed with me?"

"Have sex now, after what you've just told me?"

"Make love."

For the first three or four years of their relationship, when she was in the mood, Sophie had been the wild one. Pen had never encountered a woman who understood a man's needs so well. She would play for hours, enjoying unhurried sex in a way that had left Pen more fulfilled than he thought possible. In the warmer weather they would often smoke a spliff together afterwards, moving naked around the studio, two life models waiting to be captured in homely intimacy by a momentarily absent artist. For Pen those moments were some of the most thoroughly contented he had known.

After Alice had been born it was rare that Sophie initiated anything to do with sex. Pen understood that small children could be draining on a mother. But they had always shared the care with Alice, who anyway would soon be nine. He put it down to biology. Having fulfilled its function of pushing her into motherhood, her libido had gone into hibernation. Pen had just had to grit his teeth and wait for spring.

Sophie's news had just put another spin on things. Pen wasn't generally one to look a gift horse in the mouth but now he couldn't work out how he felt. If she had been fucking Noël no wonder there was never any left for him.

She said she just did not have any appetite. Once or twice a month Pen could coax her into having sex with him. A nice meal, a bunch of hand-picked wild flowers on the table and a chilled bottle of white wine. Throw in the washing-up or a story for Alice and that would usually do it, but it still felt like begging. Whenever she gave in and allowed him to woo her she would always come. But the old magic was no longer there. It always left Pen feeling unsatisfied and a bit sad, and he supposed it was the same for her. Anyway Pen didn't know how he felt just yet, so he took her by the hand and led her upstairs. He had decided not to inspect this horses' mouth for the moment.

It wasn't like old times but it was tender and had a quick brilliance. He had the image of a shooting star burning up as it tore into the earth's atmosphere. The sudden awareness of the frailty of their life together had drawn them closer for an instant. Pen still did not know how to feel: he was so different from what she had been used to, perhaps she had wanted to keep her options open. But right then he was too content to care. They lay spent in each other's arms. To avoid the subject that was on both their minds, Pen slipped off the bed and went downstairs to fetch the little engraving.

It came as no surprise to Pen that Sophie was impressed by the find. She had always seen his stones as rivals, vying with her for his attention, and could never get enthusiastic about them. In fact, Pen realised, very few people were the least bit interested in the stones themselves, sometimes they warmed to a bit in prehistory or cave painting, even woolly mammoths — but not stones.

This piece of bone was different. The little picture was delicately rendered in clear dark lines on the white ground. The mother's head was turned down to her fawn, facing towards us in a gesture of loving care. Her finely drawn body was in profile, yet both her eyes were visible, looking out towards the observer. The differences in her coat were clearly depicted, the line between her smooth underbelly and rougher upper body and the lie of the hairs. Her eyes were outlined with soft demarcations as in real life and the rump with its short brushy tail was drawn with a delicate realism. Her fawn was less detailed but just as well drawn, pushing its head roughly between the doe's elegant hindquarters, neck stretched up to the teat. The thrusting movement could be seen in its raised rump hiding one of the mother's front legs.

The artist who had drawn this touching maternal scene was a master. The proportions, the perspective and the detail spoke to Pen of long practice and fine observation. He would never have had a model to stand still for him for a few hours while he did his preliminary sketches.

Sophie loved it. "It's beautiful, it's a masterpiece, Pen, really!"

"Yes, and very old. It will be extremely valuable, Sophie, and there could be other stuff there." Pen's mind had gone down the fox-hole.

"Will you roll a joint, Pen?"

"Mmm, *chérie?*" he said feeling suddenly exhausted, "just give me a minute." He turned onto his side, luxuriating in the position he liked to sleep in, one knee tucked up. Snuggling up to his back, Sophie slid a hand over his belly and reached down between his legs, sorting through the recumbent tackle that nestled there.

"Pen?" she pleaded, squeezing, but Pen had gone.

She frowned to herself as she watched his shoulders gently rise and fall, the steady rhythm of the sated male. Sophie sighed and made a small effort to push away her frustration. Why, she wondered, was he always so reluctant to engage in even the most rudimentary discussions about their relationship? Or anything of an emotional nature for that matter. He always shrugged off their differences as if they were irrelevant. It seemed that they were on a different wave-length most of the time, a different planet even. Pen never seemed to want to question his feelings or analyse his motives – or, if he ever did, to share his insights with her. At first they had shared every-thing. It had been wonderful with him then. He was older than her but didn't act like it. They worked on his house together or travelled around in his truck and each could tell what the other was thinking most of the time. The way the most unusual things amused him was a little disconcerting to begin with, and his humour took some getting used to. It was as though he was mocking everything, but he was more than eager to explain things to her in his imperfect French. Their frequent love-making had been so good because of that intimacy, that communion. Examining the familiar bulk of his elegant body curled in against the post- coital chill, one leg thrown out stretching down the bed, she realised that despite their grow-ing differences she still loved this complex stranger. Pen had slowly grown more distant, wrapping himself in his work and since Alice, she knew he worried constantly about money, though even that he hardly mentioned. He became defensive when she brought the subject up, as if she were criticising his capacity to fend for them. He seemed self-contained. But she suspected that under the surface he was just a frightened little boy troubled by the loss of his father and worried about his ailing mother. He rarely talked about her now, not to mention their own fortunes — so why did he have to pretend he was so in control?

Apart from when he was with Alice, the only times Sophie saw him really happy these days was with his bloody stones. She saw them as his escape hatch: he would slip out of the house and be gone with them for hours at the most inconvenient times. Sophie had got used to eating her mid-day meal alone as often as not, with the culture pages of the newspaper spread out on the table or a novel for company. She disengaged herself from his warmth and slowly stretched her body across the rumpled bedding like a cat. She executed a few of her yoga positions, holding them for a minute or two, controlling her breathing, before rising from the bed and wondering though to the bathroom. Noël was another matter. He was gentler than Pen, softer, he seemed fragile in a way she couldn't put her finger on. She worried whether they had not made him feel inadequate in some way. It always seemed odd to her that he and Pen had become the best of friends. They had been rivals over the flints but never over her. Was that why she was considering going back to Noël? Was she jealous? Then with a pang she asked herself: could she bear losing the stability she had with Pen, his care and attention, his solid presence? That, and the fact that he worked from home and was always there for Alice which allowed her a lot of unbegrudged freedom? So many things she just took for granted but might easily miss once they were no longer there?

Automatically then of course she began to think about Alice, sweet little Alice who had never asked to be brought into this uncertain world and who had so far been protected from life's rough edges. How was she likely to be affected by a separation? She seemed to have far more of Pen in her than of her, his strong dominant genes visible in her features, his nose and almond eyes, his brow and wavy hair, his native inquisitiveness. She only hoped their daughter did not pick up his taste for field-walking — that would be the last straw. Of course she was reassured by the devotion that Pen and Alice showed each other, but occasionally felt inexplicably jealous of their complicity. The last thing she wanted was a tug-of-love over Alice or to hurt her in any way; she knew Pen felt the same. She would have to tread carefully, but despite Pen's exotic attraction and masculine good looks she knew she had never really given up Noël.

The next day was Saturday and he didn't see Sophie; she had gone out early in the truck to do her market. He needed to go to Denise's to pick up Alice who was an early riser too, locked as she was into the school rhythm. He planned to show the new find to Noël. Denise was still in pyjamas when he got there and looked slightly frazzled. He wondered if she hadn't been hitting the bottle, which gave him a twinge. But she and Alice had a wonderful complicity of their own and they whispered secrets to each other before he took her off. Pen almost regretted depriving Denise of her company. Alice was an eager little thing and asked him not to stop at any fields, please, and if she was good could they go into town afterwards and buy some magazines and things? Things meant sweets.

He didn't yet know how he felt about Noël. Strangely, he couldn't work up any anger over the old news. As he had got to know him, he began to feel guilty about taking Sophie from him. Noël showed no bitterness about it but he was shaken, as Pen knew. He thought now that somehow the separation had re-kindled their sex life and per-haps Noël was secretly grateful. He would have to talk to him about it at some point but right now he was more excited about St Léon. He decided to go into town first to keep Alice occupied; it was hard work when she was bored.

"It will have to be dark," said Noël.

Pen glanced at Alice who was playing with the kittens and sucking noisily on a dreadfully corrosive looking lollypop.

"We'll need to take shovels, maybe a pick, trowels, an axe for roots, and a saw."

"And food," said Noël. Pen could count on him to be practical. The idea had taken on a life of its own.

"Water," said Pen, "it will be thirsty work, and we'll need to be well protected, wear old clothes, and we may need waterproofs, lamps, spare batteries, perhaps gloves."

"Sophie will be home later. I'll take Alice home for lunch, and be back around eight."

"Okay, but we'll need containers if we do find anything."

"If?" said Pen. "And while we're at it why not vaccinations against viruses extinct for at least the last fifteen thousand years?"

"And a couple of bearers to carry our bags." They were laughing with the improbability of it all but also with anticipation. Alice turned towards them with a concerned look on her face and said,

"Noël, do you think Titounette is pregnant again?"

It had been dark for an hour or so when they finally arrived at the spot where Pen had parked the day before. It was partly hidden and not overlooked by any of the buildings near the château, but they did have to drive by a house on the approach to the narrow lane. They hoped that whoever lived there imagined they were on a visit to one of the other houses, and not on a mission to burgle the empty château. They were heavily loaded with their tools and provisions. If they got stopped it would not look good.

Pen had only ever taken the little animal track yesterday, once down and once back up. He had tried to memorise landmarks, but at night everything was different. There was no light to speak of but the moon would be rising shortly. They were crashing around, going downhill fast, grabbing at saplings to slow them down, snagging and getting ripped on thorns, overheating in their protective clothing. They both wore lamps on their foreheads but it was not easy to find a clear passage. Something went snorting and crashing away from them down the hill. They stopped, panting noisily. A couple of disturbed wood pigeons went whirling off over their heads.

"God, I can't see much," wheezed Noël. Pen was laughing as quietly as he could, the apprehension finally dissipating in the exhilaration of the moment. They had been spiked by the adventure all day. Noël picked up on Pen's mood and then they were both coughing and spluttering weakly, trying to keep the noise down.

"I don't remember it being so far," said Pen uncertainly, "perhaps we've overshot."

"Let's go down a bit further," whispered Noël. The sky was lightening a little as a thin moon appeared behind the trees. Pen pulled up, gesturing to Noël to stop.

"There! That's it."

Unburdening themselves of their back-packs, they rapidly surveyed the area. Then Noël started digging out one fox-hole while Pen went at the other one.

"Wait up, Noël," said Pen. "Look." He was already digging out flint and fragments of bones. "This stuff was dug up by the foxes, same as the stuff I picked up yesterday. We need one digging and one sorting through the stuff that comes out."

"Well, there's nothing in my hole anyway, so I'll sort for you and when you want a break I'll take over on the shovel."

"We'll be well outside the hearths of any settlement. To sound out the site we need to dig down to bed-rock, then work back to the cliff."

"How do you feel about this, Pen?"

"What do you mean?"

"We'll be destroying the site."

"You want to go home?"

"No, but this is what has been going on all over the world. It's called pillaging. It is not what we do in the fields. It's Iraq, Egypt, Greece."

"Yeah, but they were pillaged by America, France and England, that was alright then. Okay Noël, you go if you have qualms, but don't you go saying anything to anyone about what I'm doing here."

"Don't get me wrong Pen. I want this. I've dreamed of digging for treasure. I just feel sad for what will be lost."

"Yeah, okay. We found this site, the authorities don't have the funds to prospect, they don't even have the resources to dig the sites they already have. In the meantime it's only a matter of time before someone else comes across this — then what?"

"So that's your excuse? If we don't do it someone else will?"

"Look man, you saw the engraving. From what I can make out it is Magdalenian. There's more stuff here. An opportunity like this may never come our way again. Anyway, Magdalenian sites are the most common of the upper Palaeolithic ones — and besides, the foxes have already turned this lot upside-down." Noël didn't look convinced by Pen's attempt at justifying what they were doing, and mumbled under his breath.

"Here, I brought us a treat, man, to help us dig." Pen reached for his pack and fished out a thermos.

"Mm, tea-time."

"Tea, and something else." He unscrewed the cup from the thermos and gave it to Noël, then unscrewed the large plastic bung which could be opened: it was intended to hold the sugar. He extracted a twist of cling-film from it and said,

"You'll have to wet your finger and dab it, wash it down with a cup of tea. We can't chop out lines in the trenches, I'm afraid."

They smiled as the crushed white crystals glinted dimly in the torch light. The next six hours were wonderful. The digging was easy: the foxes had chosen well and had done half the work. The bed-rock was about three metres down and there were quite a few good-sized lumps of stone to be cleared. But as they progressed they realised that it was easier to dig out the sand to make a reservation in the wall of their tunnel and just park the boulders there.

Quite soon they saw that everything interesting lay in a narrow dark brown layer above their heads, which must have been the floor of the ancient living space. It could be clearly distinguished from the lighter sand above and below it but it fluctuated, running in and out of their grasp, dividing and disappearing and reappearing again. The conditions were cramped. The pale orangey-yellow sand filled their boots and got in to their collars and cuffs, but for them it was a day at the beach. It looked like gold dust trickling down from the roof of their narrow tunnel in the sparkle of their head-lamps.

The one who was digging passed his finds back to the other who sorted waste flakes from tools and bones broken to extract the marrow. At one point when Noël was at the front, Pen scooted in behind him and called him outside, pulling urgently at his boot. Once in the hole they could have talked normally but they whispered out of a sort of reverence. He showed Noël what he had passed to him in the last handful. In the light from their head-lamps they could clearly make out the point and double row of curved barbs of a harpoon. It looked intact and was wonderfully decorated with geometric patterns.

"Oh god," breathed Noël, his eyes two points of burning light.

The food and the tea were long gone; it was hungry work despite the little boost that Pen had brought along. The thin sliver of moon floated on its back almost directly above them; inside its curve the whole moon could be made out in the reflected earthlight. In that quiet place they could pick up the calm eloquence of the river not far away. It was a peaceful spot all right. They felt with wonder the privilege of being the only ones to have been here since the last ice age. In the hushed silence they were miniature Howard Carters making the staggering discovery of Tutankhamen's tomb.

For some time they had been tunnelling up against a huge slab which had apparently fallen onto the floor of the site, and some of the flints right under it had been crushed. Pen was worried that they would disturb the rock and it would shift, crushing whoever was under it at the time.

"We need to consolidate that block of stone, man, I don't like it, some of the smaller ones have been dislodged by our digging but imagine what would happen if that fucker came down."

"You're right," agreed Noël, "anyway I'm getting tired, what time is it?"

"I don't know, I didn't think to bring my phone, but late, three or four maybe. We need to tidy up and hide the holes, just in case someone comes by."

"Not very likely, but you're right, that law you English have — Sod's, no? Our bags will be heavy going back. I hope we find the track."

Pen felt elated, although he was thoroughly whacked when he finally got home. He took off his filthy clothes outside and left them with the back-pack. The sand had stained everything pale orange and insinuated its way into his every crease and fold. He tiptoed his way through to the bathroom and took a long shower.

As the hot water streamed over him, he thought over what he knew about the Magdalenians. He had come to think of them as the first civilisation. They didn't build cities. But at what is now the little town of Les Eyzies, which was their centre fifteen thousand years ago, they hadn't needed to. Not for nothing was Les Eyzies built in a wide canyon. The high rock faces lined both sides of a double bend in the river. In the past there had been other waterways there and the ensuing valleys made a dramatic backdrop for what he felt must have been an earthly paradise. Even now there were scores of rock shelters, some of them enormous. At various prehistoric periods there must have been hundreds of people living there, maybe sometimes even more. It was the end of the last ice age; the climate was about to change. Here on the northern limit of glacial Europe the hunting was good. The bones that they had been digging out last night, and there were quantities of them, probably came mostly from animals now extinct: aurochs, the ancestor of the cow, wild horse, the European bison and even mammoth.

They had had time to develop their culture. Though it had existed for twenty thousand years by then, it was they who took cave painting to its apogee, choosing caves with care, creating powerful sanctuaries. Pen thought of them as cathedrals, abandoned, unchanged for centuries, hidden treasures waiting for us to find. It was the carving that Pen found the most extraordinary. Thousands of bone and ivory objects had been unearthed in the many shelters that had been excavated. There were tools, hunting and fishing accessories and everyday utensils, often elaborately decorated. The various styles pointed to an enduring culture and long-standing traditions.

So what had happened? It had all suddenly stopped, the art, the specialised tool making. Pen could never quite work it out. It got quickly warmer, the ice retreated, trees covered Western Europe, much of the game died out or moved north and the human populations seemed to dwindle and disappear from the region.

He had been looking for treasure. Well, he had certainly found it, even if it wasn't exactly what he was hunting for. He had found remains of the last flowering of an advanced society that had apparently slipped into decadence and decline after thirty thousand years of brilliance. He turned off the water feeling drained and desperate for bed. Was it the climate change that wiped out their culture, or was it disease or something they did, like war, or repressive laws? They were, after all, a civilised people.

6

Fortunately for Pen it was Sunday and he didn't have to get up. He heard the girls moving around in the morning but drifted back to sleep. When he finally emerged he was alone in the house. They often visited Denise at the weekend. He thought about Sophie and Noël over tea and a roll-up in the workshop and decided that it was well in the past, that stirring it up with Noël would only cause strife. He had an image of vicious dogs twitching in their sleep; he had never got on with dogs.

Pen treasured those rare moments when he found himself alone at home. He doted on the girls, but family life had a price. Even when he was working on one of his projects Sophie could intrude on him at any moment and ruin his concentration. Having been snapped at more than once, Alice was more discreet, but being an only child and living relatively far from her friends as they were, she needed a lot of their attention. Pen picked up the hand-set for the sound system and flipped on the music: Pharaoh Sanders filled the space with his deep, round, timeless sound. It was early afternoon and a clear warm light beckoned from outside. He slid the doors open and let the music spill out down the valley. Pen's life had always been accompanied by music, a sound-track, like any self-respecting film. He couldn't imagine life without music. Sophisticated bone flutes had been unearthed in prehistoric sites forty thousand years old — they would not be the earliest ones, either. How long before that had drums existed? He put his roll-up down on the end of a work-bench to be retrieved later. He struggled with his tobacco habit, but as long as he smoked the occasional joint it was impossible to give up; there was always tobacco in the house.

He shook as much sand as possible out of the clothes he had worn last night and wondered what kind of damage they might wreak on the washing-machine. Then he picked up his grubby back-pack and brought it to his bench. He had agreed to wait for Noël to share out the booty, but couldn't resist looking. Noël said he would come around when he got up, but Pen was getting impatient and rooted through the gritty spoils in the top of the bag. Noël had taken the harpoon which was certainly the best find they had made. Pen hoped that he might find some more engraving on a fragment of bone, over-looked in the poor light last night.

Tomorrow he was due to go to Renault's, where he had started installing the mosaic. The next section was laid out in a large shallow box on trestles ready for loading into his truck. He would load up to pass the time. If Noël hadn't turned up by the time he had finished he would start washing their finds.

He saw the little Peugeot turn into the lane. Sophie was alone.

"Alice stayed with Denise, then? Good idea — they get on so well," said Pen, retrieving his cigarette and lighting it. Sophie looked troubled.

"What's happened, Sophie? Is Denise bad again?"

"No, Pen, she's okay."

"Well, you don't look too happy. Cup of tea?"

"Yes please, that might help."

They went through into the kitchen. Pen had helped Sophie decorate the house as she wanted it before Alice was born. The kitchen was festooned with hanging baskets, plants, pictures, lamps and knick-knacks. Pen felt it was too busy; it gave the eyes nowhere to rest. Almost no wall space or surface was left unoccupied, but he had got used to it: it was Sophie's presence, full of care and detail.

"Pen, I don't know how to say this."

Pen emptied the tepid teapot into a large yucca plant. Sophie looked startled by the act but didn't say anything, although it seemed to help her make up her mind.

"Noël has asked me to move back to live with him."

"When?"

"This morning."

"This morning? He couldn't have, we only got in at five."

"He didn't sleep. He phoned me about ten and I took Alice to Denise, then went to see him."

"And?"

"I don't know, Pen, he's so miserable. You know he has never really got it together with anyone else since we split up."

"What are you going to do?"

"I don't know. I'm going to Denise's for a few days to think things over."

"And Alice?"

"She can stay with me tonight. Perhaps you could pick her up tomorrow from school?"

"So you can be with him?"

"You don't want to, that's fine, Pen, I'll take her to Denise's." Her determination was evident in her flat gaze. Pen had learned that it was better not to fight her when she was in this frame of mind.

"No, for god's sake, I'll get her. Then what?"

"Then we'll see."

"Look, it's not because he's miserable that you have to throw everything up. It's how you feel that matters."

But Pen could see he was getting nowhere with that tack, he knew that resolute look so well. He poured the freshly made tea and felt his house of cards totter. She went upstairs and he could hear her rooting through the cupboards. He was in a state of shock, he decided; he couldn't begin to react, it was too sudden. He hated being given no choice. But perhaps he had made the choice when he had taken Sophie from Noël. She came down the stairs in a rush with a rucksack over one shoulder and shot Pen a look.

"I'll phone," was all she said.

"Your tea…" was his forlorn response.

Pen's first reaction when the initial shock wore off was anger at them for turning his life upside-down. God, Noël had played it close to his chest. Then came fear for Alice, who would be the innocent bystander. Not knowing what else to do he went back to bed. He was thinking of the terrible curse that was supposed to have descended on Carter and his team after they had defiled the tomb of Tutankhamen. Perhaps Noël had been onto something when he said they should think twice before digging into the ancient site. But it wasn't a burial site, and besides that was all just fucking superstition. Pen decided to drop the project anyway. It was too risky, and if they got caught who knew what might happen? He certainly would not be doing anything with Noël now anyway, that was clear.

He woke in the night with a feeling of panic; something that had been gnawing at his stomach was stuck in his throat. He read for a while, lighting both bedside lights and trying to dispel the feeling of impending loss. Unable to concentrate, he got dressed and went down to the workshop. There, surrounded by the workings of his interior life, his passions, and that maddening creativity he was cursed with, he tried to shake off the gloom. He opened the door to his little museum and turned on the neon lights. The old carpet he had laid on the concrete floor looked curiously uncluttered in the familiar little space since Renault's bloke had come and taken all the boxes. On one shelf he had piled some of the books that had helped him understand and catalogue his collection; more were piled on the floor with the little box of arrowheads with the blue fox printed on its ill-fitting lid.

He went and got a chair from the studio and sat amongst his finds, pondering the point of it all.

He thought about Vincent's collection. Vincent had nowhere near as much stuff as Pen, but it was all of the finest quality. He had all the classic pieces: Neolithic polished axes, stone daggers and beautiful bifaces, but he also had exotic stuff bought at auctions in Paris, often quite cheaply though sometimes not. He had exquisite eccentrics from Mexico, impossibly well-fashioned stylised animals flaked from attractively coloured high-quality flint. He had pieces from Denmark and Africa, eastern Europe, North America, and even some opal projectile points from Australia. One thing all of Vincent's pieces had in common was that they were for sale, at a price of course, and he prided himself on always being able to turn a good profit.

Pen had put nothing on his feet when he left his bedroom, and he was cold. Without the girls there he had not bothered to light the stove, and its warmth was conspicuously lacking at this early hour. He was glad of the rug between him and the concrete floor. Though he craved the comfort of a cigarette and a cup of Earl Grey he sat unmoving, gazing at the crowded shelves.

Was that the point? That the collection had a financial value? Certainly, these pieces would eventually find their way into other collections. He wouldn't live for ever, and someone would sell them off. Whatever he did with them they would end up percolating down to the museums, passing from hand to hand. Perhaps he should let more of them go. With the money he could buy some of those wonderful things at the auctions. It may in fact be the only way he could continue collecting. The experience of digging with Noël had been great but he realised now that it was out of the question. And although he had been lucky, there was little left to find in the fields. He could feel his life changing, sloughing its old, younger skin for a young, older one. He was working at Renault's today, and would talk to him about selling him some more of his stuff. If Sophie made up her mind to leave they would undoubtedly need some extra cash.

Archaeology had come a long way, but still the stones and a few old bones were nearly all that was left of the earlier prehistoric populations. In more recent times there was far more to go on. Pen had seen Neanderthal skeletons in museums. Though to him they just looked like any other human bones, apparently they were short, stocky, and more robust people than our modern Cro-Magnon forebears. He conceded that you could see that, when the skeletons were compared side by side. One thing was clear though — they were men and women like us. The two races had shared Europe for over ten thousand years; and had cohabited in the Middle East for considerably longer.

Pen's collection was made up essentially from Neanderthal artefacts. They had had the place to themselves for over two hundred thousand years before we turned up. They camped out on the plateaus in the same spots continually, leaving great concentrations of their tools there. We have been here for less time, but Pen had rarely found a large upper Palaeolithic site on the hillsides. What there was to be found, he had collected with increasing curiosity. The farmers who had had the pick of their fields for the last fifty years had not recognised the flake or blade tools for what they were, picking up only the far more impressive hand-axes. So Pen had been able to collect a lot. Yet it seemed surprisingly little, considering that we had totally replaced the Neanderthal culture. Didn't that imply that there were more of us around than them?

What he and Noël had found in the fox-hole had helped him understand things better. The rock-shelter contained literally hundreds of tools. They had only dug a narrow tunnel following the settlement's inhabited floor, once coming up directly under a fire-pit. They had left with both their bags full of finer things than any they had ever found in the fields.

Renault's collection had blown Pen's mind when he was first introduced to it. The huge house was decorated rather austerely with bare oak floorboards, medieval furniture, and wall-hangings. There were dark paintings of dour-looking women, hands folded in their laps in drab clothing, but surrounded with ornate gilt frames. Over the stone chimney-breasts were paintings of men in armour looking curiously vulnerable, like fleshy hermit crabs hiding in their shells. Pen felt they were out of keeping with the more recent architecture. Renault had assured him that the original building dated back to the fourteenth century, and when Pen eventually visited the labyrinth of vaulted cellars he could easily imagine the six hundred years of history crushing down on him.

Apart from the sparse furnishings the house was set out like a museum. Down the centre of each room there was a double row of back-to-back glass-panelled oak display cases, with more down each wall. The tall windows let in plenty of light, and each case had concealed lighting inside. The cases were all full of artefacts from various prehistoric cultures, and beneath each of them were piled crates of material that hadn't made it into the displays, all stamped with Renault's name and details of the contents. It was awesome.

Vincent was dismissive of Renault's collection. On their way there that first time, he had said:

"Monsieur Renault is a rich man. He decided to start collecting ten years ago. He bought stuff from everybody at stupid prices. He is bulimic; it is a sickness he can't stop. His stuff's mostly shit, he has a few good bifaces and some nice upper Palaeolithic material, and he's bought some polished axes at auction. But most of it is broken or poor quality. A lot of people have benefited from his craving and still do." It was certainly true that most of the stuff in the crates was dross, but the display cases were staggering. Renault was lacking in really top-quality pieces, but he made up for it with sheer quantity.

The whole ground floor of the slightly rundown mansion was devoted to the Cro-Magnon cultures, which were referred to as Upper Palaeolithic, which to Pen meant us. It had taken him ages to get used to the sequence when he started out, with its strange names and sub-divisions: it had been a whole new vocabulary. The twenty thousand years or so before the Magdalenian period was divided into three broad cultural groups, Aurignacian, Gravettian and Solutrean, in that order. These made up for less than a quarter of the material in the rooms. The next seven thousand years or so, the Magdalenian, made up for at least three-quarters of the remaining space. The small area left on that floor was devoted to the decline into the curiously named Azilian culture. The names so familiar to Pen now paraded beautiful artefacts before his mind's eye as he pronounced them.

The loaded truck was bumping down the churned-up drive to the big house. Pen slumped forward over the wheel in total dejection. He was trying to keep his mind off what Sophie was doing and concentrated on the collection. The big difference between Renault's collection and the national museum's was that he could pick the pieces out of their cases and handle them, which for such tactile objects was essential to understanding them.

Renault was not an academic, but had surrounded himself with people who were. He was said to serve lavish meals in his museum attended by his guests, who were invited to comment on his excessive, predominantly French acquisitions. Some of these guests were officials with the essential expert eye; they imparted authenticity and authority or, as Renault put it, substance and clout. They had put his collection on the map, classifying the material as it came in. Some were helping him expand his collection adding lacking, rarer, or otherwise more sought-after pieces. According to Vincent, all of them were after something.

Pen reflected that being rich must have its downside. All the wealthy people he knew were constantly on the go. They had employees to look after their properties; they engaged accountants, lawyers and agents to help manage their money and acquisitions; and they were suspicious of hangers-on, sycophants and parasites. They could never really switch off. Those few that Pen knew tended to be cynical and distrustful at heart.

Driving around to the back of the imposing house, Pen leaned on his horn. He would not get out of the van into the muddy yard until he saw the whites of Serge's haunted eyes; the man's unsettling Alsatian dog would be around somewhere, and Pen preferred not to meet it without the controlling presence of its master. Sometimes he had to drive around the property for a while until he found him, but he was always there. There was a large open barn adjoining one of the wings at the back of the house where the vehicles were kept. The big green and yellow tractor was parked over at the far side, next to a couple of ride-on lawn mowers, which never seemed to get much use. There were several empty jerricans lying near them and a white Citroen van with the driver's door left open. Beyond them was a utility room or workshop, where they kept an assortment of tools. Sergio came out of a door at the top of the steps leading to the kitchens and stood there watching with a cracked open twelve-bore shotgun cradled in the crook of his elbow, his dog slunk down and barked menacingly. Pen then watched in the mirror as the brute circled the truck and pissed on a back wheel.

"I need to work. Can you call your dog so I can unload?" shouted Pen from his open window. Sergio whistled once then disappeared inside. The dog bounded up the steps and was gone, leaving Pen feeling uneasy.

He once asked Vincent why Serge was such a disagreeable sod. Vincent said that the man had had a hard time as a young soldier in Algeria. Captured by a bunch of Arabs fighting the war of independence, he had been tortured for several days in retaliation for the brutal treatment the population were suffering at the hands of his compatriots. Renault had picked him up somehow when he got back to France. He was shaken up so badly that they gave him an honourable discharge and a disability pension, but he had been a basket-case ever since. Renault had given him a home and a job, and Serge was devoted to him.

Renault never answered the phone. Pen guessed he must have several numbers, but the one he had given to Pen, when it was picked up at all, was inevitably answered with Serge's abrupt:

"He's not here." But Pen knew that the loyal Sergio always kept Renault informed. He would leave a message if he needed to come to take measurements or do work, and when he arrived at the château, if he was there at all Renault would be expecting him. He found it easier to arrange appointments face to face, even if they were weeks in the future. Whatever else Pen might think of Renault, he certainly had an excellent memory.

He appeared at the top of the steps where Serge had been while Pen was putting the new ceramics carefully into a wheelbarrow. Sometimes he would ask Rémy for a hand installing the heavy or unwieldy work. Today he had to take the jigsaw apart, then re-assemble it on the board in the house before starting work. Had Rémy been here he would have saved an hour or more and he would have helped break the monotony of working alone. Renault came down to see him, over-dressed as usual and smelling strongly of cologne, careful to not get any of the slurry of drying mud churned up by the tractor on his immaculate shoes.

"You're early Pen. Have you had coffee? When you've taken that in, come to the kitchen. I want to show you something." Pen had to wheel the barrow down a ramp and through an archway that could have taken the tractor, then through the cellars lined with display cases and up another ramp — apparently made for wine-barrels or perhaps horses? — to the corridor he was working in.

In the surprisingly modern kitchen, Renault had already brewed his usual fragrant blend of coffee and was standing at the table looking through a magazine.

"Have you seen the gazette, Pen?" He was referring to the *Gazette Drouot* that advertised the coming auctions in Paris.

"No, I don't often get it."

"You should. Look, here."

Pen looked at the double page laid open on the table. It showed a fine collection of prehistory and archaeology due to go on sale in a few weeks.

"What do you think?" Renault stepped aside to let Pen see clearly. For a moment the worry slipped from him and his hunched shoulders relaxed as he looked at the magazine. It was only a matter of time, he had always known, but when it came it gave him a thrill.

"Well?"

"A jade axe."

"Yes, I will buy it. I don't want the whole collection, a few of those bifaces, perhaps a dagger or two, but certainly that axe."

"A jade axe. You can't see the colour very well, have to look on their internet site."

"The photo's not very good, but it looks intact and it says twenty-four centimetres long!"

Pen spread his hands apart to the approximate size, not too big for a polished axe but respectable. It looked large and flat. Pen thought the cutting edge showed a few chips, but that was nothing for a piece of this rarity. He immediately decided to be present at the sale.

Pen looked round at Renault. "I would like to go to the auction as well. I've never been."

"Then you must come. We can meet in Paris before the sale and have a coffee. I know the man who's running things, we shall have a private preview of the sale together." Pen had a fleeting vision of Cinderella — could Maurice Renault be his fairy godmother?

"That sounds very civilised," said Pen, "I would like to try and buy something too, perhaps a Danish dagger. I will need funds. I have decided to give in and sell you some of the things you have been asking me for."

"Ah, Pen, you will? I thought you would eventually see reason.

Can we come round before the weekend? I'll have to go back to Paris then."

Pen felt that Renault wanted to get in before he had time to change his mind. That suited him, but didn't give him much time to decide what to let go, and he had no idea about prices. Perhaps he could apply those proposed in the Drouot catalogue?

"The sale is on a Saturday, I see. That'll be a bit complicated. Sophie has her market on Saturdays while I look after Alice. She'll have to stay with her aunt."

"Are things all right, Pen? You look anxious."

"Yeah, it's okay, trouble at t'mill, as we say at home. I hope it will sort itself out soon."

"Is Sophie putting pressure on you? She will leave you, Pen, pretty young girl like that. Does she have her name on the property? She will leave you and get half of everything. She'll have you on your knees — I've seen it so many times." Pen surprised himself by grinning. There were several possible scenarios, but he was sure that would not be one of them. Renault shook his head.

"Here, let's have our coffee."

Pen didn't notice the day go by, occupied as he was with Sophie's revelation and Noël's betrayal, and Alice in all that. Then suddenly it was time to drop his tools and rush to his truck to pick up his daughter from school.

He burned his fingers making supper and to Alice's amused concern spilt half a plate of spaghetti with indelible tomato sauce over the white tablecloth. After she brushed her teeth he followed her up and read her a long story. She seemed content with the explanation that *Maman* was staying with Denise because Denise wasn't well again. Bright little thing that she was, she affected to be oblivious to Pen's preoccupation. But she could tell something was up and wanted more cuddles than usual. When she was eventually settled,

Pen installed himself in front of his computer. A large malt whisky with ice was making wet rings on the cover of a book by his elbow.

He found Drouot's site, typed in 'prehistory' and clicked 'enter'. And there on the screen was the sale catalogue. There were half a dozen or so pieces to a page, but the exceptional ones had half a page each. He scrolled through to the jade axe. It was much as he had seen it in the magazine, but the photo was quite good: you could never really trust the colour, but it appeared to be made from an opaque dark green jadeite with slightly darker veining. The cutting edge had several nicks which looked recent. He slid a sheet of photo paper into the printer. While the machine was chugging away he read the short description:

"Jadeite axe head, France, around 4300 BC, found C1900. This exceptional axe in classic dark avocado jade with a whitish bloom has been in the collection since 1965. Some damage to cutting edge but otherwise intact. Estimation: € 6000-7000." Pen found the description pompous. The patina was hard to make out in the photo but he had never heard of it being referred to as a bloom and as for "avocado", it should have said rotten avocado to include the veining anyway to him it looked more verdigris or viridian. Pen guessed the person responsible for the catalogue had never handled European jade before, which was quite possible considering its rarity on the archaeological antiquities market.

The image was spat out of the printer and Pen lifted it by its edges to avoid smudging it as it dried. Six or seven thousand euros, and it could go even higher if two or more rich collectors wanted it, not to mention the museums. There was no way that Pen was in with even a ghost of a chance. Still, he wasn't going to miss the fun.

Looking at the rest of the stuff in the sale, Pen could see that it was all pretty good. There were several other stone axes with their particular sheen from days of polishing, and although made of flint they all looked good. There were some impressive early Bronze Age flaked-flint daggers, mostly from Denmark but also a couple from

France, the ones Renault had seen. Then there was a small selection
of upper Palaeolithic material, which would be interesting. Amongst
them was a small Solutrean laurel leaf. The impossibly thin, finely
made leaf-shaped blades were probably the most emblematic of all
of the Stone Age tools. They were amongst the rarest and most
sought-after. This was going to be interesting. He blew up the photo
of the laurel leaf. It looked perfect, no breaks, neat, regular flaking
covering the entire surface and almost, but not quite, symmetrical.
Estimation: 600 to 1,000 euros. Could he perhaps try for that? His
pulse kicked up a notch at the thought. There were even some bits of
bone in the sale: two Magdalenian bone spear points with chamfered
bases in remarkable condition and several broken bits of bone with
patterns engraved on them. But what really caught Pen's eye was a
piece of a double-barbed harpoon like the one they had found. The
catalogue said it was made of antler, Magdalenian, estimated at 4,000
to 4,500 euros! The fragment was half as long as the one they had
found, theirs was intact and far more ornate.

Jeez! We've discovered a gold mine, thought Pen, and decided to
print out the whole catalogue.

Until now it would have been second nature to phone Noël to talk
to him about all this. Pen felt a pang of loss: he stood to lose so much.

He took the photocopied catalogue with him next day when he
went to work at Renault's place.

After the ritual with Serge and his dog, while coffee was brewing
he said "Look at this, Maurice," pointing at the harpoon, "Look at
the price."

"Yes, expensive, but it comes with very good credentials."

"What does that mean?"

"It means it was dug up by a well-respected archaeologist who
documented his find."

"Then sold it?"

"Not necessarily. he could have left it to his children, who could
have sold it on. Probably changed hands several times since. Anyway,

at the time people had the right to sell their finds. This piece was found before the first world war when you could buy laurel leaves and *bifaces* on the village market place."

"And that makes it expensive?"

"It's called provenance. A good provenance improves the legitimacy of a piece and therefore its value."

"Hum, I know someone who has a beautiful harpoon like this one, only his is intact. But I bet it has no provenance."

"I should like to meet him."

"Yes, well, he is a bit eccentric, he is very shy and very attached to his things, but perhaps he would lend it to me for a day and you could see it." Pen realised that the harpoon was with Noël, and he would probably not see it again himself for a long time, if at all.

The day went by in a daze again, mixing the gritty tile glue and carefully cementing the pieces of the glazed ceramic jigsaw into place; slowly the mosaic was coming to life. Around four, just before he would have to stop to get Alice, his phone went: Sophie wanted to pick Alice up from school and take her to Denise's for the night. Pen was fine with that. They exchanged a few strained words. "I am dying, hurry up and come home!" screamed Pen in his mind. They agreed to phone again tomorrow and she rang off.

P en had cleaned up his tools already and was on the point of leaving, but suddenly he had nowhere to go. He negotiated the perilous passage back to his truck, keeping an eye open for the sly old Alsatian. The brute knew that Pen was nervous of him and stalked him whenever Serge was not around. He had never been bitten, but he knew that there was a distinct possibility that one day he would be. By the time he climbed into the cab he had decided to go and take another look at St Léon. In the daylight he would see what kind of a mess they had made of the place. He would be in his truck, which was not very discreet, but perhaps he could take the bottom road as Noël had done when he found the piece of jade. He could park further away and walk up through the trees to the ploughed field at the bottom of the cliff.

When he got there he pulled off the road, parked on the packed earth and wandered leisurely up the lane towards the rock-face. The tarmac eventually gave out and the road became a dirt track. Standing for a moment looking down the path towards their dig, he could feel the river washing sedately down through the flat land to his right while the high cliff that towered close above him on his left was just beginning to be cast in shadow. The old castle brooded up there silhouetted against the gathering dusk. The poplars were still grey and yellow in the early evening light; the place held the same calm that he remembered from two short days ago — but now that seemed like another life. A pair of cooing wood-pigeons were settling down in some high branches. The sound took him, as it often did, back to a moment in his childhood that smelt soothingly of coal fires, cut grass and bright mornings with cooked breakfasts. He was thinking he had been right to come here to forget his troubles, when he was brought up by a sight he hadn't expected at all. Noël's car was there parked behind the bushes just off the lane a few metres in front of him. Good job it's not wet thought Pen, he'd never get out of there if it was. He walked up to the car and put his hand on the bonnet: stone cold. Bastard, thought Pen, he's digging, must be, this car's been here for a good while.

He made his way up to the big shattered bolder, an easy landmark from the bottom, and climbed round it to their excavation. They had made a huge heap of fresh sand. Their attempt at camouflaging it had been pretty ineffectual. If not for the big block of stone in front of it, their work would have been visible from the track. He made a note to collect some dead branches and leaf-mould to conceal it more effectively, at least from the casual glance of a Sunday stroller. When he approached the holes he spotted Noël's bag. "The bastard," thought Pen again, "and he was the one who thought this was immoral. He's taken back Sophie, he's ruining my life, and now he's ripping me off into the bargain." He felt a hot tide of anger wash through him, and jumped down into the hole, calling to Noël to come out. Pen's shout set the pigeons to flight and half-a-dozen crows to jostling and clamouring up in an angry murder from the trees. But Noël either didn't hear him or didn't want to. Seething, Pen squeezed into the hole. But with no lamp he could only wriggle forwards shouting Noël's name regardless of reverence or discretion, and came up against an obstruction.

"Oh God!" shouted Pen. In front of him the tunnel was blocked. The roof had caved in and Noël must be in there. Pen started scraping desperately with his hands and abruptly hit rock. It was hopeless. He had to call the fire-brigade or someone, and that meant the police.

"Shit! Noël! Shit!" Pen backed out of the hole, grabbed at Noël's bag and scrabbled through it. Sandwiches, a bottle of water. No lamp.

Pen hesitated a moment, then tore down the hill to the vehicles to look for something to dig with. Noël's was locked, through the window he could see the old trowel that Noël used to scrape the mud off his boots. He needed a shovel and a lamp. He raced up the lane to his truck. There were several possibilities: either Noël was dead, crushed by that great slab under which they had been digging; or he was injured and in desperate need of help — there couldn't be much air in there. Or, he was alive and well but trapped behind the wall of stone. He grabbed his telephone from the truck and called Sophie. He got her answering service — "Fucking phones!" — and left a rapid request to call him back. He climbed up into the cab and started the motor, then forced himself to calm down. Noël could have come up the bank like he did, discovered that the tunnel was blocked, left his bag there and gone for a walk. He could turn up at any minute.

His phone went: Sophie, thank god.

"What do you want Pen? We were going to talk tomorrow."

"Yes I know, I just wondered, when was the last time you saw Noël?"

"Why?"

"Just tell me Sophie, please." Something in Pen's voice made Sophie give him the answer he was hoping not to hear:

"We were supposed to see each other this morning but he didn't come."

"Have you tried phoning him?" Noël had resisted mobile phones, but had a broad-band connection for his computer and a land line phone.

"I phoned and left messages for him. He's in a state about you and Alice. I think he needs more time to think this through."

"Sophie, keep your phone handy, I may need to call you."

"Why Pen, what's happened?"

"I don't know, but he may have had an accident." Pen pulled on the wheel of his truck awkwardly with one hand as he tried to reassure Sophie without telling her anything.

"I'll call," he said, ringing off and, gunning the powerful engine, crunched up through the gears.

"This is turning into a nightmare," he moaned. He hadn't wanted to worry Sophie, but saying nothing couldn't be worse than the truth. Why did the stupid bugger go back there alone? Huh, same reason as me. Good place to be alone with your thoughts.

Pen crashed into his workshop and grabbed the big torch from his tool-box, a shovel and his crowbar. In the bathroom he took all the medical kit he could find. Finally he went to the kitchen and put the kettle on. He was running on adrenalin but it wouldn't last for ever; and when it ran out he would be on his knees. He poured himself a cup of tea the rest, heavily sweetened, went into the thermos. He prised open the plastic lid and there was his little twist of coke forgotten in the events of the last three days. Rushing back through the workshop with everything thrown into a plastic carrier bag, he picked up his head-lamp, a pack of fresh batteries, and a roll of strong cord — he didn't know what use that might be, but it felt right. He chucked the shovel and crowbar into the cab with the rest, then thought of the two warm coats hanging by the door, and was pulling out of the track when Sophie turned into it in the Peugeot. She was looking pretty agitated.

"For god's sake, Pen what's going on?" she shouted at him through the open window over the din of their two engines: "You said he had an accident."

"I don't know yet, his car is at St Léon where we were digging. Sophie, I need you here with your phone in case I want you to bring something. Give me an hour or so and I'll call you. And clean the house up, make sure that there's no dope lying around, and can you stash the stuff from the dig for me? I'll phone." Pen stamped down on the accelerator without giving Sophie time to quiz him further. The last thing he needed was Sophie getting involved if the police were brought in. Also he didn't know how he felt right now, and if Sophie was left hanging for a while so be it; it wouldn't change anything.

Back at the cliff he brought his truck right to the end of the track, jumped out and hauled his stuff, sweating with the stress of it, up to the dig. It was dusk already. If Noël was here, he might have been stuck and injured since last night, perhaps twenty-four hours — any way he looked at it, it didn't look good. He dumped the stuff next to Noël's back-pack. Typical of Noël to bring sandwiches.

He put on his head-lamp and entered the hole with his shovel in front of him. He could see now that the large slab of the roof had tilted forwards, shutting off their tunnel but leaving a cavity above it. Pen scrambled up into it, and tried digging into the sand to get behind it but came up against more rock.

He scraped away at it trying to find a way round, but it seemed pretty blocked that way. He backed out of the hole, which brought part of the roof pouring down on him, and he pulled out shaking sand from his shoulders and out of his hair. He spat a good deal and washed out his eyes with the water that Noël had thought to bring, but he was unharmed. He took his crowbar and returned to the blockage. Looking anxiously up at the roof a few centimetres from his face he guessed that it might be stable now but you could never tell. He started trying to find a purchase so that he could lever out some of the debris blocking the passage. He hacked away at likely-looking places, but nothing would give. Moving back to get a better look, he thought he heard something.

There it was again — a dull, regular throb like a machine, faint but distinct. Then it cut off. Pen moved back outside but heard nothing. He put his head back in, and there it was again. Could it be Noël? He hacked at the rock-face three times and waited. Immediately, there came a clear, dull echo. He repeated the operation enough times to be sure. Noël was in there, alive, and answering him. Pen scuttled out of the hole, stood up, and stretched: this was going to be a long night. He took his phone out of the plastic bag where he had left it, to tell Sophie the news, but he couldn't get a signal.

"Shit! These things cost the skin off your bollocks, and they never work when you need them!" He would have to drive the truck back up to the top of the track to phone, but he didn't have time now. Pen thought he could probably dig Noël out eventually, but he might be injured. He needed to think. The roof had hinged down into their tunnel like a trap-door, effectively closing it off. But the tunnel was not very large, no more than a metre at its widest, so the rock that had crashed right down to the floor of their tunnel, although massive, must be quite narrow at that point — otherwise it would have been held up by the undisturbed terrain on either side. So he needed to go round it. He poured himself a cup of tea; he was going to be here for a long time, and he had to phone Sophie. He took the lid off the thermos and prised it open; he helped himself to a dab from the package inside followed by a swig of tea, then slid back down into the hole.

This time he dug back down to the bed-rock and looked for the front of the fallen slab of the ancient shelter, which his new-found conscience told him they were defiling. He comforted himself with the thought that the last occupants of this place were opportunists who would have considered it the most normal thing in the world to exploit resources where they found them. This was very much a fortuitous situation and he couldn't begin to worry about the loss to archaeology: he was going for broke. But it was hard work with the shovel; he wasn't following the vein now, although he ploughed right through it from time to time and had to resist looking through the spoil. Pen felt his way around the fallen block in a mole's deprived dream of sand and stones; strangely, there were no worms or roots, just flint and desiccated bone.

He felt like a lost diver in that narrow subterranean world, no up nor down, little air and the only noise his own scraping; thrust, tug, slush. The tube he was making for himself as he swam through the earth was only just the size his body needed to continue pushing forward. If the tunnel he was creating collapsed in on him he would have no room at all to manoeuvre. Then he picked up Noël's knocking again, closer now and to his left. He had a moment's panic and started backing up, desperate for air. He came out gasping, realising that he was not claustrophobic — but all the same...

It was dark now outside. He had a pang of guilt for Sophie, but pushed it aside. To continue he needed to evacuate more sand. He couldn't go on in such a tight space and if Noël was injured — which was a distinct possibility — he would need more space to bring him out.

He spent the next twenty minutes widening his tunnel, taking the sand back to the entrance and dumping it outside. As soon as he had cleared the fallen trap-door he worked his way left, from time to time banging on the rock to let Noël know he was still there, but it had been a while since he had heard a reply. He was going slower now, worried about coming up against one of Noël's feet and perhaps injuring him with his shovel. But it was Noël's own shovel that he came upon first. The wooden handle was lying across his path, the blade apparently trapped under the fallen roof. Pen had to detour around it — and then suddenly there was no resistance: his spade had broken through into a space.

He widened the breach carefully with his hands, and inched forward over his shovel to get his head into the hole. He could feel cool air on his face. He hadn't realised it, but he had been getting hot with all the effort. His head-lamp showed a wide low space that angled upward.

"Noël!" he shouted up into the darkness.

"Pen, it's you." Noël was groaning and making a strange keening sound.

"Noel, are you all right?"

"Yes," came the sobbed reply, "I am now."

"Can you get down here?"

"My lamp is gone and I need a drink. There's water in my bag, it should be outside, it's all I've thought about for hours." So Pen wormed back through the tunnel, feeling the tension leaving him. Outside, he de-sanded himself, including emptying his shoes. He sorted through the things he had brought, putting the spare batteries in his pocket and the big torch, the first-aid stuff and the thermos into Noël's bag. Then after stretching a few times and taking some deep breaths — which steamed brightly in the beam of his lamp and he realised the night had become decidedly chilly — he crawled back down into the confined space, pushing the back-pack in front of him.

When he got back to the breach, he could see that it must have been caused by a fall like the one that had blocked their tunnel. An inclined plane of sandy rock led upwards; another came down to join it to his left, leaving just enough room between them for him to squirm up to where Noël was waiting.

Pen had no idea what to expect, but when he worked himself out of the gap at the top of the slope he was surprised to find himself in a musty space easily high enough to stand up in. Noël was slumped against a wall of rock looking intently at him. He wasted no time fishing the bottle of water out of the rucksack and helping Noël to drink. He looked at him as his throat worked greedily, swallowing. His hands were bloody, his fingernails broken, and blood, now dried, had run down from his head over his face.

"Whoa, not too fast Noël. I have some tea, keep a bit of that water. I want to wash your hands a bit then I will bandage them up, it will make it easier for you to climb down. Do you think you can make it?"

"I'm sorry, Pen."

"Stay cool, man, there's no problem."

"There is, Pen. I fucked up, I didn't know what to do, maybe I envied your life with Alice and Sophie, it's everything I would have wished for. Sophie had had affairs before, I didn't interfere, but she always came back to me."

"For what it's worth, Noel, things between Sophie and me have been pretty tough for a while now. She's bored with me, we argue too much. I think she only stays with me because of Alice. Here, let me look at your hands."

Pen turned on the powerful beam of his big torch and brought it round towards Noël. As he did so it swept over the walls of the prison. He was staggered to discover that they were in a narrow cavern, a cleft in the rock that seemed to go right up the cliff.

"Shit, Noël, look at this."

"You're wrong, Pen, she loves you."

"Hey man, it's okay, don't let's talk about this now." Pen took a last look up the deep well they were in, then set to work cleaning Noël's ragged fingers. They were badly abraded, but Noël seemed oblivious to Pen's ministrations. The air in the cavern smelt of decaying stone and rotting layers of compressed sand that had already lived too many lives. Pen realised the cell they were in had once been deep below the seabed.

"My spade got buried in the fall. I tried to dig my way out with my hands, but it's all rock, then I couldn't any more. I thought I would die in here."

"Hey man, don't get morbid on me. You knew we'd work it out eventually."

Pen worked quickly; he could do a better job when they were home. Noël stared off into the dark, working his jaw.

"No, Pen, I didn't. Shine your light over there on the floor." Pen looked over by the far wall for the first time and saw a half-buried tangle of roots or some kind of basket work. Noël stared at the debris, a rictus of disgust distorting his face.

"I couldn't see them in the dark but I felt them when I first climbed in here." Pen went over to take a closer look, and then he realised why Noël had feared dying in here so much. Lying tightly together as if they had been tucked up in bed, was a group of human skeletons. Time had taken its toll, but he could clearly see six skulls: no longer anatomically connected to their spines they lay, at inhuman angles, rolled away from their bodies like so many old pots.

"How the hell did they get in here?"

"I don't know, but I thought I'd be joining them quite soon. I would have if you hadn't come looking for me."

"I didn't come looking for you, Noël, I came for a walk and to see if we hadn't left too much mess. When I saw your car I thought of looking for you. but I didn't know you were in here until I heard you banging."

"Yes, I heard something. You can't imagine how quiet it can be, so long alone in the dark without any sound. I could hear the working of my joints and the pumping of my blood clear as day. And when I heard you clunking away in the distance, it was like music to me, I felt hope for the first time since I managed to get out from under that cave-in."

"When did you get here, Noël?"

"Around midnight, I wasn't tired. I have too much on my mind, there was no point going to bed. I should have, though."

"Shit, Noël, that means you've been here for nearly twenty-four hours."

"It feels like more."

"Here." Pen handed him a lukewarm cup of sweet tea, "drink this, then we'll try to get you out of here." He stowed the things and decided to leave the bag for later, it would only hinder him now. He took the batteries from his pocket and asked Noël for his lamp.

"I lost it somewhere," said Noël, gesturing down the slope. Pen took off his own lamp and fitted it over Noël's head.

Getting out was laborious. Noël had been seriously shaken up and had trouble reversing down the passage. They were facing each other head-to-head with one lamp lighting their progress, but Noël had to take rests. There was a problem at the entrance because he could not manage to turn around to climb out. Pen waited patiently, chatting about clearing the garden of the scores of tomato plants that Sophie insisted on growing every year so that she could bottle or freeze enough for a year's worth of pizzas for Alice. Noël almost allowed himself to be lulled into the familiar comfort of shared tribulations, the lines of anguish clearing from his face. Then with an effort of will he heaved himself round and scrambled out into the cold night air. He just lay there on the ground looking up at the night sky, drinking in the stars with tears washing the grime from his cheeks. Pen realised that his own face was wet too with the sudden relief.

"Come on, Noël me old son, we can't stay here. The truck's just at the bottom." But Noël just lay there.

"My feet." Noël croaked through the emotion as if ashamed. Pen gently took the lamp off his head and looked down at his feet. There was nothing to see, just sand-encrusted work boots and worn trousers. Pen was a big guy, and Noël probably weighed not much more than Sophie on a fat week. It wasn't far to the truck.

"You'll have to help, man," said Pen, dragging him into a sitting position. Then once he had him over his shoulder, it was mostly downhill.

8

Back at the truck, Pen was glad of the coats he had thrown in at the last minute. Noël looked shot and was shivering quietly. He called Sophie.

"He's all right, but I have to take him to hospital, Sophie. Something's wrong with his feet and his hands need dressing properly." Noël could hear Sophie shouting down the line at Pen.

"I'm fine, I'm okay, Sophie," he mumbled. Pen looked at him and said to her, "I'll phone you from the hospital, I have to go." Noël had fallen asleep, Pen didn't know if that was good or bad, so he backed the truck down the lane with the engine whining until he could turn round, then raced off to the accident and emergency unit at Sarlat.

On the way there, Pen racked his brain wondering how to explain Noël's condition to the interns, who were bound to ask. Potholing seemed the most feasible explanation, but where? Then he remembered the strange phenomenon of *cluzeaux* in the region. Curious about the square window-like openings he had seen peppering many of the sheer cliff faces that lined many of the valleys, he had looked it up. He discovered that throughout the medieval period in southwest France, these defensive shelters were extensively carved out of the easily-mined limestone, often high up in the precipitous rockface. The people used them to hide from marauding armies during the fanatical wars of religion in the sixteenth century. They were extensively used by the French Huguenot Protestants, who were pursued and persecuted by Louis the Fourteenth's Catholic armies. It sounded barbaric, but one had only to open a modern newspaper to realise that in many countries things hadn't improved much. There was no real official history of these sophisticated refuges and they might have been far older than the accounts that he had read claimed.

Pen had visited several of these *cluzeaux*, including the incredible so-called English Fortress not far up-river from St Léon. Accessed through a small oak doorway close to the river, it had a steep, narrow stair that turned tightly on itself to make defence easier. The stair led up to an immense natural rock shelter, a deep horizontal cleft. The huge flat open space, totally concealed from uninitiated eyes, had been modified over the centuries. Rooms had been added, cupboards had been carved out of the walls and even beds fashioned out of the living rock. It could house scores of people, at a pinch perhaps even hundreds.

Pen's mind ran on to another one on the road to Sarlat, which a farmer had pointed out to him one day when he was flinting in the fields. He had gone back later to explore it with four English friends one bright winter's afternoon. The door, set in a stone wall, built to close off a natural cave mouth, was hidden by the undergrowth at the foot of the rockface. The farmer said that you had to find a loose stone in the wall and remove it to reach the opening mechanism, a sturdy oak bar which slid through iron cleats into recesses in the walls on either side. It seemed sophisticated, but when they got inside it was just a sandy old cave. There was no sign of human habitation. They had one old bicycle lamp between them and a few cigarette lighters. As they penetrated into the gallery away from the daylight they saw that the cave system divided into two separate passages. They were examining the carcass of some unfortunate animal when one of the girls said, "Where's Katie?" They turned back and realised that she had taken the other branch. They called for her, but her boyfriend had screamed:

"Katie, don't move!" at the top of his lungs. It sounded a bit hysterical to Pen, but when they got to the girl she was standing on the lip of a well that spanned the floor in front of her. She had been holding her lighter aloft and her feet were in shadow. Pen lobbed a stone into the hole and heard it hit bottom several metres below them. Katie had looked ashen even when they got back outside, but for Pen it was the perfect story to explain Noël's accident.

He pulled up to the emergency entrance and ran into admissions. There was a glass kiosk with two women in pink uniforms sitting in front of computers. Pen stuck his head in and said,

"I have a badly injured person with me in a truck outside. Could someone help me bring him in, please?"

"Just a minute, sir," said the woman closest to him without taking her eyes off the screen. Pen took a deep breath.

"Where is your vehicle, sir?" asked the other woman.

"It's just outside," Pen said, pointing.

"You can't leave it there, sir, it's blocking the entrance."

"Well, get someone to help me bring my friend in and I'll move it."

"You can wait in there," said the first woman, pointing to the waiting area which at present held about nine frazzled-looking occupants. An almost silent TV broadcast its flickering image over its listless audience.

"I'll wait after you get me someone, madam, but in the mean time if you don't move your fat arse I'm going to rip your safe little office apart!"

"No need to get excited, sir," she said, finally taking notice of him. Looking up she saw two exhausted but very determined tawny eyes glaring at her out of a mud-caked face. Pen's hair was matted like a dishevelled dog's pelt, and most of his upper body was straining towards her through the window menacingly. She picked up the phone and said,

"Bernard, can you come out here please?" A big orderly appeared in whites from a door in the back of the office and talked quietly to the two indignant-looking women. He came out of a side door and said,

"She says you threatened them."

"Look, can we just get the injured guy in here first? Then we can talk all you want." The orderly seemed to react to his unadulterated English accent and said:

"Where?"

They wheeled Noël in on a dolly, a chubby nurse tutting at the filth of them. Noël hadn't woken up, which alarmed Pen. The orderly chatted as they tried to get him undressed.

"People who make it in here by themselves, like you, can usually survive a bit longer on their own. The girls have a lot of work to get through, and at this time of night we get a lot of drunks. We're really geared up for the ambulances, car-accidents, cerebral haemorrhaging, heart attacks, stuff like that. And you have to admit you do sound kind of funny."

He asked Pen to go and see the pink ladies to check in, then wait. Pen had a long overdue cigarette as he shifted the truck and sat in it in the flood-lit car park to phone Sophie. It was two o'clock in the morning, but she picked up on the first ring.

"He won't be out tonight, he has to have x-rays and stuff, but they say he's okay. I have the paperwork to do, then I'm going home."

"I'll be waiting for you, Pen. Take care driving, you must be tired." They were words that he should have been relieved to hear. But he just felt numb.

In the days that followed the weather turned cold but stayed dry. A bright sky seemed to widen around the workshop as the trees shed their leaves with the first frosts. Noël had come out of Sarlat hospital two days later. His feet had been badly bruised but nothing more. By chance that day he had put on his work-boots with the steel toecaps, which had saved his feet from being crushed. But they had swollen so much that they had to cut the boots off him. It was his ankles that hurt him most, and both his hands were dressed in bandages.

It was officially a fall while exploring a cave. He got some stern advice to join a recognised potholing club from the doctor who stitched up his scalp wound. He replied that he doubted that he would be taking it up as a hobby, and the matter stayed there. Sophie went to get him, bringing Noël a full set of clean clothes; but he couldn't even bear slippers on his strapped-up feet.

She brought him home to the workshop, and installed him on the large sofa downstairs. Sophie nursed him and to Pen's surprise he felt no jealousy or resentment. Noël read endless stories to Alice who was in awe of his bandages.

"You look like an Egyptian mummy in clothes," she said, looking at his hands and feet and the plaster on his head. Of course Sophie would not have sex with Pen with Noël within imagined hearing in their little house. But one night, totally unlooked for, she took him tenderly in her mouth to console him. He clamped his jaws shut to keep from crying out, but jerked and shuddered like a fish dying on the end of a line. She snuggled up tight to him afterwards with her arms round him making the contented purring sounds in his ear like the cat that got the cream. It seemed that for the time being she had made her choice, but Pen wondered if it was not just the result of having them both together under her roof.

Some of the joy had definitely gone out of Sophie though, and Pen felt she was struggling to keep her independence. She had previously been quite successful at that, but her market stall was no longer sufficient stimulation and the home and garden were never going to be enough even with Alice there. Sophie needed to get her teeth into something. She had been drifting along for too long and now, finally, her intellect appeared to be rebelling. She had become touchy, easily put out, often by small, insignificant things. She was evidently frustrated though she would never admit as much to him. Pen ached for her but trusted her to find a way out of it; he just hoped it wouldn't end up tearing them apart.

Renault and his helper came round as arranged and collected a plastic crate of second- and third-choice flints. While Serge was loading it into the car, Renault counted out a pile of banknotes onto Pen's desk. Pen knew that he was not going to find many more flints in the fields, so when Renault started negotiations and asked him how much, he looked dejected as if he was having second thoughts. Eventually Renault offered him twice what he had paid for all the stuff he had taken away the last time, and Pen despondently agreed. Renault said:

"No bill of sale, no cheque in the bank, no trail back to me. The people from the museum will find them in one of the crates in my collection and classify them, then they will officially exist, my boy. You just keep your end of the bargain and disclaim all knowledge."

Provenance, thought Pen.

He went to Noël's place and picked up the spoils from their dig. They spent a day cleaning the finds and marvelling at the quality of the workmanship. The most remarkable piece by far was the harpoon. Pen wondered if it might be made of antler like the one in the sale. He was still working at Renault's, and decided to show it to him the next time he was there. They considered letting him have it, if it was worth so much. But Noël looked pained, and they ended up deciding to wait until after the auction to see how the material from the upper Palaeolithic was received.

Maurice was due back sometime soon but he hadn't told Pen when. Then one evening Vincent turned up at the workshop. Vincent never came round unless he was after something. People spoke of him as a wily fox, but Pen thought of him as a weasel always following the line of least resistance, ever patient, ready to strike at the first sign of weakness.

"Hi Pen, I hope I'm not disturbing you. You're relaxing?"

"Yeah, just finished. You want a beer?"

"Thank you, Pen, that would be nice." Vincent followed Pen through to the house where Noël was hobbling about, back up on his feet at last. Vincent affected reverence.

"Mister Noël, it is not often that one finds oneself in the presence of the two most successful flint hunters in the region."

"Come on, Vincent, leave it out," said Noël with a grin.

"And what has happened to you, Noël? You look exhausted."

"I had a bout of flu but I'm better now," replied Noël. Aware that he was prevaricating, Vincent knew better than to push it and turned to Pen:

"Renault told me you knew of a Magdalenian harpoon. Is it true?"

"It's true," Pen conceded.

"I would very much like to see it," said Vincent, "I have made a little study on the subject and, as you know, I have one myself."

Pen remembered, Vincent did have a complete, intact harpoon, though it was small and had only a single row of barbs. He had been able to talk at length about how it was made, it's probable use based on similar Inuit harpoons and its position in the cultural sequence, apparently preceding the more recent, double-rowed version. Pen looked at Noël, who gave a slight nod, Pen said:

"I have it on loan. The owner might be persuaded to part with it eventually if the price is right, but it's not at all sure." With that he disappeared into the workshop leaving Noël to open three beers.

Vincent was for once stunned into silence. He turned the harpoon over and over in his fingers and finally, predictably, asked:

"Where did he get it?"

To which Pen replied, "It has no provenance. French!"

"Ah, well, sadly that will affect its value," said Vincent.

"We know, but he is not desperate to sell."

"Perhaps he would swap it for some nice things?" tried Vincent, magnanimously.

"I'll ask him," returned Pen, taking a tug on his beer and avoiding Noël's eye.

After he had left they rolled around on the furniture spluttering,

"Some nice things, some very nice things no doubt!" Then Noël looked at Pen and said seriously:

"If you want to sell it, go ahead."

"Listen, Noel," said Pen "you owe me nothing. I don't want you to defer to me all the time. You would have done the same for me. Sophie is another matter."

Vincent had not driven directly away from Pen's place but sat outside in his car looking at the house and thinking. Then he drew his phone from his pocket and sent a text to his most insistent client. The collector was someone he had known years ago in the army. He would not be happy that the conceited English *connard* was not keen on selling his harpoon. His contact was someone who was used to getting his own way. He wished now that he had kept it to himself: the guy could get quite difficult. Vincent scowled at the house cursing its occupants, then pulled out of the drive.

After opening another beer those same occupants had just begun talking about Noël's ordeal. He had no memory at all of the cave-in, just of the horror of being trapped there in the dark trying to dig his way out. He could feel the air up above him and eventually scrambled up there, knowing that no one knew where he was. The first thing he did was discover the skeletons. After that his imagination filled in the blanks.

He knew that he was right under the château, and guessed that the cave might have been used as a natural dungeon; he could feel the air coming down from above but did not imagine the depth of his prison until Pen had told him that it looked as if the well went right up to the top of the cliff. Whatever, those people had been trapped there like him, who knew how long ago, and had perished of thirst and despair.

"I'm going back there," said Pen, "we left the bag and besides I need to know about those others. I'm beginning to think they might have been there since medieval times."

"I'm coming with you."

"You sure, Noël?"

"I need to see where I was, it's all so vague now. I was in the dark for most of that time, it's like a dream."

"Nightmare, you mean."

"When do you want to go?"

"When can you be ready?"

"I'm ready," said Noël.

Although it was not a fortune, Pen had more money than he had ever had, so he took Noël on a shopping spree. They got proper overalls, dark grey with zips right up the front from the bottom of the leg. He bought a digital camera and got a draw-string duffel bag and a new thermos. They ended up at a builder's suppliers and bought two pairs of safety boots with steel toe-caps.

"Could you stop at the fishmonger's on the way home?" asked Noël.

"Mm, good idea." Once there, Noël insisted on paying for half a kilo of smoked salmon, two lemons and two bottles of overpriced champagne. Pen added a fresh cream-cake from the baker next door with out-of-season raspberries and from the florist he bought a bunch of yellow and white tulips with lots of ferny greenery then added half a dozen long stem red roses.

They were preparing the kitchen table with cloth and candles and table napkins and long-stemmed glasses when the girls turned up with Denise in tow. They piled into the kitchen all talking at once, ooh-ing and aah-ing over the preparations. Denise looked gay for once; she took off her warm jacket to reveal a colourful tight-fitting dress with a low neckline and a wide belt. Something had changed, Pen thought she looked quite sexy: the heels on her high leather boots lifted her bum as they were designed to, causing her to push her torso out to compensate, thus enhancing her small but generous figure. He almost blushed at this appraisal of his sister-in-law, but managed a brotherly smile. She sat next to Noël at the table, looking very concerned for him, questioning him more than he seemed comfortable with about his injuries and his brief stay in hell.

Later, sated and buoyed up with Dutch courage, both dressed in their new grey overalls and dark woollen bobs, Pen at the wheel of Noël's estate, Noël asked:

"What do you think of Denise?"

"Ah," replied Pen, "she's had a hard time recently, but she's a lovely woman."

"Funny, I haven't seen much of her since you and Sophie got together. I never really looked at her before, but she's very pretty."

Pen smiled at him: "I think she was trying to impress you this evening."

Noël swallowed: "You think so?"

"Maybe...watch it Noël you are on the rebound and Denise is a fragile girl despite appearances. I can't believe that you lived with Sophie for years and never looked at her little sister."

"If this is a rebound I must be a ping pong ball, besides Pen, nothing happened, honest man we didn't have any sex just stress and rusty lust. As for Denise she was always family, sort of, like a sister to me then."

"Evidently she doesn't feel that way herself."

"Fascinating."

"It's not fascinating, mate — it may be fate."

The spot where Noël had left his car last time seemed well enough concealed. They intended this to be the last visit to the fox-hole, and had decided not to plunder the site any more unless they came across something interesting that they really couldn't leave behind.

Pen wanted to take a good look at the skeletons of the poor devils who had been incarcerated in that subterranean cell, and try to figure out how long they had been there.

"You going to be able to handle this, Noel?" he asked at the entrance.

"I'm fine," said Noël a little too emphatically, "let's go."

Pen went first with the shovel; Noël brought the duffel-bag.

The passage was much shorter than Pen remembered; he squeezed out into the cave with Noël at his heels no more than three minutes after entering it.

"I can't believe I was so close to the outside," said Noël incredulously.

"Well it's eight or nine meters, not that close when it's through solid rock, as we discovered. You still okay?" asked Pen. Noël pulled a torch out of the duffel-bag and turned it on. By way of an answer he pointed it up the chimney, but his beam did not illuminate the upper part. Pen had retrieved another torch from Noël's back-pack left there on the floor. He added its beam to Noël's, and together they could make out a high natural cleft reaching right up the rock.

"Made by water, right?" guessed Noël.

"Yes, but it could have been millions of years ago." They ran the beams over the rock; there seemed to be a dark opening higher up, perhaps leading to the outside.

"Yes, well someone else will have to explore that one," whispered Noël. They had gone back into reverential mode. The dead were demanding respect.

With fascinated horror they turned their torches onto the shallow mound of bones. The skeletons looked devoid of any vestige of clothing or even flesh or hair, for which Pen was quietly grateful. They were apparently lying on their sides, but only the skulls, some of the ribs and the pelvises emerged from the thick coat of sand that had settled on them over the years. They seemed to move slightly, to be slowly writhing in the searching torch beams — it was disconcerting. Pen approached them carefully, so as not to step on any extremities. There were definitely six individuals, looking as if they had died snuggled up together for warmth.

"Pen, look!" called Noël, dragging Pen's uneasy gaze from the bones. He didn't see at first what it was that had excited Noël; he was just shining his lamp at the blank wall. Then he moved a step forward and it came into focus.

The walls were decorated. The entire surface seemed to be covered with a labyrinth of swirls and spirals, carved in shallow relief into the rock. The falling sand from above had built up on the ledges that had been formed, obscuring some of it — but it was clear enough to see. Pen approached and began brushing out the sand with his fingers following the lines.

"Do you know what this reminds me of, Noël?"

"It looks like Carnac or New Grange, one of those dolmens or tumuli or something. We could be inside a fucking Neolithic barrow, a burial site." Pen sank down on his haunches staring in wonder, mesmerised by the possibilities of their discovery. He was tracing the lines with his fingers to clear them. This was unbelievable.

"They're Neolithic people. Could be six thousand years old."

"We can't be sure," said Noël.

"No. But there is one way to find out. They buried their dead with their treasures, like the Egyptians, and usually with food for the voyage into the afterlife."

"They were the ones who left that piece of jade?"

"My god. Come on, take care to disturb as little as possible — but we have to look. The offerings should have been placed around the bodies." Suddenly all their good resolutions went out the window; they were about to become the most recent of that long and iniquitous line of opportunists known as grave robbers.

Working from both sides, they pushed their fingers into the soft sand digging along the edge of the bones and, almost at once, near the first gaping skull Noël found something. They examined it with their lamps, in absolute disbelief, then they looked at each other until Noël cracked.

"This is it! Shit man! This is fucking it! It's a fucking jade axe!" Pen took the tool from Noël's hands and held it in his torch-beam. It was a rich, translucent pale green, and despite a whitish encrustation of calcite on the side that had been in contact with the ground, the light was diffused throughout the stone: it glowed from within.

"What do you call that colour? Pea-green, lime-green, spinach, avocado?"

"It's not avocado or spinach, it looks more Granny Smith to me."

They began to giggle like a couple of kids around a Christmas tree full of presents.

"Well fuck knows, it's emerald green to me, and the shape, look at the way the blade splays out — we'll have to go careful, this is pristine, it looks like it's never been used."

"It's being used now." Said Noël, "they were symbols of power. This is the badge that was intended to prove to those on the other side the esteem, the place in their elite that should be accorded to these newly arrived travellers."

"This is a noble family," said Pen, his sense of awe mounting. "This axe looks as fragile as glass and as easy to chip. Come on." Laying it carefully on the bags they went back to work.

There was no way now that they could avoid disturbing the site. Stratigraphically, which is how archaeologists like to work, it was being seriously compromised. Eventually Pen had it all laid out on their bags on the floor and took hurried photos of everything. The three other jade axes, the pierced jade disk, the two huge boar tusks, the nine, very long, slightly arched flint blades of exquisite crafts-manship, the twelve large decorated gold beads, and finally the thin, embossed, plate-gold lozenge, which made up the treasure.

In a dream Pen photographed the walls and the skeletons over and over from every angle. He photographed Noël holding the two most beautiful axes, one in each hand like a bragging fisherman with an uncertain look on his face, as if to ask, are our troubles only just beginning? And in the background like a hallucination the ancient traceries wove and swirled around him enigmatically.

9

Before leaving the site they heaved a big chunk of the shattered boulder down into the hole that they had so recently borrowed from the foxes, and filled in behind it with a part of the hillock of sand that they had created. Hopefully the foxes wouldn't mind too much; there were kilometres of cliff to house them. They spread leaf-mould, stones and branches over the surface until they were sure that no one who wasn't looking for signs of an excavation would notice anything, and set off home.

"You know, Noël, I feel we've bitten off more than we can chew here," said Pen during the drive back.

"I know how you feel, this treasure is worth a fortune. But who can we show it to?"

"No one! I want to enjoy it for a while, but the only people who can handle a find like this is a museum, and we have so totally destroyed the Palaeolithic site and robbed the Neolithic one, they won't be happy at all."

"We have to invent a foolproof story before anyone sees any of this."

"You're right, but let's not worry too much yet, there's no rush. I just want to get it back to the workshop and clean it all up so that we can see what we've found."

It was after two when they got back. The girls were still up; after another glass of wine or two they were in high spirits. The boys had taken their dirty overalls off in the workshop so felt reasonably presentable. They were still flushed with the excitement of their find but the girls had other things on their minds.

"Noël," said Denise, "do you intend staying here tonight?"

"Er, I, um, why?"

"Because perhaps we could give Sophie and Pen some peace and you could take me home."

"Good idea. Not that we want to get rid of you — but Denise, you came with Sophie and Alice so you don't have a car, do you?" asked Pen.

"No I don't. What do you say, Noël?" He looked shyly at Sophie, who was giving nothing away.

"Put like that, I would be honoured to take you home, Mademoiselle," he said with a gallant flourish of his air hat.

"Come on then," said Denise, rising a little unsteadily from her chair and slipping her arm through Noël's hugging it to her bosom. To his mild embarrassment he could feel himself blushing, and grinned at Sophie and Pen. Sophie smiled and said, "See you tomorrow, then."

Neither Noël nor Pen had put their grubby bags down during this exchange, and Noël said,

"Well, I'll take this with me. I'll need to have something to look at tomorrow morning to prove it wasn't all a dream." There were kisses all round then the door to the workshop closed behind them, leaving Sophie and Pen alone in the kitchen

"A happy ending to a lovely day, darling," Sophie said, turning to Pen with a relieved smile.

"Yes, please," Pen replied lowering his bag of ill-gotten gains to the kitchen floor to free his hands.

"I'm not sure I meant it like that," she said, her grin widening.

She did not object as Pen pulled her to him and, lifting the hem of her dress, slipped his hands into the back of her knickers, she gave a little moan as his fingers kneaded. He wondered how skin could possibly feel this good.

"You've been meddling, my little match-maker. You're sure this is what you want?"

"You're not happy?"

"Oh, I think I'm going to be."

Unusually, Renault phoned Pen early next morning. For once he was enjoying a lie-in with Sophie. It was Saturday, but the season had gone quiet and she was skipping her first market since Easter. He almost didn't pick up the phone.

"Ah Pen, how are you my boy?" said Renault sounding a little over-friendly for nine-thirty, "are you likely to be coming over here today? I got back last night and there is a little matter I'd like to discuss with you."

Hmm, thought Pen: the harpoon.

Renault went on: "You'll find me in the cellar. Looking forward to it."

Woken by the telephone, Alice had come in for cuddles. She knew that Pen felt self-conscious cuddling her when he was naked, so she went to Sophie's side and Pen slipped out of bed.

After breakfast he spread out on the table all the things he had brought back from the cave. Noël had taken that first jade axe with him, but Pen had the three others. One of them resembled Noël's, but was a much darker green, the stone opaque, the blade splayed out each side at the cutting edge like an elongated battle-axe. It was a thing of beauty. For the people who made the blades, these green axes would have been a burst of sunlight and shade seen through the fresh young leaves of spring, a symbol of rejuvenation. The work involved in mining the rare minerals, at over two thousand metres up in the Alps, and bringing the roughly-formed axes a thousand kilometres by foot, the hundreds of hours of work by skilled craftsmen required to produce the flawless symmetry and perfect lustre of the finished thing — all spoke of the exceptional value placed on these remarkable works of art.

Sophie looked worried when she came down and saw the treasure laid out on the table.

"You mean you took these from someone's grave? I didn't think people were buried with their gold in France. I'm not sure I approve."

"Hey come on, Sophie, this could be our lucky break."

"Or it could get us into deep shit. Who will you be able to get rid of it to?"

"Don't you find them amazing? This stuff is thousands of years old, it's not like it's your granddad or anything. It's more like I won the lottery, a dream come true."

"They are too beautiful, Pen. I find them creepy, I mean you can't own something like this."

"Give me a break, baby. I'll lock them in the flint room for the time being while I work out what to do with it all." Seeing how determined Pen was, Sophie took her tea out into the bright chilly garden and left him with his treasure.

He was absorbed now by the two other blades that had only their flatness in common with the first one. They were made of a bright, spinach-coloured stone, they had wider blades, and were more triangular. Although they were similar and could have been cut from the same block, a pair, of only slightly different form and size. Though the stone was dark, the jade still allowed the light to pass through it, its beauty was enhanced by several paler diagonal veins. Neither of them showed any surface patina to speak of; each was as perfect as the day it was made. Pen hugged himself.

He turned his attention to the beads. Close inspection showed they were in fact made of tight spirals of thick gold wire wrapped to look like little ridged golden eggs. There was something of bees and honey about them, the gold as bright as if it had just been polished.

He weighed four of them in his hand — despite their delicacy, there was a satisfying density to them.

He knew that since the beginning of the Neolithic, gold had been sought out and worked. And all over Europe most of the native gold had been found long ago and been used over and over again — indeed there was Neolithic gold in much of the gold in circulation today. As he looked at the beads, Pen's mind drifted to the collection of prehistoric gold that he had seen in the Neues Museum in what was once East Berlin. Many of the displays had been empty, but held photographs of priceless cups and torques, collars and broaches, each with a sad label saying they had been removed by the Russians when they took Berlin in 1945. They had apparently hauled away three large crates which were never heard of again, their irreplaceable contents probably melted down.

It is said that native gold naturally contains some silver and copper, but that if it spends long enough in running water those impurities are leached out. From the purity of Neolithic gold, it is surmised that the people found much of it in water-courses. Had this gold been found in the river below the cave? If Pen did nothing to authenticate the beads, they would eventually find their way into an assay office where someone behind the counter would raise their eyebrows at the purity of the metal, then sign the forms that sent them off to be smelted into the ever-swelling flow of vulgar bullion.

He also had three of the long blades and the curious jade disk, but felt that he needed to get to Renault's and had no time to do them justice. So he put them with the rest of the stuff next door in his museum. He laid them carefully in a cardboard box on the piles of magazines at the far end of the tiny room, then picked up the harpoon from the shelf where he had left it and put it in his pocket. He was about to lock the door when on an impulse he went back in, picked the smallest of the dark green axe-heads, and slipped it into one of the old socks he kept there for just this sort of purpose. He turned the key in the lock and hid it in its groove in the architrave.

Emptying the new duffel-bag of the camera and its few remaining other bits, he wrapped the axe in an extra coat of bubble-wrap and carefully packed it into the bottom. He didn't bother with his tools as he would not be working. And if Renault didn't have anything else planned, he might even get lunch.

On the way there, thoughtfully smoking his first and most satisfying cigarette of the day, he reflected on Sophie's reaction to their finds. He was surprised that she had balked at them. He had expected her approval, praise even, but it was probably her condemnation that had prompted him to show Renault the axe. He had decided it would be the same person who let him have him the harpoon, that had entrusted him with the piece of jade. He knew full well that it would be baiting Renault, but the urge was irresistible, he had to show something from the fabulous hoard. These preoccupations meant that when he arrived around the back of the big house, he was not taking his usual care. He hung the bag over his shoulder, climbed down from the truck, and headed straight for the cellars. The Alsatian slunk around the side of the vehicle and went for Pen in a snarling rush, its large black muzzle catching him mid-thigh.

He had no time to react — before he knew it, the dog had given him two painful bites. Looking back on it, Pen was surprised by his response. He had thought that if the damn dog ever got the opportunity, it would tear him to pieces. In fact he almost got a kick in, but the dog was too quick for him. Rage welled up in him out of nowhere. The brute sensed it and ran. He turned on the dog, but too late. The problem for Pen was that the emotion was too strong to dissipate immediately and it had nowhere to go: his trousers were torn and his leg was bleeding.

He stormed into the cellar. Renault was at the far end, his head folded into one of his open display cases. The light from the neon lamp lit him from underneath, giving him a ghoulish air. Pen screamed at him from the doorway:

"Your bodyguard's fucking dog just chewed my leg!"

"Ah Pen," said Renault, extracting his head from the display, "I was expecting you earlier. How are you, my boy?"

"I'm not your fucking boy — your dog just attacked me!"

"Benji, he wouldn't hurt a fly…"

"Fucking ripped my fucking jeans! Take a look!"

Renault approached, looking concerned, "What's the trouble, Pen? You look distressed." The absurd lack of communication with Renault was defusing Pen's anger.

"Oh nothing, Maurice. Got any coffee?"

"Ah, good idea. We can see what damage Benji's done to you while we drink it. Come on, let's go up to the kitchen."

Once there, Renault looked suitably alarmed when he saw Pen's injured leg.

"Need to get that seen to. I'll take you to my doctor, just a tick, I'll phone her." Abandoning coffee, Renault rushed Pen over to Sarlat where a friendly middle-aged woman disinfected his leg and used five stitches to close the punctures.

"It will bruise and you must keep it clean and dressed. I'll give you a prescription for some antibiotics. Dog-bites," she said, smiling knowingly at Renault, "usually become infected, don't they, Maurice?" She sighed as she busied herself with the paperwork.

After the doctors, they went to a down-beat restaurant. One of the things that Pen had trouble understanding about his wealthier clients was their propensity for bad food. The workers who were obliged to take lunch somewhere cheap always complained about the quality of the food, while in the same restaurants the richer clients raved about it.

"Nothing like a bit of home cooking."

"It's all just come out of a can, Maurice."

"Yes, well. Glass of wine?"

Pen watched Renault eat. It always fascinated him to watch people when their guard was down. He had frequently noticed workers eating alone at lunch, worrying at their food with knife and fork, herding it around the plate, head over the meal, hurrying the food to their mouths, with unconscious feral glances around the room, as though someone might snatch it from them. He had decided long ago that most of us don't appreciate what we eat; it is just a means to an end. Renault was all business: he cut the precise amount of meat, chose an appropriate portion of vegetable, and conveyed the perfect forkful to his mouth without preamble. Today, the usual calculated assault did not for one minute interfere with his constant diatribe on the museum system and collectors in general, whom he considered a competitive, back-biting breed.

For the last couple of hours Pen had been clutching the duffel-bag tight to his shoulder. Now Renault mentioned it.

"That must be precious, Pen. You didn't even put it down while she stitched you up."

"Yeah, a friend lent me something to show you. I can't afford to lose it."

"Ah, the famous harpoon."

"No, I've got that in my pocket."

"What have you got, Pen? I can tell it's something important."

"Show you back at your place. Can we go? My leg is starting to stiffen up."

Back at Renault's kitchen table, Pen took the harpoon out of his pocket and handed it over. Renault's face lit up immediately. The piece was remarkably well made, impressively so when one thought that the artisan who made it had only stone tools to work with. The carefully smoothed material, whatever it was, shone a dull ivory-white in the poorly-lit room. The barbs down each side had a mechanical regularity about them. Each was decorated with fluting that Pen guessed was designed not only for decoration but for blood-letting. The thin cylindrical shaft was pointed at the tip, with two flared protuberances at the base for attaching it by a thong to the lance. The whole length was decorated with incised, parallel wavy lines.

"How much is your friend asking?" Renault asked inevitably,

stroking the thing with his thumb as if this ancient talisman was already his.

"He didn't mention a price. He wants me to tell him how much the piece in Paris is selling for, before he decides."

"Yes, but that one comes from a well-known collection."

"I told him that."

"Please tell him I am interested in negotiating with him. If you can convince him to sell, I will give you ten percent of the price. Now, what have you got in that sack?"

Pen felt a sudden reluctance to show the axe. He sensed it would cause problems. He didn't know exactly how, but he had a bad feeling about it.

"Well?" prompted Renault. Pen lowered the bag into his lap and lifted the wrapped package out onto the table.

Renault watched, intrigued. But when Pen held the axe out, the man's face flushed darkly with the violence of real passion.

For a moment Renault said nothing He searched Pen's eyes, looking for some clue as to how this treasure had found its way into his possession. He knew this would not be for sale. But he could try. He took it but placed it on the table in front of him as if holding it caused him pain.

"It makes the one in Paris pale into insignificance," he said finally.

"I wouldn't say that," consoled Pen. "Besides, even this will come on the market one day."

"I could be dead by then."

Shit, thought Pen, I had a feeling this wasn't such a good idea.

"Maurice, the Paris sale is this weekend. Let's see the stuff they have there. It all has a big advantage over these, it has provenance."

"Don't you think that when my stuff has been published it will all have provenance, no matter where it came from? I'm assembling all the clandestine collections and bringing them in from the cold. That's why some of the museum people are prepared to help me.

Don't worry, I'm not doing it because I need the money. The Renault collection will be here long after I'm gone."

"So you're looking for immortality, Maurice, and you want me to help you."

"I have quantity. I now need quality to bring it right up to national standard."

"I'll talk to him, Maurice, but I can't promise anything."

Pen limped to his truck at the back of the big house with Serge smirking from his tractor, the dog was nowhere to be seen. But Pen swore to get even, surprising himself by the hostility he felt toward not only the damn dog but also its owner.

Back home, he carefully locked the jade axe with the others in his little museum, feeling stiff and in need of solace.

Pen and Noël planned to go up to Paris by train from Brive, about an hour's drive away and with a direct line. He would leave the car at the station over the weekend: Sophie would need the truck for the market.

"I've tried phoning Noël's place for three days now, with no reply. Do you think he could be with Denise?" said Pen, holding in a breath and passing the joint to Sophie, his face showing mild concern.

"Do I? They haven't got out of bed since they left here last Friday." Did he detect envy in her eye?

"Well, I need to plan Paris. Do you think Denise can have Alice on Friday night?"

"She would love to, seeing as you are taking her Noël away." She passed the joint back.

"Her Noël — we're all one big happy family now, aren't we? It just needs me to have a scene with Denise, then we'll all be hunky-dory."

"Don't you dare do that, Pen. She's far too fragile."

"And I'm not fragile?"

"Be careful Pen — I bite harder than Renault's dog."

"I can believe that."

10

The early-morning train journey would have been uneventful, except that Pen had bought the tickets on the internet. When the ticket-collector arrived, he said the document Pen had printed out was only a receipt for payment, not the real ticket, and that he was fining him 150 euros for travelling without it. Pen and Noël cracked up laughing, but the ticket-collector didn't get the joke. When Pen said that he had neither cash nor chequebook on him, he had to sign a statement admitting his fault. He added a footnote stating that he had paid for their seats and that his credit card had been debited. This made them both crack up again, earning them a scowl from the now grumpy inspector and some chuckling from neighbouring passengers.

During the journey Pen told Noël about showing the axe to Renault. Noël understood Pen's desire to do so, but said he was content to hoard his stuff without feeling the need to be accepted into some wider community. In any case, at the moment he was more interested in talking about Denise's charms. How, he wondered could two sisters be so different? Pen looked at Noël as he gazed out of the window, stupid with infatuation

"Oof," he breathed with relief. He had been worried that Noël might be choosing the lesser of two evils, however he was evidently happy enough with the evil he had ended up with. Pen couldn't help wondering that he himself had had a very close shave.

After months and months of country living, Paris was fun. The metro was eye opening. Neither Pen nor Noël watched TV, so they laughed in a boyish way over unexpected fashions, and observed the girls with the eyes of connoisseurs; the weather was turning cold, so they were all well-covered but still contrived to look wonderfully alluring. Sitting finally at a tiny table squeezed onto the pavement outside a small bar, they watched the street over a cup of mediocre tea. Smoke, concrete and moving steel made for a lot of smelly noise, but there was a certain sophisticated elegance nonetheless. They watched a garbage truck pull up and two speedy North Africans perform an urban choreography with the bins in the mechanical fug.

Next to the bar was a row of metallic-grey, ultra-modern bicycles. Pen and Noël had not yet seen these rent-a-bike systems, and watched a moment while people turned up on foot, swiped their credit cards and took a bike, while others arrived on their cycles and poked the front wheels into the empty brackets. The machine recognising one of its own locked them in a welcome embrace.

Pen's phone rang. Renault was only a block away and making his way towards them. They were within sight of the curious-looking building that housed the Hotel Drouot auction rooms. Pen thought that even in 1980, when the place was entirely refurbished, it must have looked like an art-déco idea of the decline of future inspiration. He thought it resembled an imposing grey-red-black plastic Swiss cheese squashed between the more traditional galleries, sandwich-bars and offices — imposing, and out of place.

Renault was all smiles when he arrived, bringing his cologne and fine clothes into the rich mosaic that was turning out to be their day. Pen bore in mind that this was just a normal day for almost twenty percent of the country's population. One of Mick Jagger's lines from 'Some Girls' came into his mind: 'Life's just a cocktail party on the street', and realised he was humming it on his way to the toilets to refresh himself. When he got back, Noël went. He pulled the Drouot catalogue out of his bag under the table. Renault said they were due to rendez-vous at one-thirty with the expert in charge of the afternoon sale. Pen's eyes sparkled. If they were going to have a quick preview of the sale, he wanted to be on the ball. Spreading the catalogue out on the tiny table, they discussed merits and prices. He and Noël marked interesting lots. Renault had never met Noël, but his rustic-hippy appearance and their obvious differences in no way interfered with their appreciation of each other, which showed itself in the precise, restricted dialect of the flint-collector. They spoke the same language; they were family, distanced of course, but family all the same. It was nearly time for their visit. Maurice ordered three large cognacs. He insisted on paying for everything and left a generous tip.

They met Renault's dapper, clean-faced, energetic colleague out-side the auction rooms. He ushered them down a side-street which led to the back of the building. Here, it was all activity: vans being unloaded and dozens of men in blue jackets bustling about with trolleys loaded high with everything from Persian rugs and marble statuary to life-sized plastic Mickey Mouse cinema publicity and Marilyn Monroe prints — all of them fed into the stylish, cylindrical lifts to disappear into the heart of the building.

They took the back stairs up to the second floor. The large room that had been allotted to the sale was, thought Pen, pretty austere. The tacky feel was exacerbated by the worn, thin, grey wall-to-wall carpeting, which went up and over the low platform on which the auctioneer's dark wooden desks were arranged. Pen reckoned Renault would feel at home here. Personally he was disappointed, having hoped for a rather more grandiose setting for his first Paris auction. Against the far wall stood a row of display cases that had seen better days. Renault chatted with the organiser as Noël and Pen took their first look at flints with price-tags. Two blue-coats came in to unstack the beige plastic-and-chrome chairs and set them out in rows.

The sudden clatter in that large, unwelcoming space did nothing to quell their enthusiasm. Noël systematically went through the cases with a glossy printed catalogue from the pile by the door and started marking his personal code of desirability in ballpoint. Pen went straight to the jade axe, which had a small case to itself. Even in these drab surroundings, it was still a beacon. The colour was much like that of the one he had shown Renault, except the veining was darker, almost violet, the blade wide and flat, ground into a perfect arc. The only imperfections were on the cutting-edge, one split-pea-sized nick and two smaller ones, perhaps caused when a careless digger found the piece all those years ago. But there was no history for it marked in the catalogue, just 'circa 1900'. The 'white-ish bloom' was a light transparent milkiness that slightly dimmed the deep green in the body of the axe and ran right to the cutting-edge. It was conspicuously missing in the nicks, showing them as recently inflicted. The pointed butt looked as sharp as a raven's beak. The piece was sumptuous. Renault came over and looked at it, his body language proprietorial, his smile showing pleased surprise.

"She's a beauty," he murmured to Pen, "shame about the scars."

"The jade looks every bit as attractive as the imperial Chinese stuff I always think of when I read the word jade — and the damage is minimal, just scratches really."

"I'll buy it," said Renault, seduced. Pen was relieved. Now he could concentrate on the laurel leaf. Over the years he had seen several of these beautifully made blades in various museum collections. The most impressive had come from a deposit at Volgu, in the Loire valley. That blade had been found, with an unknown number of others, by late nineteenth-century canal diggers. At least fifteen of the surviving blades are known. The first that Pen had seen was in the British Museum, long and broad at its widest part, coming to a narrow point at the top end and a stubbier one at the base, just like a long, narrow leaf. It had been skilfully flaked from a large piece of perfect bluish brown flint and the regular flake scars textured the entire surface. But the most remarkable feature was how thin it was — twenty-eight centimetres long for a mere seven or eight millimetres thick. He had seen it long ago, but still remembered the effect it had had on him. It was the first time he had realised that the history books had it all wrong. The cavemen were not uncouth ignorant brutes at all. Some were sensitive artists, fine craftsmen, obviously from developed societies where such skills were valued. The Solutreans lived around twenty thousand years ago and produced some of the finest knapped-flint objects ever made. The enigma is that their bifacial technique, which had its origins in the Neanderthal hand-axe, disappeared from Europe with them. The next time the technique was exercised with similar skill was in the New World, several thousand years after the Solutreans had disappeared. They had lived during the coldest part of the last glacial period. Had the Solutreans somehow made it around the Atlantic ice into America?

Pen came out of his reverie when Renault said the sale was about to start. He went over to Noël, who was looking at the broken harpoon — a fine piece, darker than theirs and broken, by the look of the uniform patina, in antiquity.

"Bet it was broken in use," said Noël, who had been observing it for some time. "Looks like a frontal shock. See the way the fracture runs diagonally down the shaft? Shame, looks like it could have been as good as ours."

They skimmed over the rest of the stuff until they were politely guided to the door. Back out on the street there was a fair-sized crowd of people waiting for the doors to open. They took the opportunity for a quick last fag. When they were eventually let in the front door, Pen was surprised to see a continuation of the art-déco design in the cinema-like foyer, with oak counters and black-and-red Formica. To the left of the busy entrance-hall, they took an escalator to the second floor and waited with the crowd on the landing for the auction-room to open.

The effect of the stimulants was past its peak, but as they joined the throng of people around the display cases, they were still buzzing nicely. Noël engaged strangers in conversation as if they were old friends, talking about the exhibits, giving his opinion. Pen was amused by this new side of his old mate. They were the only two pairs of jeans in the room; everybody else were in city clothes. Apart from the three young secretaries, only two of the eighty or so people there were women. Everyone seemed respectful of Noël's views; a couple of older men in suits with dark overcoats and well-groomed grey hair asked where they were from. When Noël said Lascaux, they nodded and made appreciative noises as if that explained everything.

Suddenly everyone was taking their seats. Renault guided them off to one side so that he could see the whole room for tactical purposes. Pen was aware of the musty smell of old leather and books, with an undertone of vacuum-cleaner. The auctioneer was explaining, as if to a bunch of school-kids, that they had almost six hundred lots to get through in five hours and that no dithering would be tolerated. And with that they were off.

There was a definite charge in the air. Everyone was attentive but trying not to look it. Renault was leaning back in his chair, not looking at his catalogue but watching the room, surreptitiously checking out the competition. Pen didn't know where to look. A well-rehearsed relay of men brought the lots out from their places in the displays to hold them up before the buyers at the rate of about two a minute. Punters had little time to raise each others' bids. Pen tried to follow on his catalogue, noting the prices the lots fetched. A clerk flitted around collecting cheques from people who had bid successfully. The auctioneer was settling into a rhythm and exercised a dry humour.

"What? Nobody wants this piece? I don't want it on my hands. it would make a fine Christmas present, a fancy paper-weight. Come on, fifty euros is nothing!"

The bidding was brisk, but only rarely did anything sell above its upper estimate. Someone near the front with a shock of white hair was taking many of the cheaper lots. Renault whispered to

Pen that he was a dealer and no risk to him. When the first two
hundred or so lots had gone, the auctioneer announced a series of
eight Neolithic daggers. Pen had looked briefly at these long blades
with their well-defined handles: they were impressive, each with its
own character. A couple of the Danish ones had wide blades and
were marked 'Bronze age, imitating the form of metal daggers of the
period'. Most were made of distinctive materials, flints or cherts,
chalcedony or jaspers —all fairly common, hard, micro-crystalline
quartz silicates; but these particular ones had been chosen for their
interesting colours. The finer-quality stones had been highly prized
in antiquity, exchanged over great distances and often chosen for
prestigious work by the more skilful artisans. They were beyond Pen's
means. But Renault suddenly looked interested.

As the bidding hotted up, the auctioneer came alive, clearly having waited for this moment. One of the girls and a thin-faced clerk
were taking bids by telephone. Renault was observing everything
closely, sitting forward in his chair, his catalogue rolled up in one
fist. He seemed to have grown larger, as if his elegant jacket had been
inflated. His intent was apparent in the set of his shoulders. The first
two Danish daggers went in a flurry of furious bidding for three
thousand five hundred euros each, to one of the telephones. Renault
wasn't bidding yet: he only collected French items. A broad-bladed
greenish-grey dagger went for over four thousand euros to the same
telephone. Renault grunted but didn't look round at Pen when he
asked who it could be. The bidders in the room looked tense at not
being able to see their adversary. Each sale took only about a minute.
But to Pen the time seemed to slow considerably, and he tried to spot
who was bidding in the seats around them. But it was often subtle
and discreet, not at all obvious. A couple of lesser pieces went to a
man in the room whom Pen had noticed bidding for the other blades;
he looked relieved.

At last the first of the two French daggers came up. Renault gave
an imperceptible nod of his head and the auctioneer registered his

bid. The telephone upped him, the increments seeming arbitrary: three hundred for the first few bids, then down to two hundred. Someone else in the room dropped out. The price went over four thousand, and it was just Renault and the young secretary on her telephone tucked away behind one of the desks, bidding back and forth. There was a ten-second lull with the ball in Renault's court. The auctioneer called:

"Going once at four thousand six hundred!" Pen couldn't understand what was going on. It was a nice blade, but had nothing on some of the finer Danish ones that had gone for over a thousand euros less. "Four thousand seven hundred, to the gentleman on my right, going once, twice, three times, sold to the gentleman on my right for four thousand seven hundred euros! Now, ladies and gentlemen, I can see that you are getting into the swing of things. So, here we have a second French dagger, in perfect condition, twenty-seven centimetres long, in caramel-coloured chert from Grand Présigny in the Indre-et-Loire. And we start the bidding at two thousand euros."

Pen looked down at his catalogue. It was estimated at two to three thousand euros. Renault was used to getting what he wanted, and he would not be thwarted. It was quite exciting, but seemed somehow a bit vulgar, just a matter of who had the fattest wallet. After an intense bout of bidding, Renault claimed the second dagger for over five thousand.

It was almost a relief when a few lesser Neolithic pieces came under the hammer. Coming up was a carefully arranged collection of North African arrowheads on a board with a red cloth backing. Estimated at fifty to a hundred euros, there were at least eighty arrowheads; even if they weren't all fantastic, it wouldn't matter at that price. It was the next lot but one. Pen wanted to try for it. He started to sweat, he could feel his palms getting damp. He had never done this before, and was nervous. He had watched Renault but the organisers knew him. Pen didn't know how to get their attention.

The auctioneer raised his voice again.

"A lovely little collection of sub-Saharan arrowheads — who will give me fifty euros?" Pen made a subtle gesture but the auctioneer ignored him and said, "Fifty to the gentleman in the front row, who will give me eighty?" Pen nodded his head and tried to catch the eye of anyone on the front desk. He even started lifting up his catalogue to wave, but the auctioneer was already saying,

"No regrets? Sold for eighty euros to the man on my left. He tried to see who had got the lot for such a ridiculously low price. Furious with himself, he thought, 'Next time I'll fucking well stand up and shout!'

Noël looked at him.

"Not as easy as it looks, eh?" he muttered, raising his eyebrows in commiseration. Renault hadn't noticed Pen had tried to bid, his mind on the jade axe coming up soon.

Well, that's something, I suppose, Pen thought. Be thankful for small mercies. But he felt humiliated.

The Neolithic axes were about to begin. This was obviously going to be the high point of the auction, even though there were still some bifaces and the Upper Palaeolithic stuff to come. Pen thought the axes would fetch the highest prices. He looked around the room: some of the bidders were looking serious, almost irritated. Pen was curious about this, and Renault explained why:

"You can never tell if there is really anyone on the end of the telephone. It's common practice for unscrupulous auctioneers to take a bid off a light switch, an invisible bidder, or from the telephone, to push the price up. In some cases they will even have someone in the room to up the bidding."

"But why?" asked Pen, wondering what possible interest the auction house would have in getting a better price for one client at the cost of another.

"Many reasons," whispered Renault, "but mainly because they take twelve to fifteen percent from the seller and twenty to twenty-five percent from the buyer. But it can also be trying to push up the market value of the better-quality stuff. Prehistory is a relatively inexpensive field to collect in. The seller might have set his reserve price higher than the one stated in the catalogue, but the auctioneer starts lower to get the ball rolling, pushing the price forward himself to encourage more dynamic bidding." He would have gone on, but the next lots were being brought out.

"Ladies and gentlemen," called out the auctioneer: "It is my great pleasure to be able to propose to you today some of the finest examples of privately-owned Neolithic polished axes ever to have been offered for auction." He stopped for effect, while people whispered to each other and rustled their catalogues in anticipation.

Renault was reclining against the back of his seat, giving the air of someone relaxed and unconcerned. He didn't even bid for the first two axes that went for respectable prices; like the daggers. Then a particularly flat axe in a pale creamy flint was brought out to the front, so that no one could be in doubt about which piece was being bid for. It was well made, very symmetrical but not too big, about the same size as the jade one. The auctioneer, now beginning to look dishevelled from running his hands through his hair and his enthusiastic gesticulating, reminded everyone that this piece was considered to have been a symbol of status and power. It was too fragile, and too carefully made, to have ever been used as an axe. It came with authenticated documentation, and had been dug from a well-known burial mound in the late eighteen-hundreds.

The bidding was spirited from the start, jumping from four thousand in rapid five-hundred euro increments. The two phones were bidding, and gradually the people in the room dropped out, until it was just between them.

"Twelve thousand on my right, twelve thousand five hundred, thirteen thousand." The auctioneer was reacting to signals from the clerk and the secretary with the phones. He was twisting from side to side like a clockwork automaton, his arms swinging ahead of him, the hand holding the hammer beating out the rhythm in the stuffy air. Then to the surprise of everyone in the room Renault put in a bid.

"Sixteen thousand five hundred to Mister Renault," went the auctioneer, raising his voice like a sports journalist commenting a steeple-chase. The price carried on upward, but Renault dropped out after a few more bids, raising his hands palms outwards with a sigh.

"It's not worth nearly that much," he muttered to reassure himself. The axe went for twenty-five thousand five hundred euros. Pen was bewildered: Renault had told him that a good axe could perhaps raise five thousand — but this seemed excessive. Several people were looking put out. What would happen when the jade axe came up?

He didn't have to wait long to find out. The auctioneer was wiping his glistening face with his handkerchief as it was brought out. One of the porters was holding it above his head like some kind of trophy, while another stood a little behind him as if worried that it might slip from his colleague's fingers. They surveyed the room. The auctioneer took a breath or two, sipped some water from the glass on his bench, had a quick word with the acquaintance of Renault's next to him, then turned to face his audience.

"I will just explain, to those who may not realise, that it is the extreme rarity of these axes that makes them so valuable. The opportunity to bid for a piece like this may not arise again for many years. This next axe is even more unusual than the preceding one and even rarer. I had someone come up to me today and comment on the description in the catalogue. You can see the colour for yourselves, this jade has been famously referred to as spinach. But colour is to a certain extent subjective, so I allow you to make your own appraisals. We have referred to it as avocado in the catalogue from the colour of the flesh of the fruit, which I feel is pretty close to the colour of the jade."

"Ok, the guy is getting carried away here," thought Pen, looking over at Noël, who looked as if he could drop off to sleep. He was pretty whacked himself. It had been nearly three hours, and he needed a cigarette.

The axe started at six thousand and went up by round thousands. At one point Pen waved his hand in the air and heard:

"Sixteen thousand to the gentleman on my right, seventeen, eighteen by telephone, nineteen." Pen felt a surge of exhilaration — he had just bid sixteen thousand euros for a jade axe! The old guy with the white hair at the front was agitated and kept making noises. It sounded as though he was complaining, but no one took any notice. Renault had not even bid yet, and the price continued to climb. Then, as before, it was just the telephones.

"Thirty-five thousand." There was a small pause: the young girl on the phone could be seen to be talking to the client she was representing, then she raised her eyes to the bench and it was thirty-six, then thirty-seven.

"Thirty-seven once! thirty-seven twice!"

When Renault came in with his bid, the auctioneer looked a bit startled; the secretary signalled that her client had backed down. Now it was Renault and the other telephone.

Pen could feel the hair rise along his forearms. Even Renault could not totally hide his emotion; his face was set in determination. The sums were meaningless, abstract, like a form of poetry.

"Forty-eight thousand five hundred, forty-nine thousand." Renault would never let go.

"Going once! Going twice! Going three times! to Mister Renault for fifty thousand five hundred euros."

Pen nudged Noël and they both got up and left the room. They took the escalator, already rolling their cigarettes on the way down. Once outside they looked at each other.

"We've got four, they're all better than that one, and they aren't damaged at all," said Noël, exhaling a great lungful of smoke.

"Did you see Renault's face? He looked like a zombie."

"Don't worry about it. For him it was the financial equivalent of you paying for a couple of coffees."

"Yes, it wasn't the money. He's driven," agreed Pen.

"Well, you don't get to where he is in business by sitting around and waiting for it to happen."

"Yeah, well, he's welcome to it. He doesn't seem too happy with his lot. He could sit back and enjoy it all now that he has it."

"You know it doesn't work like that, Pen, everyone has to do something or life loses its meaning. This is just fun for him."

"Well he doesn't look like he's enjoying it very much."

"It's good to know that if we ever decided to sell, he would buy one or two of our axes, and now we know what they are worth the idea becomes suddenly quite appealing."

"Shit, it does, doesn't it?" They threw their finished cigarettes into the gutter and grinned at each other, sharing a moment of grace. Pen looked up to the narrow greying band of sky between the buildings. It looked like rain. He shrugged and said,

"Well, I'm going to try for the laurel leaf, but I'm not going to go crazy over it. Come on, let's get back in there."

The atmosphere in the room was subdued when they got back to their seats. Renault was at a desk up front talking to a secretary, cheque-book in hand. The bidding was a pale reflection of what it had been ten minutes before. There was no one on the telephones and the prices stayed well within their estimates. Renault came over and said he was leaving. He wished them good luck and was followed out of the room by quite a few pairs of eyes.

The broken harpoon didn't even sell: much to the auctioneer's apparent exasperation no one even bid for the starting price. When the laurel leaf came up there was a brief moment of activity, but Pen got it for one thousand four hundred euros. He did the calculation in his mind: plus twenty percent was one thousand six hundred and eighty. That was actually more than he had been prepared to spend, but he was thrilled. His collection was becoming quite something, even if he couldn't show the most impressive pieces to anyone. He wondered if he could do a deal with Renault to get some kind of provenance sorted out for them in exchange for his helping him buy a few nice things, the gold for example. It was a thought.

By six-thirty they were back out on the street looking for an inviting bar to start the evening in before their train. It was dusk already, and they were both tired out from the various excesses and emotions and sorely in need of a beer and a bite to eat. Pen had his new acquisition in his jacket pocket and ran his fingers over its contours contentedly, acutely aware that he was in possession of a twenty-thousand-year-old masterpiece,

"This'll do to get started," said Noël, turning into a green doorway, but a blousy blond woman tried to shoo him away saying that they were closing. "Just a beer, Madame," pleaded Noël.

"Do you smoke?" she asked him.

"Yes we do."

"Well come in and let me shut the damn door and we can have a fag. We've been at it for hours and can't even smoke in our own bloody bar with their stupid laws!" She sounded to Pen as though she smoked too much. Her loud gravely voice and dyed blond bouffant hair intimidated him, and he would have left, but Noël was insistent. The patron was a short woman with a prominent bosom straining against her white blouse. Her manner was brusque, but she turned out to be friendly enough, though it was a stark contrast to the sale rooms they had just left. Noël warmed to her immediately, and talked her into making them a couple of sandwiches. They relaxed into some comfortable green leatherette seating against a corner wall by the window. Pen was expecting to be overcharged because of his accent which she continually commented on. But he found he didn't mind much as the rain began, revealing another aspect of the city outside.

11

Later that evening they took the train back from the Gare d'Austerlitz, still buzzing from their brief immersion in the city they were leaving behind. Pen felt a twinge of melancholy for the wet streets: that cocktail party of hopes and wishes and darkly reflected lights that would go on relentlessly without them, heedless of their coming or going. Nostalgia for city life tugged at him, just once. Then he pushed his hand in his pocket and felt the hard little blade that nestled there, and smiled at Noël.

"Oof, I'll be glad to get home."

"Me too. If the rain's hammering down like this in the Dordogne, it will be just perfect for us snails."

The train was almost empty when it pulled into Brive at one twenty-six in the morning. The platforms were deserted, the contrast with Paris strangely reassuring to Pen. They were relieved to find that the car, which no longer locked very well, was still waiting obediently alone in the wet car park. An hour's drive and they would be home.

They could have stayed overnight in Paris. But today being Sunday, Pen wanted to spend some time with Alice and Sophie at home. It had been a bit like hard work lately, and with the school rhythm and Sophie usually out on Saturdays it didn't leave much time for family life.

He forced himself out of bed at ten o'clock and found Alice at the kitchen table wearing a pretty floral dress. She was observing a jam-jar of white butterflies that she must have collected the day before, probably at Denise's.

"Hi, sweetie," he said giving her a big kiss. "You will let those butterflies go later, won't you?"

She jumped off her chair and flung her arms around him as if she had not seen him for weeks.

"Papa, did you bring me any thing?"

"Alice, you mustn't expect something from me every time I come through the door." Alice looked crestfallen, but Pen slyly produced a little story-book in English that he had picked up at Austerlitz station and laughed with her at her delight.

"Maman says I can't let the butterflies go in her garden, she's still got cabbages they might eat." said Alice. "Will you come with me to the field, Papa, and we can do it together?"

"Get your coat and wellies on while I'm having a cup of tea, and I'll be with you." The familiarity of this little domestic routine was unexpectedly comforting. If only he had known how things were about to change, he would have appreciated that comfort a lot more.

They went through the workshop where Sophie was unloading her market stuff from the truck. He went to her and she smiled and gave him a welcome cuddle.

"We're going to let the butterflies out," said Alice, tramping out through the open doors to stand in the rain.

"How was Paris?" Sophie asked, looking with interest into his calm unshaven face.

"Good, very good. And your market?"

"It was the best one I've done since summer. A bit odd though."

"In what way?"

"A guy came in the morning and bought some big pots, the best wood turning I had, a lamp, and some other stuff. He spent sixteen hundred euros! Can you imagine it? I was over the moon. He said he had some friends visiting who wanted to take presents back to Paris. If I could be there in the afternoon he would bring them to my stall. I only do the morning this late in the year and the weather was *la merde*, but of course I stayed. Bugger never turned up. I stayed until six!"

"Sorry to hear that baby. That's filthy lucre for you. People assume you need it so bad you'll be prepared to do anything for it. Still, you sold well in the morning."

"It wasn't that," she snapped, "I always try to look after my clients, it's one of the reasons they seem to like me. I felt let down, I totally wasted my afternoon." She glowered at him and he could feel she would be ready to make him pay for her afternoon if he wasn't careful.

"Well, never mind. How is Denise?"

"I think she's in love, she is even more distracted than usual. Let's just hope that Noël is as well!"

"Oh, I don't think there can be much doubt about that. She's almost all he talked about on the train."

"Hmm," she mused, "And your sale?" she said, relenting: "Did Mister Renault buy it all?"

"No, but what he spent would have been enough to keep us going comfortably for a couple of years." Sophie raised her eyes and sucked in one cheek, creating some very fetching dimples. Pen couldn't resist giving her another hug, her yielding body pulled tight into his hard one until she squealed to be released.

"Are you coming, Papa?" came an impatient voice from a puddle somewhere outside.

Pen always thought of Bilbo Baggins when he sat down to his second breakfast. Alice sat with him for the novelty, her back to the stove drying her hair. She held out a glass for some orange juice but wasn't hungry. Pen poured, but for some reason the glass overflowed and soaked into Alice's dress. Her eyes went wide and she let out a howl of laughter. Pen felt his heart constrict and shook the almost empty pack by his ear. He went to get the sponge without a word. Aware of her dad's superstition and no doubt to make light of it, Alice was chattering away beside him:

"You know what mummy did when you were away, Papa?" she said, swinging her legs with an I-know-I-shouldn't-tell look on her face. "Well, she broke her bedside light."

"How did she do that?" said Pen, feigning exasperation.

"She knocked it on the floor and it broke in two."

"Well, I hope she unplugged it. I'd better take a look."

Pen was itching to get into his little flint room, but once he got in there he would no longer be available for the girls, and he was sure that Sophie was going to need some gardening done. The grass needed cutting, but it was too wet today. Pen hoped that next time would be one of the last times he would have to do it before winter set in; but there would still be wood to be cut and split for the stove. He resented having to continue cutting the grass when he started cutting wood, but there were always a few weeks in the year when the chores overlapped. There was Sophie's lamp to be looked at too. He heaved a sigh, deciding to put off the beckoning pleasures until the more urgent jobs were out of the way.

It was around four o'clock when they stopped for tea that Pen reckoned he could finally allow himself some time with his collection. He said to Sophie, "I've done almost everything for now, but your bedside lamp is good for the bin, I'm afraid."

"Don't be stupid, it still works."

"It's dangerous Sophie, cheaply-made foreign shit. It has a metal lamp socket but no earth wire — you could kill yourself with it. The socket's broken. If you knock the lampshade off it takes half the socket with it, leaving two lethal prongs sticking out. I'm going to chuck it in the bin."

"Don't you dare! Denise brought me that from Thailand. I've had it for years. It's never caused any problems, and anyway it works."

Pen knew better than to get into an argument over the bloody thing. He would have to find a safer socket and repair it. Trouble was it was so poorly made it would need almost rebuilding.

Oh well, he sighed to himself, it will have to wait.

Retrieving the key from its hiding-place, and consciously smacking his lips in anticipation, he realised that there was something almost sexual in the anticipation he felt before handling some of the beautiful objects waiting for him behind that door.

Before he got the lights on he could tell something was wrong, there was too much space, and the smell. The neon lights flickered on and he reeled with the shock of it, the floor tilted violently, and he lost his footing. The hounds of hell turned their baleful gaze on him, their great slavering snouts snapping at his entrails as his mind careered away from the bare fact staring him in the face. But try as he would to escape, he still found himself bent on his knees in the empty room. All the shelves had been thoroughly cleared; there wasn't so much as a flake of flint left. The magazines and books were scattered across the floor amid a drift of familiar, pungent, oily chainsaw chippings and dust. Pen didn't register what must have gone on there, he just knew that some enduringly passionate part of his life had gone for good. He struggled to keep his lunch down but couldn't stop the tears.

Sophie came looking for him and found him crouched on the floor, his face still wet but his sobbing over. Rocking on her knees, she held him in her arms then turned him to face the wall below the shelves where the thieves had cut their way in. They had removed a crude square of planking, stud-work and insulation and stuffed it roughly back into place after the room had been emptied. The initial shock was wearing off, but something was beginning to replace it. Pen felt he would be capable of murder. He could feel the violence rippling through the muscles of his chest and down his arms, his jaw was clenched painfully, and there was something wrong with his vision. He needed to stay calm. He needed to go and see everybody he knew who had anything to do with flint collecting. He had photographs of most of the better pieces. He needed to get them on the web with descriptions. They had to become so public that no one would be able to sell them or show them to anyone. Shaking, he all but pushed Sophie away, his eyes wild.

In his heart of hearts, he knew he had no chance of seeing his collection again. But he was not going to let it go without a fight. The first thing he wanted to do was phone Noël. He wasn't home, but Sophie said to try Denise and of course Noël was there, they would be right over. Next he phoned Renault, but Serge said he wasn't there. Pen said to tell Mr Renault that he would be over in the morning. Then he phoned Vincent, but there was no answer. So he phoned Rémy, who was silent on the end of the phone while Pen described how he had been burgled, and stayed silent a while longer.

"Nothing else was stolen?"

"No, the door was still locked. They only wanted the collection."

"I'm sorry to tell you this, Pen, but it represented a lot of money, and we all know that we're envious of each others' flints. And you had a lot. You've made someone jealous."

"Yes, but who do we know that would go to those lengths to steal my stuff? Can you think of anyone?"

"It wouldn't have been very difficult, Pen. Everyone knows everyone else's business in the countryside. Many of us knew you were going to Paris this weekend."

"But they had to know that Sophie would be at market, that there would be no one at home looking after Alice. And the noise, there are neighbours, not very close, but it was a risk to run a chainsaw at the house."

"In this season everyone's cutting wood, no one would think anything of it."

"Yeah, but you would have to be a real mean bastard or a professional criminal to pull something like this. How would they sell it? They must guess that I have photos and that I know loads of people who know other collectors who will be worried as hell when they find out, if only for their own collections."

"Yes, they could've been professionals with a buyer lined up, or put up to it by someone who knew your collection and wanted it."

"Shit, I don't get it. Anyone with the kind of money to buy all that would want to be able to show it off."

"I'm very sorry about this, Pen, it's a bad business. I'll make sure everyone I know hears about it and keeps their eyes and ears open. You never know." Pen knew better than to underestimate Rémy, but doubted that he could help much. What he really needed was influence in the wider antiquities markets. And that meant Renault. He would go to see him tomorrow morning.

Noël and Denise turned up looking shocked, wide eyed, like witnesses to a grisly car-crash. Pen had to swallow down the rising emotion that was choking him when he saw Noël.

"It's all gone, the jade, the gold, everything."

"Not everything," said Noël quietly, "I still have one jade axe, some blades, the gold lozenge and the boar tusks."

"Shit, I had completely forgotten about that, but they are yours."

"Don't be a wimp, Pen. If not for you, no one would've found them, they're ours."

"They got the harpoon."

"I'll miss your bifaces more. What can we do?"

Pen went through the conversation he'd had with Rémy.

"I need to see Renault," he said morosely. "And Vincent."

Pen felt sick again. Only a few days ago he had been wondering what was the point of hoarding a pile of old rocks. He knew now, with sudden clarity, that collecting had been more than just a rich experience: it had fed his soul. It had got him studying again, given him regular workouts traipsing through muddy fields, had honed his instincts and stretched his senses. It had taught him to understand certain aspects of the area better than most locals. It had got him out and about, meeting interesting people and visiting remarkable sites, not to mention the finest museums in Europe. It had earned him respect in some circles, notoriety in others; it had even got him work. It had, in a word, become an essential part of his life.

He knew he was still in shock. The most frustrating thing was that there was nothing to be done for the time being. He needed to occupy his mind. He couldn't go to the police. To them, though more obscure, his collecting would fall somewhere between illicit hooch-stilling and poaching. He opened the door to their little drinks cupboard and brought out a few half-empty bottles — whisky, gin and a reasonable cognac. With a hopeless shrug he squared up to his friends and forced a tight smile.

"There are also a few beers and several bottles of wine, if anyone cares to join me in a wake?"

The others were less than enthusiastic. Sophie took one glass of white wine and Denise and Noël found an excuse to leave quickly. Pen sat up trying to anaesthetise himself enough to get to sleep.

The morning rain seemed to be mocking him, and did nothing to lighten his mood or alleviate his thick head. Alice, her well-tuned little radar sensing the tension, quietly avoided him. Eyes turned to her porridge, she allowed Sophie — who was running late — to rush her through breakfast. Pen was too preoccupied to notice them leave for school. It only added to his anxiety that the girls were caught up in the inevitable repercussions. He felt, acutely, Sophie's implied recriminations in her obvious withdrawal. That was fine; he didn't want sympathy. But he could tell she thought he had brought this on himself. He sighed. He couldn't blame her, it was as if his mistress had just walked out on him: not her problem.

He had no appetite, but took tea with a couple of aspirin and a handful of blue-green spiruline tablets — just seaweed, but they had helped him out in the past so he hoped they might help now. Placebo or panacea, he didn't know; but he needed something. Unusually for him, he couldn't face a cigarette.

He was counting on Renault to help somehow. The radio came on automatically as he turned the truck's ignition key, but he couldn't listen to more lies about the interminable casualties of the current international crusade.

The aspirin hadn't had time to kick in yet. He jabbed at the switch in irritation and turned it off.

War, famine, crime, injustice, catastrophe — suffering seemed to be the norm for most of us. Shit, what a world!

His thoughts were bleak. He was dangerously distracted, he hadn't even bothered shaving, something he always did before visiting Renault. He was lucid enough to reckon that he'd do well to watch the road, but stretches of it went by with him hardly noticing.

He surprised himself by finding that he felt annoyance at Serge for not taking better care of Renault's place. What was the point of having brand-new tractors and lawnmowers to ride on and bloody strimmers and chainsaws if you never used the bloody things? In the rain, the place looked bedraggled. Pen drove around a bit blasting his horn, but saw no one. The Saab was parked around the back by the tractor, but the white van was gone. He drove close in to the cellar door and was about to climb down from the truck when he heard the dog. The animal appeared out of nowhere, howling, its yellow eyes daring Pen to come out and fight. After several turns around the truck it began to growl. Pen leaned on the horn again and the dog started barking fit to rip out its vocal cords. Pen lowered his window and did a bit of howling of his own, to zero effect. He tried the phone on the off-chance, with little hope that it would be answered. From where he was he could hear it bleating, through the din of the dog and the rain.

Not a good start to his day. Raising the window again, he phoned

Vincent. To Pen's relief he was there, and suggested he come round right away. Running as he was on automatic, his mind beating itself on the bars of his impotence, he hardly registered the half-hour drive.

Vincent's ostentatious place was immaculate. Pen always thought Freud would have had a field-day here. The large tidy house and its outbuildings didn't quite sprawl. The house was neatly linked to its annexes by tasteful walkways adorned with climbing roses and man-icured hedging. The gardens were trimmed and tamed, planted with an obsessive regularity. Pen felt more comfortable with Renault's air of opulent neglect.

The barking of another large dog, this time from inside the house, made Pen swear in despair. Vincent came out through the French windows onto the paved terrace and beckoned to him, and a large well groomed handsome collie came to check Pen over. Vincent called him to heel and obediently the dog gave one last sniff and let him be. Pen reflected that it was harder to rob people who lived in defendable stone houses protected by savage animals. The wealthy people he knew were not stupid, gullible idiots like him.

Over strong coffee in the comfort of Vincent's farmhouse chic, Pen filled him in. Like Rémy, Vincent listened in silence, his face showing deep concern which Pen didn't notice, too absorbed by his own distress. He swung between desperate self-pity and impotent vengeful violence, begging Vincent to get on the phone and compel everyone he knew to block any sale of his collection.

"Of course I'll do what I can, Pen, but I don't know what good it will do now — bit like shutting the stable door and all that."

"What are you talking about, Vincent? Do you think your col-lection is any less vulnerable than mine? It could be you tomorrow! They're still out there..."

"Yes, you were unlucky. But someone knew that your stuff would be unattended. This was planned, by all accounts."

"Your stuff is unattended every time you leave the house, Vincent.

Everyone knows you have no wife and no bodyguard to keep an eye on the place."

"No. But there's always Custer. He would never let anyone in."

Pen couldn't believe his ears: Vincent seemed so matter-of-fact.

"Look, I can't get hold of Maurice Renault. Do you know where he is?"

"I understand he's back from Paris, but other than that... He must be around."

The fact that Vincent had a couple of polished axes casually sitting on his kitchen table did nothing to help Pen's mood. Everything seemed so ordered here. A burglary would shake up this tidy little world just as much as it had his, and leave the fastidious Vincent a little less smug. He pushed up from the table and excused himself. Vincent gave a conciliatory look.

"I won't say don't worry, Pen, but we'll all make sure that everyone knows. I doubt they'll be able to sell the stuff easily." Back in the hallway Pen spotted an umbrella stand and asked if he might borrow one of the heavier, less ornate canes. Vincent looked surprised, but gave a nod of consent.

Driving away, Pen couldn't help noticing how lush everything looked. The sun had managed to push through the clouds, and the gardens, all wet with rain, sparkled in its yellow light. The coffee lay as heavily on his stomach as a lump of cold iron. Smoking his first cigarette of the day, he headed back to Renault's.

This time he drove up close to the back of the house and saw that the white van was back. He didn't bother with the horn but just jumped down from his cab wielding the cane. He climbed the steps to the kitchen-door and tried the handle, but it was locked. He battered at it with the head of the cane but there was no reply, not even the barking of the dog. But the dog was sly. If it had seen him get out of the truck, it would be likely to sneak up on him silently. He looked round, wrapped in anger, hoping that the bastard dog would have a go at him now that he was armed. It would give him an excuse to beat the living shit out of it, and soothe some of his frustration into the bargain.

Nothing. There seemed to be no one around. He was almost disappointed not to be confronting Sergio's dog. He came down the steps two at a time and backed towards the door to the cellars, expecting a surprise attack at any moment. The doors were locked. This did not surprise him as they opened from the inside, and were closed with heavy bolts, unlikely to be open if the house was locked up. Emboldened, he made his way out of the big open barn and regretted not having brought his boots. It was perfect flinting weather, and under normal circumstances he wouldn't leave the house without them; but today his mind was elsewhere. Outside the big barn roof, the tractor had churned the ground to muddy ruts. It had stopped raining, but he had no intention of wandering around looking for anyone in the mud. He was already beginning to feel exposed and headed back to the truck, his frustration growing. The vehicles all seemed to be there — but where were the people? They couldn't be far. The Saab hadn't moved since earlier. He was going to take a look at the little Citroen van when something caught his eye. Bending down he retrieved a muddied piece of cardboard. Turning it over, he recognised the blue fox.

12

In the rush of outrage that followed, Pen felt hope blossom. His trembling hands held the lid of his little box of arrow-heads. He had written things in pencil on the back of it, and there could be no mistake. He went to the Citroen and tried the doors, but it was locked. He looked in through the windows; there were only a few tools and an orange-and-white Stihl chainsaw, sitting with its jerrican of fuel on the floor behind the front seats. The space would be big enough. Thoughts were racing through his head, mostly how to get his flints back. But lurking in his mind were the first dark notions of revenge.

The surge of hope brought a ray of clarity. If he was to have any hope at all, reason dictated that he proceed carefully. His first impulse was to drive to Rémy's place and talk him into giving him a gun. He knew Rémy would be hard to convince, but he felt he needed some bargaining power. That would have to wait, though. First, he had to get his stolen collection published on the net. He needed to send it to everyone likely to see any of it at Renault's or liable to buy any pieces unknowingly or, maybe more important, knowingly. They all had to know that Pen had photos and descriptions of all his best stuff, even the hoard of grave goods, and was sending them out to everyone. Vincent had said that he would help, and there were several addresses in the auction-house gazette.

Pen drove dangerously down the wet winding lanes, heading home. He needed to contact Medea, the girl who had made up the website for him. If she didn't answer her phone, she always answered emails promptly. He would have to endure a little more close proximity with her.

He slammed into the gravel space in front of the workshop and jumped down from the cab, leaving the door hanging open as he barged into the cheerless and unfamiliar space his studio had become in the course of a day. He went through to the house and found it empty and uninviting. The stove was out, and the cold and damp seemed to rebuke him for his negligence. He told himself to calm down for the tenth time since finding the lid of his arrow-head collection.

Get the fire going first, he told himself. When the girls get back, he didn't want to scare them away. He carried an armful of logs in from outside, plumped down onto his knees in front of the stove and set to lighting it. He felt as though his stomach was beginning to feed on itself. Since the break-in he had been surviving on stimulants — alcohol, coffee and cigarettes.

Food, he thought, primal instincts managing to heave the aching blow briefly to one side. He made a quick but copious cooked breakfast, even though it was nearly time for Alice to come home from school. Then he went into the bathroom and looked at himself in the mirror. He hadn't shaved since the morning of the auction. He looked decidedly bleak: his eyes were puffy, his jaw set and aching from grinding his teeth. He decided to clean himself up a bit before they got back. In the bedroom he found the elements of Sophie's lamp on her little table by the bed. He sat for a moment and fitted them back together, the simple task steadying him.

Now the house was warmer, he was feeling a little more like himself, thinking of what to say to Medea, when he heard a car pull up behind his truck. He ran a hand over his cheeks checking to see if it was smooth enough to impress Alice. Smaller, she had grown up on a regular diet of "chin-pie", his stubbly cheeks terrorising her to giggling delight. These days she tended to refuse his kisses when he was too lazy to shave. But it was Noël who strolled into the workshop, smiling uncertainly. His friendly face and the caring look in his eye shook Pen out of his torment, and he realised that the first shock of the theft was wearing off. He was actually thinking of other things.

Over cigarettes outside in the damp garden, watching the heavy clouds rolling in over the dark woodland, Pen gave Noël a blow-by-blow account of his morning. Noël nodded at Vincent's apparent indifference, but if 'aghast' was a word that Pen would ever use, he would have said that Noël was aghast when he recounted finding the lid of his box of arrowheads at Renault's and seeing the chainsaw in the back of Sergio's van.

Pen gave Noël the outlines of a plan that was forming in his mind, a desperate one. But Pen was a desperate man; and it was the only plan he had for the moment. Noël looked worried but said he would help if he could. But he warned against taking risks that might only make things worse. Then he told Pen that Sophie had been at Denise's and was showing some pretty mixed emotions about the break-in. She was threatening to stay over at her sister's for a while until Pen had got over the worst of it, because she had found him unbearable since it had happened.

Noël looked a bit sheepish while he gave Pen this news. He said that hopefully it wouldn't come to that, and she would be back with Alice any minute. Then he brightened and said:

"I've brought you something." They walked over to the parked vehicles. Noël opened the passenger door of his car and lifted out a small fruit crate covered with a tea-cloth.

"Noël," said Pen, "is that what I think it is?"

"I would guess it is."

"Come on then, bring it inside and let's have a look."

"Sure you can handle this?"

"Noël," said Pen, "I've lost my soul, not my mind."

Noël nodded at this. They went back inside and unpacked the box onto the kitchen table.

"Neolithic, New Stone Age, why do you think they make that distinction? It's not only the stones that make the big difference between the Upper Palaeolithic and the Neolithic societies, it's behaviour. It's the fact that the Palaeos were hunter-gatherers and the Neos were herders and planters — still the stone age, but new ways of living."

"I suppose that when the polished axes started being found, I mean nowadays," said Pen, "we didn't know how the people who made them lived. Until recently, farmers who found the stones on their land thought they were produced by lightning strikes. And because they believed that lightning never strikes twice in the same place, they buried them under their doorsteps to protect their houses."

"You are right about that," said Noël, "an ex of mine found one under the doorstep of her tiny terraced house in town while she was doing some renovation work, a good one too! I saw it after she had sold it to Vincent: the price it fetched paid for her new French windows."

"Shame you weren't on good enough terms to buy it yourself after you split up." Pen had of course heard this story before. "But you can't have your cake and eat it, I guess." He ran a hand over his face and smiled.

Noël pointed a finger at Pen:

"Hey! you just smiled. I must tell Sophie you're on the mend."

"Thanks Noël. But if she wasn't here tonight it would probably not be a bad thing."

Noël was unfolding the wrappings of the jade axe. It was such a staggering piece of workmanship that their conversation ceased. Once it was unveiled, he handed it to Pen, who took it as if it were a new-born baby. But as he ran his fingers over its contours he found himself caressing it with another kind of wonder, like a new lover, his hands drawing sustenance from the contact. The perfect symmetry, the maturity and balance of its form were so harmonious, and the polish so flawless, that it was hard to believe it was made more than five thousand years ago. There was a thin crust of calcite build-up on one side where it had been in contact with the cave floor; but that didn't stop the evening sun, slanting down through a gap in the cloud cover, from illuminating the piece as if it glowed from within.

"Magic," was all Pen said. But he was thinking, that bastard Renault has taken the rest and he's going to have to pay for it, dearly.

By the time they had finished going through the stuff from the cave, the girls still weren't back.

"Take this lot home, Noël," said Pen. "I'm going to get in touch with Medea, and then I'll come round to your place."

"I brought these here for you, Pen. They're yours: You found the cave."

"No, you found it."

"It would have been my grave if it hadn't been for you."

"Take it home. I'll see you later. Perhaps we might get the rest back after all, who knows?"

Noël left looking more worried than when he arrived. Pen headed upstairs to his computer more determined than ever, a steadying calm having settled on him.

Medea got back to him almost at once. Pen had thought to use his website, stripping out all the images and replacing them with those of his collection. Medea said that she could put an email together with an attachment, a few photos, and a link to two hundred other images and brief descriptions. She could put it on line, which would be quicker and more efficient.

Pen wanted them to get started right away by email. Medea thought it essential to get together to do it.

Pen tracked down all the photos he had stored on his hard disks, plus those on his new camera. He compressed them as much as he knew how and sent them off to her. He made sure he had a copy of everything on a memory stick too, then set off for town.

Medea lived in a small modern apartment block in Périgueux, the capital of the Dordogne. Pen had always considered it a rather self-important, bourgeois country town. It was quite pretty in places, especially the old town and the impressive Byzantine-style Saint Front cathedral. It also housed the best museum he knew for prehistory. But after the many other cities he had spent time in, this one seemed rather flat, though it evidently considdered itself a cultural hub. He felt for the small student community. However it did have good internet connections and plenty of people who like him knew next to nothing about computers — the two main requisites of Medea's trade. Her apartment was on the sixth floor, and the lift was clean and quiet, although disquietingly full of mirrors. Pen knew it well, but he couldn't escape the feeling of being observed as he rode up from the street.

Medea was devastated by what had happened to Pen and wanted to console him; her hair had red streaks this time, he noted. But he was on a mission and in a hurry, and she complained that he was no fun at all. But she worked fast. In less than an hour he could leave her to finish the on-line catalogue. Anyone who received it could look at the images on the link and forward it to anyone they wanted. The introductory email told the story of the robbery and asked recipients to forward it to anyone interested or able to help. She gave him a sad hug on her landing and told him not to worry: in an hour or so it would be going out to the dozen or more addresses he had given her. Head bowed, he smiled thinly and looked at her once more. Going through his stuff on the computer had subdued him— but there was a hard glint in his eyes. He said that however it worked out, he was indebted to her, relieved to have finally got it out on the web. He felt insincere when he promised to come back and see her soon, though he had to admit she looked appealing.

"Yeah Pen, how about a meal together next time? That wouldn't be too threatening, would it? We could even go Dutch."

"No, not threatening at all, Medea. I just seem to have a lot on my plate at the moment."

"Well, throw it in the bin, then. You don't have to eat it all if you're not hungry."

"I wish it was that easy."

"I hope you find what you're looking for," she said cryptically as he stepped through the doors into the myriad waiting arms of himself and took the lift down.

The perplexed young woman watched the doors closing and stood on the landing for a moment watching her reflection in the brushed steel. He certainly was a strange one, this English client. Pen was almost old enough to be her dad, just at the age when men start to get interesting, and he sure looked good in a neglected, soulful sort of way. He didn't seem to give a damn about fashion and looked like he didn't brush his hair very often. He was clean though, at least he didn't smell bad: in fact he often smelled good enough to eat, and after two hours sitting together in front of the screen developing his site she had worked up a fair appetite. But he was already spoken for and, evidently in love. But he didn't seem very happy about it. If Medea was to be truthful he looked downright miserable. That was the trouble with love: after the first five minutes, though it gave the illusion of security, it was just a source of stress. It was all constant negotiation and unreasonable concessions that led inevitably to dissatisfaction, insecurity and boredom. She certainly hadn't met the right guy yet and Pen, cute though he was, was not going to be the one. However, though she didn't look like much, she was a red-blooded French girl and believed in charity, and he certainly looked like he needed a little saving. She decided not to give up on him yet despite his distance. Given time and perseverance she was sure she could make him feel a lot better about himself. The trick was in not letting him get too serious if ever anything did happen. First though he needed to get the bastard who rolled him over out of his system.

Medea had worked hard at university and taken to the computer like a pig to mud. She was part of the first generation to grow up with the new technology, and it had opened its secrets to her in a way that most oldies couldn't hope to follow. Afterwards she had tried working in some of the corporations that dangled glittering salaries before those with the best degrees. She found she couldn't hack it. University had been exciting, promising unending opportunity. Office routine just offered you more of the same, day in day out, and wanted you to show your constant gratitude for the privilege. She had been lucky moving back to the Dordogne, where she had managed to build up a clientele of mostly older people who just couldn't seem to get their heads around their often state-of-the-art computers. She felt it was a little like taking sweets from kids but hey! work was work and they always seemed so relieved when she had sorted them out. Medea had got used to it, but it was often pretty boring stuff. Still, she was her own boss, no dress code, no coffee machine chit-chat. Pen was different though, less formal than most, more laid-back. And from the photos on his site it looked like the way he made his money was more interesting than what she was doing. But there was something else about the guy, something she guessed he might not even know himself. He gave off the sense of there being someone else inside him, just beneath the surface, waiting to emerge if provoked, another person altogether. She wondered if he could be dangerous. He looked like a big softie but perhaps was really a caged animal. Rather than frightening her, it was this aspect of Pen that drew Medea to him.

So, Pen thought back at the wheel, one step at a time. He breathed in deeply trying to compose himself. Medea was a pretty little thing. Since Sophie's revelations of her infidelity and her increasing lack of interest in him he had to admit he was beginning to see her in another light, but right now wasn't the time. It would take the best part of an hour to get home; he had time to work out what he was going to do about this. But rather than concentrating, his mind went back to his last conversation with Noël. He hadn't been a stone picker for the last fifteen years for nothing. Who were the makers of those axes? He was occupied with these thoughts until he pulled his van off the busy *route nationale,* oblivious of the charmless grey village he passed through, on automatic, as he headed for home.

It was almost eight by the time he got home. There were two messages on the answer-phone. One from Sophie to say they would be staying over at Denise's tonight but would be back tomorrow. Pen felt irrational frustration rise nauseatingly, but the next message quashed it instantly: from Renault, to say how shocked he was to hear about the robbery and that he would be doing everything in his power to help. Bastard! thought Pen, of course you're above suspicion, Renault, you and your fucking tame orangutang! He was seething as he rooted around in the small annex that he had tacked onto the workshop to store all the stuff he didn't want piling up inside. He found the summer things he had recently put away: the inflatable paddling-pool in its big bin-liner. Down beside it was a small filter unit and a cardboard box with pool toys, a skimmer net, and various water-pistols. He chose a small hand-gun model, checked that it was all made of plastic and had no rubber seals, and took it back into the studio. Apart from being bright yellow, it looked just like the real thing. He left it on his work-table and went through into the house.

Earlier he had toyed with the idea of asking Rémy to lend him the ugly-looking rifle he had seen at his place, or the cattle prod. Rémy would probably have refused, but he realised that he wanted to involve as few people as possible in what he had planned. He took his new dark grey overalls, the woollen hat, his head-lamp and the duffel-bag out of the cupboard behind the back-door, where they had hung since this all began. He put everything into the bag, then checked the batteries on his new camera and put that in too.

"No sandwiches, no water," he said aloud.

Back in the workshop he selected the small crowbar from a shelf of masonry tools. In a random display of curios including a few odd pieces of old porcelain, sundry surgical instruments and glass objects of indeterminate nature, he found the small glass funnel he had once brought from England. It had been part of one of his student sculptures. He had always thought it might come in useful, but had he known what use he was going to put it to he might have decided to leave it behind. Well, it was too late now. Many of the local people he knew had guns in their houses. He supposed in England most farmers would have shot guns for vermin and rabbits or pigeons but here it was more widespread the gun laws were far more relaxed and rifles and revolvers were common place, town dwellers often had guns in their homes. Renaults' man Serge was unquestionably used to arms. Pen needed to be able to defend himself if it came to a confrontation, if things went to plan he intended to avoid that.

From the stained old fridge that he used as a chemicals cupboard, now decorated with a rudimentary red skull-and-crossbones, he took a plastic bottle of concentrated hydrochloric acid. And from a box on top he took a face-mask and pulled the two elastic straps over his head. Using the funnel, he filled Alice's water-pistol to the brim, turning his head instinctively as the acrid fumes licked upwards from the bottle. He checked the bung for leaks and then took it out to the garden. He removed the mask and aimed at a pile of old bricks. A thin stream of the heavy yellowish liquid shot six straight meters out from the muzzle. It smelled vile and made the old mortar on the bricks bubble and fume alarmingly. He checked the gun over once again for leaks, then went back into the workshop and put the lethal thing in a thick plastic bag — better safe than sorry. He dreaded having to use horrid weapon but if someone tried to shoot him he wouldn't hesitate. An armed aggressor dealing with a face full of acid aught to give him some breathing space. He was now as ready as he would ever be. He called Noël and said:

"All set?"

"I'm ready."

"Be with you in fifteen minutes."

He took the extra precaution of bringing some close-fitting work gloves, piled the bag and an extra pair of shoes into his truck, and set off for Noël's.

13

Noël was already outside when Pen arrived, a back-pack slung over one leather-clad shoulder, he was tugging open the heavy wooden doors of his garage. Once he had them wide enough he went in and flicked on the single suspended light bulb to reveal a mud-spattered old Yamaha 350 off-roader, with business-like chunky tyres.

"Hi," he said with a brief handshake. "Not really designed for two, but I've bolted some foot pegs onto the frame for you. You'll have to hold on tight though. Runs well, I took her out this afternoon. Bit noisy, but she'll do."

Pen asked him, "You still okay about this?"

"I don't have to do anything, do I? I'm just the driver. I don't suppose I can talk you out of it though?" Noël frowned, and added: "Let's go before it gets too late."

Pen put his bag down and drew the overalls and gloves out of it.

"Remember what I said, Noël, the girls mustn't know about this." Noël nodded with his eyes.

"Okay. Let me get this lot on first, then."

Noël produced a couple of ugly fluorescent helmets like the heads of giant insects with pointed snouts.

"Where the hell d'you get these?"

"I haven't used the bike for ages. My old helmet is a liability now. I had to borrow these from my nephew. They're all the rage with the kids, take years off you."

They chuckled nervously, a weak attempt to dispel the apprehension that had been building all day. Noël's expression was hidden inside his green and black plastic helmet, and Pen was glad they couldn't really talk any more. He was trembling slightly with the beginnings of an unfamiliar fear.

As he put on his helmet, he had the curious feeling he was back in a childhood Arthurian legend, racing off to save Guinevere, girding himself for battle. He really ought to have a sword instead of the duffel-bag with its deadly contents. Noël wheeled the bike out and kicked it over. It clattered into life at once, creating a bit too much of a racket for Pen's liking but there was nothing to be done about that now. There was no moon and the old-style yellow head-lamp seemed to shed too little light for the sinuous lanes they had to travel. He settled behind Noël, the bike's vibrations conveniently covering his trepidation. As soon as his feet found the foot rests the motor cranked up in pitch, and they accelerated away with no more warning than a brief glance from Noël over his right shoulder.

Pen was an artist. To be truthful he knew he was a failed one. That did not mean his work was less pertinent or well-done than that of other, more successful, artists. But you had to play the game, to take risks, to take your place in the arena. He hadn't done that, partly because he was still a victim of the events of his childhood but also because he had never really felt the need. He felt that all his life he had been waiting for some moment of glory that had been eluding him. During that ride, on that hurtling machine, he felt the purpose of his intent vibrating up through his loins. Was this it then, not creation but destruction, vengeance? Noël was ripping through the dark, close woodland, the motor growling like the voice of some sentient wild thing. The apprehension burned away, vaporising like morning dew under a desert sun — he had never felt so alive. Nothing he had done up to now had prepared him for what he intended to do. Renault had taken what was his and he was taking it back, whatever he had to do to get it.

The helmet had shut him into an interior world. The wind of their passage tearing at his clothing added to his sense of imminent combat. No longer a knight, more of an assassin, he felt himself growing into the task. He recognised the turning that would take them to the house and tapped Noël on his upper arm to slow him down. Noël stopped completely and turned back to Pen, talking over the noise of the motor.

"We can go a bit further?"

"Okay, but go slow, don't want them to hear us."

They idled down the lane until they could make out the drive. Noël pulled into the trees.

"Don't take any more risks than necessary, Pen."

"Don't worry. Wait for me three-quarters of an hour, no more, Noël, then get out of here."

They grasped hands, then Pen melted into the trees and was gone.

He had left his helmet with Noël and felt exposed without it, so he stopped for a second and took the woollen hat out of his bag, searching around his hand came across the little head-lamp. With the hat tugged tightly down over his ears and the lamp ready, he felt better and quickly covered the distance to the house, keeping to the left-hand edge of the drive. Most of it ran along an open plantation of larches that he could use for cover if he heard anything coming towards him.

He could see the lights of the house, which was a good sign: it meant they were not only there but still up. Pen stopped once more and took the bag off his shoulder. He found the pistol easily enough by feel and hefted it, the volume of acid giving it a reassuring weight.

He could smell the noxious stuff through the plastic bag. He stripped the bag away and put the rubbish in the duffel-bag. The gun smelled worse but it looked dry. All the same he was glad of his gloves as he handled it, making sure not to pump the trigger.

As he crept towards the front of the house he heard a faint noise; it sounded like the back-door opening. Pen made a little noise of his own, shaking some of the shrubbery along the drive to the parking area round the back. He did it again, clearing his throat at the same time.

And then he saw what he had been dreading. The shadows rippled, then one of them detached itself from the darkness and raced silently towards him up the short length of drive that led from the back of the house.

Pen didn't have time to feel afraid. He waved his weapon in the direction of the sound of rushing feet but was too slow, the dog was on him in an instant growling and snapping viciously it held back for half a second apparently recognising his adversary then lunged for him. Pen fired several times into the dark pumping the trigger wildly, trying to find the brute's head. The animal hit him hard but the attack checked as suddenly as it had begun and he heard a yelp, followed by some high-pitched whining. He couldn't believe his luck. He had expected more of a fight. He approached the stricken animal and risked a brief beam of light from the head-lamp. The dog was convulsing at the side of the road, trying desperately to breathe and pawing frantically at its muzzle. It was making too much noise, the convulsions grew worse, then the only noise was a gasping sound and the scratching of its nails on the ground. Another quick beam from the lamp illuminated pink froth drooling from the beast's mouth onto the rutted drive and a pale vapour rising from dark desperately blinking eyes. He pushed down the feelings of revulsion that threatened to overwhelm him, He must have shot the corrosive liquid straight down the animals' throat. He hoped it would not agonise for long but there was no time for remorse. If the acid gun was that lethal he decided not to use it on the men, and packed it away quickly. He sped around to where he could get a view of the back of the house. The door was open, spilling light down the steps, but by no means illuminating the whole barn area. The vehicles were in shadow over to the right. Making sure that no one was outside, Pen skirted the building, staying out of the light until he reached the tractors.

Now he was at the buildings Pen searched for courage. After his father's death, his mother, struggled on to bring him up as best she could, but she had always been fragile. The burden proved too much for her. Eventually she was taken from him too, as her mind cracked. She gave up. He never forgave her for not struggling more. He was getting over it; trying to help her when he could. Finding the treasure was a triumph, the incredible luck he and Noël had had could help them all. He was fucked if he was going to give that up. This scheming, conceited, comfortable old millionaire had chosen to take it away from him just to satisfy his vanity.

He slipped into the barn and crouched behind the lawn mower furthest from the door, just before Serge appeared in the pool of light at the top of the steps. He was whistling for his dog.

Pen froze. He had no illusions as to Serge's reaction when he found out what had happened to the brute. They were two of a kind; they deserved each other; what they lacked in manners they made up for in hostility. Serge whistled again, then cursed impatiently and slammed the door, cutting out the light. Pen was sweating copiously beneath his clothes in the dark, knowing that there was, now, no going back.

Renault had known where he was going to be last weekend, even that Sophie would be at market. He wondered how long ago the bastard had planned the whole thing. To add insult to injury, he realised with dismay that pretending to appreciate his work was probably just a manoeuvre to get his confidence.

Pen had never had to test his courage before. Apart from one deplorable occasion that he did his best to forget, he had hardly even been in any playground scraps, let alone killed a dog. He felt resolve harden in him like an indomitable nodule of flint in the soft limestone of his being. He took his tobacco pouch from his pocket and removed the lighter.

He moved through the vehicles by touch, though he doubted anyone would be out looking for the dog yet; he didn't want to risk the light. His hand alighted on one of the empty jerricans about where he thought they would be. Lucky that Serge was such an untidy, lazy bastard. Pen sorted through them, looking for one with a drop of fuel. He knew they wouldn't all be dry, but he hadn't dared hope for the half-full container that sloshed around when he picked it up.

"Perfect!" he muttered. His mind had been going like crazy, but this was the first word he had spoken since leaving Noël. It might just as well have been a battle-cry. He turned on his lamp then and looked at the lawn-mowers, one brand new just like a miniature tractor, the other older. They were parked close together right next to the big John Deere, the white van close by and the Saab tidily squared up to the back door further on.

He removed the petrol-caps from the mowers and from the jerrican, poured half the contents of the can over one, then retreated through the vehicles, dribbling a trail of fuel on the ground as he went. As soon as he was out of the barn he tossed the empty can back inside and snapped the lighter. Before he even had time to put the flame to it, the vapour took and the whole lot went up in a startling conflagration. It engulfed him first in an ephemeral embrace so brief that it hardly singed him, then ripped back away towards the interior of the barn in an explosive yellow tongue of flame that went berserk once it reached the vehicles.

He felt wild as he retreated further, moving back around to the other side of the building and keeping away from the light that was about to come on. The tyres of the big John Deere began to burn with a satisfying vengeance, crackling and hissing, sending up a pall of black smoke. He was just beginning to think that Renault and his henchman must have gone to bed when the door sprang open and Serge stood there staring at the flames, mouth hanging open, unable to decide how to act. Renault appeared next to him but Pen couldn't hear them over the increasing noise of the blaze Serge ran down the steps to the garden hose-pipe. Renault shot back inside certainly to call the fire-brigade. He appeared again moments later, struggling with a large fire-extinguisher which he brought down the steps and lugged over to engage the fire. Serge had got the water on and was out of sight, battling it from the other side.

This was it. Pen ran for the corner of the house in a crouch, then moving forward kept to the wall. He felt appallingly exposed as he ran for the steps. He needn't have worried: one glance at Renault showed him to be oblivious to anything but fighting the flames. They seemed to have reached the outbuildings now, the tall man's body a thin dark silhouette struggling hopelessly in the orange light. Pen could feel the heat on his face as he looked at them, then bounded up the steps and into the house. He had to fight the urge to shut the back door as he went into the kitchen: the longer it took them to work out what was going on the better.

The trouble was where to start. The Neolithic stuff was on the first floor of the main building. Renault's personal quarters were in this wing above the kitchens. Pen had never been up there, but he reckoned it a good bet for where he would keep Pen's stolen treasures. Perhaps he had a safe or a locked room. He was glad of the weight of the jemmy in the duffel-bag flopping against his back. He stopped for a second, just long enough to take it out and to collect himself. Some of the lights were on in the house, but most of it was in darkness.

Deciding to explore the lit parts first, he took a staircase leading up to a landing on the first floor. A corridor led away into the darkness to his left, presumably linking this wing with the main building. But to his right there were three doors, one of them ajar with light spilling from it onto the bare boards of the landing. He pushed it open and was surprised to find himself in a large, comfortable bedroom. The carpeted floor was strewn with plush woollen rugs. There was a three-piece suite in front of a fair-sized fire-place. A fire was laid, waiting for a match; crumpled newspaper and kindling over the spreading bed of ashes. Split logs filled a basket to the left of it. One of the brown leather armchairs more worn than the other was drawn up close to the grate, a pile of newspapers and magazines on the floor beside it. There was a flat-screen television on an ornate table, and dressers and cupboards against the walls. A large bed occupied the room opposite the fire, flanked by antique bedside tables and a pair of bronze reading-lamps in the shape of art-nouveau nymphs brandishing flaming torches.

Under a window to the right of the bed was a writing-desk with drawers and pigeon-holes, filled with papers. A reading-lamp lit the writing area. Pen felt renewed disgust when he recognised the sale catalogue on a pile of magazines. Lying in the centre of the desk on its tooled green leather writing-pad was the jade axe Renault had bought. Pen felt his heart leap in his chest but he didn't touch it, he just looked for a suspended moment. Then he started on the drawers. There were four on either side of the seat, some of them so full that they wouldn't close properly. The first one he opened, on the left, contained several folders marked with Renault's company name. The next held nothing of interest either, although it did contain a beautifully carved woman's hand in marble, broken off at the wrist, it seemed to be beckoning. Another drawer had some engraved bone, nothing particularly special, though Pen would have liked to be able to look at them more closely. By the time he had been through all the draws, he was getting flustered.

He looked under the bed, then went quickly through all the other drawers he could see, and all the cupboards too. Nothing!

There was a door at the end of the room, but it only led to Renault's carpeted bathroom full of the smell of cologne and talcum powder.

Out on the landing he tried the door to the right of Renault's bedroom. It was a large walk-in cupboard, its shelves filled with identical white cardboard boxes. He opened one: papers, folders with the company logo. He didn't bother opening the others and left the closet. The door opposite Renault's room was locked. Through the thick walls and covered windows he could hardly hear the crackling inferno outside, he felt he could risk a little noise. He wedged the crowbar into the gap by the lock and put his weight to it, the door sprang open. He was relieved not to have broken anything; he reminded himself that the longer it took them to work out what had happened, the better. He didn't put the light on, but could see that it was another bedroom, less luxurious than Renault's and with no bureau. He went in and looked around with the aid of his lamp. It looked disused. He pulled open a few drawers — either empty or full of bed-linen. Pulling the door closed behind him, he turned to the corridor. Other doors led off it to the right. He threw them open and looked inside as he passed. They were smaller rooms than the other two: some were bedrooms, one a toilet with a high wall-mounted cast-iron cistern, another a bathroom with a large enamelled bath in the centre of the unadorned room, its ball-and-claw feet gripping the bare boards, brown stains running down from the taps to the plug-hole.

Pen emerged into a large space at the far end of the hallway and realised that he was in the main building on the first floor, where the Neolithic collection was kept. He cast his lamp over the display cases, four rows of them in this room alone. He hurried from one to the next taking in nothing, simply ascertaining that his finds were not on show and flipping open the top of the crates positioned under most of them to see if he recognised anything in the pale beam of his lamp. He had looked over most of them and had found nothing, before he heard the sirens wailing in the distance.

"Already? Oh shit."

He shot through into the next room: more of the same, case after case of large worked flakes, scrapers and blades with the occasional dagger or polished axe, some horn and bone, and in one corner some large chunks of stone from a burial mound or Neolithic tomb. No jade axes, and no gold. Pen could have pillaged the place, could have taken Renault's jade axe when he was in his bedroom, but the thought never crossed his mind. He wanted his own finds, wanted them more than anything. And time was running out.

The fire-engines left their sirens on right into the courtyard, spiking adrenaline into Pen's veins and sending him hurtling down the wide staircase heading for a small doorway to the right of the main entrance on the front of the house. He had never used it, but knew that it would be furthest from the action. He tried the bolts and they drew back easily, but it was locked and the key was not in it.

"Shit, shit!" He ran back the way he had come and checked the front doors. The key was there but it was an exposed way to leave. He turned out his lamp, opened the door a crack, and looked out gingerly: one of the fire-engines was right outside, its lights strobing orange. There was no one in sight, and he was about to chance it when a black-clad knight in a gold helmet came charging around the corner. Pen squatted down instinctively but didn't dare close the door for fear of alerting him by the movement. He heard the big engine roar outside, then move off around the building. When he looked again there was only the reflected flickering light from the trucks — or the fire, he couldn't tell. He looked out, then crept outside. He pulled the door shut and leaped off the top of the steps. He hit the ground hard, dropped his bag, and rolled over. He snatched up the bag and was on his feet and limping for the shadows surprised to feel no more than a little throb in his right ankle. He hopped then ran through the bushes to where he had last seen the dog. The fire was bigger than he expected, and looking up he saw why: the roof had caught.

He found the dog by smell. It had not moved far, but it was off the track, which was lucky or the firemen would have seen it. Mercifully it was dead. He grabbed it by its hind legs and dragged it as far as he could into the trees. He then crossed back over the track and ran through the tree cover to where he had left Noël.

All that for nothing! Shit! He had no idea what time it was. Would Noël still be there?

"Shit!"

"Pen!" he heard Noël hiss from the dense shadow of the trees, but he couldn't see him.

"Here, Pen, come on, hurry!"

"What time is it?"

"I don't know. What the fuck's going on, Pen? What have you done? Let's get out of here."

Noël kicked the motor, careful not to rev it too loudly. Pen jumped onto the pillion and they wheeled out onto the track, moving slowly until they reached the road. Pen's back crawled all the way with the sensation that Serge had a bead on him with his hunting rifle. He looked back and saw the glow of the burning house above the darkness of the trees, and then they were on the road. Noël opened the throttle and they thrashed away into the night, kicking up gravel and dust.

Too little time for fuck's sake! thought Pen furiously. What had he expected — that his stuff would be just lying around waiting for him to walk in and take it? He groaned out loud for being such a fool. Noël pulled the bike off the road and into a narrow lane just as a pair of headlights crested the hill they had been climbing. This wasn't the moment for them to be seen by anyone. Pen had not bothered to put his helmet on; he was carrying it awkwardly in his elbow, which made it difficult to hold on to Noël. He was getting a buffeting, and tucked his head into the lee of the slim body in front of him. He didn't even feel satisfaction at setting fire to Renault's place.

"So, you found no sign of anything?"

"No I didn't. Curiously, though, his new jade axe was in pride of place on a desk in his bedroom."

"What's so curious about that? I'd have had mine in the bed with me if I didn't have Denise."

"No, I mean if he had our stuff, why didn't he have it at least within fondling distance?"

"Your stuff must have taken up several crates. It wouldn't have been that easy to dissimulate even in amongst his own hoard."

"I only managed to look at one floor. There's another whole one, plus the attics and the cellars."

"Well, it's fucked now."

"Yeah, fucked." Pen took out his tobacco and, gazing into the dark, rolled himself a cigarette. His life had changed dramatically since he had come across that bloody little cave, none of it for the better. Not caring to spend the night alone, he sat up for most of it, smoking and talking things over with a very uneasy Noël.

14

It was a cold dawn that was breaking as Pen finally pulled his truck into the drive. There was no sign of the Peugeot. A hot shower and some tea would be nice, but first he needed to get a fire going outside. He had a lot of rubbish to burn, and tough shit for the ecological implications. Once the bonfire was going well, its heart burning bright as a furnace, he took out some of the contents of his bag and started throwing them on. The overalls had the effect of dousing the flames for a moment, but then began to blacken and smoke and reluctantly catch fire. The water-pistol back in its plastic bag caught instantly, but a cloud of noxious white smoke erupted from the molten yellow mass, making him retreat to a safe distance fearing for his lungs. Perhaps he should have emptied it first, but he didn't want to have anything more to do with the thing. He even threw his hat and his old shoes into the flames, wondering if the police might be considering a criminal origin for the fire, and be looking for footprints at this very moment. There were only the little crowbar and his camera left in the bag now. He took them out and threw the brand-new bag into the fire: the act had an air of finality about it. He prodded the embers with a garden fork, making sure everything was thoroughly burned before going back to the house.

He was expecting the police at any moment and was far too

nervous to go to bed. So he turned on the computer and looked at his mail for something to do. There was a sweet message from Medea inviting him to supper whenever he wanted, and telling him she had finished the job and that the catalogue of his misfortunes was out on the worldwide web. Several people had replied already. Some he knew but others could only be friends of friends. He opened one of those first and read:

> Dear Pen,
> I was shocked and saddened to read your email.
> You don't know me, but we collectors need to stick together.
> It is frightening to realise that we might be targeted by crim-
> inals because our collections have begun to take on value.
> I will be sending it on to all my acquaintances in the hope
> that one of them might eventually hear something and that
> you may get your beautiful flints back.
> Good luck in your endeavours, Francis Piñata.

So, word was getting around. He opened a few others; all were in the same vein. The flint-collecting world was small, and most people would be informed before very long. It would make them nervous — of course: who knew who might be next? Pen hadn't hoped to get results so soon. He opened a new folder, called it 'Rip Off', and slid all the emails into it along with a copy of Medea's original. Then he opened the folder of photos he had gathered of his collection and looked through them, feeding his sense of tragedy.

It was then, with the early-morning light streaming in through the east window and the smell of smoke and ashes still in his nostrils, that he was stricken with a potent sense of nostalgia. Leaving the computer running, he got up and went to the kitchen. He chose an apple and half a packet of chocolate-wholemeal biscuits from the larder. He took a bottle of spring water, checked that he had his tobacco, picked up his wellies and climbed into the truck. He didn't have to think about where he was going. He automatically took the old familiar route he had taken so many times before with a stone-picker's eagerness.

He drove slowly through thick mists in the lowlands, but they thinned out as he got higher and had cleared completely as he climbed up out of the trees towards the freshly worked farmland. He pulled over and parked on the side of the road, making no attempt to hide the vehicle. He clambered out and looked over one of the most promising sites in the region. Keeping to his ritual he changed out of his shoes and rolled a cigarette by the van, savouring the moment. Then he passed through a sparse hedge and set out across the uneven surface of the well-scoured, deeply-cultivated field.

He had always found it curious, the way the best sites were often quite close to the roads, especially those that followed the ridges along the hill-tops. The valleys were cut deeply out of the high land, creating loads of roughly parallel folds running in every case down to the rivers. The easiest passage through this deeply corrugated terrain was to keep to the highest land following the ridges to points where they joined to change direction.

Originally those routes were used by animals long before we arrived. As Pen strode out into the field he came across the cloven hoof prints of several large deer running parallel to the road: if they were anything to go by, they were still using the same tracks. The Neanderthals must have used them too, following the game as would have all the succeeding cultures each benefiting from the advantageous views afforded by their elevation. Not to be outdone, we built our roads along them: they were after all the obvious routes, requiring the least amount of earth moving. How many sites must have been destroyed by all that road-building?

Pen's practised eye picked out the waste flakes of countless centuries of knapping strewn around him in the freshly washed earth. A short distance from the road was a Neanderthal campsite, a big one, with a wide fire-pit at the heart of it. The burnt stones that had surrounded it were brought to the surface by the plough. The larger ones were red on the side that had faced the flames, but there were plenty of smaller quartzite cobbles which were entirely red. The pot-boilers, they were put in the fires until they were almost red-hot, then transferred to suspended skins of water or other liquids like soup, or into waterproofed hollows scooped out of the ground to heat up their contents, dyes perhaps, or medicines. Pen had tried them out, and they worked. Heating them permanently changed their colour from crystalline white to dark pink. Such stones could be found at many sites: obviously no one thought them interesting enough to pick up, perhaps because of their weight; but he had a pile of them at home. For him, they were imbued with a magical history, and spoke eloquently of the ordinary daily life of people who had vanished so long ago. He had found dozens of good bifaces around this spot.

Conspicuously, there were no other footprints in the field. Pen had been told that the farmer wanted no one on his land, and apparently his words had been taken to heart — which suited Pen fine this morning. He felt his troubles gradually slough off him like a layer of grime in a hot bath after a hard day's work. His thoughts went out to the people whose summer camps these had been. They must have gathered in some numbers, if the quantity of their leavings was anything to go by. This was the highest spot for miles around, a crossroads where two main ridges approached each other at right-angles. He could look down and away into the shrouded valleys on either side of the road, and raising his eyes he could see successive ridges flowing off into the distance. The valleys were still filled with the torn white rags of dissipating mists. From where he stood he counted seven hills on one side and six on the other. Those views, combing themselves out before him in the pale morning light, soothed him greatly and eased his bruised soul.

This was what field-walking was about, stepping into the skins of those who had made the artefacts that he was finding and trying to feel their presence. They had been right here where he stood, and undoubtedly also marvelled at the world. He just stood for a while, looking and listening, smelling the damp earth and watching the low cloud rolling across the high brightening sky of that wide, airy place.

Fuck it all, so what? He thought. Worse things happen. I'm still in love, and I've got a wonderful little girl out of it. I've got sickeningly good health, never had a day's illness in my life. I've never had to go to war, I'm living in the best period ever, since the end of the last ice age anyway. Sod the stones, let them go!

As he thought this, Pen heard a car pull up with a sharp squeal of breaks in front of his van. Who's this then — Noël? I'll bet my next biface on it. But when he looked, it wasn't Noël's car. Two angry-looking farmers were climbing out of it.

"What are you doing on my land!" shouted the older one, his temper barely concealed. The younger man ran across the field and adopted a classic Hollywood kung-fu pose in front of Pen.

"Sorry, pal, but you're going to have to pay for all the rest, we're sick to death of you scum!"

Pen smiled pleasantly at the burly young fellow, while what he supposed was the father strode up to them, his eyes like cocked guns.

"Turned out nice, eh?" said Pen, his eyes turned skywards in an effort to break the ice.

"Who gave you permission to trample over my fields?" The older guy was short but looked robust, and probably not much older than Pen.

"Hey, stay cool, man," said Pen, raising his hands placatingly. The young guy, whom Pen now felt he recognised from somewhere, made a rapid crab-like lunge at him. Pen stepped back easily and avoided him, and couldn't help laughing. The two of them advanced on him. Pen said:

"I'm not causing you any trouble. What's wrong?"

"It's theft! Empty your pockets! Come on, show us what you've stolen."

"Are you telling me you are stone-collectors? Wow, you sure have a good site here! You must have a fantastic collection — I'd love to see it."

"He's fucking with us, Papa, let's kick the shit out of him."

The father ignored his son, but still insisted that Pen empty his pockets. Pen shrugged and reluctantly complied with this rather intimate request, producing a dirty tissue, his tobacco, and a few coins.

"What else have you got?" screamed the son.

"'Fraid that's it," sighed Pen, who was getting bored, and started to wander off, eyes to the ground as usual.

"Hey!" shouted the young one again. Pen rounded on him, the frustration that he had been trying to bury suddenly boiling back to the surface.

"What, what the hell do you want? You looking for a fight at eight o'clock in the morning? Well come on, man, I'll take on both of you." He squared up to them, looking for weaknesses. He wasn't scared and was deciding that perhaps this was what he needed. But he held back, waiting to see how it would go.

"It's illegal to take the stones," said the father, the wind going out of his sails.

"Why don't you look for them yourselves?" asked Pen.

"We don't know what to look for."

"Oh god!" exclaimed Pen, "take a look in Périgueux museum one day. It has the best collection I know. It's not like they're hard to recognise, you've just got to get down off your fucking tractor sometimes!" Pen realised that he was tensed up for a fight, he allowed his shoulders to drop and shrugged.

"Now. I'm asking you, may I *please* walk across your field?"

"No you fucking can't," said the son.

"Well, you can't say I didn't ask," said Pen, walking off over the field away from them.

"You're looking for trouble, and you're going to find it," said the father, turning and leaving the field. Pen ignored them; he had spotted something interesting.

The son wasn't finished and was waving his arms around, his hurt pride making him unable to let go, but the father was already at the car. What Pen had spotted looked like a biface, but he could hardly prise it out of the ground with the stupid lout gesticulating next to him.

"Ok mate, keep your hair on, come on, let's go." Pen took out his tobacco and started rolling a cigarette. He sat in the cab of his truck as they roared angrily away. He pretended to be on his phone when their car came back, as he knew it would. It slowed as it passed, and the farmers glowered at him through the windscreen.

He made it as quick as he could, but it took a moment to locate the spot. He didn't drag it out, but just snatched the stone from the ground, noting that it was quite a large one, and was back in his truck and starting the engine before the adrenaline from the whole silly encounter hit him. It was ludicrous: peasants wanting to fight him over a bunch of stones they didn't collect or even know were there. They had well and truly messed up his morning: he was pissed off again and mumbling angrily. He wiped the mud from the flat triangle of flint with his hand. It looked intact, an almost perfect isosceles triangle in white stone, with black patches like a Frisian cow.

That's rare, he thought, I've never found anything like this before. Those idiots — why don't they take an interest. The next machine they run over the field would have smashed this little beauty to gravel. It was well made but the style of it looked ancient. It might have been lying there intact for more than a hundred and fifty thousand years. La Ferrassie perhaps? Despite the interruption he couldn't help speculating.

The general misconception was that there had been a gradual refining of forms and craftsmanship over time. But in fact, Pen was sure, there must always have been some skilful craftsmen who stood out, their work throwing up new variations, sometimes of exceptional quality, even far back in time. At some sites one could discern the hand of a flint-knapper in several different pieces. Conversely there must always have been a whole lot of inferior flints made with poor-quality material and little consideration for aesthetics, even in more recent times. After all, symmetry was not a prerequisite for efficiency.

Pen felt bleak. He had had it. His new-found assurance was shattered. For all the pleasure it had brought him over the years, he finally felt that he had had it with the stones. This tantalising piece opened one more door to the world of conflict in which he would have to survive to continue. He was over it, he didn't have the energy. He would tell Sophie, whenever she came back. She would be relieved to hear it, and at least all this might end up making someone happy. He was being unfair to Sophie perhaps, but he was feeling so wretched he hardly knew who his allies were any more. He was still muttering miserable thoughts to himself as he pulled the truck onto the road. Suddenly he felt extremely tired.

He slept all the rest of the day. He was woken sometime in the evening by Alice shaking him and asking him if he was ill. Going down the stairs, a wonderful smell of cooking greeted him. The kitchen was warm and cosy with Sophie's presence, and there were flowers.

"Sleep well, darling?" Sophie asked, turning from the sink to smile at him. As she dried her hands on a tea-towel he noticed a bottle of white wine sitting in a cooler.

"Yeah, sorry, I didn't sleep so well last night." He tried a smile, and then Alice was between them.

"You know, Papa, Denise says she wants to have a little cousin for me."

Pen's smile widened and he looked at Sophie.

"Well," said Sophie, "it's a bit early to decide anything like that just yet. But it is true, she did say it to you."

Their conversation was relaxed, and stayed away from delicate topics over supper. Pen read to Alice at bedtime, putting on all the voices and delighting her with special effects like earthquakes, until he remembered that he was supposed to be lulling her to sleep. Sophie was taking a shower when he got back downstairs. He poured the last of the Chardonnay into their glasses — all but flush to the brim, emptying the bottle completely; he gave a little smile — and sat wondering where this good fortune had come from. Sophie eventually appeared wrapped in a towel, another around her hair. She picked up her glass:

"I suppose you've had enough sleep and will be down here doing things for hours."

"Er, actually, I'm still quite tired, I was just thinking of brushing my teeth." And that was it: they were back in each other's good books.

15

Pen awoke, alert, eyes wide in the dark lying on his back dead still, listening. There was something wrong. He heard the footfalls softly on the stairs and called out, "Alice, are you all right." Then the room was lit with the narrow beam of a torch sweeping back and forth from Sophie, already sitting up, alarmed, then blindingly into Pen's eyes. He hit the floor by the bed, pushing up onto his feet, when the blow fell.

"What did you do to my dog? you bastard!"

The pain on the left side of his head had Pen struggling; he coughed up something, then put all his effort into lunging at his aggressor. The next blow caught him on the right side of his face, knocking him down again. He struggled with a wave of nausea. He was aware that the light was on in the bedroom and glimpsed the white form of Sophie rise from the bed, but he couldn't shake off the thick blanket of pain shrouding his other senses. Serge (for who else could it be?) grabbed viciously at Sophie's body, and he heard her scream. There was a crash and the light went out. Pen vomited on the floor where he lay, bleeding from the side of his face, but he was coming round. Suddenly there was a grunt and an explosion ripped the bed apart beside him, something sent a burning sensation through his ear and the side of his head. He could hear screaming.

Serge's torch was swinging around, mostly on the ceiling. Pen had to do something; the maniac was going to kill them all. He couldn't clear his head, pain and nausea had blurred his vision, and he found that he was sobbing. The vision of little Alice cowering in her room jolted him, and with a surge of adrenalin he reached out and found the hilt of his kukri hanging by the bed. He jerked the vicious weapon free of its sheath and went for the lamp hoping it was on the bastard's forehead.

"Down on the floor Sophie!" he howled in English as he slashed in the darkness. He felt the heavy blade hit something, glance off and bury itself in what he hoped was a shoulder. The bed erupted again, and a stink of spent powder and burnt bedding filled the little room. Pen could hear Alice sobbing and struck again hard.

"Fuck! We need some light!" Pen grabbed the man's head-lamp. He turned it on to his face. It was unrecognisable: Something was very wrong with him, apart from all the blood: the man's eyes were glazing over.

"It's okay Sophie, go to Alice!" Pen cried. But Sophie didn't reply.

Pen shone the torch where he expected Sophie to be. But she was tangled in the sheets on the floor. He couldn't see her face. He looked back at the man, and felt a cold shock when he saw the shotgun still gripped in his hand. The bastard had shot her. He raised the kukri again, then thought better of it and grabbed for the gun. The man let it go and keeled over, off the bed. Pen needed the lights on. He tried the wall switch, but it didn't work.

Off at the mains? He put on the head-lamp, scrambled into his boxers then grabbed the inert body by the ankles and dragged it out of the bedroom. With the strength of desperation, he bundled the man down the stairs.

"It's going to be all right, Alice. I'll be back in a minute. Just stay in your room. I'm going to put the lights on." He couldn't risk leaving the killer on the stairs. So he threw the big blade ahead of himself and dragged him through into the workshop. He could feel the heavy body beginning to revive, so he retrieved his weapon and hurried to the fuse-box. The trip-switch was down, he switched it back on, found the light switch and illuminated the big room. The attacker had his eyes open and was observing Pen, but was obviously badly injured. Blood ran down his face from a nasty head wound and one shoulder was in poor shape — blood dripped from his fingers. Pen raised the large blade again.

"Shall I give you another one, you bastard? Or are you going to hold still?"

He needed to get back to Sophie. There was no time to waste. He raised the blade to give the bastard a maiming blow, but recognised the voice when it said,

"Stop! I'll keep still," the man groaned. "I'm not going anywhere."

It was Serge he must have shaved his beard off and tucked his hair up in a woollen cap. He looked older than Pen remembered.

"You move, I'll find you and hamstring you, you mad fucker."

Pen ran through the house, picking up the phone. His mouth tasted disgusting and he hurriedly rinsed it out over the kitchen sink, then, raced up the stairs. He called softly into Alice's room and she rushed out into his arms. He gathered her up and went into his bedroom and turned the light on. Sophie was sitting on the floor wrapped in the sheets. He fell to his knees beside her and looked her over, checking for injuries. She looked down, refusing to meet his eyes. One pillow had been shot to ribbons and duck down was drifting around the room at every movement. Pen's side of the mattress was blackened. The shotgun lay among the mess and the sheets were bloody. Sophie's bedside lamp lay on the floor in bits, the top-heavy red lampshade over by the door, the two lethal prongs sticking out of the lamp socket.

"Are you hurt, Sophie?" She didn't answer; he looked down at the lamp.

"Sophie, you didn't...?" Sophie did not look injured but she wasn't responding well. He kneeled down next to her and looked into her eyes, Alice clinging round his neck.

"He hurt me," she sobbed, "he was squeezing my breast so hard, I knocked the lampshade off and stuck the lamp in his face, but I got the shock myself." She was weeping now. Alice let go of Pen and wrapped her arms around her mother, whispering comforting words.

Pen was beginning to shake when he phoned the police. He outlined the attack and asked them to send some ambulances, He went back into the workshop, his head throbbing. Serge had gone. Looking down at the floor he could see the wide trail of blood leading into his desecrated little museum. The door was closed and the key was gone but Pen kicked it hard and it smashed open. He could see the rear half of Sergio protruding through the chain-sawed hole in the wall. Pen kicked him as hard as his bare feet would allow.

"Get back in here you mad fucker, or I'll use this blade on you!" He kicked Serge again and the man squirmed back slowly into the little room, his breath wet and ragged.

"You're a fucking rapist!" shouted Pen, kicking him again.

"Stop! Stop! You killed my dog!"

The guy was a mess. Half of his face was hanging open. One blow must have caught him on the side of his head and cut down his cheek, just missing the eye. Pen thought he could see some teeth glistening through the blood even though the man's mouth was closed.

"Why do you say that?"

"Because, because he bit you, who else would do that." The man was sobbing now, his hands hovering near his face but not daring to touch it.

"That's almost a good enough reason to kill the vicious brute. Now listen, Sergio, you stole my flints. I'm going to give you one chance to tell me where they are otherwise I'm going to start cutting you." Pen held out the blood-stained blade to show he meant business. Serge glared back at him.

"You would not be the first person to do that to me."

"Oh, and do you find it to your liking?"

"You don't scare me half as much as those Arabs."

"Where are they?"

"Dead I hope." Pen lifted the kukri.

He found he didn't have it in him to chop the old guy up in cold blood, even though only minutes ago he had discharged a shotgun into his bed twice and would have probably raped Sophie — and god only knows what would have become of little Alice.

The decision was taken out of his hands as two large policemen came through the house into the workshop, one of them with his service automatic held out in front of him.

Alice, was showing signs of shock and clung to Sophie in the ambulance. Pen was made to lie down. He had several shotgun pellets in the side of his head and his face was disfigured with bruising. There was a large gash up by the hair-line where the gun must have hit him. He didn't feel so good and was regretting not avenging himself more on Serge.

"He was the guy on the market, the one who bought all those things last Saturday," said Sophie looking accusingly at Pen. "You know him, don't you?" Her voice was flat, demanding.

Pen was beginning to hurt badly now that the pressure was off, but he owed Sophie a lot, and replied as well as he could:

"Yeah, he's Renault's handyman. But he has shaved his big red beard off and tucked his hair away. I didn't recognise him until he spoke to me."

"What did he want?"

"He was the one that ripped me off. We didn't check but perhaps he was in the house during the robbery. I think he might have been after you."

"Are you kidding?"

"I really don't know."

"What did he say about a dog?"

"I don't know, his dog bit me."

"Pen?" He took refuge in his pain for a moment, groaning, but he knew that she wouldn't leave it alone.

Alice was beginning to look panicked. Sophie snuggled up to her, but her eyes were somewhere else.

The police inspector who came to see him in hospital was called Bardot. Pen was just lucid enough to realise that some flippant remark about Brigitte would probably not help his case. Anyway he seemed too cheerful to be a policeman. He had a broad salt-and-pepper moustache and a twinkle in his eye that gave the disconcerting impression that he knew more about Pen's affairs than Pen would like. His partner was less imposing: grey suit, thinning on top and a long face. Pen didn't retain his name. The man remained quiet but vigilant. In Inspector Bardot's experience, people who got attacked in their homes usually knew their assailant and the reason. After the preliminaries, Bardot asked, "Why do you think he did it, Monsieur Williamson?"

"He was deranged?"

"Yes, that could be one reason, his military record shows that he was tortured in Algeria. There were repercussions... but apparently you know him."

"He is one of my client's hired help."

"He claims that you killed his dog."

"Did he give any reason why I might have done that?"

"Says his dog bit you."

"Well that's true enough, vicious brute, I had stitches."

"So, did you kill it?"

"As a matter of fact no, though I'm not sorry to hear that it's dead. But let's say, for argument's sake, that I did what he accuses me of, would that justify him coming into my bedroom in the middle of the night and discharging a shotgun into my bed, not to mention sexually assaulting my wife?" The inspector was no fool. This foreigner, who expressed himself fairly well in French, was concealing something from him. But what? and why?

"I understand that you are not married, sir." He ventured.

"What has that got to do with anything?"

"Nothing I suppose. And you are right, it's a bad business. You and your family are lucky to be alive. You stuck up for yourselves admirably." The inspector seemed sincere, but Pen got the impression that he was being accused of being attacked.

"There was an element of luck involved, but it was Sophie who saved us."

"Yes, she told me. A resourceful woman, your, wife, it would seem. You defended yourself also very well, if I may say so, Monsieur Williamson. Your attacker will be in the hospital for some time. He lost a lot of blood."

"It was all I could do to stop myself from whacking him a few more times."

"Yes, shows great restraint. You keep a formidable weapon by your bed. When he attacked you, apart from the dog business, did you get the impression that he was after anything other than to hurt you?"

"Yes, I think he wanted to rape Sophie."

"With you in the house?"

"He had a gun, Inspector."

"Yes well... What makes you think he was after her?"

"The way he grabbed her tits after he had clubbed me half to death."

"He says you had found a treasure, Monsieur Williamson."

"Does he now? And what type of treasure is it supposed to be?"

"He says gold and precious stones."

"And he came to steal it, or to make me tell him where it's hidden?"

"Something like that."

"And what do you think, Inspector?"

"I don't know what to think."

"Look." Pen dragged in some air as he gathered his thoughts. "The guy is off his rocker. Did Sophie tell you that last Saturday he came to Sarlat and bought over a thousand euros' worth of arty souvenirs from her stall?"

"No, she didn't. That is certainly a lot to spend on trinkets. You are right about him being deranged, Monsieur Williamson. But we will have to get to the bottom of this. I will let you get some rest, but I will be back in touch with you soon. I'll bid you good day for now."

Inspector Bardot smiled reassuringly as he left the room. But the policeman could tell that the English guy was worried about something and not hiding it very well. Bardot's silent partner scowled at him, giving Pen an ominous premonition.

His head was still pounding. The gendarme had put the wind up him. That crazy bastard Serge was trying to take Pen down with him, without mentioning the theft and knowing that Pen couldn't say anything himself.

He phoned Medea from his bed.

"What about our meal, Adonis?" she replied, as soon as she saw his number displayed.

"Medea," he croaked trying to get control of his voice, "I need your help again."

"Yeah, well, you're going to owe me big time after this, sweetie."

"Wait until you hear what it is. I need you to track down all those e-mails we sent out, and get rid of them."

"You're a crazy man, that can't be done."

"Yeah, it can. I've heard about a virus you can programme to destroy specific targets."

"That's probably illegal and will only work safely on stuff on the web, not things that have already been downloaded."

"That's a start. How long will it take to do?"

"Whoa there, I didn't say I would do it."

"You have to, Medea. I'm in deep shit. I could be prosecuted if the police get hold of it."

"It's by no means as easy as you imagine."

"I don't imagine anything."

"Well, it would be no guarantee that they won't get hold of it anyway, if they know what to look for, even if I'm successful. But I'll try my best."

"Thanks, Medea, I'll really be in your debt if you can do something."

"Hm, haven't I heard that one before somewhere...?"

Sophie had been sent home with Alice, but Pen had to stay in for an extra night. He had been shot and beaten about the head, and was suffering from concussion. Now that he could let go, he felt like a jelly about to slide off the plate. He needed to get home and delete all the stuff on his computer before the police decided to take a look at it.

He was discharged the next day. His face still felt as if a branding-iron had only recently been removed from it. Although his head was clear, he still couldn't work out a strategy to deal with the insistent Inspector Bardot, or what to say to Sophie, or Alice for that matter. He called Noël.

"Noël, they've let me out of the hospital. Do you think you could come and get me?"

"Périgueux? Sure."

"Thanks mate, I'll try to find an internet place while I'm waiting, but I will be in the hospital foyer in an hour."

"Pen, you have to know, Sophie and Alice are at Denise's again. Sophie is really pissed off and I can see why. You need to talk to her."

"Okay, Noël, see you in an hour."

He was pushing through the rotating glass doors of the reception area when he saw Renault coming in. He ducked his head, but Renault spotted him anyway and hurried over to intercept him. Pen raised his hands to ward him off, but Renault looked genuinely concerned.

"Pen my boy, you look terrible." This was hardly an exaggeration. Pen had a bandage around his head covering his ear, one side of his face, and his scalp wound. The exposed part of his face was swollen and disfigured, purple and yellow bruising ran down to his jaw on the right side.

"I don't want to talk to you, Renault," said Pen, trying hard to look menacing but with little effect.

"You have every right to be upset, Pen. When the police came to see me and I heard what had happened to you, I immediately felt responsible. Please accept my apologies. I knew Sergio was deranged, of course, but I have been trying to help him over the years."

"He could have killed us all! You realise that?"

"Pen. I was his commanding officer in Algeria. He was captured there and tortured atrociously during the war. He had to be discharged. After that he couldn't settle, and got on the wrong side of the police a couple of times. On one occasion I was asked to be a character witness, and I ended up adopting him."

"I don't give a toss about all that, Renault!" Pen spat. "I'm glad he was tortured. What I want is my collection!"

"Yes, I heard about that as well, and of course anything I can do..."

"Just give it back to me, you fucking megalomaniac!"

"What do you mean Pen? I certainly don't have your collection."

"Your man Serge stole it from me, so you must have it, Renault. What do you take me for, a cretin?"

"I assure you, Pen, I know nothing whatsoever about this. I have had my own troubles. There was a fire at the house, caused lots of damage. I haven't been following what's been going on since."

"Yeah, well, we all have our troubles. Bye Renault." Pen turned to go, but Renault put out a hand to stop him:

"What do you mean, Sergio stole your collection?"

"Don't play innocent, you can't expect to me to swallow that shit. Your man cut a hole in the side of my workshop with one of your chainsaws and ripped me off while I was in Paris with you. He even went to Sarlat to check that Sophie would not be home, all right? So I know. You'd go to any lengths you nutter, but it won't do you any good. Everyone will know my flints by now."

Renault's mouth dropped open, but for once he had nothing to say. Pen turned away from him, shoulders hunched, and walked briskly through the parking area, desperate to get away. Renault shouted after him a couple of times, but let him go.

Pen was sweating. He would have liked to kick Renault's teeth down his throat. But he had hardly even insulted him. There had been something unsettling about his attitude. He didn't doubt that Renault would be skilful at dissimulation, but he seemed a little too shocked. Why had the old guy come and hunted him out at the hospital?

There were two *lycées* close to the hospital, high-schools with hundreds of pupils catered for by cheap burger joints and kebab houses and several cyber cafés. Pen went into the first one he came across, bought a coke, settled in at a screen, and checked his email.

"Shit," was his first reaction: a dozen messages referring to the theft. What could he do to stop them? He scanned through them quickly. One stood out:

> Quit whining you little shit! They are gone. So, there is no use crying over spilt milk. If you make trouble about it now you will regret it later. You have been warned.

No signature, and Pen's own address as the sender. Pen was too shaken already to feel shocked. He said "Crank!" out loud, causing the youngsters who had stared at him when he walked in to bury their heads even deeper into their screens. But in some dark recess of his soul he knew the threat was real. Pushing aside a wave of apprehension, he picked out all the others and did a general 'reply to sender' to the lot:

Hi,

Thank you all for your kind thoughts and consideration. It has been a great comfort to me over the last few days.

The situation has become even more complicated, however, and it would help matters enormously if the whole thing could disappear off the web for a while.

So could everyone please stop sending the emails around.

I am still searching for my collection, but it seems I'm not the only one!

Pen.

PS please inform your colleagues.

He pressed 'send', and decided it must be time to go back to the hospital. His whole face ached after the small effort of walking to the cybercafé, and his head had begun to throb as well. The nurse had offered him some codeine with his cup of tea at breakfast. But he was worried it might slow him down and had opted for a couple of paracetamol instead; but they weren't doing the trick.

Noël was already waiting outside when he got back.

"God, Pen, you look awful."

"I feel awful." He had gone beyond looking for sympathy, but felt in danger of going to pieces. Noël's familiar face helped pull him together. "The gendarmes came to see me, Noël. Renault's fucking guard dog has told them about our treasure."

"Why would he do that?"

"Because he's a vindictive bastard who is going to prison for a long time and has nothing to lose. He has guessed it was me who killed his dog but he can't possibly know, no one saw me."

"No. But say they think the fire was an accident: how would they account for the dog?"

"God knows. Even if he suspects something he can't have been sure it was me. I don't know why Serge came to attack us, but I have a feeling that someone out there is pretty pissed off about me publishing the photos on the net."

"That nutter's got it in for you for some reason, that's for sure. Maybe for someone as twisted as him that's enough. Or maybe someone else is twisting him, he didn't do this on his own. What did you say to the police?"

"Nothing. But they are not going to go away. Another thing: Renault came to see me. I bumped into him as I was leaving the hospital. I confronted him about my collection. He seemed genuinely shocked that I should accuse him."

"Why did he come?"

"Good question. Perhaps because if he was innocent he would be concerned for me and feel responsible for his man, and visiting me would be the most normal thing to do. He wants to appear innocent so he acts normal. Perhaps he was just fishing for information. He has my collection now, and he guesses I'm not letting it go without a fight."

Noël looked at Pen's ruined face and shook his head "I wish we'd never found that Neolithic burial. We're cursed, we should have left them in peace, Pen. Do you realise, everyone who comes into contact with those jade axes has something horrible happen to them?"

"Why, what has happened to you so far?"

"Apart from being buried alive and losing most of the treasure, you mean? Don't worry, Pen, Renault will get his share."

"Okay, let's go shall we? I have to face Sophie next. You could be right about a curse. Whatever happens, Noël, no one must find out about the fire or I'll find myself sitting in a cell with Serge. I'm beginning to understand the French expression *un sac de noeuds*, a bag of knots."

16

Pen walked into the kitchen of what had been his home for the last fifteen years. The warmth and the colour seemed to have been leached out of the place, leaving an empty crime scene with barely cleaned-up chalk marks and blood-stains. The bedroom was a mess, and stank. Someone had unplugged the broken lamp and placed the red lampshade next to it on Sophie's bedside table. The mattress would have to be taken to the recycling bins, along with all the bedding. The gun had gone and a feeble attempt had been made to clean the floor. Pen felt sick. He went downstairs and called Denise.

"Pen, darling, how are you? You can't imagine what a shock all this is for us."

"Yes, I can imagine. I'm fine, Denise. Can I talk to Sophie please?"

"Pen, I'm sorry, but Sophie needs a little bit of time. She's had a terrible shock."

"You mean she doesn't want to talk to me."

"Give her a couple of days, Pen, she'll come round."

"And Alice. I need to see her, Denise."

"Noël says you look awful. Are you sure she won't be frightened?"

"About as frightened as when Noël was recovering from his ordeal. Denise, I'm coming round."

"Okay, but leave it one more day. That way Sophie might be a bit less angry."

Pen felt helpless.

"All right, Denise, tomorrow. Can you tell them I called, please?"

He walked through into the workshop, where a half-hearted attempt had also been made at cleaning up. But there was a long stain trailing from the door to his empty museum; it had soaked into the raw concrete floor. He opened the door to the little room. The magazines and books had been carefully stacked on one of the shelves and the missing piece had been pushed back into the wall. Pen wondered what the gendarmes must have made of that. He felt he was painting himself into a corner.

On his computer, he searched out the flint collection files and deleted those that had any association with the theft, and all the photos from the Neolithic cave. Then he went to the 'Rip-Off' file with all the email correspondence and burned it onto a disk. He deleted that file from the computer too, and finally he ran his cleaner program. He wrote 'Electric Lady Land, Hendrix, 1968' on the disk, took it downstairs and put it into an already occupied CD cover marked 'Nicks' Play List'; he slipped this into the unruly unused ranks of music CDs lining the shelves by the sound system. He was sure that anyone who knew enough about computers could find the deleted files, but felt he had done all he could.

His phone went. It was Renault.

"Don't put the phone down on me, Pen, we need to talk."

"Okay, Renault, but make it quick. I don't have much patience with you."

"Look," replied Renault, "I believe you that Sergio stole your collection, though I don't yet know why. Can we meet? I could come over and see you. We need to talk."

"We already talked, Renault. For me, that's it."

"I saw your email, Pen."

"Ah, I'll bet that took the wind out of your sails."

"On the contrary, my dear boy, it's an excellent idea. But Pen, those jade axes and the gold — is it wise to be publishing stuff like that? You always were full of surprises, and I may be able to help. Can I come around to see you?"

Pen had to admit that he was curious. Why was Renault so interested in him, now that he had what he had always wanted from him and more?

"No, I'll come to you. I'll be with you in half an hour if you are at home."

"Good boy, see you then."

It was the same old road that he had taken feeling on top of the world so many times, and then just a couple of days ago on the back of Noël's trail bike. But it was a very different destination that was awaiting him as he rounded the bend in the drive that exposed his recent night's work in all its dreadful glory. The roof of the Renault house was still intact from the front, though a little blackened. But when he took the truck round to the rear of the building he was taken aback: even though his intention had been to cause damage, the scale of his success was a shock. The whole barn was gutted, the fire having apparently climbed up the wall, entered the house under the eves and set the attic aflame. The gaping hole in the roof had been covered with a large blue tarpaulin. The damage looked to be just above Renault's bedroom.

The Saab was in its usual place, apparently none the worse for wear. But the other vehicles were burnt-out wrecks. The big new tractor had been mostly plastic and rubber, and its blackened skeleton lay amongst the rubble and sodden ashes like a giant insect that had died defending its young.

Renault appeared at the top of the kitchen steps, as immaculately dressed as usual, just as Pen clambered out of his truck. He was stiff and, suddenly, felt older. Renault extended his hand and Pen had to fight against an urge to return the friendly gesture.

"As you wish, Pen," said Renault ruefully, "but you are wrong about me. I had nothing to do with Serge's behaviour. He's never liked you, and when he gets a bee in his bonnet there's no shaking it out."

"So, why am I here?"

"Yes, yes, so impatient. Can I offer you coffee? I've just made some."

Pen felt like refusing, but surprised himself by accepting. He drew his tobacco from his jacket and rolled a cigarette as he followed Renault up the steps to the kitchen.

"Pen. Just for the sake of argument here, let's say that I was not the recipient of your collection. The question seems to be what did Serge do with all your stuff. There was a lot of it."

"For the sake of argument, Renault, I suppose it would have filled the bed of his van and he must have known where he was taking it."

"He could have hidden it here amongst all my stuff. It would have taken a while before I noticed anything. But I was away for two days. And knowing Serge, I would guess he was not acting alone."

"So we are back to the pre-argument hypotheses."

"Listen Pen, all sorts of people come here. Sergio got to meet many of them, and I am often away in Paris or Brussels. There was plenty of time to work out a plan with some unscrupulous accomplice. The question is who, and what would be in it for Serge?"

"Money?"

"Serge spends almost nothing. His needs are looked after here. This place has become his home."

"If it wasn't you, who would want to rob me?"

"Has anyone shown any interest in your stuff besides me recently?"

"Well, no, apart from Vincent."

"Ah yes, Vincent." Renault had been looking into his coffee, but he raised his eyes and looked at Pen before going on: "Vincent was in our regiment in Algeria as well, you know. He was a corporal. He too got into a bit of trouble over there, for being unnecessarily brutal to the locals. But he was not discharged, just sent home to paint the parade ground for a while. I don't think he knew Sergio personally until he met him at my place. But he knew about him, and they had some experiences in common and got on. Sergio looked up to him."

"So?"

"Look, Pen, I don't want to accuse anyone. Vincent inherited the manse at some point, and at least one other house, but he has hardly ever worked and is always short of money, despite appearances. The archaeological business has been a real source of income for him even though he's as hooked as the worst of us. He's always tried to hold onto the best stuff, but ends up letting it go when the price is right or money is tighter than usual. I have had a lot of good stuff off him."

"So you think he might have been desperate enough to put Serge up to it?"

"If it was Vincent, it would not be for himself. He has contacts all over the place, even abroad. I should know: the first time he sold me something it was in Belgium and apparently he sometimes goes to see someone in Switzerland."

"If you are Belgian what were you doing in the French army?"

"You might not think it to look at me, but my father came from a very poor mid-west American background. He came over with so many others at the end of the first world war. He had the good sense to fall in love with a Belgian girl, and when it was all over they stayed in touch. To cut a long story short, he eventually came back and they married. He took French nationality when he realised he was not going back. I was born just before word war two. We lived near Rouen when I was younger, and it was bleak. I only took Belgian nationality when my business took off — they have a more accommodating fiscal system than France." Pen blinked, it was unlike Renault to confide in him.

"So you are saying that my stuff could be out of the country?"

"I'm not saying anything. I'm just trying to look at all the angles. Believe me, I know what that collection meant to you, and if I can help you in any way at all to get it back you have my word I will."

Pen was getting confused, an uncomfortable creeping feeling was telling him that he might have made a terrible mistake. He observed Renault's reaction from under worried brows as he asked,

"How did the fire start?"

Renault looked exasperated but resigned:

"Something with the old lawn-mower apparently, something electrical. The insurance people have been but say it's not too clear because there was a lot of fuel around, cans everywhere. As you may have noticed my man Sergio is not the most organised of workers. A nuisance, but I'm more than covered. Nothing important got damaged, but it was a close thing. The biggest problem is the water from the firemen, which made a terrible mess. Some tapestries and carpets and furniture got spoilt, but nothing important got burned."

"Apart from the roof and the barn."

"Yes, but they can be replaced — unlike your collection. Where did you get those jade axes, and was that gold? Those photos looked like they were taken inside a Neolithic chamber of some sort."

"I regret putting those images on the net now. I showed you one of the axes, but I showed no one else, so they couldn't have been the motivation for the theft, if as you say it wasn't you. Whoever has them will be over the moon. You paid fifty thousand for a damaged one, but those I had were in pristine condition."

"I'm going to try to talk to Serge this afternoon. As his employer and closest thing he has to kin since he came back from Algeria, I may be allowed to see him. We have to find out where your things have got to and try to get them back."

Pen didn't know what the hell to think.

"Okay then, Monsieur Renault, perhaps we should keep in touch."

"I'll give you my mobile number so that you can reach me," replied Renault. "But I'll phone you when I know anything."

Pen left in a daze. His mind often went off at a tangent when he was behind the wheel, it did now. Renault's analysis sounded feasible, but all three of them being in the same army thing was weird.

Algeria had been independent for years — they must have all been kids at the time. Wasn't that always the way though, Pen sighed. He reflected, that he had never had to live through a war, never had to do national service. He had always been able to do more or less what he wanted. Born lucky, it would seem. But so many had no choice, they were just dragged off to die horribly or to suffer life-changing trauma in the cherry of their youth. Not that that excused everything. The colonies had always been immoral, theft, an unnecessary evil, totally inexcusable, and war seemed to bring out the worst in some people. Demobilised soldiers who had seen action could be dangerous men in a peaceable society. But then who was he to criticise? He had, only just this week, killed a dog in an unbelievably gruesome manner and committed, it now appeared, unwarranted arson.

Pen thought, what a hopeless race we were. In his mind, if the Upper Palaeolithic clans had peopled the childhood of our species, then we were now going through our adolescence, and a difficult time we were having of it. He imagined the kind of lives the Solutreans must have lived. Extreme winters, huge herds of reindeer, horse, bison, mammoth, and redoubtable predators like roaming packs spotted hyena. A hard life for sure, but straightforward compared with the kind of choices we have to make today. Should we ban nuclear power? What happens when the oil runs out? Are genetically modified organisms really dangerous? What becomes of our powerful armies and weaponry in peacetime because we dare not dismantle them? Every day a new moral dilemma raises its ugly head to grin at the species and say:

"You created me. Now what you going to do about it?"

Pen tended to be an optimist at heart. He trusted that when we eventually grew up, after a few more millennia, we would learn to see the errors of our ways — or, more to the point, the solutions to them. But, some days, it was touch and go.

Back in the empty house, Pen was trying to tidy things up when he heard a car pull up outside the kitchen door. He heard two car doors slam and then two more. He left the mop and bucket and went to the door. Through the panes of glass he could see two uniformed policemen. He had known they would be along sooner or later. When he pulled open the door he took in the grim expression on Inspector Bardot's moustachioed face. Then he checked out the other stern plain-clothes man standing behind two armed officers, who were observing him intently as if he might try to make a run for it.

One of the uniforms asked him if he was who he was, to which he said yes. Giving Bardot an exasperated look, he said:

"Come in."

He retreated into the kitchen. He could hear some words being exchanged, then the two plain-clothes men followed him through. Inspector Bardot said that the other man, Detective-Inspector Merle, was attached to the Direction Régionale des Affaires Culturelles and had come to have a few words with him. Pen looked at Merle and saw a dour, refined face with a long thin nose and a hard, disapproving mouth that made him look as though he was reacting to an awful smell but trying not to show it. He had on a well- fitting if slightly rumpled dark suit which Pen felt was more intimidating than the gendarmes uniforms. The Detective inspector reached into his brief-case and brought out a pink folder, which he held against his chest.

Merle had spent twenty-two years on the force, ten of them in cultural affairs, and was well aware that apart from the art thieves, most of the offenders he had to deal with did not consider themselves criminals, this made him dislike them even more. It was rare to catch anyone pillaging archaeological sites, and they were difficult to deal with if they were not caught red-handed, especially at an unknown site. Merle hoped that the fact that this was not your typical villain used to evading the police meant that it was going be easy to put pressure on him. He assumed a practised air of righteousness and authority.

"Monsieur Williamson," he said, looking at Pen with gimlet-grey eyes. "The email in which you describe the theft of undeclared archaeological artefacts that were in your possession has come to my notice." He placed the folder on the table. "This is a print-out of that communication with photographs of over two hundred objects that I would like information about. Especially some that look very much like a Neolithic treasure of considerable value, both archaeological and financial." Pen felt a slow chill creep into his gut. Keeping his face neutral, he said:

"Appearances can be deceptive, Inspector."

"Granted, Monsieur Williamson. So could you elucidate this for me?" He opened the folder and showed him the grainy photos taken in the cave, not brilliantly clear but good enough to get the idea of a large cache of what could quite easily be jade, some beautiful long flint blades, and perhaps gold, all laid out on what were evidently two flattened canvas bags. In the green glow of the flash a few swirly lines were discernible in the background.

"Well no, Inspector I can't, not right now. I can only say that it is not what it seems."

"That is a shame, Monsieur Williamson. You see, your aggressor insists that you had found a treasure of some importance."

"And you take the word of that nutter?"

"The evidence is building up against you, Monsieur Williamson. I have a warrant with me to search your premises and impound such items as may help with my research. I also intend to take you in for questioning, sir."

With that he called in the two gendarmes.

Pen had appealed to Bardot, but the older inspector had stood by unmoved as the gendarmes handcuffed him and put him in the back of the car. They then searched the house. Bardot waited with him, leaning against the vehicle. Pen asked if he might wait out there with him to have a smoke. Bardot graciously allowed him:

"Make the most of it, lad, you may well not be smoking for the next few days."

One of the mildest forms of persuasion, deprivation, old as the hills — poor, irregular meals, a cold, hard cell, humiliation, no outside contact. Well, two could play at that game. Pen had a stubborn streak: they would get nothing out of him like that. He said to Bardot,

"I am under medication and have to have my dressings changed tomorrow. May I get what I need, or is that also going to be used to persuade me to capitulate?"

Bardot looked at him and said,

"We have a doctor who will look you over if you need it."

Somewhere within the imposing white concrete walls of the Périgueux police headquarters, a meeting was taking place. Dominique Pasquier had dragged Max Poteau from another meeting at the museum in Les Eyzies to look over some images that he had been sent. They had been downloaded from a link discovered in the outgoing email folder in the computer of this English suspect, Pen Williamson. Pasquier and Poteau had worked together some years ago. A farmer had bulldozed a Neolithic dolmen in one of his fields to make it easier to plough. They managed to get a conviction, but to their consternation the farmer only had a small fine to pay. Max had been unable to salvage anything useful from the flattened site. The case had not ended well for either of them. The ageing archaeologist was close to retirement now. Pasquier understood that he resented being put out to grass, but that was how it worked in the civil service. He had done a lot of interesting work on the circulation of prestigious materials during the Neolithic and was officially considered an authority on the period. Pasquier had been heading up the Département des Affaires Culturelles in Aquitaine for the last six years. They both happened to be in the Dordogne now, and Max seemed the logical choice to investigate what this was all about. But Max's reaction was unexpected. He obviously considered the photographs, apparently taken in some kind of underground cavity, highly significant. He had become quite agitated while studying the dossier, and raised his voice unnecessarily when Pasquier said it looked like a recent clandestine discovery by some bloody local treasure hunter. Max was moaning on about the grainy nature of the images — a tantalising out-of-focus glimpse of a fabulous pile of Neolithic grave goods. They were both agitated, but not for the same reasons.

Pasquier put his hand on the archaeologist's forearm in a placating gesture, quite out of character for him. But he needed an objective professional opinion on this, and did not expect a show of emotion. He was aware, though, that for an archaeologist like Max these photographs might represent the chance of a lifetime – if, of course, they were genuine.

"Max, this is all we have to work with. What do you think, is it authentic?"

"Why? Shouldn't it be?" Max looked round and their eyes met. "Dominique, if this is what it looks like we have to do everything in our power to recover it. I have never seen a hoard of this apparent quality. Can I talk to the fellow who found it?"

"It is not as simple as that. If our chap did find this stuff, he will deny it straight off if we accuse him."

"I know what you are thinking, Dominique, and you're right, these people should be sent off to the galleys. But in a case like this don't you think we have more to gain by working with this fellow than by alienating him?"

"I can't stand them, Max. They're a self-seeking mercenary breed. I want to try it my way first."

"Ok ok, I know, but if all else fails I would have to advocate some kind of deal for the fellow, at least to secure the site. It *is* important, Dominique, and wherever it is, it may have lain undiscovered perhaps for ever if not for this stroke of luck. Bear that in mind."

"We'll see, Max. Merle brought the guy in earlier on. Let's see how he reacts before we make any decisions. But he is going to get a serious shake-down before it comes to talking of concessions." It was evening when they wandered out of the building together into the sodium orange glow of the damp city and shook hands at the top of the steps.

"He'll be here in a chilly cell for the night, with Inspector Merle's boys for company. We'll see how he responds to that. He's not a hardened criminal by all accounts, that type never is. We can always hope that he will repent. I'll be in touch when I have something for you." Max nodded, preoccupied, his head bent against the fine drizzle as he walked off to find his car, his mind drawn to those jade axes. The tantalising chance of that one last discovery and the research that it would throw up meant that he might yet go out in a blaze of glory.

It looked to him that they had only taken the computer from the house, apparently not interested in drugs, thank god. On arrival at Périgueux he was taken down two flights of stairs to a cold, bare, suitably intimidating cell, a white porcelain toilet with no seat set against one wall. It only took him a second to take it all in: the bed was a concrete shelf protruding out of one grey wall with a thin canvas and kapok mattress chucked over it. There were chipped white tiles on the wall that housed the toilet, but no graffiti. The people who were incarcerated here had nothing with them that could make a permanent mark. His own pockets had been emptied: they had taken his tobacco, his money, his phone, his shoe-laces and his belt, but – and this made him chuckle — left him enough bandage to hang himself from the sturdy-looking iron lighting fixture over the door. He sat on the hard bunk, the obnoxious stink of human waste and misery hardly disguised by the raw smell of bleach. He was working out how to deal with the next few days, when the door was pushed open noisily by a bored-looking gendarme in shirt-sleeves who asked him, almost politely, to follow him. He was led back up to another featureless grey room, this time with a table, three chairs and a two-way mirror on the wall, and locked in. Pen sat reflecting on the austere environment in which the police tend to work and on what an unglamorous job it must be, when the door was banged open again. Pen noticed already that, being deprived of outside stimulus, every sound took on unexpected dimensions: right then they seemed to be echoing from the end of a tunnel in the harsh white light.

It was Merle with another suit who did not bother to identify himself. Without preamble, Merle said:

"Listen to me, Williamson. We know that you found something. What we want is for you to tell us where you found it and where it is now." Pen did not look at the policeman but said quietly:

"You have got absolutely nothing on me, Monsieur Merle, the word of a would-be murderer and rapist and some photos off the internet. Get realistic — I can ride this out. You need more leverage than tobacco deprivation and a few cold nights courtesy of the Republic."

"You are not listening to me, Williamson. You would not be the first person to go to prison on evidence supplied from the internet."

"Well, first you have to have some evidence that will bear scrutiny. What makes you think it is not a hoax?"

"Your house was burgled, from what your email said. We saw the breach in the wall of your workshop. It leads into a small room with lots of empty shelves and piles of archaeological publications."

"It was a storeroom that I'm thinking of enlarging."

"All of those photographs on the internet came from you, Monsieur Williamson."

"Yes, well, that's true. But originally it was an email that someone else sent to me, asking me to forward it on to anyone who might be interested. And I still think it was a hoax."

"We are getting nowhere like this. Perhaps a few days in the cell downstairs might help jog your memory."

"Perhaps. But I think you are wasting time for all of us. Might I see a doctor, please? My dressings will need changing."

"It is too late now. It will have to wait until tomorrow."

Merle got up to go to the door. But the other man, who had so far said nothing, piped up:

"Just a minute." He turned to Pen and continued, "Look I work for the Musée National de la Préhistoire. As you can imagine we are very interested in your discovery."

"What discovery would that be, Monsieur? I'm sorry, I didn't get your name."

"No need to be sorry, I didn't give it. Look, we have seen the photos and to us they look like one of the most important hoards of Neolithic grave goods to have been found in France in recent years. We would be very interested in recovering it and excavating the site. Most of the more interesting sites were pillaged around the end of the nineteenth century. This could be a unique opportunity."

"You must be joking! This oaf is threatening to throw the book at me."

"Don't push your luck, Williamson," said Merle, glowering.

"I need a cigarette to think about this," said Pen.

"Well, you will have to do without."

The suit broke in:

"Wait a minute, Inspector. Monsieur Williamson, would you be willing to talk?"

"I have to remind you that I don't know who you are."

"Sorry. I am Dominique Pasquier, assistant director for regional cultural affairs, affiliated to the Musée d'Aquitaine in Bordeaux."

"Well Monsieur Pasquier, I would like to know what charges are being brought against me."

Merle spoke up:

"You are being held on suspicion of the illegal excavation of important archaeological remains and criminal dealing in archaeological artefacts for financial gain."

"For Christ's sake, Inspector, how do you expect to make any of that stick?"

"Don't you worry. We have your computer. Let's see what we can wring out of that first."

"I have to admit I am also curious to see that," said Pen, feeling sick again.

"Monsieur Williamson," said Pasquier, "we have certain powers. That is, we may be prepared to drop certain charges for your help in this matter."

"Wait a minute!" Merle was getting upset: "You can't go making deals with this kind of customer!"

Pen looked at them both:

"I'm not sure I could be of any help to myself let alone anyone else at the moment. First," he went on, "I would like a cigarette and access to my medical cabinet, I need pain relief and to change my dressing."

Merle interrupted him:

"I vote we throw him back in the cells until tomorrow sometime, then discuss this after we've had a good night's sleep." Pen showed no reaction to the suggestion. It was after all what he had been expecting. But Pasquier was not to be put off.

"I'm sorry, Inspector, but I was brought in rather precipitously on this case, when the importance of the find became evident. And I have hardly any background information. Can you give me an outline of Williamson's previous criminal record please?" Merle didn't seem to like the way things were going, but then neither did Pen. The idea of not spending a night in the guts of the commissariat was too appealing. He knew that was the intention of this manoeuvre, to soften him up and get him to admit to something for which they only had circumstantial evidence. They didn't know where the site was so how could they claim he had robbed it?

"He has no police record in France," Merle almost spat.

"Then it could be difficult to detain him on the evidence at our disposal, couldn't it?"

"We can detain whoever we want for at least forty-eight hours without having to inform anyone under the anti-terrorist laws."

Merle looked smug and menacing, a tedious spider at home at the hub of its inelegant but intimidating web.

"Just take me back and perhaps I can sleep the headache off on the concrete bunk," said Pen. Pasquier remained predictably silent. Merle called in the gendarme, who ushered Pen from the room and returned him to the cell, it seemed even colder in there than before. And of course there was no blanket.

The last thing Pen had imagined when he found the hidden fox-hole was that it would lead him here. The thing that surprised him the most was that he hardly felt frightened by his situation — resigned was the word. Even a sleepless night or two in a cold cell with nothing to distract him and no fags hadn't crushed him. He was determined to brave it out with Merle. As for Pasquier, Pen wouldn't trust him as far as he could throw the cracked porcelain toilet he had for company.

It was the door rattling open that woke him suddenly from a terrible dream. Sophie was covered in blood, she had been screaming at him, but he couldn't hear what she was saying. Alice had been abducted... and then he was awake. The white light was still glaring at him from above the door, he was disorientated and cold, with a terrible taste in his mouth and a crashing headache. Apart from that he felt fine. It was another gendarme this time, with a plastic mug of watery coffee, no milk, no sugar. As he left he tipped his head and bid him good morning with a knowing smirk. Merle must have given orders to keep him under pressure.

Half-an-hour later the coffee boy was back. He collected the empty mug and told Pen to follow him. He was taken to the same featureless interrogation room as before, where Pasquier was waiting for him alone. He looked agitated.

"Monsieur Williamson," he began, then looked down at his shoes for a second as if gathering his thoughts, "has the night brought counsel?"

"Very well thanks, and you?"

"Monsieur Williamson," Pasquier started again, "yesterday we got off on the wrong foot. Inspector Merle likes to get his way — this is his territory after all. Please take a seat. I have brought you some cigarettes." He held out a new packet of ready-rolled and produced a lighter.

"Well, you have learned your role well, Monsieur Pasquier, which is lucky for me. I thought you might have forgotten the cigarettes." Pasquier watched in silence as Pen lit up, inhaled, and exhaled long and slow, savouring the smoke as only the dependant can: "Monsieur Pasquier, although I am grateful for the cigarette, I'm afraid I feel absolutely no inclination to inform you about anything that may incriminate me."

"I understand that. However my colleagues at the museum believe that you may have stumbled upon an exceptionally important Neolithic burial site. The grave goods look to be outstanding and to indicate immense prestige, the Neolithic equivalent of royalty if you like. We want to excavate that site and I am here to negotiate the location with you."

"Well, I don't negotiate anything from a prison cell. If you had anything on me, I would have been charged by now. So your bargaining position is rather weak, wouldn't you say?"

"We are prepared to drop any eventual charges that are associated with this case in exchange for your cooperation."

"Don't you think I can see through that, Monsieur Pasquier, or do I get it in writing?"

"Better than that, Monsieur Williamson. This is what I propose…"

An hour later Pen was at home standing under a hot shower, his head wounds protected by an improvised shower cap. He was wondering what he had got himself into.

17

France's national prehistory museum, the Musée Nationale de la Préhistoire, is situated in the tiny town of Les Eyzies, only a handful of kilometres from Pen's home. He had removed his bandages leaving a sticking plaster up by his hairline covering the stitches. But his face was still alarmingly swollen and vividly coloured, as if painted in by an Impressionist on a bad day. The scabs of the shotgun wounds itched atrociously. The paracetamol had helped, though, and he felt almost normal as he walked up the steep little lane to the entrance of the astonishing modern edifice that had been carved out of the rockface to house the collections and the research facility.

Pen had always loved visiting the original museum next door, installed in a remarkable medieval château also built high up in the cliff. It had been designed to initiate a visiting public into the captivating world of their recently discovered ancestors. It was also a treasure house of beautiful things.

The new building seemed to house a self satisfied hymn to archaeology, an altar where all the great French archaeologists past and present had their most important work displayed. When Pen had brought some visiting friends along shortly after it had opened, they had been politely bored by it all. Pen couldn't blame them. He found it a bit pompous too, big and airy and light, and devoid of many of the treasures that he had so enjoyed in the old one, but to an initiate it was a remarkable place. He had got into the habit of going there with finds that he had trouble classifying. He would usually have a few flints in his pocket that he would try to match to something in the huge perplexing panoply of artefacts.

He was met in the large entrance hall by a disturbingly eager Pasquier, who had been talking to two bespectacled archaeologists, the older one sporting a neatly-trimmed, mostly grey beard. The younger one peered myopically out of his carefully neglected beard framed by abundant curly light brown locks. Pasquier introduced them both as specialists in Neolithic studies. The older one, looked dour but his young partner was all smiles, almost reverential, which made Pen feel uneasy.

"Well, it all seems okay so far, Monsieur Pasquier. But I don't see the lawyer."

"He'll be here soon. Don't worry."

They went through the foyer to a corridor and a suite of offices. The younger of the two archaeologists addressed him respectfully:

"We really appreciate what you are doing, Monsieur Williamson. We saw the photographs and were most impressed."

"I haven't done anything yet, and I'm not likely to if the lawyer doesn't turn up soon." Just then a young woman pushed the door open. Clinging lightly to it, she swung the top half of her body into the room, and, sotto voce announced the arrival of the tardy advocate.

"Hello everybody," said the tall, smart, dark-suited lawyer. Pen thought ominously that he looked more like an undertaker than a solicitor. He made no apology for being late but shook everyone's hands and exchanged glances with Pasquier. He took in Pen's impressive colouring, but made no remark.

"Down to business then," he began, digging into his briefcase.

"Monsieur Pasquier, I have drawn up the document that you asked for. It just remains for all of the signatories to read through it and sign and date each page, and it will become legal and binding."

The essence of it was that the cultural authorities would drop all potential charges against Pen in exchange for the location of a site of which he had knowledge. There were five copies of the three-page document. Pen still didn't like it, but he tried for one more condition before signing.

"If you are happy with what you are about to get, may I be involved?"

"On the site you mean?" asked Pasquier.

"Yes, in any eventual excavations."

Pasquier looked at the older archaeologist, who raised his neat eyebrows and said he would be honoured to have the *inventeur* of such a potentially prestigious site present at the excavation — indeed he thought his presence might be invaluable.

The archaeologists looked smug, and little wonder. They were about to get the site of a lifetime, even if it had been defiled, given to them on a plate. He had always seen archaeology as the most romantic of the sciences, though curiously it was rare to read an analysis or a report that was willing to interpret the findings in any but the most rigorously barren terms; there was never any poetry there. Pen wondered if they regretted denying themselves an artist's insight to help transform the mountain of information they had accumulated over the last hundred and eighty years, into the tangible image of a series of socially active cultures. For the Neanderthals the evidence pointed to a developed society, with territorial limits and long-range exchanges between individuals. There was no quantifiable proof of the higher cognitive skills of those early prehistoric people or the uses they put them to: language or music for example, or art, dance or medicine. Although they obviously had them all, there was no irrefutable evidence. As far as science could tell, they may have been just one step away from other socially grouping animals.

Archaeologists today were the ones who had the right to contradict unfounded flights of fancy. Hypothesis followed hypothesis until finally the accepted theory had become "we just don't know". Pen felt this made the discipline melancholic. Max Poteau certainly looked melancholic, though his younger colleague still seemed keen.

There ensued much eager signing. Pen still felt nervous, but threw caution to the wind and signed anyway. He had called Sophie's mobile earlier and tried Denise too, but with no luck. He did get through to Noël, who suggested that it was still too early to talk to Sophie. Pen asked him to explain what was going on, or at least how they were. Noël told him that they were recovering but Alice had not been to school and Sophie was livid when she wasn't in tears. He was silent when Pen recounted his night at the police station and his deal with Mr Pasquier. Noël seemed shocked. He croaked, "Don't trust the bastards." But that was exactly what Pen was doing. He just hoped his amnesty held.

Pasquier now glared at Pen, and said:

"What did you expect, the police to come pouring in and drag you away as soon as you had signed? You could have made this deal yesterday and saved yourself a lot of trouble."

"Behave as badly as you wish, Pasquier, the way this is worded you still have nothing on me."

"You could always go back to Merle if you prefer his company," said Pasquier. The archaeologists looked shocked by this exchange.

"Dominique," said the older one "what are you trying to do?"

"No. You are right. But Monsieur Williamson has driven a hard bargain. I just thought that he should not expect to get away with everything without a rap on the knuckles. But don't you worry Monsieur Williamson, my mistake. We will of course keep to our deal."

"Yeah, well, when do I get my computer back?"

"That is Inspector Merle's domain, I'm afraid, not mine."

"Well I'm off home you can stuff your little game Monsieur

Pasquier." Pen snatched up the papers from the table and headed for the door.

"Okay, okay, Monsieur Williamson, I'll see what I can do."

"Listen to me and listen well. I don't give a flying fuck for you and your team of ghouls. Go and find your own pile of bones. I'll take my luck with Merle. At least we understand each other."

Max spoke up:

"So much of our work begins with fortuitous finds like yours, Monsieur Williamson."

"People like him have been pillaging the best archaeological sites here for a hundred and fifty years," said Pasquier, "to me, he's just another grave robber."

"The problem lies with the rich market," said Max, "not with the poor diggers. If there were no buyers ready to take the stuff, people would not be so ready to hunt it out."

Pen rounded on the archaeologist: "Hold on a minute! I don't sell anything. I'm a serious collector and a passionate amateur palaeontologist, and I didn't hunt the site out, it was a chance discovery." He found himself telling an abridged story of the fox-hole. He left out Noël's part in it and the location, but mentioned the piece of jade found in the river and finding the first flakes of flint.

The three people in the room with him listened without interrupting, apart from grunting their disbelief as he took them down the fox-hole, claiming that it was he who had been trapped, had dug himself out, then gone back the next day better-equipped. He described how he had found the six skeletons and the swirling patterns on the walls. The two scientists looked thrilled and exchanged excited looks, but Pasquier looked shocked. Pen ended with a description of the treasure.

"Everything was taken as soon as it was found, stolen by that mad bastard that works for Renault. I have no idea what the hell he did with it, nor why he tried to kill me."

Now that he had got it out, he felt drained. The truth was that he realised he wanted people to see his discovery. He had never seen how he would be able to own up to knowing about the site without incriminating himself — but that problem had solved its self.

"Where is the site?" asked Pasquier.

"Even if I tell you, you would never find it."

"Allow us to draw our own conclusion."

"No, I will take you there. But even well-equipped for pot-holing you may find that you're a little large to get through the tight passage to the chamber."

As he left the museum, Pen felt lighter in a way he couldn't put his finger on. After the attack, he somehow couldn't really take Merle's threats seriously. He was worried about the girls, though, and needed to see them now. In the village just below the museum there was a café with a covered terrace. Pen didn't know what time it was probably just after lunch time but he ordered a double-whisky with ice. At the bar, he called Sophie's mobile number. To his surprise she answered.

"I thought you were supposed to be coming to see us yesterday." She sounded distant, still turned against him.

"Yes, well, I got detained."

"It doesn't matter much, Pen. I won't be coming back to live at your place. I couldn't bear it after all that's happened. Alice is so scared she'll never go back there. At the moment she's seeing a child psychiatrist. She refuses to sleep alone, because she's frightened to go to sleep. What did you do, Pen, to bring that man into our lives?"

"I just worked for Renault. He was Renault's man, he didn't like me. But he was mad, Sophie, I didn't have to do anything to make him do what he did. And besides he's been put away, he won't be coming back."

"Don't call me again, Pen. I'll call you when I feel better about it but I think we should both get used to living our own lives." And she hung up.

"Sophie!" he called. But the line was dead. He looked around the café, now more or less empty. He chucked back his whisky, left a note that more than covered it on the bar, and hurried out to the car park. The cards were still pilling up against him. Sophie should have been worried about him, caring, he had been beaten and shot for Christ's sake. To add to his disquiet, she had never apologised for cheating on him, it was as if she considered it her right. He couldn't help wondering if there had been others.

Back on the road, he went through all the events that had bred this nightmare. Would it ever end? None of it had anything to do with the treasure, although it had begun with it. The robbery would still have been committed, and he would still have been just as determined to get his stuff back. He certainly regretted killing the dog, it made him sick just thinking about it, he wondered if that had actually pushed Serge over the edge. It looked now that the fire had been a mistake. He regretted mostly not injuring the madman more though, to shut him up. There would be a court case, more police. And it could all get even more complicated.

He had no intention of going home. He was sick and tired of the whole affair and needed a bit of time away from it. He was trying to decide where to go when his mobile rang. He looked at the screen: Medea. He nearly didn't answer, then had a change of heart.

"Hiya, Medea, you don't call me often."

"Not for lack of wanting to, I can tell you."

"Can I call that a compliment?"

"I call it lust."

"Don't tempt me, Medea."

"Hey Pen, what's up? You sound a bit frayed there."

"Yeah, well, I've been having a bit of a hard time of it recently."

"Well, you and I have a long outstanding engagement, remember? How about coming to Périgueux? There's a new Japanese, just opened. I'll pay."

"You will not! I owe you, remember?"

"Does that mean yes?"

"I would be delighted to, Medea, but I warn you: I don't look my old self."

"I'm sure you'll do."

"I'll be about an hour." Pen surprised himself, but what harm could it do? — as long as Medea didn't get any big ideas into her head.

He got into the little city just as everyone was pouring out. Tangled up in the rush-hour traffic, he cursed his luck again. The town had three single carriageway bridges allowing one to cross the narrow river to its south and there was a string of choked up roundabouts leading to each. Pen was in no hurry. He just had no patience with it all.

The lift up to Medea's increased his sense of something illicit about this visit. It was the first time he had been there for any reason other than work. She let him in when he rang at the street door, and when he stepped out of the lift she opened the door to her apartment and came to greet him. But she stopped short of kissing him on both cheeks when she saw his bruising.

"Okay, so you've been fighting, or was this just a car accident?"

He gave a sad smile and said, "You should see the other guy."

"No. You're serious?" Pen just looked at her until she shook her head and ushered him into her tiny flat.

"Drink?" she asked.

"Yeah, I already started."

"Good boy. Whisky do? I don't have a great choice."

"Whisky is good."

"Listen, Pen. I did what you asked but there are so many recipients of that message by now that the only way to really stop it is to contact each one and ask them to stop sending them around. And even then, the web has a life of its own."

"Don't worry your pretty little head about it, Medea. The police had it already." Looking at her Pen realised that she was really a very pretty girl in a slutty-chic sort of way. Her hair was all black now, shoulder-length, but she had done something to give it a sort of spiky volume; she had on a short black military-style jacket over a low-cut tight white top. A red tartan pleated miniskirt matching her lipstick, worn over her thin black leggings accentuated the look. She was petite but well formed, and seemed less chubby than Pen remembered. He guessed that she had dressed to provoke, rather successfully.

"Oh god, it wasn't them that did that to you?" she said, gesturing at his face.

"Medea," he said: "do you mind if we talk about this another time? I've had it up to the back teeth for the moment."

"Lucky 'it'," she said, handing him a generous glass of whisky, no ice, but there was a bottle of water on the low table in front of her sofa. They sat down, her with her black clad held knees primly together. He grinned despite himself.

"Why don't you have a boyfriend, Medea? You seem obsessed by sex."

"I love sex, but most men are such jerks when it comes to relationships. I'm still waiting for Prince Charming. I'm still young you know."

They ate Japanese in an empty restaurant, in a minimal pared-down décor of grey and red that reminded Pen of the Hotel Drouot, where only a week ago he had watched Renault buy that jade axe. He realised that Medea was dressed to fit in, a perfect Manga princess. They drank saké and laughed together, and walked back to Medea's apartment through the empty streets.

In the lift Medea did something with the buttons and it came to a shuddering stop between floors. She smiled at Pen and snuggled up to him, putting her arms around him and pressing her hard little body against him. Her eyes catching his, she turned her face up and kissed him. He opened his lips and let her tongue find his. She tasted slightly sweet from the saké, and he realised that he wanted her. She was giving off a mild musky scent, intoxicating him far more than the alcohol. Their images melting away into the distance multiplied the bodies that he was taking blissful pleasure in undressing.

Lying in bed smoking together next morning, he asked her:

"Have you made love in that lift before?"

"Not exactly, but I have often fantasized about it. And once I worked out how to stop it between floors, I masturbated in there."

"You what?"

"I was so excited it didn't take a moment."

"Well, consider me naïve, but I never imagined girls like you would masturbate in public places."

"Well, so now you know."

They thought they would go to a café for breakfast, but when they got there they found it was one o'clock in the afternoon and all the croissants were finished. So they went for a light lunch of poached rainbow trout on toasted brioche with lamb's lettuce and a dry white wine, then back to the apartment to luxuriate in each other's arms.

Life could have gone on like that for Pen, but while they were dozing the afternoon away, his phone rang from somewhere in the pile of clothes on the floor. When he finally sifted it out, there was a text from Renault:

Have news, call me back.

Medea watched him dressing with a cheeky smile on her face:

"Well, you look a bit better than you did when you washed up on my doorstep."

"I feel better Medea. Am I allowed to come back some time, or am I just another jerk that will get a rating on Facebook?"

"You can't help your gender, but I might just let you back in — if you don't keep me waiting too long." He grabbed the duvet and pulled it up to her chin, covering those inviting breasts with their delectable dark little nipples, then kissed her on the nose, as he would Alice, and went out to find Renault.

On his way back he called in at Alice's school. It was home-time and the children were starting to come out. He saw the Peugeot, in need of a wash as usual, parked with the other parents' more cared-for cars. He pulled the truck into a vacant space and went over, but Sophie must have already gone to the gate to get Alice; so he waited by the car. When they turned up, it was Denise holding Alice's hand. Alice dropped her achingly sweet little satchel and ran to him with her arms outstretched. Pen swept her up and they did a little jig together, Alice giggling with a gap-toothed smile brightening up her face, him with relief that felt like coming up for air after a long held breath.

Denise was smiling as she said, "Pen, you look much better than I expected."

"I feel better than I expected to myself. And now that I have seen my little *écolière* here, I feel on ze top of ze world." He spun Alice around again, but she looked seriously at him and said, "Papa, what will happen to the man who attacked us?"

"He has been shut away in prison for ever, Alice. We will never see him again." She searched his bruised face for the truth, then buried her head in his shoulder and sobbed.

"Where did you go, Papa?"

"I went to hospital, then I had to help the police, sweetheart."

"Mama says that we are not going home."

"Well, it is my home, Alice. And when I've finished cleaning it up and redecorating it, you will be back."

"But not to sleep at night," said Alice, eyes wide.

"Not if you don't want to, Alice." Denise looked at him pityingly and said:

"You could take her out at the weekends."

Pen smiled and put Alice down. He said, "Give Maman a big kiss for me," and tapped her on the bottom. "I'll phone tomorrow." He watched as they got into the little car. Alice was wiping her eyes with the back of one small hand and smiling at him through the window as they drove off. He took his tobacco out and stood there smoking for a while, thinking about how he regretted not hacking Sergio to pieces.

18

On the phone, Renault said the police had not let him see his handy-man who was still in a locked hospital ward and apparently in a bad way. Strangely, that gave Pen no joy. The police had questioned him about the email that was circulating. But he had been unable to help them and they had let it drop. Renault went on to tell him that he had been to see Vincent, and that something had happened at the manse. They needed to meet up and talk.

So he went round. Renault took him into the kitchen and produced an expensive-looking bottle of Burgundy. Pen didn't care to get befuddled around Renault, but he felt he owed him something and no longer wished to seem ungrateful.

"All right, Maurice," he said as he took the glass: "I'm ready to accept that you had nothing to do with the theft. And I'm sorry I accused you."

"And I, dear boy, I feel responsible for everything."

Pen's injured forehead crinkled painfully as he acknowledged his mistake. He had certainly misread this unusual old man; but then reading people had never been one of his strong points. He was regretting it now, he had always been too impulsive. He could only justify himself by re-examining the evidence. It had all pointed to Maurice Renault. The old man looked pained, and Pen had the irrational fear that he had just read his thoughts. Then Renault began going over the essentials of his visit to Vincent's place. Vincent had come out to meet him on the steps with an ugly bruise discolouring one side of his face — nothing compared to Pen's, but all the same. When Renault pressed him, Vincent had explained that he had done some kind of stupid deal with a wealthy Swiss collector that had gone sour. The guy had turned out to be influential and ruthless, and had sent a couple of heavies around to sort it out. Vincent had muttered something about never trust the bloody Swiss. He was at a loss to what the trouble was about, and the guys didn't bother to explain themselves. They just collected all the stones and bone implements they could find in his house to compensate for whatever it was, and when Vincent protested one of them hit him. His dog Custer had gone for the assailant and been hit so hard with one of the stone axes that he had lost the use of his hind legs. Before leaving, one of the thugs had said that Vincent should consider the dog's fate, sprawled as it was on the rugs in his parlour with a broken back, as a warning of what would happen to him if he thought of contacting the police.

Unable to help himself, Pen muttered,

"Custer's last stand."

His guess about the deal that had gone sour was that it was his stolen collection. He no longer had the will or the wherewithal to do anything about it. He had already discovered that he was a stone-picker, not a commando. But he would take serious pleasure in visiting Vincent and rubbing his face in it.

Thoughtfully, Renault took a mouthful of wine. Savouring it and gazing into his glass, he said:

"Listen, Pen, Serge was not a bad sort. Unsophisticated, a bit rough, but he was honest when I first knew him. He was once taken prisoner for a week. It was Vincent who eventually found him. Did some terrible things to get the information from some of the local people, but nobody respects human rights in wartime. It came out later that both sides were torturing prisoners, sometimes raping them, either for information or, just from brutal lust. It seems Vincent was involved in that too. In the end we took three jeeps into the hills and pulled Serge out. They were holding him in a tiny village. Kept him tied up with a sack over his head the whole time. They wouldn't let him use the latrine. From time to time they poured water over the sack, which made it hard for him to breathe but kept him alive. He had been cut up a bit, but it was the sack over his head that drove him over the edge. The thing is that no one spoke French in the village apart from a little boy, so he wasn't interrogated. But the boy said they wanted revenge for the desecration of a nearby shrine." Renault's face seemed to droop with the memory, his skin sagged like melted wax, his eyes were fixed on the sheen of the wine in his glass.

"You see, it was my fault. I had sent him there to go and check out a promising site I had heard about, with this other young soldier. He came back with stories of magnificent marble statues and carvings all over the walls. When it all came out, I was sent home too and didn't see the others for over a year."

Renault paused a moment, then took a deep breath and continued:

"Anyway, someone had beaten us to it. The marbles had gone when Serge and I went back together. Then he was taken at gun-point by some Arabs, and I did nothing to help him. I was worried that if I went after him that they would shoot both of us, or worse. I've been trying to atone for it for years."

Another pause.

"The next day we went storming up into the hills and dragged back some wretched shepherds, who eventually put us on the right track. It was Vincent who was really responsible for finding him. He doesn't look like it now, but he was a vindictive, cruel bastard in those days, and like many of our lads hated the Arabs."

Renault looked up to see if Pen was following. Pen held his gaze steady. Renault took a deep breath, but made no effort to drink. Devoid of his confident air of control he suddenly looked an old man. Pen broke the silence:

"He still is a vindictive cruel bastard. On top of it all, you know your man Serge has put the cultural authorities on my back. They've seen the photos on the internet and they're insisting that I lead them to the burial cave."

Renault said:

"They'll be looking for the grave goods too. That would put the wind up whoever it is that has your stuff. No museum would touch any of it, and with the photos flying around it will be untouchable by anyone but criminals, and even then at only a fraction of their real value."

"It may be difficult to convince any non-collector of their real value," Pen replied.

"You're joking. With the report on the last Drouot sale, anyone can find out with three little pecks on a smart-phone."

"If they know where to look."

"Oh come on, Pen."

"Hmm."

"Maurice," said Pen later, when the bottle was empty, "can I take a look at your jade axe?"

"Yes of course, come on up. Feel free to spend as much time with the collection as you wish."

Pen wandered around the glass cases, opening them and taking pieces out to look at in the shrouded cabinet lighting, while Renault disappeared into his room.

He discovered that he was taking little pleasure in this new-found liberty with the collection. Pieces that might have sent him into raptures before now failed to stir his emotions.

Renault returned with a tray and another bottle of the same wine and their glasses, and some smoked ham, cheese, bread, and dark grapes. He set it all carefully on a table in the gallery. Wrapped in a white tea-cloth was the dark green jade axe. They sat in silence, while Renault uncorked the wine and Pen let his hands run over the soft contours of that voluptuous, ancient treasure — until finally, un-bidden tears of loss and frustration began running down his cheeks.

Renault affected not to notice and poured, helping them to food and pouring again when necessary. Eventually Pen left, unexpectedly alleviated.

19

Merle phoned early next morning, waking him. Pen had a thick head, due to last nights red wine. The phone was in the next room, but with all the recent events Pen felt disinclined to let it ring — it might be Sophie. He stumbled through, naked, feeling wretched.

"Yes?"

"We need to see you today."

"Who's we?"

"The archaeologists are getting impatient."

"You mean you want me to take you to the burial cave."

"We have a deal."

"I have a hangover."

"Tough!"

Pen hung up. The phone rang again two minutes later.

"Who the hell is it?"

"Do we have to come and get you, Monsieur Williamson?"

"Yes, but you will need protective clothing, lamps, a shovel and lunch somewhere nice. Oh, and a pair of overalls for me too."

Pen showered, put the kettle on and put two aspirin into a glass of water. He didn't shave: it seemed that it was something self-respecting archaeologists didn't need to bother with.

He knew that the flints were an extension of his obsessive child-hood tendency to classify and collect. He couldn't see how collecting them might be detrimental to others; he never hunted on any offi-cially recognised pitch or known site. Yet here he was, trying to work off a hangover and supposedly preparing to pay for being the most successful Neolithic treasure-hunter in recent years. It infuriated him; but he couldn't work up any guilt.

He had never suffered a nervous breakdown. But now, as he watched the two cars pulling into his track, he wondered whether he might not be losing it.

Merle climbed out of a dark blue Peugeot and stood leaning on the open door as Pen came out of the house. There was another person in the front of his car, behind which were the two archaeologists in a white, long-wheel-based LandRover Defender. Merle opened the back door of the car for him and said:

"You look rough, Monsieur Williamson."

"I'm not well."

"Self-inflicted."

"Life's not been easy of late."

"Brought it on yourself."

Pen turned on his heel and headed back to the house. The other door of Merle's car opened and a large, serious-looking man with close-cropped hair climbed out. At the same time the younger of the two archaeologists jumped out of their LandRover smiling, non-committally.

"Monsieur Williamson, how nice to see you again," said the curly young man: "we would like you to travel with us in the LandRover if you don't mind the discomfort."

"Sounds lots better than travelling with Punch and Judy over there, thank you I will."

The archaeologist studied the ground on the way back to their vehicle, while Merle glared at them peevishly. The fat guy watched from the other side of the car passively, his hands in his pockets. Pen reached for the door before anyone could open it for him and climbed into the passenger seat. The curly-headed archaeologist clambered into the back with the shovels and other gear.

"You haven't locked up your house, Monsieur Williamson," said Max, looking into Pen's ruined face with concern.

"Call me Pen, please — there is nothing left to steal in my place, you should know that. Take the next left, we are going to St Léon. Can you tell me why Merle is here? I expected Pasquier."

"Monsieur Pasquier is occupied elsewhere at the moment, and Inspector Merle was worried that you might not keep your side of the bargain if he didn't insist." Merle was following close behind. Pen guessed that not being in control was pissing him off; but at least Max and Curly were civil. This was after all quite an occasion, and he didn't intend to let Merle spoil his moment of glory. He folded his arms tightly across his chest to hide the slight tremor in his hands that he had noticed since Merle's phone-call.

Curly piped up from the back as they turned down into the lane that led below the château.

"La Rochette, Max, that's René's dig. It's along this rock face somewhere, towards the far end, mostly Aurignacian, I think." Max turned to them and grinned. Pen could feel their mounting excitement. It was infectious; he was feeling slightly better himself.

"You can take this vehicle right up to the foot of the cliff," he said, realising that Merle's car would have to stop when the navigable track ran out.

They were getting into their overalls when the two officials turned up. Merle looked to be in a dark mood but he didn't say anything. Pen grabbed a shovel and led the way up the overgrown embankment. The great boulder of fallen rock was a clear landmark. But Pen did not comment on it even when, rounding it and reaching the foot of the rock face, he was standing on the pile of spoil from their digging. He wanted to see how well they had camouflaged their work, and wondered if the archaeologists would spot anything. There were quite a lot of new fallen leaves which helped hide the mess. They had done a good enough job. Without his help, the archaeologists would be hard-pressed to find the entrance.

"Excuse me," said Pen to the younger of the two, who was eagerly scanning the cliff before them, "I'm sorry, but what's your name? We were introduced at the museum but I've a terrible memory for names. I'm tired of thinking of you as Curly."

"I'm Daniel," the man smiled, reaching out a callused hand, "pleased to meet you." Pen shook his hand, pleasantly reassured, and smiled.

"We'll have to dig, Daniel, and there's a rather large boulder blocking the tunnel which will have to be moved."

"Where exactly?"

"Right here," said Pen, planting his shovel in the packed yellow mound of rotted sandstone on which they were standing.

It was hard work convincing Daniel and Max that it was no use going through all the flakes that the 'foxes' had already picked over, but they finally got the point. When they got down to the rock blocking the tunnel, there was a bit of a dilemma. There was obviously no room for both of them to squeeze into the hole to lever out the boulder, and neither man was strong enough to lift it out alone. They were discussing enlarging the hole towards the down-slope to create a ramp to walk the block up between them, when Merle's silent companion stepped up to the edge of the hole. He removed his jacket and handed it to Max.

"Give me a little space," he requested, in an unexpectedly soft voice. Pen scrambled out of the hole as if there were a nest of scorpions down there, and Merle's companion hopped lightly in and took his place. Looking down on him as he stooped, Pen realised that the minder, whom he had taken for fat, was in fact powerfully built.

So that's why Merle brought him, thought Pen, not to intimidate me, but to save time. He was feeling really alive again, and took up a position near the hole checking his foot-hold ready to help with the boulder as the big guy hauled it up. Daniel was standing back a little to watch.

The sturdy man seemed to struggle down there for a second or two, straining and jostling as if the thing was alive and fighting him, his shirt stretched tight across his bowed back. Then, with a soft grunt, the chunk of stone was sitting up on the lip of the hole as if it had always been there. Pen reached his hand down with a grin and helped the guy out of the hole, but his help went completely unacknowledged. Merle's colleague now went discreetly to the back of the group, where he brushed off his hands, crossed them over his crotch, and stood quietly to watch the proceedings.

Pen dropped down into the hole again. By the time he had removed half-a-dozen shovels of sand, he disappeared into the tunnel. He resurfaced almost immediately and called for lamps and trowels.

"And, Daniel," he added, "get yourself some gear and follow me." With that, Pen wormed himself back into the claustrophobic depths under the towering rock-face.

Daniel was close behind him. Pen helped him negotiate the rock-fall. They then had only to squeeze through that last gap, and they would be up in the cave.

It had been late morning outside, the sky clear with a tang of autumn chill. A slight breeze had been enough to make the dead leaves spin in lazy drifts down to the valley floor. It was even cooler in the lingering shadow of the cliff and a little damp, but in the cramped space under that mass of rock Pen could feel the sweat trickling under his t-shirt; his face was hot and damp. Scooting up the inclined slab first, he wriggled through into the high, open cavity. He took the pack Daniel had brought, then tugged on the archaeologist's arms to help his more corpulent body squeeze through.

They swept their lights over the walls in silence, each lost in his own world. Pen looked for the skeletons, but couldn't immediately comprehend what he was seeing: part of the floor had changed. He crept across it, careful this time to disturb as little as possible, but something was wrong: the skeletons were no longer there. He let out a low groan.

"What? What is it?" asked Daniel, emerging from his reverie.

"I'm not really sure," said Pen, not knowing what to say or how this new turn of events might change things.

He asked Daniel for a more powerful light, and was passed a big, flat torch. Pen shone it up the shaft above them and saw a pale area of fresh rock about four metres above them.

"The sandstone is rotten in places," he said. "The skeletons are over by that wall, but they must have been buried under a fall since I was here." Looking around, he could see that the whole floor had been sprayed with debris, mostly sand but also some large chunks of rock. It made him feel suddenly sick. He guessed that the digging with Noël, plus the rock-fall that Noël had provoked, and then opening this closed space to the outside air, had somehow changed the balance that had kept it stable for the last few thousand years. They could so easily both have died in here.

"This is a dangerous place to hang around. We don't know how much more is likely to come down."

"Wait, I have to take some photographs." Daniel rooted around in his pack and brought out a sophisticated camera. Pen retreated to the opening, shining the torch up the shaft on the lookout for signs of imminent trouble. Daniel's gaze followed the beam of light and he exclaimed,

"My god, look at that! The shaft must go right up to the château above us."

"Yes, and there seem to be other openings up there. Look, hurry man, I don't like this one bit," said Pen. The archaeologist looked disappointed, but finished quickly, stowed his stuff away in his pack and scuttled down into the tunnel behind him. A minute or two later, they were back outside.

It had been a blow to Pen that the skeletons had been buried, but it didn't seem to faze the archaeologists. They chatted excitedly while Daniel looked at the images on his camera. Merle came and looked over their shoulders, then turned to Pen and said:

"Bear this in mind, *mon petit*. I catch you pillaging any more sites and you are going down. They'd love you in prison. And remember this: if any of that stuff surfaces we are going to be looking into it — and if it can be traced back to you our deal is off."

Pen felt weak as he watched the policeman shake the archaeologists' hands gravely and head off down the slope, followed by the large minder.

Max turned towards him, his head bowed the better to collect his thoughts. But Pen could see that he was preparing to give him the benefit of them. He held up both hands in defence, "Now you've got what you wanted, I hope you are not going to lecture me."

Max's eyes blinked behind lenses of his glasses as he looked up.

"Look," he began with obviously restrained reproach, "we know your field-walking does no harm to our work. On the contrary you are salvaging things that would be irrevocably lost otherwise. But you could keep a record, work with the museum on an informal basis. You and your friend's knowledge of the open-air sites could be invaluable to us and form the groundwork for an unprecedented study. But digging out virgin sites like this one!" He shook his head. Pen looked defiant. It was a long walk home, but he had been expecting something like this.

"How about a bite of lunch after all that excitement?" said Daniel, smiling broadly. "I know just the place. We'd very much like to hear the whole story, Pen. What was it that drove you to take the terrible risks to push on right through to the chamber?" Max sighed, shrugging off his annoyance.

Pen moved away from them to strip off his overalls and reached reflexively into his pocket for his tobacco, his earlier enthusiasm gone. He must absolutely see Noël, and soon.

The rock-fall in the chamber had, providentially, obliterated their foot-prints. One of the things he had been worried about was that it would have been evident to a trained eye that there had been two people in the cave. Noël seemed safe enough — for now, he would just have to take care not to trip himself up.

Max took them to a restaurant in Les Eyzies, close to the museum. A steep road led high up the cliff into a deep, extremely wide rock-shelter, a natural excavation made by the elements hundreds of thousands of years ago. The vast natural ceiling, discoloured by countless years of hearth-fires and other human use, curved outwards and sheltered them as it had the earlier inhabitants for thousands of generations. Up here on this spectacular terrace, there was room for a car-park with turning space, two private homes and a large restaurant with three dining rooms. Pen wondered what the Magdalenians would have made of the electricity and glassed-in walls, or the sophisticated food. It was a curious feeling to be seated at a table in one of the most ancient continually inhabited dwellings on the planet.

"So they stole everything," said Daniel wistfully: "Nothing from the burial chamber remains to you?" Pen paused for a moment before answering.

"The curious thing is that there is no way the thief, or the recipient of the stuff could have known that we — er that I, had found the treasure. It was pure luck. Serge knew of my collection because he had visited my place with his boss, Renault."

"Ah yes, the famous Renault collection," responded Max at the mention of the name.

"Yes, what can you tell me about him?"

"Well," began Max, his animosity forgotten, "Mr Renault has been extremely successful in business, and has put a portion of his fortune into building what must be the largest private collection of prehistoric artefacts in France, perhaps the world. He only collects French or French-related items. But in the last ten years he has amassed so much stuff that it will probably never all be catalogued.

He's one of the most important private benefactors the museum has. He has donated hundreds of thousands of euros to us in recent years. But he's very jealous of his personal collection, and hasn't ever let us have so much as a waste flake from it despite our entreaties. Some of us have been helping him with cataloguing, so we are getting to know it. He has suggested bequeathing it to the museum at his death."

Pen said: "He told me he wanted to assemble all the thousands of local collections that are still sleeping in farm-houses and barns all over the countryside."

"An impossible task," said the archaeologist. "He's been moderately successful, but he often just gets the leavings after other less scrupulous people have already skimmed off the cream. Mind you, from an archaeological point of view the leavings can often tell us more than the better stuff anyway."

Pen thought about that for a moment. It neither confirmed nor denied Renault's innocence in the matter. He had talked to him earlier about Vincent, but that had proved nothing apart from the fact that Vincent was a dangerous fool. He had more or less decided that Renault was not implicated in the theft, but still felt the man knew more than he was telling. He wouldn't get any more out of him for the moment; but Pen wouldn't be letting it go.

"How do you intend going about the excavation of the funeral chamber?" asked Pen, after swallowing a mouthful of his *gratin de noix de St Jacques*.

"Yes, it will certainly be complicated," said Daniel. "In some cases we bring in specialist engineers to make the site secure for the archaeologists to work in. There was one time where a dangerous shaft over a particularly interesting painted cave site was closed off with a sort of great inflated airbag that was made specially. A cheap and quick solution, while something more permanent could be worked out."

No wonder they didn't seem too bothered, thought Pen.

"Listen, guys, do you need me any more today? I have something I have been putting off that I really have to do."

"You will have a little dessert before you go, Pen? Their *ile flottante* is marvellous, or a little fresh-fruit charlotte?"

"Thanks, Max, but I have to get back. Can you drop me off? I must go and see how my wife and daughter are. They have been really shaken up by this filthy bloody affair, and until things get smoothed over between us, I will be useless for anything else."

"Of course, by all means, you must put your family first. We'll take you home. When you have the time, come and see us — I'll give you my number." Pen took out his phone and saw he had two text messages.

On the drive home he was quiet and pensive. He took out his phone to look at the messages again. The one from Medea he had already decided to open later. The other, from Denise's cell-phone, said:

Where the hell are you? Worried sick, Noël.

So Denise had got through Noël's enduring rejection of cell-phones! Or, more likely, she had written the text in his name. He called her number, but couldn't get a connection and decided to wait until he got home. He loved the Dordogne, but vast rural areas obviously aren't profitable enough to provide with decent Internet or mobile phone cover.

He felt like going back to bed when he walked through the still-open kitchen door into his cold neglected house, but resisted the urge and dialled Denise's number on the land-line. She answered immediately:

"Pen darling! Where are you, we tried to get you all morning!"

"I'm at home now, Denise, but the police have been quite insistent and came to get me far too early today. I just got back. Denise, can I speak to Sophie please?"

"That's one of the things we wanted to talk to you about, Pen, she has gone."

"Gone where?"

"To Mum's. She left yesterday with Alice, said she needed to get away from all that reminded her of what happened here."

"But Alice has school and I'm still her dad! Don't I have a bloody say in anything that goes on?" He realised he was shouting, but couldn't contain his frustration.

"Pen, Alice has not been well since the attack. Her teacher says that she is no longer the happy, curious little girl she's used to, she often weeps."

"What she needs," said Pen trying to calm his voice, "is to see her home intact with her two parents there to love her. She'll get over it in time, and running away won't help."

"Well, I'm not sure Sophie sees it that way. Pen, you can come here come for tea, come and eat with us tonight, we want to see you. Noël is very worried about you too."

"Thank you, Denise, you are very sweet. But there's something I need to do right now. Tell Noël I'll be all right. I'll stay in touch. I promise."

His mood darkened like a brewing storm as he realised how helpless he was. He stood in the suddenly oppressive space of his kitchen trembling with the violence that he hadn't known was in him. He dialled Renault's mobile number. Renault replied after several rings.

"Yes."

"Maurice, it's Pen. Are you in the Dordogne still?"

"Yes, I was planning to leave tomorrow morning. Why?"

"I need to see you."

"Well, I'm at home."

"Okay, I'll be half-an-hour."

"Fair enough, Pen. You sound distraught. Take care on the road for goodness sake."

Back in his truck, still trembling, Pen grabbed the wheel, closed his eyes, and lay his head on his forearms for a few minutes, shoulders hunched against the pain in the core of his being until the spasm passed.

"Oh god," he breathed as the motor kicked into life, "someone's going to pay for this."

In Renault's tidy kitchen Pen felt disorientated. The drive had hardened his resolve; but it had also given him time to think. He needed Renault's support and had to avoid alarming him. Accepting a cup of coffee that he didn't want, he began:

"Yesterday, when we were talking about Vincent, I got the feeling there was something you were holding back."

"Like what?"

"Look at my face, Maurice. I've been beaten and shot, I spent the morning with a fucking vindictive cop and his intimidating gorilla, and he didn't hesitate to threaten me with prison. My wife has been hurt and terrified and so has my eight-year-old daughter. As a result she has left me and says she isn't coming back, and I don't know what I'm going to do about it. All this because that cunt Vincent put your man Serge up to stealing my collection which now looks as if it might have been worth at least half-a-million euros! Why?"

"Well, I can't be sure, Pen. But I do have an idea who might have been ultimately responsible for Vincent ordering the theft — if indeed it was him."

"I hope Vincent doesn't think he's going to get away with it. I've been thinking, Maurice. You could go and tell him you've seen Serge, who's refusing to take the rap alone and that he has implicated Vincent — and that you will go to the police unless he gives you the name of the guy who he sold the stuff to."

"I have also been thinking, Pen. Remember me telling you that in Algeria I was hoping to acquire some Greek or Roman marble statuary, and perhaps some other un-guessed antiquities from a ruined temple? And that Serge and another chap went off one day to reconnoitre the site? Thing is, the other chap, the soldier who went with

Serge, came from a good background. Jacques DeLauro. I looked him up. His mother was Swiss, from some banking family, not a very important scion at the time, but well-enough connected to impress our Mister Vincent. They certainly knew each other, they were both in the regiment. It turns out that these days he is, among other things, an assiduous collector of high-quality antiquities, and he supplies museums around the globe. I guess, now, that they worked together to double-cross me on those temple marbles."

"Where does this guy live now?"

"Geneva."

"Vincent's Swiss client?"

"I didn't make the connection at the time, and anyway we were all in trouble except DeLauro. Pen, I have no proof, but it seems likely that it was him." Renault's jaw was set like concrete. Pen's expression didn't change either. He just said:

"I need to go and see him, and if you'll give it I'll need your help."

"He's a powerful man now, and seems to stop at nothing to get what he wants. Haven't you suffered enough?"

"That's just the point Maurice: I have suffered too much."

20

With a little coaxing, but also prompted by guilt, Maurice Renault eventually agreed to Pen's plan to confront Vincent. He arranged to go and see him directly before leaving for Brussels the next morning. The two men sat in Vincent's large glassed-in conservatory on the comfortable antique chairs with the tasteful floral upholstery. Renault affected to be totally shocked and unconvinced by Serge's disclosure, but said he was finally obliged to acknowledge that, cornered and abandoned, Serge felt he now had nothing to lose. As a result, Renault said he had no alternative but to believe the story. Vincent vehemently denied any knowledge of the theft, and called Serge a lying little toad. Renault then changed tactics and became angry. He said that if Vincent didn't come clean, tell him the truth and reveal where the stuff was now, he would be advising Serge to tell his version to the police. Vincent looked shocked. But as Renault turned to leave, he began speaking in a terrified whisper:

"You don't know him, he will have me killed. He thinks he is untouchable. He thinks he can get away with anything. They killed Custer, I had to have him put down, Maurice. For Christ's sake, Maurice, believe me, they mean business."

"It's DeLauro, isn't?"

"You knew?"

"Isn't it?" Renault repeated.

"Yes, damn it, it's that bastard DeLauro. I've gone out of my way time and time again to find him the things he needs for his clients, and this is how he repays me." Vincent was close to tears. Renault had no wish to witness them, but could not resist staying to find out what had happened:

"Fine, Vincent. But the jade axes and the Neolithic gold were worth far more than the occasional box of bifaces. How did you value them?"

Like a cornered cat, Vincent spat: "I didn't want the bloody treasure. It was the harpoon that DeLauro wanted. He had a museum badgering him for one, but that arrogant English bastard wouldn't sell it to me and after all that it wasn't even there. I don't know what happened. Serge went over the top when he couldn't find it and took everything he could lay his hands on."

Renault had finally become sick of the avaricious idiot snivelling in front of him and responded with disgust.

"No, he wouldn't sell it to you. But he might have eventually sold it to me along with part of that inestimable treasure, which is no doubt lost to everyone now. Where is it?"

"DeLauro's men took it."

"You make me sick!"

Vincent was weeping with self-pity, and sobbed:

"How can you say that to me, Maurice? I have always been generous to you. I've helped you out with your collection dozens of times."

"For money again, like this bloody fiasco for your own financial benefit. You double-crossed me on that temple in Algeria and were ultimately responsible for the torture that Serge endured."

"It was Jacques who organised that. I just helped with the logistics — and as for Serge, at least I managed to get him back."

"Yes, you got him back, but in what condition? You'd better move house, Vincent, and change your name while you're about it. Because I wouldn't like to be in your shoes when DeLauro finds out you gave his name to the police. Either that or you go to the police yourself. Maybe they'll give you protection in exchange for evidence against him."

Vincent looked aghast: "You wouldn't! You said if I told you…"

"This is not for Pen. It's for your betrayal in Algeria."

"But it was so long ago!"

"Tell that to Sergio."

Renault felt soiled after leaving the manse, but there was also a feeling of righteous satisfaction. And at least Vincent had fair warning to get out, which was more of a chance than either Serge, or Pen.

Renault called Pen just before his flight from Bordeaux. His intuition had been right, he told him, it was DeLauro who had received Pen's collection. Maurice had been seething. Vincent confirmed that it was them that had fucked him over in Algeria as well, twice damning Serge. Vincent had it coming.

Pen had asked Renault to find out as much as he could about DeLauro. He needed background on the guy. He may never get his stuff back or even prove to the police where it was now — but he would try. And if not, he was determined to take his revenge on the bastard.

Pen shuddered. For a second he could picture himself, bitter and full of violence. He could hardly recognise the hunched figure he had become since finding those damned jade axes. He had changed. How had he managed to kill Serge's damn dog in cold blood and set fire to Renault's house with them there, and then deny it all, even to Sophie? He should be rushing to her, to be with her and Alice in their distress, and beg her forgiveness. He needed to rebuild their confidence in him before it was too late. Instead, he was busy planning the next terrible step in this decent into hell. He didn't even want to see Noël for the moment: he dreaded his old friend's disapproval. It was clear that Denise was waiting for Pen to pull himself together and sort things out with Sophie. But all he wanted to do right now was to squirt a pistol full of hydrochloric acid into the loathsome face of this Jacques DeLauro, whoever he was. He felt the tears spill over his eyelids and run down his beaten face. Fighting the urge to give in to self-pity, he dashed them away. But his heart was swollen and painful, like a bruise in his chest.

Pen needed his computer, but the police had yet to return it. Refusing to allow that to interfere with his intent on vengeance, and needing to do something, he raced off to Périgueux to get a cheap lap-top and fill up on whisky and other essentials.

Later, at the unfamiliar screen at his desk upstairs, and ignoring the neglected piles of pressing bills and other correspondence, he typed 'Jacques DeLauro' into the search engine. The DeLauro family name had dozens of entries, mostly to do with the banking firm General Finance, or GFB. There were several mentions of a Jacques DeLauro in some sort of incomprehensible executive capacity on one of several boards of directors. But the one that caught his eye was an entry for Eden Holdings, which offered warehouse space for rent in the free port of Geneva: managing director, Jacques DeLauro.

"What the hell is a free port when it's at home?" So Pen looked that up next. "Well, well, well, I suppose I should say bingo!" Many of the entries were about art smuggling.

He discovered that the interesting thing about free ports, of which of course there are many dotted around the world, is that merchandise stored in their warehouses seems to cease to exist. Generally the owners' names are withheld and no customs declarations are required. No taxes are payable on items held there, as they are considered to be in transit. However, hefty fees are payable for the guardianship of the often sensitive and sometimes fragile, valuable objects stored there — typically art-works, antiques, fine wines, and jewellery. There have been several scandals about art treasures looted during the second world war being stored for decades before being turned up in free ports by diligent sleuths. Predictably, hundreds of valuable plundered Italian, Egyptian or Greek grave goods have surfaced in rare but well-documented police raids authorised on irrefutable evidence.

There was no photo of him, but this must be the DeLauro he was looking for: it stank of him. However the various sites that enumerated the advantages of the premises for hire looked daunting. Guard-dogs he was used to, but there were also high perimeter fences and closed-circuit TV cameras, not to mention the top-security buildings themselves. All had built-in fire-control, steel doors, heat sensors — you name it.

Still, it was a start. He would have to see what Renault could come up with. He went down to the kitchen, his mind turning over the events of the last few days, and poured a hefty whisky. He cracked out some ice-cubes and piled in as many as the glass would take, then started to roll a joint but thought better of it: since this whole thing began he had been feeling emotionally fragile, and smoking dope seemed to make it worse. It was a hard habit to break, but he settled for a cigarette. He would eat later if he still felt hungry, perhaps.

He had fallen asleep in an armchair and felt just awful when the telephone woke him, jangling his frayed nerves like more bad news. It was Renault; he seemed genuinely concerned about Pen's state of mind.

"Never mind about that, Maurice. Have you found out anything about him?"

"Well, I have a friend in one of the museums here who told me last night that DeLauro doesn't have a very good reputation with the European museums because the provenance on his stuff is often shaky, not to say downright spurious. It is rumoured that he puts doubtful items through the more reputable auction houses in London or elsewhere, then buys them back through one of his various company accounts to give them credibility before selling them on to the very lucrative American, Asian or European markets. The paperwork must be excruciatingly complicated, but it seems that one of his companies has shares in part of Geneva's free port area which must make it feasible."

"And all this is common knowledge?"

"Well no, it's gossip in certain circles in the museum world. They have to look out for themselves, and you wouldn't believe the quantity of dodgy stuff that is circulating."

"Do you have other friends in the museum circuit, Maurice?"

"Well yes, I do know some people, some in France, a couple in America, Italy, Belgium of course, and I have a good friend in London."

"Listen please, Maurice, this is important. I would like you to contact them, at least those who you know you can trust, especially any who may have reason to dislike DeLauro. Tell them, I don't know, that he has offered some antiquities to a friend of yours and, er, you've been told he can't be trusted, and what do they think? Improvise."

"Why?"

"I looked him up on the internet, Maurice. He does have a place in Geneva's free port. My guess is that that's where my collection is being held. I need to work out a plan to get inside, and I will need all the help I can get."

"You need to realise that DeLauro is not playing games? He has a lot at stake and plenty of resources, far more than us. And he's on his home ground. And I'm warning you, Pen, he will be a dangerous man to cross."

"You said us. Does that mean you're going to help me?"

"That depends on what you intend to do. I won't help you get into even deeper trouble, if that's what you mean. But let me remind you once more, Pen, I've been on your side from the outset."

"All right, thanks for that, Maurice. I'm sorry I haven't been in my right mind since all this happened. Listen then, I have the bones of a plan, but it all pivots on renting some space in DeLauro's warehouse in the free port. I'd like to store some valuable antiquities there. It will be expensive and I sure don't have that kind of money."

"If that's all you need of me, Pen, I'm sure it is going to be simple."

"That's not all I'm going to need of you, Maurice. And I can promise you it won't be simple. One important thing is that you should have no contact with him whatsoever. And he should never know who I am."

"That'll make the operation a little difficult, don't you think? Do you intend to bring someone else in on this?"

"Not if I can help it, Maurice — though as I said, I'll need plenty of help. When are you coming back? I think we should start getting used to talking face-to-face from now on or not at all. I don't like using phones unless we can work out some kind of code."

"Now you are sounding melodramatic."

"What, you don't think Merle will try to find out where the treasure went? Or that if we get it back DeLauro won't use all the considerable resources that you talked about to wreak some terrible revenge? I don't see this as a game, Maurice. If it works out only half as well as I imagine it might, it will be as messy as hell. I want to put him in prison."

"Then make your plans. I'll be back on Monday. We could eat together in Sergeac."

"Chez Paulette?"

"Chez Paulette at eight."

Pen called Sophie and left a contrite message begging her to relent and talk to him, but she did not reply. He made tea and went up to his new computer. Shit, he thought, it's a laptop — I might as well use it in the kitchen — freedom! Well, sort of, he still had to be plugged into a phone line until he worked out how the wifi access worked, but it was progress. Logging on to his mailbox, he saw that the number of messages related to the theft had exceeded his expectations. Dozens of people had written to commiserate and to tell him that they respected his wishes to limit the propagation of his email but feared that it was probably too late. What was wrong with them all? Shit, now he had loads of new friends!

Medea had sent two very sweet messages suggesting that she might look after him if he was at a loose end. He replied that he would certainly see her in the next few days but that he was tied up just now. He felt guilty that Medea was far from the top of his list. She was just the most comforting person available to him at the moment, but he didn't want to burden her with any more of his troubles. What's more he had no intention of benefiting from her sweet nature only to dump her when Sophie came back. But the flesh was, as he knew so well, extremely weak.

He composed an email to Martyn who would be on one of his regular pilgrimages to Benares or trekking in Nepal:

Hi Martyn,

Um,

Do you know of an English guy around my age and height who would be prepared to lose his passport for 2,000 quid?

He must not declare it stolen for at least a month.

He should not know my identity.

If you deal with it, all expenses paid. Same if you have to employ someone, say, 200 quid for you.

Cash by Western Union as of your reply, to the bank of your choice.

Time is of the essence.

I shall be eternally grateful.

P.S. eat this after reading.

P.

He pressed send, then deleted the message from his server and ran his cleaner. He guessed it could be some time before he heard anything back. But it would be an essential part of a plan that was slowly beginning to take shape, and would depend on so many uncertainties.

He sat back in the chair. He would have to pose as an art collector or dealer bringing objects into DeLauro's warehouse, if there was any available space to rent there. The stuff would have to be flown in from some credible source country, which would mean getting it to that country in the first place. DeLauro or one of his employees would probably want to look at it, so it would have to be authentic. He would probably need to make several visits to get the people used to him and, hopefully, into his confidence.

So many things that could go wrong — and he hadn't even got to the part where he steals his flints back. He needed to see Alec and his wife Cath, to talk about some of the technical aspects of the shipments. They had all sorts of obscure expertise, some of which would be essential if he was going to make his scheme work. He needed to set up an account with some of Maurice's money, because he would probably be spending a fair amount of it before the end of all this.

The familiar rattle of the big door sliding open in the workshop disturbed his thoughts. A few seconds later there was a tentative knock at the inside door.

"Yes, Noël," he called out from his place at the table, and Noël came through looking apprehensive, his face drawn.

"Pen," he started from the open doorway. But Pen got up from behind the table and went over and gave him a crushing hug.

"God, you look like shit."

Pen held Noël at arm's length and said:

"You don't look so good yourself." It was a relief to see his old mate, but they both looked grim.

"I had a feeling that hoard would bring us nothing but trouble," said Noël, his blue eyes dulled with worry.

"Well, if it brings trouble to whoever possesses it that might be a good thing. But it means you'll have to give up your part of it, Noël."

"What do you mean by that?" said Noël, visibly withering.

"Tea?"

"Okay." Noël cleared a chair and sat across from the computer, while Pen put the kettle on.

"The police have the photos I took in the cave, Noël. They aren't very clear, but you never know what they might be able to do with them to identify the stuff." A shadow crossed Noël's face; he looked resigned, and Pen suddenly found him strangely small and vulnerable.

"It's my fault, Noël, but they went down fairly hard on me, and I took the easy option. Perhaps it was that freezing cold cell with the light on all night and no pain-killers or change of dressing. I've discovered that I'm not as tough as I thought I was. I suppose I was feeling sorry for myself. It was as if I was the killer, not the victim. They wanted the burial cave and I'm afraid I gave it to them. I was offered immunity in exchange for the location and I took it. I'm sorry."

"Don't concern yourself about it Pen, I don't care a toss about that. It's you that we've been worried for. I came here a couple of times but you had disappeared. We often phoned."

"The police have warned me that if any of the stuff we found surfaces, anywhere, I will be held responsible. It would probably mean prison. We have to give up the last jade axe, Noël."

"Yeah, I'm sorry too. I guess I got kind of attached to it. It is an awesome thing, emanates an irresistible power, but I knew it was not mine. Besides, it worries me. I would hate Denise to suffer because of it. You going to give it to the police?"

"No, the museum. I'll need it all, Noël, the blades, the tusks, and the gold thing too."

"Yeah, okay."

"Now tell me about Sophie and Alice."

"Alice has been sleeping badly, waking up in the night screaming. Sophie tried to put her back in school but she couldn't settle, so she took her out."

"Poor little thing. Sophie blames me for everything and with good reason."

"Thing is that Sophie is not herself either. She doesn't talk unless she's spoken to, she's closed in on herself as if the light has gone out of her."

"She won't reply to my phone calls."

"Go and see her, man."

"I intend going later today. How does my face look? I don't want to frighten her mum if I can help it."

"You look awful, Pen. But the old woman is probably tougher than we give her credit for. Don't let that stop you."

"I think I might be losing my grip, Noël. Sometimes I just find myself crying."

"That's normal, man, after what you've been through."

"It's not normal for me."

They talked for a while longer. Pen told Noël about the rock fall in the cave. It made Noël shudder and he looked even more pained. He insisted that Pen come and stay with him and Denise, and Pen said he would think about it. But after Noël had gone, he realised that he had been unable to reassure him. There had been an unfamiliar awkwardness between them. Their mutual company only served to remind them of what they had just been through and of the terrible repercussions, like shock waves still rippling out from the cave.

Pen didn't go to see Sophie that day, and by evening was getting impatient to see Renault. He had already had a couple of whiskies before going to the quiet country cottage that was now a restaurant, but he was early and ordered another. Maurice Renault turned up behaving as if he owned the place, as Pen had come to realise was his manner. He left generous tips and was well-liked. He kissed Paulette on both cheeks and asked about the summer season, her grandchildren and the weather, then came and sat across from Pen.

"You don't look well, Pen," was his first remark. "What's up?"

Pen laughed out loud at this, making one or two heads turn. His exotic colouring had already drawn a few looks.

"I'm fine, Maurice. And you?"

"I'm famished. I didn't have time for anything at lunch. Let's order."

A young woman came over. Renault ordered a bottle of Bordeaux red, and Pen stuck to whisky. He was wound as tight as a watch-spring, and kept looking around the dining room to steady himself. The restaurant had been converted from a homely farmhouse with its courtyard and barns into a successful local business well before Pen knew it. It had quite a reputation, but on a Monday night in early autumn it was quiet enough.

"Well, Pen," said Renault in that annoyingly patronising tone he used so often: "What's the plan?"

Pen was aware that he had been drinking, more perhaps than he had intended, and that Renault was not the enemy. He forced himself to calm down.

Over a meal of Paulette's simple farmhouse cooking, he outlined what he had worked out so far. He needed Renault's help finding some antiquities they could put through the free port to get him started. Renault knew the curator of a museum in Italy who had borrowed some Greek ceramics from an American museum for study. They had just finished with them and were about to send them back. Renault's friend didn't mind them travelling via Geneva, especially if it meant that Renault would take care of the shipping costs.

Pen started to relax. Maurice was in on this with him, and was prepared to put up the money for the passport as well. He only hoped that Martyn knew of some English backpacker who was desperate enough for a bit of extra cash to go for his offer. Then came the question he had been dreading:

"So, Pen, what do you do once this has all been set up, assuming everything goes to plan?"

"Do?"

"Well, assuming you meet DeLauro eventually, how are you going to get your stuff back or manage to incriminate him?"

"I haven't got that far yet, Maurice. But perhaps I could bring in a shipment of flints heading for a wealthy private foreign collector who is not too fussy about provenance, and make sure DeLauro knows that. To get the ball rolling, you know? Then take it from there."

"Where does this shipment come from?"

"In for a penny, Maurice."

"I see that you've thought this through," said Renault with a smile. "Dessert?"

"No thanks. There's a way to go yet though. It all hangs on the passport for the moment. I need it to open at least one bank account, to buy plane tickets and probably to get into the free port — plus DeLauro will surely ask for ID. Renault looked at him, raised his glass, and said:

"If I had one piece of advice to give you, it would be go easy on the whisky. It doesn't mix well with heartbreak, and you look like you are suffering from a fair dose of that."

"What would you know about heartbreak Maurice? It's not what you get when someone bids you over the odds on something you want but can't get, you know."

"You'd be surprised what I know on that subject, young fellow."

That was when Pen realised that he knew nothing really about Maurice Renault. Only that he was helping him when he didn't have to, after he himself had almost burnt the man's house down. While Renault didn't know that and never would, Pen was suffering regular pangs of guilt about it. This time he hoped he was planning to attack the right person.

"Okay, I'll take it easy. It's true I miss my family, but until this is sorted out they're better off without me."

"Do they have a bit of money to be going on with?"

"I have no idea — she won't talk to me."

"Send them some."

"I think they need love and affection, but I don't have much of that at the moment, so I could do as you say, Maurice. Thanks for caring."

They agreed they would only call each other if there were any important new developments, in which case they would arrange to meet to discuss them. There was plenty for both of them to be getting on with and they would eat together in two days' time. Renault booked a table for that while he paid the bill. He had arranged to be around for most of the next month, as the work was starting on his house. There were the repairs to his roof and rebuilding of the barn, and he no longer had Serge to help with anything.

21

The following day there was a message from Martyn. It read simply:

Will Scottish do?

To which Pen wrote back:

Anything like me? If so which bank?

An hour later he received:

Height and age. My name, Everest Travel Centre, Kathmandu, Nepal will be fine. Stay safe.

And that was that. In theory he could have the money to him in two days max, and if he sent it airmail the passport shouldn't take much more than a week. He was in business. He would set up a bank account in Bordeaux, one-and-a-half hours away along the new A89 *autoroute* and big enough to be anonymous in. He would have to put several cash deposits into the account to avoid a trail back to Renault, but afterwards he could do all his banking on line from any internet café. He would need an address. He could just set up a PO box, although a flat would be more practical.

While he was being anonymous, he intended to make a donation to the Musée d'Aquitaine. Max and Daniel would not be very happy about it, but he assumed there was cooperation between their institutions. He phoned Denise. She was her usual sweet self, as always so concerned. The traumatic events seemed to have drawn her and Noël even closer. She made him promise to visit Sophie, and then said, "Here's Noël." There was a quiet mumble on the end of the line, and Pen said:

"Noël, we need to see each other. When will you be at home?"

"Half-an-hour if you want." Noël's voice was barely more than a whisper.

"Don't forget anything!"

"Hmm."

"See you there then."

Noël looked as if he was being led to the gallows. He had a cardboard box on his table in front of him, and for an instant glared accusingly at Pen as if it were an orphan about to be given up to the brothel.

"Look, Noël, it's over. Let's face it — these were never intended for us."

Noël looked up at Pen and forced a wan smile. "I know," he said. "It's a relief really. They were haunting me. Maybe now they'll let me forget about the cave and get on with it."

Pen found waiting for the passport intolerable. He phoned Sophie's mum every day to talk to Alice, who seemed much like her old cheerful self now that she was away from the scene of all the horror. She chattered on about the big swimming-pool in town and always asked when he was going to come. He had no answer to that, so made thin excuses which, in her young wise way, she affected to accept. She never pushed him, sensing perhaps that until Sophie was ready it might reopen wounds that were still all too painful.

He spent long hours scrubbing the blood stains out of the bedroom floor, the stairs, and the kitchen floor. He took the mattress to the dump and bought a new, deeper, firmer model of superlative comfort. But he slept no better on it. He tidied and cleaned and repaired the breach in the workshop wall, but did not go to see Sophie nor insist on speaking with her.

He had been to the restaurant twice more with Renault. He had little appetite. Renault was concerned and said he was losing weight. He had arranged for the shipment of ceramics to fly from Naples to Geneva when the time came, and looked into Eden Holdings, DeLauro's company. Apparently they had space to rent in their warehouse in the free port, and were still waiting for a name to confirm the booking.

The time difference with Nepal got on Pen's nerves. He checked for messages ten times a day. Martyn received the money with no problem and sent the package by registered airmail, which Pen felt was a bit risky. So he was relieved to hear the postwoman beeping her horn, wanting a signature.

Joseph Fircloth ("Joe"), British citizen from Sterling, was almost exactly Pen's age but a little heavier, and darker and bearded in the photo. The passport was due to run out in three years so the photo was seven years old. The only disconcerting thing was that apart from his entrance visa into India most of the other stamps were from Mexico, including two recently. Could that lead to suspicion? Pen would just have to wait and see. He thought a wig would be best, better than dying his own hair, and perhaps a false moustache; the eyes were dark, which was perfect. Good old Martyn, he had earned his money on this. Necessity may be the mother of invention, but in Pen's case desperation was doing a reasonable job of engendering this new-found ingenuity. He tried a few signatures, and settled for a simple flourish that he could easily repeat.

He phoned Renault and said, "Maurice, I'm ready to roll."

The next week went by in a flurry of activity for both of them. When his bank card came through it was sent to his new address, a tiny one-room apartment in sight of the St Michel cathedral in the centre of old Bordeaux. He had had the phone line installed and bought an answer-phone.

He found dozens of wig-makers on the internet, and agonised over his appearance before deciding on a staid, slightly wavy mid-length city conformity with a left-side parting, in pure human hair, and a moustache to match. The wig would be fixed with grips into his own hair, the moustache would have to be stuck on with theatrical adhesive. Never mind: he would have to get used to it. He bought a couple of suits and some shirts, and a pair of shiny brown town shoes.

He had only a kettle and a mug, an inflatable mattress, a sleeping-bag and a down pillow in Bordeaux, and travelled to and fro with his laptop. It was murder parking his truck, and he often ended up walking miles in the autumn chill around the busy town. At last he was on a mission. He started eating properly again and slowly began putting back on the weight he had lost over the last three weeks.

He was Joe Fircloth now, and once he had the wig and moustache, he wore them around Bordeaux until he came to feel at home in his new persona.

He used Joe's bank card to book a cheap Bordeaux-Geneva flight on-line to keep his first appointment with Eden Holdings. On his way over France, he reflected on the last disastrous month of his life. That he no longer recognised himself came as no surprise: he no longer was himself. His creamy oatmeal suit wasn't quite businesslike enough, he decided, but it was distinctive — easily dirtied and already rumpled; and his scalp itched. But he felt comfortable as Joe. The only part he couldn't get used to was the moustache. He was tempted, while he was travelling at least, to keep that and the glue in his pocket. But he decided it would be too risky, someone might just spot the difference when he stuck it on. He was play-acting again. He had been good at dressing-up before his father died and his mother became hopelessly dysfunctional. It wasn't just the disguise, he hardly recognised him self any more. Sadly he realised that he could no longer sense any presence of the little boy he had once been, hiding away somewhere inside. Perhaps when this was over and Pen was back, he would manage to coax him out. But he had done his crying. What he needed now was revenge.

He smiled to himself as he thought of typing out the spurious explanation that he had attached to his donation to the museum in Bordeaux. The finds, which Joe Fircloth had handed over the counter in the large entrance-hall, all carefully cleaned of fingerprints and any possible genetic evidence, were claimed to have been in his family since the nineteenth century. They had been discovered in the Gers near Toulouse, in 1865 (by workmen who broke into a tomb while they were digging in a quarry), along with several other equally beautiful objects all now lost. The treasure had been quickly sold off, but his great-grandfather had tracked some of it down and managed to buy it. He had always wanted it all to end up in the museum that had given him so much pleasure throughout his long life. He had left no signed document. Pen knew that the photos in the cave were far from clear and he doubted that a definite match could be made between them and the objects he had handed in — peevish, he realised, but it felt like one in the eye for Merle. At least they could not be linked back to him.

From the plane window, Pen vaguely registered the already snow covered distant peaks, but was too distracted to feel any thrill. He felt a twinge of nerves as the plane touched down juddering noisily. But before they had finished taxiing up to the busy terminal the nerves had, curiously, left him. It wasn't quite skiing season yet so it could have been worse: he was just another harassed businessman rushing somewhere. He had no baggage, just his laptop and some moustache glue; coming up the escalator after the bottleneck of identity control, he found a free silver-grey Mercedes E series taxi waiting in the rank. He gave the driver the address of the offices where his appointment was scheduled that afternoon. The well groomed man got out of the car to hold the door open for him. Pen wondered at the immaculately pressed suit that looked as if it had cost far more than his own. So this, he thought, is Switzerland. Then he was being whisked out and along the lake to a large, heavily fenced-in area with several uniformed guards at the gates.

No doubt used to taxis ferrying the free port's clients in and out, they waved him through without looking too closely. The road became a wide concrete apron, stained and oil-splattered. He saw blocks of huge modern warehouses and offices lined up along it, articulated trucks and commercial vans parked outside of many of them, and cars flitting about. A plane took off from the nearby runway and passed just overhead with an ear-splitting roar. The taxi threaded its way between ranks of buildings to the back of a grubby white concrete-and-pressed-steel warehouse, with three tiled steps leading up to some wide glass swing-doors. The words 'Eden Holdings' in chrome lettering were the only thing he could see that spoke of any class: certainly no air of banking here. But he knew his collection was in there somewhere; he could almost taste it. And there was something else as well — the cloying metallic tang of impending vengeance. He pushed the vexing thought to the back of his mind: this was not the moment for passion to spoil anything.

He paid the taxi, went in through the glass doors, and passed through the foyer to an open-plan office area with no one around. He went up two more steps to a deserted reception desk. He was aware that he might be being filmed, so made it look casual but exasperated. After a while a door opened in a wall beyond the desk and a smart-looking, youngish guy in a dark green suit came out and said, in Swiss-accented French:

"Hello, can I help you, sir?"

Pen replied: "Joe Fircloth. I have an appointment."

The guy took out a phone and spoke into it briefly. Pen thought he looked rather bored.

"Sorry for the delay sir," he said, slipping the phone back into his jacket pocket, "Mister DeLauro is here this morning and wishes to deal with your account himself."

Pen felt it was too good to be true: he was at last going to meet the author of his nightmares. His wig was long enough to cover most of his fading wounds, but a month after the attack the right side of his face was still slightly yellowish. He hoped DeLauro would be more interested in his merchandise than his face. There was a risky link to Pen there, but he found he didn't care.

When DeLauro appeared, Pen was surprised to find that he was a small man, elegantly dressed with silver grey hair longer than Joe's wig and brushed over from the left to cover a bald patch. He smiled at Pen, extending a small, well-manicured hand in a gesture of welcome.

"Mister Fircloth. I trust you had a good flight."

"Only an hour or so. It's more hassle going through the airports than the actual flying."

"Terrible places, they're just gigantic up-market bazaars. We are herded into them hours before our flights in the hope that we will spend money on things we don't need. It is scandalous."

So this was Jacques DeLauro. Pen hadn't expected him to be so, well, charming.

"Come through to my office, Mr Fircloth," he said in English: "Tell me, how did you hear about our little enterprise, if you don't mind my asking?" Renault had given Pen the name of someone who worked in antiquities in Brussels and had used Eden Holdings a few years earlier, and had filled him in on the workings of the place. Pen didn't know exactly what the deal was. With any luck Renault had asked him for a reference for Joe, but Pen couldn't be sure. It was one of the many areas of his plan that he had been rather sketchy about. So Pen decided to play hard to get, and said:

"I have an acquaintance who used your services a while ago and considered them adequate."

"We have the highest security and total discretion here, Mr Fircloth. I think 'adequate' is a rather weak adjective to describe us. Don't you?"

"You were given the highest recommendations, I can assure you, Mr DeLauro."

"Good, good. And may I ask who your acquaintance is, Mr Fircloth?"

"Call me Joe. I suppose there's no harm in telling you, although I too believe in discretion, Mr DeLauro. It was Justin Pradel in Brussels."

"Who works for Brussels art auctions?"

"Used to."

"We haven't seen him here in a while. But he did use our services, I remember him."

Shit, thought Pen, let's hope he doesn't decide to call him up.

"Well, Joe, how can I help you?"

"I'll be receiving some rather fragile antiquities from Italy that I would like to transit here for a little while before sending them on to a client in the States."

"Hmm, if you know Justin you know that I have a special interest in antiquities, Joe. I wonder if you'd mind telling me what kind of antiquities they might be."

"Well yes, of course. But as I said, I'm counting on your utmost discretion." DeLauro gave a solemn nod, but impatience flickered momentarily across his smooth features as Pen continued: "It's a group of Greek ceramics from Sicily. You know, calyx-type vessels, and red figure vases for the most part."

DeLauro was taken aback: "There has been a lot of trouble with Italian antiquities, I have to tell you."

"Don't worry, Mr DeLauro," said Pen. He was beginning to feel a bit hot and sticky and had a sudden horror that his moustache was slipping. He put his hand up to stroke it as he continued: "They all have authentic provenances and my client knows that they are on their way, so I won't inconvenience you for long." Pen had a sudden uncomfortable need to pee and took a slow breath in through his nose.

"Call me, Jacques, please; we are all friends in this business."

Ah, thought Pen, relaxing a little, here's the DeLauro I was expecting to find.

"You realise we have to be careful Joe. Would you mind me taking a look at your passport?" Pen had been told that they would be thorough, so he took the passport from his pocket and handed it over. DeLauro flipped through the slightly battered document.

"India?" Pen had not bothered doing his homework on that entry, and answered:

"Yes, a holiday really, although I did look at some early temple carvings from the Khajuraho region. Beautiful work, but I have no one I can trust there to do the handling." Pen had once taken a book out of the library at art school and had been charmed by the wealth of explicit erotic carvings that covered the temples in that area.

"According to your passport it would seem you have more success in Mexico." Pen had spent some time looking into the pre-Columbian cultures of Central America and bullshitted as best he could:

"Yes. Nasca pottery mostly, a few Tumaco and Narino statuettes, some wonderful flaked-stone tools and sacrificial knives, that sort of thing — there's enough of it on the market." It was his intention to develop in that direction in the weeks to come: the simple forms of those ceramics had grown to become an essential part of his plan.

"Yes. But they're beginning to clamp down on that now, too. Do you bring any of those things to Europe, Joe?"

"I have a contact in Lisbon. But from there it gets complicated. Do you think I might be able to have the stuff sent by road or train from Portugal to transit through Geneva?"

"As long as your merchandise has legitimate provenances, the paperwork is all in order, and you have someone to sign as the owner of anything you bring here, of course. That is our function: items may be stored here almost indefinitely."

DeLauro told him that the vaults were on the subterranean levels. But for Joe's purposes he thought a ground-floor unit would do to start with, and be the most convenient. He took Pen to look over their storage facilities, explaining that he himself used this level for bulky items or for acquisitions which would not be staying long. They approached a formidable security door with complex locking systems, which DeLauro opened with several keys from a bunch that hung on a golden chain from his belt. The door slid quietly back into the wall. As they entered the wide corridor, Pen couldn't help thinking how daunting it all looked. He would hate to be locked in, on the wrong side of these doors. He forced himself to concentrate as he was shown around a few of the rooms currently available. The smallest were empty cupboard-sized spaces with smooth concrete floors and block-work walls with set-in steel doors; others were much larger.

At the end of the corridor was a larger pair of high-security doors leading to a vast hangar with iron beams that supported a rolling gantry and sliding doors opening onto the apron outside. Up on the loading-bay, on the same level as the rooms they had looked at, a small rank of gas-powered fork-lift trucks were parked, each with its domestic-type gas-bottle slung behind the driver's seat, waiting to service the intercontinental traffic loading and unloading there.

Pen was most taken by a room of about forty square metres in the heart of the warehouse which looked as though it had recently been partitioned out from a larger space. The dividing wall and ceiling looked and smelled like fresh-skimmed plaster-board, and there were splashes of hastily wiped up plaster on the floor. The large doorway looked like it was designed to accept a fork-lift, which would be practical when his stuff started arriving. Outside wide corridors were lit with rudimentary strip-lighting and hung with the occasional CCTV camera. Smoke-alarms, the iron piping of a sprinkler fire-control system and a few ventilation grills made up the rest of the visible services. Pen supposed that there must also be heating and sanitary services in there somewhere, with drainage and evacuation pipes and god knows what other warrens of conduits and ducts running through the walls and under the floors.

They had come across no one else in their wanderings, and Pen noticed an air of disorder in this part of the complex — cables hanging unattached in places along the corridor, and even a small pile of builder's rubble in one corner. DeLauro explained that they were renovating some of the rooms and that the work would be finished soon.

They ended up agreeing that Joe Fircloth would take room, D14a. The door to the left was D13. The next one, on the right, was D14b. In any case, he felt the room was going to be perfect for his needs. He finished the paperwork in DeLauro's office, requesting a table and at least two chairs in the room, and shelving on the walls opposite to and on the left of the door. DeLauro said he would arrange it all. Pen signed a cheque for six months up front. DeLauro reminded him that, for a fee, Eden Holdings could handle incoming deliveries, which could either be stored in D14a, or be held until his next visit; and they could look after any subsequent shipping of articles stored with them. When they shook hands, DeLauro took Pen's in both of his and said that he thought that it was going to be "a pleasure working with you, Joe". And then he called for a car to return his new client to the airport.

It was as easy as that. So why did Pen feel so uneasy on his way home? He was wary of the evil old bastard: the man had sent thugs to Vincent's place and was obviously used to getting his own way. The only scheming Pen had ever done in his life, until this last month that is, had been to soft-talk his way into Sophie's pants. As Joe, though, it seemed to come more easily. He hoped he wouldn't develop a taste for deception.

22

Back at the workshop, wandering its few empty rooms and breathing the familiar air with unaccustomed difficulty, Pen wondered if Joe Faircloth's identity hadn't become more appealing than his own free of any past, a virgin future stretched before him like a primed canvas. Still no word from Sophie, and even Medea seemed to be giving up on him. She had sent just one email:

Where are you?

He knew beyond a shadow of a doubt that Sophie would not approve of Joe; but what would Medea make of him?

Renault had not been idle during Joe's first outing. He had been to an antiquities auction in Toulouse that Pen had spotted on the net, and managed to buy five good Nasca pots. Two of them were bottles with arched handles and narrow necks. Pen was enthusiastic: the workmanship was good, yet basic enough for him to try his hand at copying them in his workshop.

The idea had been to gain DeLauro's confidence and give Joe credibility by showing him the valuable museum pieces of Italian stuff. Pen never found out how, but Renault had arranged for three lesser but nonetheless authentic pieces to be bought and sent on with the shipment that Joe could leave in Geneva, to give the impression that he was starting to build up a stock there. They would then fill up the room with passable facsimiles. The Italian and Greek ceramics were all but impossible to fake. But the more recent, highly collectable pre-Colombian pottery was cruder, the technique simple, and it was baked at lower temperatures. Pen was going to try his hand at various different models. He felt confident that he could reproduce their beautiful stylised decoration, using the same minerals for the colours as the originals.

He was acutely aware that they didn't have much time. Once the real Joe Fircloth declared his passport missing, Pen would no longer be able to use it. That gave him two-and-a-half weeks at most; he must set to work. He had quantities of coarse red clay from the ceramics he had been working on for Renault. He would need to make plaster slip-moulds for some of the doll-like deities of the Olmec and Inca cultures. But most of the pots could be thrown on his old potter's wheel. He needed a couple of dozen closed, hollow vessels that looked the part. He could get the earthy oxides from the local builder's supplier, and some fine sand from a nearby stream. Leftover barbecue charcoal, oak chippings or sawdust could be added to the kiln during firing to create wood smoke, giving an authentic, uneven look.

With two large trestle tables set up to accommodate the various stages of production, Pen worked as if possessed. The real pre-Colombian vessels were installed as models on his desk, swept clear of his undealt-with paperwork. He had dragged his old wheel out into the centre of the room, and was lost in the primeval, earthy odour of wet clay. His fingers had no trouble remembering the timeless gestures that his consciousness had barely known. His feet worked the rhythm that transformed the lumps of raw clay into delicate forms on the heavy, spinning disk in front of him.

It was like waking from a dream when, two days later, he surveyed the fruits of his labours set out on the two trestle-tables to dry in the hot air from two electric fan-heaters abetted by the wood-burner. In the last four days he hadn't shaved once and had barely eaten. He had drunk tea but no alcohol, and had scarcely, he was surprised to realise, smoked a fag.

He mixed the ground colours into some of the translucent clay slip using iron oxides for the strong reds, yellow ochre and manganese for the black, and a small quantity of tin oxide for the white. These were the colours of the past that he was familiar with: they had been used since prehistoric times. Pen realised that Joe had departed for the moment: there was no place for him in the workshop — this was pure Pen.

The pots he had on his desk had been burnished before they were fired. This had given them a distinctive warm sheen very different to the glassy glazed finishes Pen was used to. He knew of the ancient technique, but had never tried it: it consisted of polishing the surface of the dry clay with a smooth pebble and a little water or oil. It was the last step before decorating them with the simple geometric designs of fish and animals that he would copy from the printouts he had made from the net. His gas-fired kiln was small for the task of baking all those pieces. It would need at least three firings to get everything done, which meant getting in several more gas cylinders.

He planned on cooking the pieces just enough to stop them dissolving in water. Too much, and the lustre he had given them would dull. He reckoned a number eighteen cone would do it. These potter's cones were designed to melt at different temperatures, placed in the kiln so as to be seen through little viewing holes as they glowed incandescent and keeled over — telling you when it was hot enough inside.

Daylight was leaking in through the branches of the trees surrounding the workshop and Pen realised that, once again, he had worked through the night. A noisy dawn was breaking. His work was almost finished. He was getting ahead of himself, though. A bit more drying was needed, and meanwhile Pen needed to see Alec. The guy had a load of special expertise and some knowledge of chemistry, and Pen was going to need both. It was still too early, so before he went over to see him he went online to order packaging materials — heavy-duty cardboard boxes and a roll of bubble wrap to start with. He found a company which promised two days for delivery. The whole operation was becoming quite expensive, and he thought, not for the first time, that if Renault had not been backing him he wouldn't have had a hope in hell.

Alec was manoeuvring his powerful little forklift, loaded with several heavy black iron girders, when Pen arrived at his chaotic workshop. He noticed that the forklift resembled those in DeLauro's warehouse, and made a mental note to ask how it worked before he left. The ever good-hearted Alec didn't remark on Pen's haggard appearance. There was a self-conscious moment when Pen felt he ought to have washed and changed out of his sweaty clay-stained clothes; but it was fleeting. He was invited into Alec's office-cum-kitchen for a cup of tea.

"What's on your mind?" asked Alec, turning from the sink with studied nonchalance.

"My flints," said Pen looking up as Alec put the kettle on: "If I can't have them, I want to try and make sure that nobody else can. Your Catherine still does fireworks, doesn't she?"

There were some elements of his plan that Pen had not yet worked out. Perhaps the hardest was going to be where to find the confidence to pull it off at all. As for the rest, that first visit had been easier than he expected, wearing a wig, dressing-up, travelling around and talking people into things — would you buy a used antiquity from this man? Most of it was kid's stuff to Pen, at least the role playing aspect was, if he ignored the risks he was taking. Being used to working with all sorts of materials and employing his accursed creativity, he had managed to overcome many of the other difficulties as they cropped up. There was at least one thing, though, with which he was going to need some enlightened help.

Like her husband, Cath had a relentlessly cheerful disposition. For the wrong reasons, perhaps, Pen was glad of that; it's easier to wheedle something out of a happy person than a grouch. She had a broad handsome face that had seen plenty of wind and sun and her unruly ginger hair had flecks of grey that she did nothing to disguise. He guessed that she would not be far short of fifty now, but she didn't look old to him, she seemed girlish. He realised that his perception of old had shifted of late. Girls somehow contrived to look like women these days, but older people rarely looked young. He decided it was more a question of attitude.

Alec of course knew about the theft at Pen's workshop and the subsequent late night attack, but Pen had not wanted to discuss his present project with him. He had given him the bare minimum, not going into the details, and had eventually managed to talk the accommodating Alec into convincing Cath to help. But it turned out to be hard work getting what he wanted. Being the practical sort of woman she was, Cath kept trying to get him to go to the police.

"I can't explain this to you yet, Cath," he begged shamelessly: "But believe me, there are reasons why I can't go to the police. You'll have to take it on trust. I have a plan — not just mindless revenge, okay? And I promise both of you," — at this Alec raised his bushy eyebrows with interest — "I have no intention of hurting anybody, I just may need a distraction." Cathy had been working with fireworks off and on as long as Pen had known her. She travelled all over France during the fine months setting up displays, and occasionally worked on special effects for the cinema and theatre. Her clients paid well and often came back for more, which enabled her to put a bit of jam on her bread, as she liked to say. He had seen some of her work but had never thought to wonder about what went into it. Cathy could tell that he was getting close to the end of his tether. He was having trouble keeping the frustration out of his voice, as he made it clear that this was an essential part of some carefully thought-out back-up plan. He hoped that a little initiation into basic theory and some minimal help with logistics would be enough. That was it, he did not want to implicate anyone else, least of all them. Cathy finally caved in, reluctantly agreeing to show him a few of her tricks. The worst part about that was seeing the worry on her face: he had known that she would give in and help him in the end, but he took no satisfaction from it. He knew that she had seen it for what it was: obsessive, desperate. She was so serious about her explanations, repeating everything to him several times over and making him go through the motions until she was sure he had taken in all the dangers. Alec beamed a big smile and gave Pen a wink of confidence. Pen left, feeling unexpectedly guilty. He would have to try and make damn sure he didn't let them down.

They were cutting it fine. But along with the original five pots Pen now had thirty-two slightly grubby, well-made fakes. Most of the pots were closed, round-bodied bottles, some with two or three spouts. A couple were of a pornographic nature, true to the archaeological evidence that Pen had looked up, with scenes of joyful sodomy worked in relief into the handles and necks. Others had stylised fish or animals painted on them. The doll-like figurines looked as if they had been baked out of bread, like fat buns with large head-dresses, or hydro-encephalic children. There were also several bowls. One or two of the pieces were slightly damaged and some were restored. He gave them all a fine coating of earthy patina to age them. Now that he had finished getting them ready for packing he realised that they were surprisingly heavy, but it was difficult to gauge the thickness of the walls of most of them — and anyway, Pen reckoned, large or thick ceramic objects are generally heavy and he decided not to worry.

He wanted to call Sophie's mum and find out how the girls were doing. But he was so focused on his obsession with DeLauro that he couldn't trust himself to keep calm enough to talk to them. He felt on the verge of hysteria most of the time. So he settled for a phone call to Denise:

"Hi."

"Pen! God, where are you?"

"I'm at home, Denise. I'm sorry I haven't been in touch, but I've not been well."

"What do you mean?"

"I think I'm depressed."

"Come and stay with us, Pen. You know that I'm used to the blues. I have some good medication that might help you."

"No, Denise, there's only one thing that can help me." He knew how Denise would interpret that; Pen only hoped that it was what he meant.

"Listen. They're both well. Alice asks after you, but they still say they don't want to come back to the house where all those terrible things happened. You can understand that, can't you? Give them time. You know they'll change their minds eventually."

"I hope so. But right now I can't count on anything."

"Our house is open to you, Pen. You can count on that."

"That's sweet of you, Denise. Give my love to Alice when you see her, tell her I phoned."

He rang off feeling worse than ever, and lay on his bed for a while staring at the bare ceiling he had so carefully painted. Near the window he noticed two spots of blood that he had missed in his clean-up, and cursed the cold slippery, bastard who was responsible for his torment.

He had been a spoilt child, doted on by his parents, and he knew it. But they had deserted him so young, destroying his world and shaking his confidence in others to the point where he had hardly ever trusted anyone. He had slowly learned to let his guard down. But then suddenly, out of the blue, the tsunami that was DeLauro had hit him full in the face.

"I'm on my way, Jacques!" he shouted loudly, and levered himself up off the bed, too preoccupied to rest.

He needed to pack the pots, drive them down to Portugal, and get them on a train to Geneva. Then he needed to get himself to Geneva to see to the Italian stuff, which was to be sent on to Boston. His phone went down below in the kitchen. He took the stairs two at a time, picked up the handset, and sat heavily at the table.

"Hey! You're home! Where've you been? You don't even answer your emails any more. I know you've got your troubles, but you could drop me a line once in a while."

Pen smiled:

"I thought people of my gender were beneath your notice."

"Hey come on, Pen, you know I'm fond of you."

"Medea," said Pen, on a whim, "you don't speak Portuguese by any chance do you?"

"Spanish, they sound a bit similar but in fact they're quite different. What now?"

"Are you free at the moment? I have to drive down to Lisbon and would love some company."

"Oh how romantic, a honeymoon! How many days?"

"Just there and back in my truck. Appeal to you?"

"Might do."

"I'll phone when I'm ready. Probably pick you up around eight tomorrow morning, okay?"

"Why not tonight?" She sounded petulant.

"All good things are worth waiting for, sweetheart." He realised that he would like nothing better. But there was still a lot to do before he could leave.

"Okay then, great" she sighed, resigned.

The fact that he would be seeing Medea again cheered him up. Perhaps he was clutching at straws, but theirs was the only uncompromised relationship he had to cling to at the moment. He hoped that his bad luck wasn't going to spill over onto her. He took an open pack of milk out of the fridge. He upended it into the whisky glass on the marble worktop. To his satisfaction it filled the glass to within a couple of millimetres of the top. He downed the milk in one deep, cool, rich draft, which tasted better than all the whisky he had been putting away of late. He had gone three days without a single cigarette, almost without thinking about it, and now decided he was going to kick the habit altogether. Joe Fircloth was a non-smoker. Pen told himself that he wasn't on a suicide mission, and this was how he was going to prove it.

It was only just getting light when he pulled up in front of Medea's building. She was waiting for him, sitting on one of the bollards that stopped people parking too close to the entrance. She was dressed in a black bomber jacket over a full white sun-dress like something Marilyn Monroe might wear, her toes pointing in towards each other in mid-calf lace-up black Doc Martens. Pen had forgotten how good she looked. She was chewing gum, her jaw working and her bright-red-painted lips were closed in a suppressed smile. Her thick black bob was cut shoulder-length, the fringe just above her impish eyes. Pen glanced at the large suitcase on the ground beside her and said,

"Shit Medea! We're only going for two days, three at the outside!"

"You've got a truck, so where's the problem? Besides, a girl's got to have a change of clothes. Who knows what might happen?"

"He snorted at that and gave her a warm kiss, hugging her yielding body tight. Then he stowed her heavy case in the back with his 'merchandise'and she hopped up into the cab.

"Got your passport?" he asked.

"Identity card's enough, driver's licence even. This is Europe, don't forget."

Yes, thought Pen, Europe — a fine idea in theory, but it was proving difficult to put into practice. Though it made sense he couldn't see it ever working unless they organised some kind of federal government, like in the States: nobody seemed to be able to agree on anything. It had seemed great not having to change money within the member countries. But as most people paid with plastic anyway these days even that minor advantage was lost. The euro was always in dire trouble anyway: it was better to have your money in flints, he reflected bitterly. Medea slumped back in her seat turned towards him, chewing, and said:

"I hope you're planning on stopping soon so that we can catch up on all that stuff we've been missing out on."

"You're such a predator, Medea."

"Well, somebody has to take the initiative, and you're so — preoccupied."

"Yeah, well, sorry — but it'll all be over soon one way or the other, I hope."

They stopped in one of the service stations heading south on the A 63 north of Bayonne for a pee and a coffee. Medea found him seated by the window at an impracticably small plastic table in the crowded cafeteria. He was gazing out at the petrol station lost in thought, nursing his cup.

"She's a lucky girl to have someone who cares about her so much."

Pen looked up at her. "I'm not thinking about Sophie."

"Well why do you look so miserable then?"

"You're a nutter Medea," he said conceding a reluctant smile.

"Look, I want to drive a bit now. You look tired and if we keep at that snail's pace of yours we'll never get there."

"What do you mean snail's pace? It's a van, not a BMW coupé, you sausage."

"No need to drive like a pensioner in it though, is there? Look, I've brought my driving gloves." Medea produced the flashy fashion accessories from her bag, unexpected but unsurprising, Pen realised. He dropped his shoulders in resignation.

"Okay then. But just don't get us into trouble or worse still kill us. I'd never be able to explain to Sophie what I was up to."

True to her gloves, Medea drove aggressively. She stayed in the outside lane with her foot down, shifting only reluctantly when powerful cars impatient to overtake flashed them from behind. They made good time shooting into Spain hardly registering the border. But Medea kept Pen on tenterhooks, her antics better suited to a video game than a goods vehicle, until he cracked and told her that she drove like a maniac; if she couldn't give him a less stressful honeymoon, he would file for premature divorce on the grounds of unwarranted cruelty to his gearbox. She was tired herself by then, and was briefly subdued. She gave him a dark scowl but brightened when she saw the signs for Portugal.

Pen had prepared a story for the customs. He was an artist working in France, taking some of his work to a craft fair in Lisbon. He even had a printout of the flyer found on the net. But neither the Spanish nor the Portuguese bothered him. Nonetheless it was a gruelling drive, and by the end of it even Medea's ardour was dulled if not entirely dead. The road and rail freight offices were well and truly closed when they arrived, so Pen decided to look for a hotel for the night. Medea seemed to perk up at the prospect.

"And we'll need some sleep! We're driving back tomorrow."

"I'm just looking forward to taking a shower to wash our travel-weary bodies clean for each other."

Pen was glad she had come: she was frivolous and gay, altogether just what he needed. Though a small voice called out from somewhere in his conscience just loud enough to dampen any real joy he may have gleaned from her presence.

He had sorted out the transit papers with Renault, and had DeLauro's forms for admission into the free port in Geneva. Medea's Spanish came in useful because the efficient woman from the freight office spoke Spanish, but not English or French. He had packed his boxes onto a wooden pallet in the back of the truck, and then wrapped the whole thing in cling film. One of the ubiquitous fork-lifts unloaded it easily and whisked it away into the bowels of a dark, windowless warehouse where it would await transport.

"Cheap, too," thought Pen as they drove away. The whole operation was turning out to be pretty costly, and he raised an imaginary glass once more to Renault.

The drive back was uneventful, perhaps more so than Medea would have liked. But when they got over the French border into Biarritz, Pen relented and said that they would do a bit of shopping there and find in another hotel.

"With a bigger shower than the last one please, or a bath," she said.

By that time she knew all that Pen was prepared to tell her about his friends Joe Fircloth, Maurice Renault and Jacques DeLauro. But she did not know yet that she had actually met the first of them.

"I wanna help," she had said around a mouthful of gum, but Pen didn't know how dangerous it might be. Two girls that he loved were already suffering lasting psychological damage because of him; that was more than enough. But it did not stop him buying her a severe-looking business-suit with an almost knee-length pencil skirt split by a long vent up the back and a fitted, single-breasted jacket to match with cloth-covered buttons and padded shoulders. To Pen's surprise, when she tied her hair back and gave him a preview in stockings and heels, she looked more provocative than in any of her sexy gear. Bewildered, he ran his hands through his hair and blew out a lungful of air.

The next day, he dropped her off in Périgueux outside her building. They lingered over their farewells, and Pen promised to call her when Joe got back from Geneva.

23

Pen saw Maurice Renault to plan the next step. It was important he somehow get himself into DeLauro's confidence. Since he couldn't bank on the man necessarily being there when he visited the free port, he decided to announce his visits by telephone and ask for the boss each time, hoping that curiosity would get the better of DeLauro to the point of wanting to see what his latest client was importing.

Back home, he put a load in the washing machine. Hunting around for something to keep him warm, he found the lightweight jacket he was wearing when he was bitten by Serge's dog, hanging behind the kitchen door. He put it on and slipped his hands into the worn pockets. It'll do for now, he thought. With a start his fingers brushed against the unmistakeable serrated form of the bone harpoon that he had shown to Maurice that same day. He pulled it carefully out of the folds of cloth and gaped at it. He had presumed it stolen, gone with all the rest. He must have forgotten it, driven out of his mind by the rush of events after the discovery of the cave. He marvelled again at its perfection. This was the object that had started all the trouble. Vincent had tried to have it stolen to sell to DeLauro. Pen turned it in his fingers and could feel the missing pieces falling into place.

He still had the laurel-leaf he had bought at Drouot. It and the harpoon were both seriously respectable pieces of prehistory. The laurel-leaf even had its own history inscribed on a little paper label glued on the bottom of one face. He would take them with him tomorrow and show them to DeLauro. He could pretend a contact was offering him a collection; but he had no idea of their authenticity or their value, and could DeLauro please advise him? Because if they were good, Joe had the perfect client.

Once more as Joe, he settled into his flight. He felt that he ought to be flying business-class. He was sure Renault wouldn't bat an eyelid, but couldn't bring himself to pay the extra.

He had to put a bag in the hold this time, as he had brought the harpoon and the blade and several tools to deal with the boxes of ceramics, they wouldn't have made it through in his hand-luggage. So he was held up for a while in baggage reclaim. Out on the concourse there were no taxis right away and he could feel his impatience building. But eventually he was making the short run once more in the back of a plush Mercedes along the lakeside to the free port.

In the empty foyer he just stood for a few moments, confident that someone would be aware of his arrival. Sure enough the door behind the reception desk opened, and the same bored-looking, foppish guy in the dark green suit came to greet him.

"Hello, Mr Fircloth. Mr DeLauro is expecting you. You have your key? He will be along to your room shortly." The man fiddled with the locks on the security door and let Joe into the corridor. The transformation from his previous visit was heartening. He walked confidently down the wide corridor, although he was still aware of the cameras following his every move. The shelving and the table and chairs were welcome additions to his room and when DeLauro arrived tapping at the open door Joe was installed comfortably behind his laptop at the table.

"Joe, nice to see you! Your merchandise arrived from Italy three days ago. I'm having it brought up now."

"Thank you, Jacques. How are you?" DeLauro smiled. Giving him no time to reply, Pen launched into his prepared pitch:

"I'll be unpacking the items to check that they got here in one piece. If you have time later on, I would appreciate you passing your expert eye over them to tell me what you think. You can never be too careful these days, and two heads are better than one."

"I would love to see them Joe, I'll pop back later then."

DeLauro left, and moments later one of the orange fork-lifts turned up at his door. The uniformed warehouseman called over his shoulder:

"Mr Fircloth?"

"Yes, please bring it in. Over by the shelves, if you would."

"Sign here, please sir," said the man, shoving a form at him.

Joe signed, and watched as the fork-lift on its soft, wide wheels swept out of the room, the driver barely glancing at the controls. It seemed easy enough, though Pen guessed it might be harder than it looked.

The pallet was piled with wooden crates, and Pen immediately worried about the cardboard boxes he had taken down to Portugal. Would they have survived the journey? A bit late to worry about that now.

In the holdall he'd brought with him he had a craft knife, scissors, a big felt-tip pen, Havana packing-tape, a pad of writing-paper and his Leatherman. No jemmy and no screw-gun. When DeLauro came back to the room expectantly, Joe asked for some tools. DeLauro looked at the wooden cases and motioned for him to follow.

He took him down the empty corridor to the loading-bay, where the security door had remained open. On the left there was a maintenance area with a cage of gas-bottles for the fork-lifts, a work-bench, and a tool-locker. DeLauro told him to look for what he needed and to be careful to put it back when he had finished. Joe took a screw-gun with a selection of different heads, a small crowbar, and a hammer. He didn't miss a thing. The surveillance cameras obviously covered the various areas he would have to pass through. He realised he'd better have a damn good reason to be seen in the loading-bay. There was no hope of creeping around in there.

Back in his room, Pen cursed the silly moustache under his breath: it made his lip sweat whenever he was nervous, as he was now. He would love to know how many security staff there were, the positions of the monitors, and so many other things that might make it possible to take a look in a few of the other rooms, starting with D14b next door.

He unscrewed the lid of the topmost crate and carefully levered it off, to reveal a layer of thick corrugated cardboard and swathes of bubblewrap. The crate held a single, breath-taking piece of fine terra-cotta pottery. Joe lifted it out carefully and stood it on the table. It was a large double-handled vase made of red clay with a series of finely-drawn, near-naked figures dancing around its wide belly in shades of red on a black background. It had been visibly restored, but that had diminished none of its presence. Joe heard the door next to his open and close. DeLauro put his head round Joe's open doorway to see if everything was going okay. Lost as he was in contemplating the beauty of the astonishing artefact, Pen didn't turn round or in any way acknowledge his host.

"My god," he heard DeLauro say, drawn into the room by the power of the handsome vase, "You know what that is Joe? A calyx krater, they were used from Mesopotamia right through to Western Europe for mixing strong wine with water. It's Greek, probably fourth or fifth century BC. Goodness, it's beautiful! Do the other boxes hold pieces of this quality?"

"More or less," said Joe, who had no more clue than Pen; but he realised he was having the hoped-for effect. "You've had stuff like this through here before?"

"I've got some," said DeLauro, "but not of this quality. May I stay a moment while you unpack the rest?"

"If you wish, Jacques. But I'm only checking that everything is intact. I'll be packing it away afterwards. Most of it has to be sent on to Boston this week and I won't be back before my first shipment gets here from Lisbon."

"So all's going as you expected," said DeLauro lightly, all business and smiling again.

"Well, the first lot seems to have got here okay. The others should be here sometime next week." Pen had got the cover off another crate and exposed a smaller vase, also with two handles set low down on its elegant body, exquisitely painted in the style of the first. DeLauro was in awe.

"This stuff is worth serious money, you know."

"How much would you say?"

"Well. It's no secret. A piece like that first one, a bit bigger and in remarkable condition, sold for eight hundred thousand dollars to the New York Met some years ago." Pen glowed with satisfaction. Renault had really pulled his weight this time — although he wouldn't like to know how much he was paying in insurance. He must really want to drag DeLauro down. Well, now it was up to Joe to see that they did indeed do so. As he continued to unpack, searching for the three marked vases that he was to keep, he noticed DeLauro had gone quiet. Catching him unawares, Joe saw the emotions struggling in a face that was darkly suffused with blood. But what startled Pen, and nearly made him forget he was Joe, were the eyes. They were alive with craving, reptilian, cold and unscrupulous. Pen coughed to hide his sudden panic, and then DeLauro was under control again, his face once more passive. Evidently having seen enough, he said:

"Impressive, very impressive. Come and see me when you've finished, Joe, I'll be up in my office." And with that he left, leaving Pen struggling with the enormity of what he had got himself into.

He locked up and went along the corridor to the foyer. The

security door was open there, but the space was empty, although he knew he was being watched. He knocked on DeLauro's door trying to look casual and was called in. DeLauro was behind his desk. Pen recognised a more noxious, amoral version of Merle, a manipulative spider aware of its power, waiting expectantly at the hub of its web. He felt his unease crank up a notch, but told himself this was hardly surprising. He gave DeLauro a sheaf of papers with the address of the museum in Boston, the inventory of objects, the customs and tax forms and all the other formalities that Renault had sorted out for him. DeLauro looked his old charming self again, apparently quite satisfied with the paperwork:

"Seems all in order. Curious, though, Italy doesn't usually like letting such valuable antiquities out of its borders. You must tell me your secret one day." He smiled and promised to have the shipment sent on, taking all necessary precautions for its delicate handling.

They were preparing to say goodbye when Joe seemed to remember something.

"Oh, hang on a second. I was wondering if you had any ideas on this." He put his holdall down on the ground, stooping to hunt around in it until he came up with a padded envelope.

"One of my French clients has some prehistoric flints and stuff and has offered me a modest collection. I trust him of course, but I don't know this stuff well and have no idea if they are what he claims, I wondered if you could tell me." He unwrapped the harpoon and the laurel-leaf and handed them to DeLauro. He saw something flicker momentarily across DeLauro's face, but this time the eyes were as flat and emotionless as two stones. He turned them over briefly in his hands and handed them back to Joe with little enthusiasm.

"Not my field, I'm afraid. Could be worth something, but you would have to know what you're doing. France, you say? Might be illegal to export them, even with proof of ownership." Pen had a sinking feeling. He was afraid the flints had aroused the spider's suspicions.

Oh well, he thought, back to the drawing board.

It was late when he got back to Bordeaux. He bought a prepaid cheap cellphone at the airport and slipped it into his breast pocket. Then he broke his rule and didn't go to the flat to change. He drove from the airport directly to the impressive Pont d'Aquitaine suspension bridge that spanned the wide river Garonne, thus avoiding the city centre and saving more than half an hour. He rode straight up and over, for a moment hanging in the sky with the city lights sprawled out below him as if he were flying.

How did we manage to do all this? he pondered: the industry, the technology. Who coordinates it all? How does it all keep working? He caught himself marvelling once more at the world and was momentarily heartened. Heading home, he considered stopping over in Périgueux but thought better of it: he needed to see Alec first.

The thing that was stoking Pen's hope was that there was no camera in his room at the free port. He was thinking he might be able to drill a small hole through the partition between the rooms somewhere out of the way, up in a corner where it wouldn't be noticed, and use a little web cam hooked up to his computer to take a look next door. He had heard DeLauro come out of that room and he was hoping it might contain some of his personal goods.

He showered and had French toast, or eggy bread as his mum used to call it, quick and easy, and thought of turning on his laptop. But in the end he just went to bed and crashed out, exhausted.

He was woken the next morning by the telephone bleating insistently from the next room. But by the time he got there it was too late: whoever it was had rung off. He dialled the service to see who had rung, hoping that it might at last be Sophie. He was getting exasperated by her refusal to talk to him, and was worried by how it might affect Alice. The thought brought on a wave of sadness. The electronic voice came on with a click and told him the number that had called was that of a mobile phone that he did not recognise. He was given the option to call it back and he took it. But he was immediately sorry when he heard the self-righteous tones of Inspector Merle.

"You been playing silly bastards with me, son?"

"What now?" replied Pen, almost slipping into Joe's persona to hide.

"You told me that all the stuff from that cave had been stolen from you."

"And?"

"Some of it has turned up in Bordeaux."

"You must be over the moon."

"What do you mean?"

"Well, case solved, no?"

"No, and you bloody well know it isn't. Bordeaux's claiming that it's nothing to do with us, says it was bequeathed by some old collector, and it was all found near Toulouse in the eighteen-sixties!"

"That means it can't be from the cave, then, doesn't it?"

"Listen, laddie. I told you that if any of the stuff from that heist turned up you would be going down. But what I meant was that if you had any of it left you should hand it over pronto."

"But I didn't have any of the stuff from the, er, dig."

"That's what you say. But the things that have turned up in Bordeaux look suspiciously like the ones in the photos you took in the cave. Why couldn't you be as good a photographer as you are a liar-boy?"

"I don't know if I should take that as a compliment."

"I've got my eye on you, lad."

"I noticed."

Merle cut off. Pen felt weak. He wanted to laugh and cry at the same time. God, life was hard just now.

He made a pot of tea and called Alec, who answered on the third ring.

"Alec. You busy?"

"Depends what you mean by busy."

"I need to see you, man. I can pay you for your time."

"Hey, stay cool, man, I'm never too busy to see you."

"Can I come now?"

"Sure. You okay?"

"I'm fine — or I will be when this is over."

The morning had gone by the time they had finished. Pen called Renault.

"Hi Maurice, how's it going?"

"Ah, Pen. Not too bad, the work on the house is painstakingly slow, but it is advancing. You?"

"It's hard, Maurice. Can I come and see you."

"When?"

"Now."

"Ok Pen, I've got a meeting but I'll put it off till later this afternoon. You eaten?"

"Not since last night."

"We'll have lunch here."

"Thanks, I'm on my way."

Pen told Renault how in Geneva they had both been blown away by the Greek terracottas and how they were to be sent on to Boston this week. Renault looked noticeably relieved. Then he told him of DeLauro's reaction to the harpoon.

"Pen," said Renault carefully: "whatever you do, don't underestimate DeLauro. He's ruthless. If he thinks you're a danger to him, he won't hesitate to take whatever action he feels necessary to protect his interests. Remember Vincent. I think you should pull out."

Pen had gone too far to pull out now and said as much. Renault countered with:

"You're on his ground out there and you have no backup, no one who could help if you get into trouble."

"That's why I've come to see you, Maurice. Take down this phone number. When I get back there I'll phone you before I go into the free port. If I don't phone you again three hours later, call this number and tell them everything."

"It sounds like madness, Pen. Look, we can get out now while we're ahead."

"No!" shouted Pen, "that bastard is still destroying my life, now as we speak. If you want to help, say you'll call that number exactly three hours after I tell you I'm going in, and don't let me down."

"Who are these people, Pen, and why is the time so important?"

"They're my backup, and the time is so I know where I am in my negotiations. He's not going to get away with this, Maurice."

"Maybe, Pen. But surely it isn't worth getting yourself killed over?"

"I don't intend to do that, Maurice."

Then he called Medea.

"Hi Medea, you ready to try out that suit?"

"Why not? The weather's cold enough for it." It was true, the temperature had dropped. But Pen hardly bothered with heating; if he felt cold he just put on more clothes.

"Can you be ready tomorrow morning? This will be a paying job, you realise?"

"Why not tonight? There's a new Bengali restaurant just opened here, and you can keep your money."

This sounded tempting. Pen gave an audible sigh into the telephone.

"Sorry Medea, I still have loads to do before tomorrow. But if it's any consolation I am starting to get seriously attached to you."

"Hey, Pen, you don't want to do that. I was just beginning to like you."

"So, see you at eight tomorrow morning then. Oh, and, er Medea, bring a change of clothes, can you, something casual? And remember, Switzerland isn't in Europe — you'll need your passport."

"Mmm..."

She was wearing her suit. Although her hair had streaks of white, it was done up in a bun: but the shorter strands at the front had refused to be captured and hung out framing her face fetchingly. Pen couldn't help noticing once again that her high heels had changed the architecture of her anatomy and that her stockings had seams. He pushed away the image of a garter belt and the smooth stretch of bare thigh above them. He was glad to see that she was carrying only a single, in-flight case.

"You look the part, Madame," he said when he greeted her.

"You're not bad yourself, boy. You could do with fattening up a bit though. Have you had breakfast? C'mon, let's get coffee and croissants before we set off."

So they sat in a busy bar and he told her that she was shortly to meet his friend Joe. Then they talked about music. After twenty years in France Pen had developed a growing dislike for French music. There was something unsuited to the language for anything other than rudimentary generic folk, it couldn't rock at all. Anyway they were far more interested in the text than the delivery. Apart from rap or rai, Pen thought it all sounded like variety or music-hall. He hardly ever listened to French bands. He could take Edith Piaf in context, for the nostalgia, and a miniscule amount of folk accordion for the ambiance; but that was about it. To his surprise Medea partly agreed with him, although she knew he was old-fashioned — he even listened to jazz! She had a thing for electro. On the trip to Portugal she had seen the external jack on his CD player, so this time she produced a USB drive to plug in so they could listen to Tricky and Nitin Sawney on the road to Bordeaux. Pen had never noticed that he could do that; he was still on CDs.

As they climbed the stairs to his tiny flat, Pen could sense that something was wrong. He had his holdall in his right hand and his flight-bag over his shoulder. Medea was one step behind him when he stopped. He turned and, in an urgent whisper, told her:

"Get back outside — now!"

She retreated a step, but stayed put as he went up the last two steps to his landing. The door to his apartment was ajar. He shrugged the bags off and barged into the room.

Empty. The mattress was still inflated under the window, with the sleeping-bag and his one luxury, a down pillow, on it. But the bare room had been visited. The bathroom door was wide open. The door to the cabinet above the sink had been forced. The steady red light on the answer-phone showed there was at least one undeleted message that had already been listened to. He pressed the button. Just one, telling him he had been selected to win fifty thousand euros and that he should ring the following number to find out more. He nearly erased it but realised that would put the little light out.

Pen tried to think. Medea came up and stood in the open door-way looking around.

"Looks like they took everything," she said, wide-eyed.

"They took nothing," Pen replied through clenched teeth. "Shit, this changes everything. C'mon, let's go."

"What's going on for Holy Mary mother of Jesus Christ's sake?" Pen surprised her by smiling.

"I always thought you were a closet Catholic, Medea."

"So? I did my catechism at thirteen, and then I discovered drugs and boys so I sort of lapsed. But I enjoyed it at the time."

"Come on, we're going to hire a car and I need to get my suit cleaned."

"That suit looks clean," she said pointing to the few items of clothing hanging on a simple rail.

"Yes, but I can't risk them working out that I know they've been here." Pen was getting used to Medea by now, so was unsurprised that that she required no more explanation. She just raised her eye-brows and retreated down the stairs.

Pen ended up buying a new suit as the cleaners told him they couldn't have his crumpled one ready before late afternoon. Despite

Medea insisting that they would look more the part in a new Mercedes or a big BMW, he hired a Ford Mondeo estate. But she was happy enough when she saw the four-way sound system and the USB dock. Pen groaned and hoped there might be something good on the radio. Realising she was going to have to take on more importance in his fast-changing plan, he told her to drive so she could get used to the car. They had already shared the driving down to Portugal, and it was no surprise that in the powerful Ford she was an even more aggressive driver. She kicked her shoes off, hiked up her skirt to unclip and remove her stockings, and drove bare-legged with the heating on.

She felt Pen looking at her and stared back.

"What?" she said, smiling at him.

"Look. First, slow down a bit. we don't want to die just yet. This is going to be dangerous enough without a pile-up. They broke into my flat and they're on to me. I think my best bet is to try and get them to think I'm some sort of undercover police or Interpol agent. It might protect me a bit. You, young lady, are to stay well away. But if I call you, you've got to be ready to drive in and pick me up."

"I thought I was your secretary."

"Not any more you aren't. Thank god I didn't go back to the flat and leave my stuff there when I came back last time. If they'd found the wig and the moustache, I'd be cooked."

"Come on, Pen. When am I going to meet Joe, he sounds interesting."

Medea crinkled up her eyes lewdly but he didn't laugh. He looked out at the heavy traffic heading out of Bordeaux and said:

"The wig is hot and uncomfortable but you get used to it. The worst is the moustache, always worrying it's going to slip sideways or fall off altogether. I should warn you that Joe is not me. He's someone else completely. I inhabit him when I put on his clothes. I don't even know if he likes girls, especially not punky ones."

"Punk!" she retorted, "that post-hippy nihilist crap! They had some good ideas but their music was shit. At least when we dye our hair or pierce our bodies we do it with taste. I like the way the Japanese do fashion."

"If you say so — and I agree with you about the music. But you look sort of punky, they did set some trends."

"Too anti-establishment for me. Can you imagine what it would be like if they ran the country."

"Probably be post-apocalyptic by now, I should think."

Pen had one more idea as they stopped at a garage to fill up and buy chocolate and drinks for the drive. Medea bought some sunglasses and he bought and filled an orange five-litre plastic jerrican with petrol and he stowed it in the back.

Geneva wasn't as far as Lisbon, but it took all day to get to the Swiss border, and Pen decided they would find a hotel in France for the night. They booked in at what at any other time Pen would have considered a charming imitation Tyrolean-style chalet overlooking a still, dark lake surrounded by tall pines, a half-hour drive from the border. He had lost some of his self-assurance, and Medea didn't seem able to coax him out of his distracted mood.

24

Next morning Pen was brighter. Dressed as Joe Fircloth he had a freshly determined look, with his personal assistant Medea beside him. She was back in her stockings and high-heels but had her red sneakers handy for driving. At breakfast she kept shooting him looks of disbelief, holding her napkin to her mouth to hide her incredulity. He didn't only look completely different; he even behaved differently. To the others in the dining-room they probably looked like a couple who had had a tiff. Joe was wired, ready for action, and wanted to get going. He knocked back a couple of coffees while his girlfriend had scrambled eggs, hot buttered toast with marmalade and orange juice.

Just outside Geneva they pulled into a fuel-station. Pen got out and stretched in the cool alpine air. Medea sat behind the wheel in her dark glasses looking every bit the part, but complained that it was too cold to get out. Pen was sorry Joe Fircloth didn't smoke, and avoided the rather more pertinent considerations such as the wisdom of what he was doing and what he might be getting Medea into. He climbed into the back seat across from his driver, and reminded her to get rid of her gum before they arrived.

With the car not being an airport taxi, the efficient-looking free port checkpoint guard stopped them and looked them over. Medea pulled forward to bring the rear window level with the guard, and Pen produced his British passport. The man looked it over and gave it back. Medea held out her French one, but seeing the country of origin was enough for him, and he waved them through. Pen now made a quick call to Renault, saying he was on his way in and reminded him to call back as arranged in exactly three hours. He gave the number to Medea and told her to enter it under Joe and said to phone it if he was not out inside three hours. He then gave her his own phone. He realised that maybe he should have bought a new phone for the occasion, because if that one fell into the wrong hands it would finger everyone — but then that would have meant having to many phones to worry about because he still had the throwaway he had picked up at the airport last time on him.

"I might need you in a hurry," he told her. "I can't say when, but I'll be in there a while."

"Why can't I come with you, Pen? It's so boring waiting."

"You stay out of this — and don't call me Pen!"

She looked sullen but said no more as he directed her to the warehouse entrance, where he got out and told her to stay out of sight.

As he watched her drive off he regretted his outburst. Then he shrugged and pushed into the building, slipping as easily into Joe as into a lukewarm bath. Pen was gone, it was someone else who pointedly did not look up at the cameras, who waited impatiently for attention. The door opened and DeLauro's manager came out looking a bit flustered:

"Mister Fircloth — we were expecting you yesterday."

"Yeah. I missed my plane. Sorry I didn't call you."

"Mister DeLauro isn't here at the moment. How can I help you?"

"My shipment from Lisbon should have arrived. I'd just like to check it over."

"Okay, er, just a moment, I'll just go and check." He retreated behind his door and Joe waited. In two minutes the young guy was back, looking more anxious than ever, and said:

"Yes. It's in the loading-bay. But we don't have anyone here to bring it through for you right now."

"That's all right," replied Joe, "I can take a look at it where it is. I do have a fork-lift licence, so if you will permit me I might move it myself. I'm afraid I don't have such a lot of time this trip. My plane leaves in about three hours."

"Well, that would be a bit irregular. I'll try to get Mister DeLauro on the phone, but he's not answering at the moment." Joe couldn't believe his luck and waved off-handedly:

"Oh, don't bother him. I can handle it. Could you open up so I can take a look?"

The young man fumbled the security door open with his bunch of keys and Joe set off down the corridor towards his room. The manager went past him to open the loading-bay.

Once in his room, he placed his holdall on the table and looked around the bare room. He spotted the new camera above the door and was careful to make no reaction.

So, he thought, no drilling through the wall then — shit! This guy is quick. Pen was careful to look neutral and not talk aloud. He went to the loading-bay. The big outer doors to the hangar were closed. The only light filtered through the dirty overhead skylights, long sooted-up from countless intercontinental flights. The dramatic slanted rays filtering through the dirt partly illuminated the huge, deserted space. There were several loaded pallets of merchandise waiting in the half-light on the concrete pad to be sent on. He saw his, the second pallet in from the corridor. To get to it, he would have to move the first one out of the way.

Only three days ago Alec had given Pen a quick lesson in forklift truck driving. But he had said that his was an old model, now they had all sorts of fail-safes and security measures. Although Pen was confident that Alec's was the same make, size, and shape as the machines parked in the deserted hangar, he crossed his fingers anyway to be on the safe side. He turned on the gas feed of the closest truck and climbed up into the driver's seat. The key was in the ignition, so he depressed the brake pedal as Alec had shown him, made sure the gear-shift was in neutral, and turned the key. The motor turned over, which so surprised him that he took his foot off the brake and the truck stalled.

He told himself he needed to calm down. He was on- screen somewhere — not that they would see much in this light; but if he fluffed things someone would come running to stop him causing damage. Then suddenly a bank of strip lights flickered on, and he could see what he was doing. He tried again and got the motor running. He backed out from the parking slot and, using the handle on the steering-wheel, manoeuvred over to the first pallet. He remembered what Alec had said — too low, and you catch the bottom plank and push the pallet forward or break the plank. He took his time and slipped the forks carefully between the boards, then pulled the lever back for a slight lift of a few centimetres, tilting the pallet back towards him. That would do, he decided, but when he backed the little vehicle out the forks rocked forwards and scraped the floor. Sweating under his wig he lifted a bit more, and succeeded in moving the tightly wrapped pallet out of the way. Carefully, he deposited it far enough away on the wide platform that he could take out his own pallet without hindrance.

This time he was smoother. But just as he was turning into the corridor, his own pallet on board, the motor spluttered and cut out. He tried the key but though the starter turned over nothing else happened. Pen looked at the gauges and saw that the gas-bottle was empty. Swearing quietly, he climbed down to unhitch the bottle and remove the pressure fitting, as he did when changing bottles on his kiln back home. On his way back from the cage where the spare bottles were stored, the young man from reception arrived, obviously in a flap.

"Mr Fircloth! Clients aren't insured to use the equipment! If anything were to happen — I am in charge while Mr DeLauro isn't here — I really must insist!"

"Hey, no sweat! Jacques DeLauro said I could use the equipment as long as I put it back when I've finished," said Joe, securing the full bottle into the cradle and attaching the feed. He turned the valve on and climbed back into the seat. He turned the key, remembering to step on the brake pedal just in time, and the motor puttered into life. He smiled at the anxious manager and said,

"I'm afraid I don't have much time and I need to get this done."

The fork-lift was still in his room but he had already unpacked several of the pots, careful to keep his back to the camera. The pallet was out of the way, tight up against the party wall, and one or two of the original pots were on the table. He had had a fair bit of time but was not surprised when DeLauro and another guy came into his room unannounced.

"Ah, Jacques, how are you since my last visit?" Joe lifted his head from his work and smiled warmly: "Thank you for dealing with the previous shipment so promptly. My client has not yet received it but I am informed that it is already in the USA."

DeLauro did not answer immediately, but looked at the Nasca pots on the table. He picked one up and turned it over in his hand. Then he raised his reptilian eyes to Joe Fircloth's and said,

"Who the hell are you?"

Pen looked at the man with DeLauro. Somehow he was reminded of the guy who had been with Inspector Merle that day at the cave. Not the way he looked, but the way he held himself. He wondered if it was him who had beaten Vincent black and blue.

"I'm a businessman like you, Jacques — not in the same league, but I try to live by my wits."

"I have taken the liberty to look into your background, Joe. There is nothing there. No one has heard of you. To have the kind of clients you have you need to have been in the business for years, believe me I know. But no one has ever come across you before. So who is running you?"

"Listen, Jacques. I have been into antiquities in a small way for long enough, bronze mostly and a bit of oriental, but it is impossible not to take a wider interest in things. I got lucky with the Greek stuff, so I decided to try and make a bit more profit out of it. If you know anything about collecting you know that it gets under your skin. I promise you I have done nothing illegal on your premises, neither here nor abroad. My hope is to build up a little collection of the better stuff for myself here. If I can do that away from the eyes of most of the taxmen on the planet, then it will be thanks to you."

"There is something that worries me about you, Joe. I think we ought to have a little discussion in my office. This is my colleague Jason." The man didn't even acknowledge that his name had been mentioned. "Jason was in special services in the army before working for me. His particular speciality was close combat, so don't try to run off on me." Pen looked up at the video camera and realised that it worked both ways: he supposed that if DeLauro was going to get rough he would rather do it off-screen.

"Oh, and you'd better give me your telephone. We don't want you calling any of your little friends."

Pen spread his arms and said:

"I forgot my phone. Ridiculous, I know. But true." Jason searched him deftly, rubbing him down with practised hands. He raised his eyebrows but didn't deign to say anything.

"That is one more strange thing about you, Joe, to add to my list. Come on, let's find out who you are."

"Ok," said Pen, showing no signs of alarm, "I'd better just put this fork-lift back in the hangar."

"That won't be necessary, Joe, you can leave it for now."

"Well in that case I'd better turn the gas bottle off. They can be dangerous, you know." Still wittering away about security and his fragile Nasca pottery, Pen moved towards the machine. DeLauro showed no interest and was starting to look impatient. Joe went to turn off the gas but deftly half unclipped the feed at the same time. The gas had not been entirely shut off. He could hear it hissing out into the room and raised his voice to cover the sound. He turned to the door raising his voice even more and said:

"Ok Jacques, I can't say I'm happy about this but I can see that you have some unfounded suspicions about me, so let's get it over with."

Pen pushed out into the corridor. To his relief the others followed him. DeLauro's thug put a heavy hand around Pen's left arm just above the elbow, gripping him tightly. But Joe turned back slowly and reached for the door handle with the other hand, fastidiously latching it closed behind him.

DeLauro was already marching ahead of them, his small frame hunched forward purposefully inside its expensive suit. Jason pulled on Joe's arm. Pen yielded immediately, not wanting to provoke his escort who might have far less consideration for his screen image than DeLauro, who now stopped in front of one of the small rooms and brought out his keys.

"This will do for now," he said, "no need to mess up my office." He had found the right key and began to open the door when Joe suddenly dropped to the floor. His legs seemed to go out from under him and his full weight dragged his elbow free from the tight grip. But he instantly shot up again from a low crouch and rammed his head backwards. He connected with something and heard a grunt, but didn't wait to see what he had hit. As he lurched forwards, a hand shot out like lightning and grabbed him by the hair. He didn't even feel the tug as the wig detached, just the cool air over his damp scalp giving him wings. DeLauro had been too confident. The fool had left the security door open. Pen raced through it into the empty foyer and pushed out through the glass doors into the cold exposed avenue, looking around desperately for a way to escape. He ran but heard the glass doors clang open again as his pursuer raced after him. Adrenaline was pumping through his veins. He was going to have to fight. He looked over his shoulder and thought he saw blood on the gorilla's face. What the hell chance did he have?

When he heard the squeal of tyres from a fast-moving car, his heart sank in his chest. He put on a spurt towards the corner of the nearest warehouse. He was a good runner and was drawing away from DeLauro's minder, but he couldn't keep it up for long.

He wasn't scared that he might die. He had a curious sensation that things were happening in slow motion, and could hear the sluggish blood pumping in his ears. He looked down the canyon between the buildings and saw a vehicle approaching fast through the deep shadow.

He felt a sudden mixture of horror and joy when he recognised the Ford. Medea looked grim behind the wheel in her dark glasses. She aimed between the two men, but just before she reached them she jerked up the hand brake and pulled the wheel hard over towards Joe. The effect was dramatic: the car spun on itself, the rear end slewing around so violently that two wheels left the ground. Medea had stopped inches from Joe, and as the wheels slammed back down she revved the engine in an urgent signal for him to jump in.

Jason had been narrowly missed by the back of the car, but he was a professional and leapt onto the vehicle trying to reach Pen. Medea reversed violently, throwing him off, and then raced forward, slowing for Pen who yanked open the back door and dived into the seat. Jason was after them but Medea stamped hard on the accelerator and watched him in the rear view mirror bent over with his hands on his knees.

"Medea, am I glad to see you!" Pen sobbed through shuddering breaths. "Give me your phone," he said urgently, "your phone, quick." Medea was efficient but she had just been scared half to death and was not functioning as well as she might. She fumbled around in the foot-well for the phone that had been ejected from the seat beside her in the fracas.

"Your phone!" screamed Pen from the back. Then he heard a heavy crump followed by what sounded like a series of small explosions.

"Drive between those two buildings," he said, pointing out a trajectory that would give them a view of DeLauro's warehouse.

"What about the phone?" asked Medea petulantly; but she did as he asked. Looking back, Pen could see a pall of thick smoke rising into the sky, apparently right above Eden Holdings.

"Shit! Head for the gate but take it slow through the checkpoint, Medea, we don't want anyone getting suspicious. But be ready to go for it if they try to stop us."

Medea turned and looked at him, but said nothing. He realised he was dealing with delayed panic and it was not over yet. He smoothed his short hair and sat up in the back trying to look cool. He needn't have worried: perhaps DeLauro had more to think about right now than phoning through to the gate-house. He said,

"Follow the signs for the railway station."

"The station?"

"We have to ditch the car."

"What, are you mad? How will we get home?"

"Train."

"First class?"

"First class."

They parked up against a high concrete wall in an empty part of the lorry-park some distance away from the passenger terminal. Pen felt safe here. They changed out of their suits and left everything in the car.

Medea's casual clothes were the short red plaid skirt she had worn on their first date and her bomber jacket with red sneakers. She had kept her stockings on and Pen sighed. Her hair was down. She popped a piece of gum into her mouth and offered one to Pen with a smile. He declined and told her to go to the passenger terminal and wait for him there. They were standing between the wall and the dark blue Ford. She put her face close to his, then reached up and ripped his moustache off. Grinning, she said:

"Can I keep the shoes?" Pen couldn't see why not. She stuffed the stilettos into her flight-bag, tugged out the bag's handle, and walked off wiggling her red skirt as it rolled along behind her.

Pen was in jeans, a sweat shirt, and the thin green harpoon jacket. But he still felt undressed. The suit had become his battle-dress and it was warm. He reached into the car, turned on the ignition, lowered his window, retrieved his tie, and then slammed the door. He unscrewed the cap of the jerrican and the petrol reek filled his nostrils. He poured most of the contents into the car through the window, making sure to cover their suits and the passport. He removed the car's petrol cap and threw the keys into the car. He soaked half the tie with fuel and threw it over the wall, then chucked the empty can in through the window as well. He scrambled over the wall, landing on a quiet pavement behind a group of buildings. This was an industrial part of town. But it was daytime and he felt exposed. Checking out his most likely getaway route, he picked up the tie, lit the damp end of it with his cigarette lighter, threw it swiftly over the wall and walked away. The deflagration was impossible to ignore but he refused to run.

Getting between the buildings, he made his way as quickly as he could to the station. Once in the crowd, he felt better but was trembling. He made for a tobacconist's and bought some tobacco and papers. When Medea walked up to him he was sitting on a bench rolling a cigarette.

"I thought you were giving up smoking," she said looking down at him. He had nothing to say to that. She relented and said:

"It's fun working with you."

"I've retired."

The sound of sirens brought relief to Pen, who realised he had been worrying about the fire, though they might be heading for Eden Holdings.

"Let's get out of here," he said, lifting himself off the bench and drawing hard on his fag. "I won't feel safe until we've put a few kilometres between ourselves and DeLauro, not to mention the Swiss police."

When they consulted the departures screen they realised that they would have to run if they were to catch their train. They boarded the one from Geneva to Lyon, then, taking the risk of being noticed bought two second-class tickets from the conductor, much to Medea's disgust. But Pen felt safer in a crowded carriage. It was only ninety minutes on the TGV, one of France's plush ultra-high-speed trains. From there they took first-class seats to Bordeaux. Pen intended never going back to the apartment, but he needed his truck. They had a compartment to themselves and bought little bottles of champagne and hot *croque-monsieur* toasted sandwiches.

Pen couldn't tell how he felt. He had survived. But had his efforts had any other effect than to put the wind up DeLauro? He would have to wait and see. Medea snuggled up to him and rubbed his shoulders and stroked his chest; and under her gentle hand he felt the rage that had been driving him begin to subside. Thinking back over the last few hours he asked,

"How long was I in Eden Holdings. Do you know?"

"About two hours if that. I wasn't expecting you out so soon." Pen swore quietly, then his face brightened:

"And how the hell did you learn to drive like that?"

"My driving instructor had a crush on me, taught me handbrake turns and skid control. He gave me extra lessons for free, but I've never used them until today."

"Did you like him?"

"Who, the driving instructor? Bloody wanker, but he could drive. Why? You're not jealous, are you?"

"Yeah, of course."

"Listen," said Medea: "I'm mad about you, but don't go getting soft on me. You are not free at all, you're still in love with Sophie, and we both know it. Besides, you're fifteen years older than me and nowhere near rich enough. So let's just keep it friends, okay?"

She took his hand and slipped it under the hem of her skirt, encouraging him to stroke the smooth bit of thigh that bulged slightly above the top of her stockings. He glanced at her, his eyes wide, and whispered,

"You monkey — you're not wearing any knickers!"

25

"I'll pop round with your well-earned pay one day soon," said Pen from the open window of his truck: "Don't make a fuss. You know it's not my money, and Renault will think it well spent."

"Don't worry about the money. Just come and see me or I'll plague you with viruses."

"You wouldn't."

"I could."

"I wouldn't put it past you."

"New Bengali restaurant, my treat."

As he drove off he pictured the goddess Kali, tempting him, her many arms writhing in the lift. It was getting light already and the ghost of a large moon, pale between the clouds, hung low over the horizon. They had travelled through the night and he was whacked. Now he was alone in the truck, he couldn't trust himself to keep his eyes open and opened the window to get a rush of cold air over his face. He put his hand into the front pocket of the dashboard looking for a tissue, and his fingers found the last triangular biface that he had picked up, lying forgotten where he had left it. He pulled it out and glanced at it, black-and-white like a Frisian cow.

"Ha! Noël hasn't seen this — he's going to be absolutely green!" He put it into his jacket pocket and yawned. He could sleep for a week. He could have stayed over with Medea but he knew he should get home. He needed to create some sort of an alibi against the unnerving event that someone linked him with the goings-on in Geneva.

Before he went up to bed, Pen lit the wood-burner in the kitchen, then sat down at the table and turned on his laptop. He typed 'Interflora' into his search-engine and ordered a dozen red roses and six yellow ones to go to Sophie's mother's address.

He added two messages. For the red ones he wrote:

My wounds have all healed
But my heart still feels like a cold peeled potato
Please come home and make chips.

And for the yellow ones he wrote:

I'm thinking of buying you a small puppy
Who will grow into a great big guard dog.
To keep you safe.

He hoped he could count on same-day delivery. He knew Sophie's mum would make sure they got vases full of water and wouldn't let Sophie throw them out. He thought the girls would be happy to get flowers as a first step towards negotiations.

He considered making tea but was too drained to bother. He knew he ought to phone Renault soon, but it was still early. Although he felt thoroughly flaked, he realised that he felt less tense than at any time since the robbery. He climbed the stairs and collapsed across his bed fully dressed.

His cell-phone woke him, ringing in his jacket pocket to intrude on his dreamless sleep like a bad conscience. He answered it automatically, cursing himself as he did so; but he was still far too anxious to let it go unanswered.

"Yeah?" God, his mouth was dry.

"Well. You're alive then?"

"Maurice. Sorry, I'm asleep. We need to meet. Can you come here?"

"Give me an hour."

"Make a lot of noise when you get here — I might easily go back to sleep." He pulled the biface out of his pocket where it had been making overtures to the left side of his rib cage for the last few hours.

Pen felt briefly guilty for not showing some sign of life sooner, even if he had been afraid to talk on the phone. Fuck it, he thought, too late to worry about that now.

He awoke again seconds later, with the phone sounding off like a fire alarm. Why couldn't he have a lullaby for a ring tone? It was Maurice, and he was downstairs. He had let himself in which disconcerted Pen who badly needed to pee. Maurice had made a pot of tea.

"I took the liberty, I hope you don't mind. It would seem our relationship has become more of a friendship over the last few weeks." It wasn't a question, but an assertion.

"Maurice, what happened. Did you wait the three hours before you called the number I gave you?"

"Oh that. Well, I tried. I was so agitated I may have called a little early. I thought you might need help but it made no difference, there was no reply. I tried at least half a dozen times and always got engaged."

Pen didn't know what to make of that. All through this nightmare, events just kept taking their own course regardless of planning.

"Well, Maurice, believe it or not you may well have saved my bacon. Either that or nearly killed me."

"Oh, how?"

"I might tell you one day. But for now, just let me say that we need to watch the news, especially anything coming from Switzerland."

Pen stifled a yawn and went to the bathroom. As they drank their tea, He explained that DeLauro was indeed onto Joe Fircloth as Maurice had feared. Without going into too many details, he told him he had escaped by the skin of his teeth. Renault was surprised to find Pen not particularly upset that his collection was now irrevocably lost to him.

"It's gone, yes. But we knew that from the beginning, Maurice. I had no viable plan to get it out of DeLauro's lair. But you never know — we may just have struck a serious blow against the evil bastard. I'm counting on the curse of the treasure to finish what I started."

"What's all this about a curse, then? I didn't know you were superstitious, Pen."

"Look, I'm going to let you into a bit more of the background of this story. I feel I owe it to you." Pen knocked back the last of his tea and chewed at his bottom lip, wondering how much he could say. He had already decided to take Maurice into his confidence, and he began to explain the strange conclusion he had reached.

"The truth of the matter," he said, looking pointedly at Renault, "though this is not to go beyond this room, is that it was Noël who first found the cave. He was on his own when he discovered it. There was a fall-in and he was buried alive."

Renault looked appalled as Pen went on.

"He was in there for twenty-four hours before I dug him out. His feet had been crushed, he was dehydrated, it was only sheer luck that I found him at all. He could have died in there and the treasure would have been lost with him, end of story. Nutcase — he should never have been digging on his own. Anyway, I found him and took him to hospital and brought the deadly stuff home to my house and we both know what happened to me, and to poor Sophie: she absolutely hated the treasure from the start, wouldn't have touched it with a clothes prop. Then there was Serge. How's he doing by the way?"

Renault looked resigned.

"His wounds are healing up well. He'll have some nasty scars though. But he seems to have regressed, he doesn't talk really and is much like he was when we rescued him in Algeria. He doesn't respond well to captivity. I'm worried that when this eventually comes to trial they will lock him away in an institution for the criminally insane and throw away the key." Pen thought that would be a good idea, but didn't say so. Instead, he continued:

"The next one to handle the grave goods was Vincent. Any idea what he's up to now?"

"I haven't seen him at all and don't want to. But an estate agent in Montignac tells me his two houses are up for sale. Whether that means he's moving away, I don't know."

They looked at each other gravely. Pen was thinking that Vincent had got off rather lightly. But if he was driven away from his family home and the village where he had been respected and looked up to for a lifetime, that would certainly be a personal catastrophe for him.

"So now it's DeLauro's turn," said Pen. "He's had the stuff longer than anyone else, so we can only hope he suffers the most."

"Men like DeLauro are protected by all sorts of systems that their money affords them, Pen. Believe me, I know about that." Maurice Renault had shown various changing faces to Pen over the years, especially this last month. Gone was the aggressive, self-interested businessman, giving way to a benign presence of unexpected integrity, now elegantly drinking tea at Pen's kitchen table. Pen felt as relaxed with him as he would be with Noël, and he realised at last that he liked Maurice Renault. Pen hadn't finished:

"I have to remind you that you also saw just one axe for ten minutes, and look what happened to your place..."

"Perhaps," said Renault, "but a curse, isn't that going a bit far?"

"Well maybe. Don't think I haven't thought through the logical explanations for what is probably only an unfortunate, unlikely chain of events, good luck, bad luck, misery and greed. But you have to admit it is a remarkable coincidence that everyone who's ever been in contact with the treasure has met with mishap just afterwards."

"Okay, so by your logic DeLauro should be in for some serious bad luck right about now."

"With a little help from the late Joe Fircloth, yes I do. By the way, I've still got his bank card. There must still be at least three thousand euros left in the account. What should I do with it?"

"Burn it. It could be dangerous to use it. Being in banking, DeLauro may well have ways of following any transactions you make."

"And the cash?"

"Let it go. Talking of money, Pen, you know I no longer have anyone I can rely on in the Dordogne. I was wondering if you might be prepared to work for me."

"I already do, Maurice."

"Yes. But I mean full-time, on the payroll. The insurance people are asking for me to take all sorts of measures now that I no longer have someone living permanently at the museum. It seems my two ineffectual security cameras and sweet-shop burglar-alarm system are no longer enough. I wondered if I couldn't tempt you."

Pen looked pained.

"Maurice, it's true I've never had enough money. And also that any hope of having any flew out of the window when Serge cut his way into my house with a chainsaw and ripped off my collection. But I could never give up my liberty to be the guardian of your collection."

"Don't look at it like that, Pen. You could have a well- equipped studio at my place and apartments for you and your family. We could hire a gardener and a housekeeper. I would be prepared to give you a reasonable salary with all the usual perks, medical insurance, pension, a vehicle if you need one. And of course you'd have free run of the collection. Besides being a presence there, your job would basically be to keep the place running — dealing with the tradesmen, picking me up from the airport when I need it, that sort of thing. And help catalogue the collection when you've a mind to. You'd still have plenty of time to pursue your own projects."

"Jesus, Maurice, you sure do know how to sweet talk a gal. Give me time to think about it, will you? I will have to discuss it with Sophie of course."

"Mmm — how are things with Sophie?"

"Bad. I don't know. I sent her some roses this morning. I hope she is getting over it all, but she was terribly shaken and it may take time. Strange thing is that I never thought she was so fragile. She blames me for everything, and of course she's right. It's one of those if-only! situations. But what's done is done and we're all going to have to live with the bloody consequences."

Renault was leaving, but they still had many things to settle and Pen promised to visit the following day. He thought briefly of the two hitherto unknown video cameras in Renault's museum and gave a mental shudder. Still tired, he toyed with the idea of going back to bed, but felt he had too much to do; it was well past midday already. He took a long shower and automatically thought fondly of Medea. She had turned out to be a real gem and had been more than a friend. Whatever happened now with Sophie, Medea was in his life. Perhaps the girls would get on, he could see certain similarities between them.

He was sitting down to eat when the phone rang. To his joy it was Alice.

"Thank you for the roses, Papa," she began, bringing an immediate lump to his throat.

"Hey, they weren't nearly good enough for you, sweetie, but they'd run out of the solid gold ones." Suddenly he was stuck for something to say. Their conversations were usually about mundane things, but he needed answers to questions that he couldn't ask her.

"Is it true you are going to get a puppy, Papa?"

"Well, I don't know, poppet. Would you like one?"

"Yes, can I come to choose it? When are you going?"

"When can you get here?"

She didn't answer immediately, and he could hear excited words in the background. Then she said,

"Papa, I don't know. I'll put Maman on."

"All right, Alice. See you soon, lots of love, sweetie."

And then Sophie came on the line:

"Pen, how are you feeling now?"

"Good, much better for hearing your voice, anyway. You know, there's a lot we need to talk about and I would love it if we didn't have to do it over the phone. I was wondering, do you think you're ready to come home yet?"

"You've got to be joking Pen, but I've decided I'm no longer entirely rejecting the idea of ever seeing you again. Mother is driving me nuts. I can't stay here much longer — I would end up strangling her."

"Ah, well that wouldn't do. If you need to burn off some energy, the garden here is a mess."

"Great, so that's why you want me back."

Ignoring the remark just in case she was serious, Pen said:

"I'm just trying to be friendly, Sophie. I miss you, and Alice needs to get back to school."

"Pen, I'm still not interested in living in that house."

"Yes, well that's one of the things we need to talk about. When can I see you?"

"I'll call you. Thanks for the flowers, I thought you had forgotten about us."

"Sophie…" he called plaintively into the phone. But she had gone.

Pen was in a daze. Was that all it took, a bunch of flowers? Why hadn't he thought of it sooner? Because he hadn't been ready to, he realised, simply that. He couldn't have handled normal family life with all that rage eating him up. For good or for worse it had burned itself out now. He only had to hope that it would stop there and that he hadn't brought anything else down on them all.

He needed to do some shopping to be ready if the girls did eventually come back. He wanted to replace Sophie's lamp. He could go to Montignac for all of that, and drop in on Noël if he was home. He called to make sure: like a rock, dependable old Noël was there, delighted to hear from Pen, looking forward to seeing him, and sounding relieved. Denise and he were inseparable. He said she was trying to domesticate him. Oh, and he had a few new flints to show him. Pen had the new biface in his coat pocket. Although it was lovely, he couldn't seem to work up the old enthusiasm. But he would of course take it with him.

Pen went into the town first, picked up a newspaper and some bread and a couple of bouquets of flowers. Then he went out to the huge supermarket that had all but destroyed the commerce of the pretty little market town that straddled the quietly flowing Vézère river. Fortunately Montignac had been able to struggle on thanks to the tourism that the facsimile of the Lascaux cave, Lascaux 2, had brought in. Cheap, poor-quality produce had replaced real service and care, and so quickly! Pen reflected on how the economy had affected the quality of people's lives even here. He hated the music, the lighting, and the vast range of merchandise in the big store. But he did his shopping there because there was nowhere else left to buy half the things he wanted. Despite his annoyance, though, he found he was smiling at the hope of the girls coming home soon, and chose a bottle of Bourgogne white and a bottle of Veuve Clicqot champagne with its distinctive orange label — the perfect accompaniment for pizza, he thought. And some soft drinks of course, for Alice whenever they turned up. He suddenly wanted a cigarette. He always ended up spending more in the bloody supermarket. Weren't they supposed to be cheaper than the high-street shops?

He parked outside Noël's little house, picking up one of the bunches of flowers from the passenger seat as they came out to greet him. Noël and Denise looked so perfect together. Pen wondered why they had taken so long to get it on. Denise looked radiant.

"Pen!" said Noël with a smile, "You look great! What's happened to cheer you up so much? Has Sophie come home?"

"No, but she did talk to me on the phone."

"That's good news," a serene smile was lighting up Denis's face, "she didn't say that she had softened towards you when I spoke to her yesterday."

"No, I don't think she knew herself then." Denise held Pen at arms' length evidently liking what she saw, then drew him to her and gave him a gentle hug.

"Pen, we have some news as well. It's supposed to be bad luck to talk about it so soon, but you're family. Guess what — I'm pregnant!" Pen gathered her back in and hugged her tight. He felt a bit awkward with the flowers dangling from his hand, so disentangled himself and presented them to her. Her happiness was infectious and they laughed and chattered for a while. Then Pen remembered something. He put his hand into his pocket and drew out the harpoon.

"Here you go, Noël, something to show your son or daughter to illustrate the story of the most remarkable Neolithic discovery of the century." Noël looked shocked.

"I thought that was lost, Pen. I thought Renault got it."

"Man, have we got a lot to talk about, but not just now. First, show me your new flints."

"But I can't keep this, Pen. It's all that's left of what we found."

"Of course you can, Noël. It's not Neolithic, so it will have no bad joss attached to it. Don't tell me you don't like it? Oh, and by the way — Denise, does Sophie know you're pregnant?"

"Yes, of course she does. But she hasn't told Alice yet. We thought we'd wait at least three months for that."

"Very prudent of you, but I'm sure it's not necessary. Well, look, perhaps tomorrow night we could have a get-together at my place, nothing extravagant, I'm planning pizza. Denise, you won't be drinking alcohol or smoking for at least a year, eh? But I hope you don't mind if we do?" She chuckled and said:

"Two years, Pen. I intend to breast-feed the little fellow as long as I can."

"Enjoy her while you can, Noël, the competition will be fierce."

"There'll be no competition," retorted Noël, "he can feed while I'm out flint-hunting, and then make room for me when I come home."

Pen sighed. He knew something had subtly changed inside him, that he would never be the same again. While Denise went off to find something to put the flowers in, Pen took the opportunity to ask a question that had been bothering him for days.

"Noël: did you show the jade axe to Denise?"

"Well, no, we had other things to occupy us at the time," he replied self-consciously, "and then somehow with all the trouble they caused I kind of left it on hold. Besides, she isn't interested in prehistory at all. Why do you ask?"

"Why do you think?"

"Yes, I know, I didn't even keep it in the house." They looked at each other, silently counting their lucky stars.

Noël was stunned by the black-and-white hand-axe. He grinned as he said:

"The first piece in your new collection, Pen?"

"I don't think so, Noël. I think I'm through with flints."

Noël obviously didn't believe him, and showed him his own most recent finds. Pen still couldn't work up much enthusiasm, and felt a little sad. He could hardly believe that only yesterday he was running for his life from a professional thug. Still very tired, he remembered that he needed to sleep for a week.

Before he left, he asked them if the police or anyone else wanted to know where he had been, if they wouldn't mind saying he had spent the last twenty-four hours sleeping off a hangover at Denise's place.

"What was the occasion?" asked Noël.

"I'm depressed," said Pen with a conspiratorial wink.

26

He slept. He went to bed at four that afternoon and woke at nine-thirty the next morning. It was already getting late to go and see Maurice if he was going to cut wood and tidy up after himself. If they were ever going to work together, Maurice was going to have to learn to use the computer, at least for email. He called him. He seemed delighted to hear that Sophie seemed to be coming round. He said:

"When you have the time, turn on the telly and watch the news. Something quite odd seems to be happening in Switzerland." Pen wanted to ask what, but they had rules, so he just said:

"I'll try and come over tomorrow, Maurice," and turned on the radio.

There had been nothing about it in yesterday's paper, and he had missed the current affairs programme that he liked to listen to. But it was nearly eleven and the news would come on shortly. He was kneading dough for pizza when it did. The headlines were about France's lamentable performance in international football, followed by the latest on paedophilia in the Catholic Church. Then came conflicts involving France in North Africa, then the wobbly World Bank and various financial collapses, some national and European politics — all after the football, of course. The final report was one about a certain Jacques DeLauro, international art-dealer and managing director of Eden Holdings in Switzerland, currently being held by the authorities there. There had been a mysterious explosion in his warehouse in Geneva's free port. The Swiss police, who had been watching him for some time, had taken the opportunity to follow the fire services into the building, and found a cache of stolen art treasures on his wrecked premises, including hundreds of articles purportedly from Herculaneum and Pompeii. Many of the priceless objects had been damaged in the explosion and ensuing fire, but more than enough had been saved from the flames to incriminate the crooked art-dealer.

It looked to Pen as though the curse was not only very real, but getting more virulent by the hour. He had stopped kneading the pizza dough to listen, and found he was still holding it in his hands. He threw it up in the air and then slapped it down hard onto the marble worktop with satisfaction. He was still staggeringly out of pocket, but all the people who had had a hand in turning him over had come to grief, and that was worth something. He was finally able to placate some of the demons that had been wrecking his peace of mind and gnawing at his duodenum, since this whole thing began.

The phone rang again — Medea.

"You did it darling! I'm so proud of you!"

"We did it, you mean. Listen, Medea, I'm going to be held up for a while because I need to see Sophie and Alice. There is a lot to sort out. But I was wondering if you would care to come for supper here one night and meet everyone?"

"What! Come to your place, meet your family?"

"Have I shocked you?"

"No, I would love to come, Pen. Send me a formal gilt-edged invitation when you're ready."

"I still don't actually have a family at the moment but I know Alice will be intrigued to meet you. Oh, and Medea, we might just have one last shopping spree to do together if you fancy it."

"Well," she answered, "you know me. I'm a simple girl at heart, simple pleasures. Why not? I'll come provided I can drive."

When she rang off, Pen was unable to hide from himself how good it was to hear Medea's voice. One thing he could count on was that his life wasn't getting any less complicated. He hoped the girls would end up getting on.

John Martyn was playing on his old-fashioned CD player and the house was full of the warmth of wood fires and cooking. Though the flowers created a welcoming display on the freshly laid table for Noël and Denise who agreed to come and bring some life back into the place, Pen was unable to get into the mood for it. He was mournfully surveying his handiwork when he threw down the dishcloth he was using, grabbed his jacket and rushed out to his truck. He called Denise on the road and explained he was sorry it was such short notice but he was postponing their celebration. She was more than happy when she heard why.

It was a three-hour drive to Sophie's mum's. But he had so much on his mind that it did its usual trick of wandering off and the familiar long journey was over before he knew it. He sat outside the house in the vehicle trying to build up the courage to face Sophie's rejection, wishing again that he had not given up tobacco. Sophie's mum spotted him from a window and opened the door — then Alice dashed out and he climbed out to meet her

"Papa!" She leaped into his arms. She was really getting too heavy for that, but he swept her up and rubbed her playfully with his chin.

"You got no whiskers, Papa."

"Of course not, I shaved for Sophie — I hope she notices!" Sophie didn't seem to care one way or the other but she seemed happy to see them together. She and Pen were a little shy when she approached him, and they gave each other a chased peck on the cheek like distant friends. Pen let Alice dribble out of his arms down onto the front door step, and the thought came to him unbidden: how simple it had been with Medea. He could tell by Sophie's attitude that it was going to be a long haul this time: but she allowed him hope.

Unsurprisingly, she had been distant that evening, closed in on herself. By tacit agreement they hadn't talked at all about what had happened. In any case Alice and Sophie's mum chattered away for the four of them at supper. But later, when Alice was tucked up in bed, and the old woman had tactfully left them in peace, they talked in the kitchen. They were both too agitated to sit together so were standing by the old stone chimney enjoying the heat. He told Sophie about Maurice Renault's job offer, though he insisted that he didn't want to leave the house unless there was no alternative. She was shocked at first and it showed in her averted body, as though she resented this facile solution to her objection to coming home.

"Isn't it great that Denise is pregnant?" he said to change the subject.

"You knew?" she asked, turning to look at him.

"This morning, yes, she told me. They didn't waste any time."

"Nothing could be better for her, though it seems too soon, they have only been together a little over a month."

"Come on Sophie they have known each other for years. But you look sad about it. I suppose Noël is lost to you for good now, is that it?"

"No, I don't know, it's everything..." She turned into him, put her head on his chest and sobbed. He held her gently as she wept. He wished he could do as much; he had cried over his damned flints, for god's sake.

Lying in the spare room in the darkened house on his own again with his eyes open, he wandered back through the dappled grove of his life and realised that there would always be a dark wig and a tube of moustache glue there now, a deadly, broken lamp and of course the forty kilos of highly explosive sodium-chlorate domestic weed-killer-mix packed into some very good facsimiles of antique

Mexican pottery. And there would be a cheap mobile phone with an electric-firework igniter wired to the speaker terminals. He meant to thank Alec and Catherine properly: perhaps they ought to come to dinner with Medea, and why not Maurice and Noël and Denise? It was curious how it had all worked out, the gas-powered fork-lift had been pure chance; he had never counted on it, but in the end it had probably been more devastating than his home-made incendiary bomb.

Alec had warned him to make sure that the volume was turned up to maximum on the telephone before connecting the igniter, and to install the rigged phone at the last minute to avoid accidents or detection by scanning devices. His last piece of advice had been: "And don't forget to charge the battery!"

He thought that when he emptied Joe's account with Medea they would go somewhere far away from the scene of the crime. Perhaps to Toulouse for the day, the so-called Pink City, built largely of red brick, with a pretty town centre and a Mediterranean feel, very different from Bordeaux. And they should do it soon, too, while DeLauro was still in custody: because knowing the kind of influence he was likely to have, he would be out on bail soon and screaming for blood.

He wanted to return to Bordeaux, though with Noël this time, if he could prise him away from Denise. He had read an interesting article in yesterday's paper about a new acquisition on show in the Musée d'Aquitaine — a prehistoric treasure of capital importance believed to be a small part of what must be one of the most spectacular Neolithic finds ever in southwest France. Discovered by quarry-men in the eighteen-sixties, the treasure had been sold off and dispersed. But a determined collector had soon tracked down and bought an impressive part of it. An anonymous descendant of that long-deceased collector had recently walked in and donated it to the museum. According to the article, amongst the exceptional articles making up the treasure there was a jadeite axe of outstanding quality...

Alice was up with the lark as usual and came to find him in the spare room.

"Sleep well, Alice?" he asked as he buttered her toast for her.

"Yes, but when are we getting my puppy?" she asked.

"We'll have to look into it Aly. Can't rush into something like that, you know." Shit, he thought, what have I got myself into now? Oh well, anything to make amends, I guess. Pen found he couldn't bear being so close yet so far from his family, he would have preferred a migraine or toothache, but Sophie obviously still needed time. So he chose to head back to the Dordogne that morning. But not before he heard Alice say to her:

"When are we going home, Maman? I need to help choose my puppy."

Rattling around, back in his empty workshop, Pen felt at a loss. The last month had been so intense, he found his mind was still busy elsewhere and he couldn't settle. He decided to go out for a drive, see how the dig in St Léon was doing. He called Max, who told him that Daniel was running the show over there. They had just started, and had brought in some heavy plant to shift the rock-fall. They would be on-site in the afternoon if Pen cared to lend a hand.

Aha, he found himself noting with satisfaction: lend a hand, not just come and watch. But he had mixed feelings about it all now. His confidence had taken a blow and his interest had waned considerably. His collection and the stone picking had been his raison d'étre for the last fifteen years. He still knew every piece he'd picked up while roving the hills he had grown to love. He had studied them in depth. Improbable as it seemed to him now, he could call to mind almost each of the individual locations he had picked them from — many, sites that only he knew of. Those were the things that had driven his passion.

Pen had been granted a privileged glimpse into the lives of the distant communities that inhabited the hills long before he set to wandering them. There were few people who could claim as much.

He had been brutally amputated from that intimate contact and the loss ached like a phantom limb. Now that Max was extending a conciliatory hand he hesitated, chewing it over, but not for long. Of course he'd go, he needed to. But he realised that he no longer cared to be involved. From now on he would be an observer, nothing more. The romance was over. He was left with a couple of small, but exceptional pieces, and the exquisite little Magdalenian engraving. They were more than enough. Their lives would never be as they were before Noël found that little piece of jade. He would just have to trust that they would find their way. They would heal and there would be other equally engrossing things to discover in the intriguing new version of the dappled grove that was beginning to unfold around him.

The treasure described in this book is not only real but is called *Le Trésor de Pauilhac* and may be seen in the wonderful Musée d'Aquitaine in Bordeaux. While I have tried to give an accurate account of the prehistory it is a changing discipline and I take total responsibility for any inaccuracies. This novel is by definition entirely a work of fiction and unless otherwise stated any resemblance to actual events or real persons, living or dead, is purely coincidental and unintended. Any misapprehensions or errors are entirely my own.

ACKNOWLEDGEMENTS

Even though writing is a solitary affair I can hardly begin to list all the people who have had a hand in making this book what it is. From the occasional chance conversation that changed the course of the story, to the kind curious person who took the trouble to read the book in its fledgling form and give me their feelings and point out discrepancies and innumerable mistakes. There have been many of you, you know who you are and I thank you all for believing in The Stone Picker.

There have also been other more intimate helpers along the way and I will try to mention them in chronological order. If I have overlooked some of you please excuse my omission and know I hold your contributions dear. So to Tim Neal, thanks for being the first to check my prehistory facts, I hope you finally finished your doctorate. Roger Hurst and Pauline Birghoffer you read the first rough, rough draft and still speak to me. Adam Lawrence was next, lovely man. Theresa Towle you kept me on the rails and stroked my fraying ego bringing metaphorical tea and sympathy, I couldn't have done it without your help and advice. My first proofreader was Caroline Barnes, Merci Caroline. Duncan Caldwell thank you for sharing my passion for field walking, for your invaluable proof reading and encouragement. Ella came and threw her spanner in, ta for that. Bob Lesage often brought his underrated technical wizardry to my aide, thanks Bob. Martin Walker gave invaluable counsel, which subtly improved the structure of the story. My undying gratitude goes to my most sympathetic editor and excellent word smith Michael Woosnam-Mills who so kindly took on the daunting project of refitting, refining the mechanics and tweaking the tuning to make the book an object to be proud of. Mike I can't thank you enough for your modest erudition and your boundless patience.

Patrick Pian is a prince amongst men I consider my self privileged to call him my friend, I hope he forgives me for taking liberties with his knowledge. And Daniel Lebeurrier credit must go to you for your particular insight. The most recent unexpected interest has come from Julie Erskine and Andy Evans who both suggested the independent route to getting this book out to a reading public. Thanks, without you The Stone Picker would still be lying dormant in my computer. Mika, thanks for your priceless help at the end of the long road.

Finally my Heart felt gratitude goes to those members of my family who put up with me along the way. Much love to my long suffering children who often had to wait patiently in the car whilst I checked out a soggy field or two.

Printed in Great Britain
by Amazon